THE WINTER WARRIOR

THE WINTER WARRIOR

A NOVEL OF MEDIEVAL ENGLAND

JAMES WILDE

PEGASUS BOOKS
NEW YORK LONDON

THE WINTER WARRIOR

Pegasus Books LLC
80 Broad Street, 5th Floor
New York, NY 10004

First Pegasus Books cloth edition November 2013

ISBN: 978-1-60598-484-1

10 9 8 7 8 6 5 4 3 2 1

Printed in the United States of America
Distributed by W. W. Norton & Company, Inc.

For the ravens and the jackdaws

CHAPTER ONE

23 June 1069

The End-Times had come, and the world was turning from the light.

Over the wetlands, the sun was setting in a crimson haze. Black clouds of midges danced across the reeking marshes and, among the ash trees and willows, shadows pooled as the pack of silent English warriors herded their stumbling captive south, like a pig to slaughter. Spear-tips jabbed into the Norman soldier's back. On his sweat-stained tunic, blood-roses bloomed. His hauberk and helm were missing, long since tossed into the sucking bog. His double-edged sword, though, that had been claimed by one of his hated enemies. Like a chastised dog, he snarled, his eyes still darting towards that prized blade after each burning prod into his bruised skin.

On the causeway, he tripped and fell, tearing his hands on the flint. 'Stand. Or die,' one of his captors barked. If he understood the tongue, he didn't show it. But the spears jabbed again, more insistent this time, urging him to return to that breathless pace across the desolate fenlands. He showed a cold face to the detested English, ten of them, their pale eyes flickering with the fire of the vermilion sky. Then he swallowed and hauled himself up on weary legs to lurch on.

Once they had reached the next wooded island, Hereward raised his right arm to bring the long march to a halt. He was the leader of the English group, a Mercian by birth, his fair hair and blue eyes marking him out as of Danish blood. The tattooed spirals and circles of the warrior rippled across the flexing sinews of his arms.

As his weary men crumpled, drawing in huge, juddering breaths, he watched fear carve lines in their faces. They were hunters, but the hunted too. He glanced back along the path into the deepening dark. Death was near, and drawing nearer by the moment.

'Water, rest, put fire back in your hearts,' he called as he moved among the slumped warriors. 'The road has been hard and you have run it well, but we have dogs at our back and we cannot slow.'

On the edge of the war-band, the captive brooded. Hereward narrowed his eyes, scrutinizing every move the man made. Like stone, these Norman bastards were, hard, and cold too, he thought. But they would break, in time. The hammers of the English would never still.

In the tilt of the prisoner's chin he saw the arrogance of the invaders who had laid waste to England over three long years since William the Bastard had stolen the crown. In the unflinching gaze was the brutality that had spilled the blood of men, women and children, burned whole villages to the ground, and stolen the livelihoods of those who kept starvation at bay only through grinding toil. He shook his head, contemptuous.

Moving into a copse of dolorous willows, Hereward wiped the sweat from his brow with the back of his hand. His men sluiced water down their throats from skins, and splashed it on their burning faces. That summer had been hotter than hell. The heat crushed them down in the day and choked them during the sweltering nights. And there they were, only at the Feast of

8

St John, with the prospect of many more weeks of the warm season still to come. Perhaps this cruel weather was another sign of the End-Times, as all the old women warned.

As if his prayers had been answered, a cooling breeze whispered through the rustling leaves. He looked across the glassy waters of the fenlands that blazed scarlet in the ruddy light. Black-headed gulls seemed to be calling *Flee! Flee!* as they wheeled overhead.

Hereward swigged a soothing gulp of water. While he wiped his mouth, he caught sight of Swithun slumped at the foot of an oak. Pity stung him. The young warrior's face was ashen, his brown hair lank with sweat, his eyelids fluttering. The left side of his tunic was black and sodden with his blood. Hereward strode over and squatted beside the wounded man.

'Not far now to Ely,' the Mercian murmured. 'Keep the fire in your belly. The leech will soon be mending you with his foul brews and pastes.'

Swithun smiled wanly, reassured by his leader's words. But after a moment, he shook his head, his brow furrowed. 'You must leave me. I am a burden.'

Hereward rested a comforting hand on the young man's shoulder. 'We leave no one behind.'

'But I slow you all down,' the wounded man protested in a voice like dry leaves. 'Fromund must all but carry me now, so weak am I. If the Normans come, you will not be able to outrun them with me like a dead pig on your shoulders.'

'We leave no one,' the Mercian insisted. He held Swithun's gaze, adding warmly, 'Of all our battle-wolves, you fought the bravest. Without your spear, we would not have our captive.'

Swithun smiled again, closing his eyes and leaning his head back. Hereward rose and turned away to hide his concern. The battle-sweat staining the man's tunic was still spreading too quickly. Time was short for him.

He strode back to the willows, eyeing his men as he passed. In the hunched shoulders and drawn faces, he saw their exhaustion. They had been running too long, with death always only a whisper away. Many feared they would never live to see their homes again, he knew.

'The captive is hiding something. You can see it in his eyes.' The whispered voice belonged to Alric, the monk. In the seven summers since they had first met on a bitter Northumbrian night, his thin face had lost its callow blandness. Worry now lined his brow and a scar marred his temple. He nodded towards the captured soldier and put his hand over his mouth so the other men would not hear. 'Hereward, I am afraid,' he breathed. 'We are beset by enemies on all sides. What if we march into a trap?'

'Every step we take now carries risk,' the other man murmured. He kept his face impassive, but his eyes continually searched that lonely land of water and wood. So many places a threat could hide. They would know nothing until danger was upon them. He smiled. 'Let them come. My sword, Brainbiter, thirsts for more Norman blood.'

He could see his bravado had not eased his friend's worries as he had hoped and he turned his attention back to the captive. The Norman fighters always believed themselves superior to the ale-addled, weak-thewed English, but this was different. Hereward watched sly eyes searching the clustering trees. A smile flickered across the man's lips, gone in an instant as he muttered something under his breath, a prayer or a curse.

'Do not harm him,' the monk insisted as if he could read the Mercian's thoughts.

'And you think the Normans would show us the same kindness, when they cut off the hands and feet of any who even raise a voice in defiance of their rule?'

'Would you be a Norman, then?'

'I would not be a monk,' Hereward baited, his tone wry. 'The only man who can turn a feast into a funeral.'

Alric shook his head wearily. He was used to his friend's taunting. 'You are much changed since we first met. No longer the wild beast that would tear out a wolf's throat with his own teeth. A wise man,' he said with an overstated note of incredulity, 'who is not afraid to show kindness. A good leader. Would the English have risked their necks against the king's men here in the east if any other warrior had called them?'

Hereward grunted, embarrassed. The monk knew his weak spot. 'I kill Normans. That is all I do.'

After his chuckles had died away, Alric grew serious once more. 'Is it wise to have taken this prisoner so far from our home? You know as well as I, the Normans are like hungry dogs when they have been defied. They will not cease until they have taken their man back, or they have avenged him. I have never known a kind like them.'

'Once we have loosened his lips, we will gain greatly from all he knows of the Norman defences, their numbers, their supply tracks, their plans for crushing our fight.'

The monk fixed a doubtful eye on his friend. 'There are Normans aplenty within a morning's walk of Ely. Why not one of those? And then you would not have to march through the night, and give our enemies time to hunt us down, out here where we would find it hard to defend ourselves.'

'You are a warrior now, too, like some of those Norman priests I hear so much about?' Hereward gave a sardonic grin.

Alric furrowed his brow, refusing to lighten the mood. He turned slowly, looking past the lengthening shadows to the still, silent marshes and pools and woods. 'You laugh, but I have spent enough time in your company to know when something is crooked. Can you not feel it? My skin is like gooseflesh, my stomach like a butter-churn.' He swallowed. 'Our enemies are out there somewhere, I am sure, watching us, waiting for the moment when they can tear us apart.'

'You must have faith, monk,' Hereward replied, enjoying his joke.

'If the Normans attack now, we are dead men, all of us.'

'There are risks in everything we do. And there will be more, until we have enough men to take this war to the king. Our numbers are growing, but still they are far from what we need,' Hereward said in as reassuring a tone as he could muster. How

11

to bring the English together and build an army, that was his greatest worry. Time was growing short. Soon William the Bastard would turn his full attention to the east. Neither Alric nor any of his men understood that the rebellion hung by a thread until he had found a solution to that problem. And this night, he hoped, would help. He rested a hand on his friend's shoulder, adding, 'We gamble or we lose. That is the simple truth.'

'Aye, but whose lives are at stake when you make your wager?' Hereward didn't need to answer.

Once Alric had returned to the column of men, Hereward nodded, and the warrior at the front jabbed the captive once again, forcing him to set off. Leather soles rattled loose flints as the group followed the causeway through the treacherous bogs.

The night came down.

Among the willows there was little moonlight to guide their way. They could risk no naked flames for fear they would shine like beacons across the sea of dark. As the pace slowed, Hereward's thoughts raced back across the summers. The peaceful days of his youth, fishing and drinking with friends around his father's hall at Barholme, sometimes seemed to belong to another man. He missed those times – though he did not miss his father's fist or shoe. He winced, trying to turn his mind's eye away from the old man's face, but instead he glimpsed a flash of his mother lying on the floor of the hall, bloody and beaten to death. That memory brought a surge of hot anger.

Then he pictured that bastard William sitting on the stolen throne. He knew nothing of the new king's looks, but oddly it was his father's face he saw swimming there beneath the crown. His anger burned hotter still.

When they rested again, he leaned against the still-warm bark of an ash tree, listening. He heard the screech of an owl far beyond the water, and glimpsed the flutter of a bat overhead. The men clutched their spears, knuckles white in the gloom, heads bowed so no one could see the fear in their faces. Yet the captive watched them all with a lingering wolf's eye as he squatted at the foot of a willow. He was seemingly untroubled by his wounds. His breathing was steady, his shoulders at ease.

Hereward rested his hand on the shoulder of the nearest man, Godfrid, still only sixteen summers old and as raw as all the others who had taken that journey north. The young warrior nodded in reply to his leader's silent communication. Dropping low, he crept along the track ahead to scout the way.

After a few moments, Alric stiffened. 'I heard something,' he hissed.

Hereward looked around, but it was impossible to see more than four spear-lengths. He could smell the monk's fresh fear-sweat. 'The water never stops moving. The mud sucks and belches. You are still not used to the moods of the land around these parts,' he replied.

'No, I heard a hard sound,' Alric insisted. 'Like iron on wood.'

Hereward cocked his head and listened. As the night-breeze dropped, the faint crack of a fallen branch echoed from away to the east. He whirled, whistling through clenched teeth. His men crouched so they were harder to see. The captive only grinned. One of the English stood up and planted a heavy foot into the man's ribs. The Norman glowered, but said nothing. He knew that his life would be lost in an instant if he dared draw attention to their location.

'Kill him now,' one of the men urged. 'He will only slow us down.'

'Our enemies may have only crossed our trail and not yet know where we are,' Alric whispered, his voice hopeful.

'They know,' Hereward growled. He darted to the captive. Drawing his sword, he raised the iron blade until the tip pressed at the man's neck. 'Slow your step for even a moment and I will leave your head here for your kind to find.'

The Norman held the warrior's gaze for a moment until his eyes flickered away and down. Keeping his blade against the man's back, Hereward thrust the prisoner forward until they were running. From the back of the column, he could hear

Fromund's ragged breathing as he lumbered with the wounded Swithun. The dying man's prophecy had come back to haunt them.

Hereward swept out his left arm. As his men slowed, he squinted into the dark ahead. With senses long accustomed to the whispering fenland nights, he felt his skin prickle at something unfamiliar. He prowled forward alone. Barely had he gone a few steps when he glimpsed a grey shape among the trees.

A Norman scout, he thought, though the moment the notion passed through his mind he knew it was wrong. He crept forward a few more paces and the pale figure came into focus. It was Godfrid, the look-out, spreadeagled across a hawthorn bush. Blood dripped in a steady patter. His head lay at an unnatural angle, attached to the torso by little more than a strip of sinew and flesh.

The Normans were on every side.

CHAPTER TWO

The English warriors reeled away from the slaughtered man. Breath caught in narrow throats as eyes searched the enveloping dark for whoever had slain their brother. Then shields snapped up and spears levelled, and, as one, they squatted and listened. A breeze stirred the leaves and the blood dripped into the sticky puddle under the fallen man's feet, but no other sound reached their ears.

Hereward crouched beside them. He saw their white knuckles and their drawn expressions and knew he must quickly move to calm them. Fear bred errors and with these inexperienced men that would soon lead to a messy death. 'Godfrid gave his life for us,' he whispered. 'We must not let his sacrifice come to naught. Haste now. We will take the narrow track by Dedman's Pool—'

Flames flared in the eastern dark. His reassuring voice drained away as he watched the flickering light. A brand had been lit. Their enemy no longer saw a need to hide under night's cloak.

'There.' Alric pointed to the west. Through the swaying branches, another torch burned. As he turned in a slow arc, more lights crackled into life all around them, five, ten; he gave up counting. How many of those bastards were out there, Hereward wondered? Fifty? A hundred? The Normans had sealed their trap, biding their time until they were sure their prey was at the centre of their circle. The monk looked over, but he kept his wits enough not to give voice to his thought: that there was no way out.

'Keep low and run,' the Mercian ordered. 'This is our land. We still have a lead on them.'

The captive laughed silently as he looked around the unsettled faces. Hunstan, the eldest there, spun round, bristling as he jabbed his spear. 'He will betray us. We must kill him.'

'Let him go,' Hereward said.

The warriors turned to look at him, baffled. Aghast, Alric stuttered, 'Godfrid gave up his life for us to learn what this Norman knows. And if he goes free, he will draw the enemy to us within moments.'

All around the bobbing flames were drawing closer across the sea of night. He could hear the clang of iron now, and the bark of harsh voices. The Normans' blood was up. They were ready for a slaughter. 'Set him free,' Hereward ordered.

The captive glanced around, unsure what was happening. Hereward grabbed his sweat-soaked tunic and hurled him back along the track with a sharp kick up his arse for good measure. The Norman fell, flashing one murderous look back at his former captors, before he scrambled to his feet and raced away into the dark.

Alric snatched his friend's arm. 'An act of kindness for your enemy? This from a warrior who has hacked off hands and burned faces for a wrong word.'

'Has it not been your mission in life to teach me to be the lamb and not the wolf? All your labours must have worked,' Hereward said, ignoring the monk's suspicious gaze.

The invaders beat iron swords on mail as their death-march drew nearer. Their guttural war-song rumbled across the desolate fens. Dread was only another of their weapons and they used it to good effect.

'Run,' Hereward exhorted before his men had time to take full measure of the threat they faced, 'as if the Devil were at your backs.' Taking the lead, he pounded along the track until he saw the bent oak that marked the spot where the narrower path branched away to the left. It was more treacherous still: barely wide enough for one, it snaked through deep bogs where a wrong step would plunge a man to his death. To take that way would slow their pace, no doubt, but the Normans could come at them from only two directions.

'I admit, more than once I have worried that madness has claimed you,' Alric gasped between heavy breaths. 'But this time I truly think you have lost your wits.'

'It is my curse to listen to your wittering through day and night until I die. I know that,' Hereward grumbled as he searched the dark ahead. 'But I would spend a day on my knees in your church if it would buy me silence for the rest of this night.'

'You have likely killed me anyway so you have no more need to complain. Why did I not stay in Ely?'

'A good question,' the Mercian said, his jaw taut.

Through the clustering willows and ash trees, he could see the wavering flames dance closer. The circle was drawing in tighter still. In his head swam the stony face of Ivo Taillebois, called by his own men the Butcher. Though he had glimpsed the Norman sheriff only a few times while spying through a wall of branches, he could never forget the creator of so much of the misery that had been inflicted on the fens. How that bastard must be laughing now. He had been ready for the English foray, that was clear. Perhaps he had even been praying for it. Losing one man would signify nothing to him if it meant he could follow the secret trail back into the well-guarded heart of the English fortress.

Ahead, torches bobbed where the track reached solid ground once more. Hereward hissed and the men came to a halt behind him.

'We are trapped,' Alric whispered.

'Monk,' Hereward cautioned, waving a finger. He nodded to a shaped stone standing upright at the edge of the track. 'The waters are low this time of year. Beneath the surface a

17

ridge of higher ground runs south. If we are careful we should be able to walk along it and keep our heads high enough to breathe.'

'And how will you know when you are following the line of the ridge?' The monk's voice wavered.

'When I am not, I will be dead.' Hereward heard his friend swallow and he allowed himself another grin. Silence at last. 'You have two choices,' he whispered. 'Put your faith in God, or for now put your faith in me. I have not let you die yet, have I?'

Before Alric could respond, he slipped into the cold slime next to the shaped stone. The clutching fingers of the reeking bog dragged his feet down. Bubbles gurgled and burst around his groin, his waist, rising higher and higher still. When the pungent mud reached his chest, he felt his foot settle on solid ground. He waded forward a few paces, every iota of his wits focused on the sensations from his feet. Tapping one shoe in front of him, he felt the bumps and hollows for the narrow path of the ridge. As he moved on, he turned his head to see Alric immediately behind him and the rest of the war-band following in his wake, easing into the bog one by one. He made out the silhouette of Fromund with a barely conscious Swithun, and watched briefly as Fromund held the wounded man's arms and lowered him into the marsh, where clutching hands guided him in and supported him. As Hereward worked his cautious way onwards he felt pride at how Swithun's brothers were prepared to risk their own lives to bring the fallen warrior home.

Once before, when he was a boy, he had taken this path, though his chin had barely reached above the surface. But then he had been filled with the stupidity and bravado of youth. He remembered the sludge gushing down his throat. Choking, fighting for air, the dark closing over his head. His panic as he realized death had him in its grip. He shook himself back to the present.

Hands scrabbled for his back, almost throwing him off-balance. Hereward wrenched his head around. 'If you pitch me to my death, by all that's holy, I will drag you down with me.'

'Forgive me,' the monk replied in a tremulous voice. The Mercian could see he was shaking and would likely soon make a fatal error. He grasped the man's shoulder and whispered warmly, 'Have faith. All will be well.'

Alric forced a worried smile, his teeth pale in the gloom.

In silence, they waded into the dark.

Enveloped in the stink of rotting vegetation, they heaved against the sucking mire. With each step the silt licked up until it reached their shoulders, and they began to shiver from the cold despite the heat of the night. Hereward glanced back at the trail of warriors snaking into the marsh. The end of the column was lost to the dark, but the faces of those nearest were taut with stark concentration. Everyone there knew a wrong step could be the end of them. 'Slow and steady will see us through this,' he hissed in encouragement. Yet time and again he heard a muted splash as someone snatched at the man in front for support when his feet slipped off the narrow ridge. Alric's muttered prayers droned out, the words laced with mounting desperation.

As they rounded a spur of land dense with trees, a torch glimmered among the branches barely ten spear-lengths away. Hereward hissed for his men to halt. Norman voices rang out through the dark, drawing nearer. He squinted, watching the light gleam off helms. Five men, he guessed, exploring the finger of dry land reaching into the marsh. Hereward watched the light from the lofted brands dance across the gleaming surface of the mud towards the huddled English. Once it revealed them, they would be easy targets for the Norman archers.

Closer the light glimmered until Hereward could almost touch it with his hand. It wavered there, taunting them. The voices chimed louder, insistent tones mixed among the barked orders. Had they been seen? He wished he understood more of that strange tongue than the few words he had gathered. His chest tightened.

After a few moments the orange light began to ebb and the voices receded as the Normans retreated back into the willows. Alric let out the long sigh he had kept trapped in his throat. 'God watches over us,' he whispered.

When he was sure the king's men had gone, Hereward uttered the order to continue. It rustled back along the line into the dark. He watched the torches wavering through the trees all around, like fireflies. The Normans had the scent of their prey. They would not give up until they had fresh heads to perch atop their gates.

As he advanced, he heard low voices behind him and he glanced back. Alric listened to the next warrior in line and then leaned in. 'Swithun's wounds were too great,' he murmured. 'The cold has sapped the last of the life from him.'

Hereward bowed his head for a moment, then said, 'Let him go.'

'We should take him home for a Christian burial—'

'I will not risk another man's life. Two is enough for this night.'

Alric hesitated, then nodded. He passed the order back. As the warriors released Swithun's body to the mud, the monk intoned a brief, sombre prayer in the Roman tongue, adding in English that the warrior had finally escaped the suffering and would be welcomed in to the peace and plenty of heaven. That small comfort was welcomed by the other men, Hereward saw. The monk had done well.

They heaved on around another spur of land, and then finally the mud began to recede. Hereward glimpsed the familiar silhouette of the three broken ash trees where he knew the second stone marker stood. With a low hail to his men, he waded ashore.

The English collapsed on the dry bank, heaving in gulps of warm night air. Hereward allowed them a moment, but his gaze never left the constantly moving torches.

'We can follow a track home from here, yes?' Alric whispered as he wiped the mud from his face with a dock leaf.

The Mercian shook his head. 'No home for us yet. Now we fight.'

Alric gaped in horror. 'We barely escape from the enemy with our lives and now you would take the fight to them with a handful of weary men. You *are* mad. You will kill us all.'

CHAPTER THREE

The moon crept from behind the clouds, painting the willows silver. Through the dark shadows pooling around the trees the English ran, spears held low. The sound of their feet was barely a whisper on the turf. All around, the torches of their enemies ranged. Alric could see no clear path through their ranks.

The monk struggled to keep up with Hereward's loping gait. 'Are you hell-bent on damning all of us?' he hissed between gasps.

'I told you: trust me.'

Alric scrabbled with his hands to fight his way through a curtain of hanging branches that his friend avoided with ease. He looked back at the other men, who trusted every word their leader uttered, and prayed they would be well. *Have faith*, he thought bitterly. If only Hereward knew how much faith he had shown on their long march together.

A waft of burnt wood made his nose wrinkle. He peered into the dark, searching for any sign of a settlement, and soon glimpsed the outline of buildings.

'Where is this place?' Alric gasped as they emerged into a circle of six thatched houses around a green in a clearing.

'Norham,' Hereward replied without glancing back. He kicked open the nearest door and peered inside. The hearth was dead, the ghost of woodsmoke lingering in the air. Alric glimpsed no sign of life within. Had the whole village fled the Normans?

'Burn it down,' Hereward yelled to his men. 'All of it. Do it quickly and let us be away.'

'Stop,' the monk whispered in protest. 'These are our people. You cannot destroy their homes.' He threw himself in front of the Mercian, ducking from side to side to keep himself in between the warrior and the dwelling.

With a grunt of frustration, Hereward grabbed his friend's tunic and dragged him around the back of the house where the air reeked of rot. Choking, the monk pressed the back of his hand across his mouth and nose. Rough hands propelled him towards a pile of cordwood. As his eyes grew accustomed to the gloom, he saw it wasn't firewood at all. The bodies of the villagers had been piled up in a jumbled heap, men, women and children. The blood had long since dried brown, but the gaping wounds spoke of sharp swords.

'They will no longer miss their homes,' Hereward hissed.

'How long have they been dead?' Alric gasped.

'Five days now,' Hereward growled. 'Word reached me before we set off north.'

'What did they do to offend the Normans so?'

'They helped our fight against the thieving king.' The warrior spat. 'Sometimes they offered shelter to those who travelled from afar to join us, or a bite of bread to the hungry.' His voice lowered, but it remained iron-hard with anger.

Alric gaped at the heap of bodies. However many times he witnessed the brutality of their new masters, he never failed to be sickened.

Without another word, Hereward returned to the front of the crudely thatched building and snatched a newly lit brand from one of the other men. He hurled it on to the dirty reed thatch and within a moment the flames licked up. The crackle became a roar, orange sparks whisking up into the night sky on the swirling black smoke. 'Let this be their pyre,' he bellowed into the dark, 'and a beacon too.'

Alric stumbled over the rows of herbs growing beside the house and scrambled to his friend's side. 'What good is burning the village?' he protested. 'It will only draw the Normans to us.'

Hereward shielded his eyes against the glare from the conflagration and watched as his men set fire to the other houses. 'Let those stinking curs come,' he murmured. For a long moment, he seemed caught by the spectacle and then, as if waking from a dream, he thrust a fist towards the heavens. 'Follow me,' he yelled above the roar of the flames. 'We have two more villages to burn. Let us lead those bastards on a dance before death comes.'

Alric felt queasy with worry. He gripped his friend's arm and whispered, 'Do not drag these good men down with you. If you see only doom here, let you and me face it alone.'

When Hereward turned to him, the monk recoiled. With the fires burning behind him and flames dancing in his eyes, Hereward looked like the devil himself.

A dark grin spread across the warrior's face. 'The Normans would sit in judgement of the English,' he said. 'Let them come and I will judge them.'

CHAPTER FOUR

The night was filled with fire and fury. In the black gulf of the fenlands, the burning village glowed, torches flickering all around like sparks caught in the smoke-eddies. The warm breeze smelled of endings, sharp and tarry. Silhouetted against the orange luminescence, two men stood on the higher ground, watching the grey wave of Norman fighters wash towards their prey. At their feet, the hunched villager sobbed. Blood caked his face and soaked his tunic from the long beating he had received.

'See, it was all for naught.' William de Warenne had to shout to be heard over the roar and crackle of the fires, the drone of the war-chant. With cold contempt, the Norman noble looked down his nose at his captive. 'The English warriors have decided to stand and die anyway. If you had told what you knew of them, you might have saved your worthless life.' He was a fighting man, his brown hair cropped and shaved at the back like the mail-clad warriors he had battled alongside when the king had taken England. In a show of virility, he had thrown his purple cloak over his right shoulder to reveal the sword hanging at his hip.

Glowering from beneath a low brow, the other man kicked the captive in the side. He nodded in appreciation when he heard the howl as another rib broke. Ivo Taillebois, now the sheriff, had gained his byname from King William himself: *the Butcher*. Dressed all in black like the men he commanded, he showed none of the flamboyance of his companion, nor the aristocratic profile. Swarthy-skinned, his heavy features spoke of generations of toil on the land. Yet through a strong right arm, animal cunning and a brutal nature, he had clawed his way to undreamed heights. 'You betray the king, you pay the price,' he grunted to the broken villager. 'How hard is it for you English to learn this lesson?' He turned and called into the dark.

A warrior ran up, his own tunic stained with blood. 'I should have you whipped for letting the English take you captive,' the Butcher said to the man Hereward had set free earlier that night. 'But you guided us to the path these rebels took and we now have them in our grasp. So it seems I should reward you.' He placed one foot upon the whimpering villager and shoved him down the mound. 'Gut him and dump him in the bog. And you might find a skin of wine on your bed when we are back in Lincylene.'

The warrior grinned. He hooked a hand in the back of the captive's tunic and dragged the screaming man away into the dark.

'Bring Hereward to me alive,' William de Warenne said once the screams had died away. 'I would break him in front of the English, until he sobs like a child and pleads for his life. Then we shall see how many raise arms against us.'

'You will get your wish. It was only ever a matter of time before he fell.'

The two turned to watch their men close on the English rabble.

All of this Harald Redteeth saw as he cloaked himself in the dark of a copse near by. The fires shimmered off his helmet and glowed from the black pools of the eye-holes. His wild hair and beard were stained red. And under his mail, he reeked of sweat, the smell of an honest man.

The Viking took the king's coin as an axe-for-hire, but that didn't mean he had any respect for his Norman masters. They knew no honour, only the value of things that they could take by force and covet like magpies, and honour, as his father had told him time and again, was everything. Though he had sold his axe to any who would pay since he had left the cold northern lands of his home as a boy, that had always been his code. Blood for blood above all.

And he knew that if anyone took Hereward's head, it would be he.

More flames erupted further to the north, in a clearing among the woods. Another village set alight by the rebels. What possessed them? Were they demanding their own doom?

'You will be avenged, Ivar,' Redteeth muttered, plucking at the skulls of birds and rodents that hung from his hauberk. His gaze flickered towards the grey figure that followed him everywhere, unseen by any other man. He had grown used to the unblinking stare of his long-dead companion, burned alive by Hereward in the Northumbrian wastes all those years ago. The shade did not frighten him. It was a reminder of his duty, nothing more. 'Hereward will fall under my axe, Grim, and I will take that monk for good measure. If he had submitted to the law, my law, I would not be here and you would not be dead,' the Viking murmured. 'The Mercian denied you the Hall of the Slain by the manner in which he took your life, Ivar, but I have vowed to break the shackles that bind you to this world, and so I will.'

He eyed William de Warenne and the Butcher as they discussed their tactics. Christians both, praying in their stone churches. Their lives were like those cold, dismal places. Where was the feast and the song? Where was the hot blood of life gushing over your chin?

'You would speak with the old man now?' Taillebois was saying in his rumbling voice.

William nodded, and the Butcher yelled into the night. A moment later a Norman guard escorted a stooping figure up the mound. The man leaned on a gnarled staff, his skin ashen, his cheeks hollow, his body like a winter hawthorn beneath the frayed woollen cloak. His thinning, silvery hair and frail appearance suggested a man much older than his fifty summers.

'Welcome Asketil Tokesune,' William said in a cheery tone that made no attempt to hide the inherent mockery. 'Though thegn no more, you still carry yourself as a man above men. That is good to see.'

'What news?' the old man croaked, his voice like pebbles on ice.

'Your son is as good as dead,' Taillebois grunted.

Despite the bluntness of the words, Asketil only nodded. 'Then all is well.'

'We are in your debt,' William said, smiling. 'Without your aid, we would not have learned the secret paths in these parts, nor would we have understood your son's ways.'

'Speak no more of my son. He should have been throttled at birth. Like a mad dog, he was, from the moment he clawed his way out of his mother's cunt. He robbed his own, he fought, he killed, and there was nothing I could do to tame him.' The old man's knuckles grew white where he gripped the staff. 'His own mother died because of him. He has been a stain on the honour of my kin. Let him be gone, and forgotten, and then I can hold my head high once more.'

'You have been a good friend to us,' William continued, 'and our king has ordered that all friends among the English be welcomed. You will be well rewarded for this, Asketil.'

The old man grunted.

'Take him back to the hall and feed him what is left of the goose,' Taillebois said to the guard. William de Warenne and Ivo Taillebois did not even wait until the old man was out of sight before they laughed at his back.

Of all of them there, Redteeth despised Asketil the most. The old thegn had betrayed his own kin for some scant reward, even though the Normans had cut off the head of his youngest son, stolen his hall and all his gold. Even though they had stripped

28

him of all he had earned in his long life and tossed him into an existence of near-starvation, begging for scraps from his new masters' table. Harald Redteeth spat. No honour had he.

A column of flames roared up from a third village, the spiral of golden sparks reaching up almost to the stars themselves. The Viking leaned on an oak and let his eyes drift across the three blazes. They were a strange people, these English under Hereward's command. The Mercian had shaped those mud-spattered ceorls and soft-bellied merchants and all those spears-for-hire into a fighting force more rapidly than Redteeth would ever have imagined. But once he was dead the rebellion was over, and King William could sleep a little easier.

While William and Taillebois laughed and schemed, the Viking crept out of the copse and slipped through the swaying willows to the edge of a still pool. Among the brown reeds, he squatted, and then pulled a handful of leathery dried toadstools from the pouch at his waist. The creamy gills of the white-dotted scarlet caps seemed to glow in the gloom. He popped two toadstools in his mouth, wrinkling his nose at the bitter iron taste. Soon he would be walking along the shores of the great black sea, and, if the gods were willing, he would return with the knowledge he gained there.

'Walk with me there, Ivar,' he whispered to the rustling reeds. 'And I will make my vow to you again. Vengeance and blood, to free you from the shackles of this world.'

As the night drew on, Harald Redteeth felt the familiar nausea churn his stomach, and then the tremors and the sweat. Finally, peace descended on him. He sensed the *alfar* stirring in the willows all around him. Their eyes burned away in the dark as they judged him. The beating of wings enveloped him, and he took flight with the ravens, soaring high above those black fenlands, with their gleaming, dark mirrors that gave passage to other worlds. He looked down on those three burning villages where the fugitives cowered. He saw the tide of iron washing towards them. And higher he climbed, and higher still, and across the land and across the sea.

Months passed, years, and though he did not see his father, he spoke long with Ivar and the others he met on that silent shore, until he felt the pull of home.

As if swimming up through dark waters, he emerged into his hunched body among the rushes, his stomach as raw as if he had eaten sour apples. He had learned much that would serve him in the days and weeks to come. But as his senses settled upon him, he realized something was amiss. Shouts in the Norman tongue rang out through the trees from all sides.

His pupils so dilated his eyes seemed all-black, Harald Redteeth hauled himself out of the reeds and strode back up the slope. He gripped his axe, Grim, and allowed Death to fill his skin.

On the higher ground, he looked across the night-cloaked marshes and ditches to where the three burning villages shimmered. The roar of the fire filled his ears. Out in the dark, something was stirring. He wondered briefly if he had left the doors to the otherworld open and the dead were marching through to reclaim the life they once knew. Apparitions rose from the watercourses and the bogs. Skull-faced they were, the shrieking hordes of Hel here to drag all men back down into eternal torment. The supernatural force swept out of the night, their death's-heads glowing in the gloom.

Beware, the *alfar* cried. *Beware!*

CHAPTER FIVE

Out of the woods, the deathly figures ghosted. From the ditches, and the marsh, and the still, silent pools where they had been waiting. Across a landscape that had seemed empty only moments before, the wraiths swarmed. Their features were smeared white with ash, their eyes dark-ringed, and the black mud of the fenlands caked their arms and legs and bare chests so that they bound the night around them. The Normans came to a lumbering halt. Gazes flickered across the apparitions. No mortal army, this. A Devil's Army, that came with the night and the mists and left only bones in its wake.

As they advanced, the English rebels were backlit by the flames leaping up through the trees, a hellish sight that no man there could ever forget.

An axe-blade sang. A head leapt from its shoulders. A spear driven with ferocious force plunged through mail and squelched into the soft flesh beneath. Blood sprayed in a glistening arc.

Hereward smeared wet ashes on his own face, grinning as he watched the horror etched into the Norman features. Their advance had stalled and now they milled in confusion. As he had long planned, the fires and the released captive had drawn his enemy to the place where he needed them to be. The English had kept their hiding places well, settled deep into the ditches and the woods, silent and watchful, until the final ravaged village had gone up in flames.

He unsheathed his sword. As he glanced at Alric, lit orange by the blaze, a smile flickered across his lips at the monk's look of astonishment. He had revealed his plans to no one, not even his closest companion. Too many lives were at stake for even the faintest risk.

Throwing back his head, he bellowed a battle-cry that would curdle the blood of his foes. Then he bounded away from the crackle and roar and heat into the marsh-reeking night.

His eyes quickly grew accustomed to the dark. The king's men were milling around among the reed-beds and willows. Some stumbled into the bogs, screaming as the mud sucked them down to their deaths. Others splashed into unseen flood-lakes or tumbled into ditches and watercourses, made easy targets for spears by their slow-witted response. Yet surprise would work its magic only for a short while. The Normans were too seasoned, too well trained, to be wrong-footed for long.

He sprinted down a narrow track and threw himself from a bank with a cry. Beneath him, a Norman recoiled at this phantasm falling from the night. As the king's man struggled to bring up his long shield, Hereward swung Brainbiter in an arc. It hacked into his foe's exposed neck. The head flew.

Sparks glittered as he clashed swords with the next warrior. When his enemy staggered back, his helm dislodged, Hereward smashed his forehead into the man's face. The cheek shattered. With a snarl, he cleaved the man's head in two.

The thing inside him cried out in glee at the killing. He allowed that blood-lust to rise a little further.

He raced along the track and out of the trees to where fingers of land probed the edges of lethal marsh. He knew every furrow, every bog, every pool, as did all his men. At his orders, they had spent the last days studying the lie of the land while they waited for him to arrive. His gaze roved over the weaving gleams of Norman torches and their glinting reflections in the water.

Though the light saved their necks from the hostile territory, it made them easy prey for the stealthy English.

Through the din of battle, he heard the Butcher's furious orders ring out. They were having some effect. The bobbing brands began to draw together along a narrow line of grassy ground between the edge of the marsh and the wood. Hereward grinned. The Normans still thought they were on the broad downs of Wessex. When the commander barked the order to retreat and regroup, the iron-clad invaders stumbled back into the trees. But the undergrowth was too dense, the trunks too tightly packed for easy progress.

'Bows!' Hereward called.

The men he had trained with their hunting bows nocked their shafts. Grey shapes in the night, they steadied themselves against the back foot and raised their weapons as he had seen time and again on the battlefields of Flanders. The torches wavered along the tree-line as the Normans struggled into the wood.

'Loose your arrows!'

The first flight whistled through the air. With grim satisfaction, Hereward listened to the cries as the shafts drove home. Brands fell, setting alight the dry grass and underbrush. As the flames licked up, he yelled the order for his men to advance. The Normans had slaughtered the best of England. Now it was the time for vengeance. When the echoes of this night rolled out, the king would have no choice but to take notice.

The skull-faced English warriors raced forward, driving a wedge through the centre of the king's men. Hereward looked to the far side of the marsh where the right flank of the enemy was being herded towards an area of bog that appeared to be dry land. In the woods, the remainder of the force had realized their error. They turned to engage the rebels, but their ability to fight back was hampered by the trees.

Hereward shouldered his way through his men to reach the heart of the battle. Some were still but boys, others grey-haired and hollow-chested, yet all had a fierce gleam in their eyes. Familiar faces loomed out of the night on each side. There was Guthrinc, more bear than man, ramming his ham-like fist into a Norman face and laughing as he felt bone shatter. There was Hengist, his pale eyes as cold as ice, his ash-streaked face filled with the bitterness of a man who had seen his family and neighbours cut down by the invaders. Kraki the Viking, once the most feared warrior among the huscarls of Earl Tostig of Northumbria, gritted his teeth and swung his axe. No humour lit his features; battle, like life, was a serious business.

And then Hereward glimpsed apple-cheeks and a mop of curly brown hair, an innocence that even gritted teeth could not mask. Redwald, his brother in all but blood. Though he was not a fighting man, he stabbed his spear as furiously as any other there. For a moment, their gazes locked. Caught in the fury of battle, Redwald appeared oddly blank. But as he looked into Hereward's eyes, he grinned, making a show of grinding his spear-tip into a Norman face.

A wall of flame crackled along the tree-line. Panic flared in the faces of the king's men. The higher ground was tinder-dry, and Hereward saw his enemies start to realize that if the woods caught alight, they would be caught between two different kinds of hell.

The heat brought a bloom to his flesh and his breath quickened. At that moment he wanted to see the conflagration consume them all, perhaps all England, burning away the darkness and the misery in the fires of purification. He stood calm for long moments, caught in the flames' spell as the battle raged around him. He heard no clash of iron, no screams of the dying. He saw nothing but the gold and amber and scarlet.

Then dimly he heard a voice calling his name. He stirred from his dream and glimpsed Kraki pointing past the milling bodies. Silhouetted against the sheet of gold stood a familiar figure, axe raised high in its right hand, the left clenched in a fist of defiance.

Death, he thought.

Distracted, he hacked his blade into the neck of a foe without a second thought. With a snarl he kicked the dying Norman out of the way and pushed on through the melee. All his men knew to alert him to any sign of the hated mercenary Harald Redteeth. Never would he forget how the Viking had taken the head of his friend Vadir, across the whale road in Flanders, and never would he forgive. Only death could end their blood-feud.

Rage flooded him. His sword whirled over his head, never slowing. Two more Normans fell, gouting blood. Hengist finished them off with thrusts of his spear. Only when no one stood between him and his prey did he slow. 'Redteeth,' he bellowed above the deafening roar of the fire.

The Viking turned towards him, unconcerned by the searing heat. Charred twigs flickering with tiny flames showered all around him from the burning branches overhead. His eyes appeared all-black as if he were possessed by some devil. Amid his dyed-red beard a gash appeared, broken, stained teeth showing in a satisfied grin. He lowered his shoulders and let out a bestial snarl.

The two men flew at each other. Harald Redteeth swung his chipped and blood-stained axe for the Mercian's neck. Hereward ducked and thrust with Brainbiter. The sword only glanced off the rusted hauberk in a trail of golden sparks. Pivoting on the ball of his right foot, he allowed his weight to carry him through and spun behind the heavier, shorter mercenary. Whisking his blade up, he drove it down towards the back of the Viking's neck.

Harald Redteeth seemed to sense the strike. He lowered his head as the sword rammed down. It gashed a clean line across his tarnished helm. Without glancing back, the Viking whipped his axe around behind him. Hereward danced back at the last instant. The blade swept by, a whisker away from opening up his guts.

For long moments they battled like wolves trying to tear out each other's throat. Sweat soaked through Hereward's breeches and his skin burned a fiery red from the furnace heat. Thin trails of smoke rose from his hair where burning twigs had fallen on him. Wounds bloomed on both their bodies and blood spatters sizzled on flaming fallen branches. Hereward gritted his teeth against the pain of a gash above his eye. The Viking wiped away the sticky gore from the slash that had opened up his left cheek.

A crack like thunder resounded through the wood's edge. In a torrent of burning branches, an ash tree splintered and fell. Hereward wrenched his head up. A firestorm hurtled towards them. If Harald Redteeth was aware of the danger, he cared little. His black eyes narrowed, and with a lupine pounce he swung his axe for Hereward's neck.

Golden fire rained down as the blade swept in. Hereward closed his eyes, accepting that his moment had come. The roaring faded away. The heat no longer seared his skin. Time seemed to stand still as peace filled his heart. But the blow never struck home.

Instead, the full weight of Harald Redteeth slammed into him and the two men flew backwards. The burning ash tree crashed only a spear-length away. The ground shook. Flaming branches engulfed Hereward. Heat seared his lungs.

As he fought to free himself from the inferno, someone grabbed his arms and dragged him out. Choking, he looked up into Redwald's face. He scrambled to his feet and searched around for his enemy. Through the wall of flame, he glimpsed the Viking with Redwald's spear protruding from his side. His beard and hair were afire. With eerie detachment, he gritted his teeth, grasped the shaft with both hands and snapped the spear in two.

More burning branches crashed down, and the fire surged towards the heavens. As a thick cloud of smoke swirled through the woods, the last thing Hereward glimpsed was Harald Redteeth's black eyes glinting.

Hereward lurched in the Viking's direction, but Redwald grabbed his arm. 'Would you roast yourself like a Christmas ox?' he demanded, concerned. 'That bastard's wounds are too great for him to live.'

'He will live,' Hereward snarled as the other man dragged him away. 'Only I can kill him.'

The two men stumbled out of the burning woods into the relief of the night-breeze. The inferno lit up the battlefield. The wetlands beyond glowed a hellish red in the reflected light. Hereward blinked sweat from his eyes, feeling his throat and chest burn. 'I owe you my thanks, brother,' he grinned, clapping a hand on the other man's shoulder.

'I look out for you, as I always have.' Redwald smiled shyly.

The din of battle had moved away from the fire, but Hereward could hear it was already dying down. Norman bodies littered the edge of the bog. A few English men lay here and there, but nowhere near as many as he had expected.

Redwald squinted to pierce the dark surrounding the remains of the battle. 'The Normans' strength comes from their ordered ranks. Faced with the wildness of the wolf, they cannot cope and are torn apart.' He paused, seemingly unable to believe what he was seeing. Then he turned and looked to Hereward with bright eyes. 'We have won.'

'Not yet. Not until William de Warenne bows down before us and the Butcher's head sits atop a spike for his sins. But this Devil's Army has its blood up. Now let us drive the Normans before us to their end.'

CHAPTER SIX

Flakes of black snowed down on the gathered warriors. Whisked up by the sour-smelling wind, the charred remnants of the burning villages settled across the wetlands far and wide in that quiet time before dawn. In the gloom, ash-streaked faces glowed, death's-heads haunting the tattered remnants of the Norman force. Here was the fate that awaited all men, but them sooner than most.

The English stood on the bank of the Great Ouse. On the far bank, the invaders licked their wounds. Bloody heads and gashed arms were dark against pale skin in the wavering torch-light. Hereward watched the turned-down faces and smiled with satisfaction. He could almost taste the desolation of these warriors who fought in the most feared army in all Europe, yet who had been rent apart by a rag-tag band of mud-spattered English with straw in their hair. This matter was far from done, but here was a cry that would reach all the way to the king.

He narrowed his eyes at the hated enemy and walked to the river's edge. Raising his sword in defiance, he said in a loud, clear voice, knowing full well that the Norman nobles and knights understood the English tongue, 'These are the men who have put women and children to the sword, broken families, stolen food and livestock, carved up lands, and murdered loved ones. These are the men who tried to steal the very soul of the English, putting castles and stone and ledgers in its place. No more. We have whipped them like curs, and we will do so again and again until they flee these shores and return to their God-forsaken home.' He looked around at his men, serious faces all as they hung on his every word. 'We have been failed by our leaders, betrayed by all those who seek their own benefit from power. And I say again, no more. Now it is time for the English to fight back. All the English, together. One voice. One spear. Let us drive the invaders out.'

The skull-faced men raised their fists and bellowed Hereward's final exhortation.

The Mercian turned to the grim-faced Normans across the black river. At this point, the waters moved too fast for the English to try to wade across, even where they were shallowest. 'William de Warenne, do you hear me?'

A long silence followed, filled only with the rushing of the river. Hereward called again.

Finally, the Norman nobleman stepped out from among his bedraggled men. He raised his chin and attempted to show a brave face, but even in the dancing torchlight, Hereward could see his features were drawn and pale. 'I do not answer to the baying of a dog,' he called.

The English laughed. 'These hounds have run you ragged,' Hereward mocked. 'You will answer to us now.' He squinted and could just discern Taillebois standing at the back of his men. The Butcher was too proud to show his face in defeat.

'Gloat now,' William de Warenne called, 'but you will come to regret this day.'

'We are men of honour here,' Hereward said in response. 'Knights, both. Let us end this like knights. Cross the river. Face me, man-to-man. I challenge you to a duel.'

The nobleman laughed. 'I should trust your word, outlaw? I see no honour in any English. You are like snakes, lying still until you bare your fangs and strike.'

Yet as William's false humour drained away, the Mercian saw the Norman's troubled look. He knew he had now lost face, after the humiliation of his men's defeat. Hereward had driven the final blow home sharply.

With sullen demeanour, the Normans limped away. The English watched them go until the last man had shuffled off into the dark, and then they let out a cheer. 'Run like curs,' Hereward yelled after them. 'Lick your wounds. You will never break the English. Tell your bastard master that.'

CHAPTER SEVEN

The great stone feasting hall loomed up against the blue sky. On the pitch of the roof, high overhead, a young man balanced, his arms outstretched as if worshipping the golden orb of the midday sun. Balthar the Fox looked up at the towering building, marvelling at how quickly it had been constructed. A new palace was rising from the ashes of the squat timber-and-thatch buildings where old King Edward had held his court. And a new England too.

He watched the mason shield his eyes against the glare and survey the sprawl of Wincestre and the green fields of Wessex beyond the walls. He seemed unconcerned by his precarious perch. Satisfied, the builder prowled back along the roof, ducking down here and there to check the last of the new tiles.

Balthar shook his head, smiling to himself. What wonders to behold. Stone buildings, erected with such speed and expertise, like the ones the Men of Rome had constructed in summers long gone. Never would he have thought to see this day. He was not a tall man, but he was strong, though he carried more weight across the belly than he ever had in the days before the Normans came. When William had ridden into Wincestre and taken the crown near three years gone, he had feared the worst, but life had been good to him. Though the grey of forty summers streaked his hair, he no longer felt the years. His tunic was finest linen now, not harsh wool, and expertly dyed the colour of autumn leaves. He worried not from where the next meal would come. All was well.

Content, he lowered his eyes to the swarm of activity in the sun-drenched square in front of the feasting hall. Within the palace walls – stone ones, no less, not the wooden palisades of Edward's soon-to-be-forgotten days – the finest craftsmen from across Europe bustled. Masons shaped blocks of creamy-grey stone. Their mallets fell in steady rhythm as they chanted their songs of distant lands in strange, rolling tongues. Saws sang through timber. Strong men shouldered the trunks of oak from the wood-pile beyond the walls. Carts rattled, laden with lime for mortar. The boys who ran behind were as white as if they had been caught in a winter storm. The earthy aroma of stone-dust whipped up in the sweet-smelling woodsmoke from the fires burning the off-cuts. King William made the world his way, and for that he could only be admired.

A young boy forced a path through the milling labourers, his unruly red hair flying. Balthar noted his determined expression and felt a jolt of excitement. Here was his meat for the day. The boy sidled up, glancing around with all the suspicion of a seasoned informant.

'What have you for me, Felgild?' Balthar murmured.

'The king has guests from the east. They smile, but their eyes are worried.'

Balthar nodded. 'Good lad. I will have a coin for you.'

As they walked towards the palace, Balthar slowed his step when he saw two men striding through the crowd, chins held high. One was blond-haired, lithe and strong, his hand resting easily upon the golden dragon-head hilt of his sword. The other was a horse-faced, balding man.

'Who are they, and why do your eyes narrow when you see them?' Felgild whispered.

Balthar chuckled. 'I have taught you well.'

'Who are they?'

'They are the old world, Felgild,' he replied with a sly smile. 'The tall one is Edwin, Earl of Mercia, once a force to be reckoned with in the land, when you were still playing in the mud instead of scrabbling for coin. The other one, though few could tell by looking at him, is Edwin's brother, Morcar. He was once earl of unruly Northumbria, a poisoned chalice for even a strong leader. And Morcar was far from strong.'

He bowed his head as the two earls passed, but they looked away, pretending not to see him. Balthar chuckled again, untouched by the slight. 'So proud, so haughty, with no good reason to be.'

Felgild kicked a chunk of stone in a looping arc. A cry rang out and he ducked behind the older man, keeping his head down.

'If those two were braver or wiser they could unite the broken-backed English into a force to be reckoned with,' Balthar continued. 'And so King William keeps them close, deep in the heart of his court, trapped in a prison of fine food and whores and wine. The monarch flatters them that they still hold some value in this new England that he is building, and they bow their heads and accept his way of seeing, for to believe otherwise is unthinkable.'

'They would do well to heed you,' Felgild said with a nod. '*You* are a force to be reckoned with now.'

Balthar could not disagree.

Once the lad had scurried off to see to his chores, Balthar hurried into the king's hall, cool after the heat of the day, quiet after the pandemonium of the builders' yard. The sound of voices speaking in the Norman tongue he had worked so hard to learn echoed dimly from the recesses. He slowed his pace so his footsteps would not give him away. He was not a moment too soon. More footsteps approached, small ones and rapid, accompanied by the sound of short breaths. He pressed himself into the shadows under an arched doorway.

A pretty, blonde-haired girl of some eighteen summers

hurried past, glancing over her shoulder in the direction of the Norman voices. She was scared, perhaps, that the king would find her away from her duties. Godrun was her name. Balthar smiled to himself as he recalled how she had caught his eye the day she passed through Dungate and arrived at the palace at the beginning of the hot season. She was hungry, abandoned, with dirt under nails and more besmirching her roughly made dress. Yet she had been raised up with alacrity, soon serving the table of the king himself. Balthar had not been surprised at that. Her beauty was pristine. What man would not want such an angel at their right hand? In her pale face, he thought he had seen an innocence that would need protecting amid the random cruelty and base desires of the court. It was a task he would gladly take up.

Once she had passed, he eased out of the shadows and hastened towards the vaulted hall, still fragrant with the aroma of fresh stone and newly cut timber. Sumptuous tapestries hung on the walls, their bright colours illuminated by the hissing torches. Slipping through the open door, Balthar darted to his right and found his favourite hiding place behind a screen showing an image of the Christ ascending to heaven. He held his breath and peeked around the edge.

William sat on his throne, leaning forward and pointing at two men who stood before him. Balthar had quickly learned that with the king appearances could not be trusted. He was enormously fat, his belly straining against any tunic made for him. Yet he was as strong as an ox, still vital for a man of some fifty summers. No warrior was powerful enough to draw his bow, it was said. Balthar himself had seen the king lift a nobleman who had angered him above his head and hurl him across the hall. And though he was quick to find good humour, his temper burned fierce. Lives were snuffed out on a whim. Many had been sent to their doom, even in the heart of the palace.

Balthar recognized the two guests: Ivo Taillebois, a brutish man with a low brow who had been dispatched to bring order to the Fenlands, and William de Warenne, one of the nobles who had been rewarded with land in that area.

'Did I not send you fresh men?' the king was saying, his brow knit.

'You did, my liege,' the nobleman replied, with a twitching half-bow.

'And horses? And gold?'

'Yes, my liege.'

Taillebois stepped forward, clasping his hands in front of him. 'The prey we run to ground is not short of paths for flight and has a well-protected lair.'

The king leaned back in his throne, steepling his fingers. 'Hereward, yes? The English dog you assured me would be swinging from a gibbet before the spring waters had ebbed?'

'Aye,' the Norman commander grunted. 'My tongue outran my wits. I should have taken my time to get the lie of the land. Then I would have seen that even a child could stay out of our grasp in that God-forsaken place.' Balthar watched him bare his teeth in frustration. 'It is a place of bogs and forests and floods that shift with the weather. That cur knows its moods and uses it well to hide his tracks.'

William de Warenne held out an imploring hand. 'With more men we could harry him at every turn. Drive him out into the open.'

'Surely he has no more than a handful of men out in those empty wetlands?' the king said. 'How, then, can he be responsible for so many dead?'

'Men join him by the day, from all parts of this land. Weak, they are, yes,' the nobleman replied, 'little more than scraps of meat and bone in filthy rags, but the numbers swell.'

Peeking around the edge of the screen, Balthar studied the curve of William's smile. It was hard, not easy. 'And this is the Devil's Army I have heard so much about?'

'They are poorly armed, true,' de Taillebois muttered, 'but given time, and enough men heeding this dog's call, they could force us back by weight of bodies alone. Our swords are sharp, but our men could not cut down those saplings fast enough.'

The king beckoned past a helmed guard to a figure waiting in the shadows on the edge of the hall. Balthar saw it was Godrun who had at some point returned to the hall with a pitcher. She poured a wooden cup of red wine and hurried to place it into the king's hand. William eyed her a little lasciviously, Balthar thought. She bowed her head and retreated to the shadows. The two guests remained silent as the king swigged back his drink. When he was done, he wiped his mouth with the back of his hand and sighed, 'After three years this place still bubbles like a stew-pot too low on the flames. I would be back in Normandy now, but this business of the English will not set me free. Here, there and everywhere I am called to deal with spears raised against my rule, and fists and axes and angry voices. Even among the womenfolk and the children. I put my faith in you to bring peace to the east, a wild place, a quiet place so I am told, and yet you come here with words of failure?'

William de Warenne flinched as if he had been struck. The Butcher remained impassive, but he lowered his eyes. 'Not failure, no,' Taillebois began after a moment, 'but this drags on and with a few more men we would be done with it by the time the snows come—'

'The Fox! Where is the Fox?' William called over the other man. 'And more wine,' he demanded, waving his cup.

Balthar jumped and moved swiftly towards the door, which lay out of the king's line of sight. He sucked in three breaths in rapid succession and scrabbled his fingers through his hair to make it seem he had been hurrying. As William continued to call his name, he scurried towards the throne. 'My lord?' he enquired, breathless.

'The Fox,' the king boomed, throwing his arms wide and grinning. 'How is your wife, Gertrude?'

'Well, my lord.'

'And your two boys?'

'Both well, my lord.'

46

'Balthar the Fox advises me in the ways of the English more wisely than any Norman ever could,' William said to his two guests with a ghost of a smirk. 'I named him well, for he is cunning, and slinks unseen through the shadows. Balthar is my eyes and ears among our new friends.'

'You honour me, my lord,' Balthar said with a bow.

'I do, indeed.' The king covered his smile. He waved his cup again and Godrun scampered forward from the shadows. Balthar saw her look towards him for no more than a fleeting moment, yet he felt a tingle of satisfaction at the recognition of a kindred spirit that he thought he glimpsed there.

'So many times we have spoken here about the unruly nature of your kinsmen,' William continued, showing the face of a concerned father with a lightly furrowed brow and downcast eyes.

Balthar nodded, hiding his bitterness. He felt stung by the resistance of the English. What gain was there in fighting a lost cause? Better to welcome the many benefits William's new rule promised. Peace, stability, a chance to heal all wounds.

'I thought when I had seen off that pretender to my crown, that Edgar Aetheling, there would be an end to these troubles,' the king added, a crack in his voice despite his attempts at equanimity. 'Now the north is demanding my attention again. And the west and . . .' His left hand clenched on the arm of his throne, but he forced a tight smile. 'And now I hear a flea in the east is continuing to bite, a flea that should have long since been crushed.' He narrowed his eyes at his two guests. 'Tell me, Fox, what should I do about this Hereward?'

Balthar pressed his palms together as if praying. 'News has reached me of the Mercian, my lord,' he began in measured tones. 'There is no love lost between his kinsmen Edwin and Morcar and him. I doubt they would ever rally to his banner.'

'You agree that the north remains the greater threat?'

'I do, my lord. Northumbria has always been a nest of vipers. The poison will spread if those snakes are not put to the spear—'

47

'The spear, you say,' William cut in, raising his head thoughtfully.

Balthar felt his chest swell that the king – the king! – was hanging on his words. 'Hereward is but one man, my lord, for all the lost souls who flock to his banner. Without his leadership, they would be nothing. One man, and by all accounts of his time at Edward's court, a poor one at that. Scarcely more than a wild beast, baring his fangs at friend and foe alike, more red rage than wise head. In truth, my lord, he is naught but a hungry cur, not worthy of your time.'

'Once again, Fox, our thoughts are in line,' the king said. 'Keep the English in their place. Surround yourself with men you trust. That is all I heard when I took this crown. But I knew there was much to gain by throwing the doors wide and calling wise heads such as yours to gather round the fire. A fox always watches for its next meal, does it not?' He laughed. Balthar flushed with pride and bowed his head.

William turned to the two Normans and said, 'No more men for you, nor gold. I will need all I have to . . .' He hesitated, smiling, '. . . put the vipers in the north to the spear. You must deal with this Hereward with what you have, and that is more than enough for a wild dog.'

Balthar caught sight of Ivo the Butcher glowering at him and he shuddered.

'How do you counsel, my lord?' William de Warenne asked.

The king shook his head slowly, his face hardening. 'I would counsel more wit and less whining,' he snapped. 'Look to the Fox here. Learn from his cunning. If this Hereward uses trees and water as his weapons, would you stand on the ramparts shaking your sword at the tides, or the wind? His home is an island. Turn his castle into a prison. Creep through shadows, watch and whisper, and only when the time is right, strike. Find the cracks in his defences and prise them apart.' He tapped his index finger on his temple, then jabbed it at the visiting Normans, demanding thought. With barely concealed contempt, he glared at the two men. 'What do you say, Fox?' he asked.

'Wise words, as always, my lord.'

'The Fox has spoken,' the monarch growled. 'Now leave my sight and do not return until you have words I wish to hear.' The Butcher nodded his head while the nobleman bowed and scraped. 'It seems there will be no peace here until a tide of blood has washed the land clean,' the king added. Before Balthar could consider what he meant, William tossed aside his cup and stalked from the hall.

As the two guests sloped away, Balthar slipped out of the small western door. He felt that odd mix of fear and pride that he always suffered once he had left the volatile monarch's company. Leaning on the stone wall, he took a deep breath to steady himself.

'The king smiles upon you.'

Balthar whirled to see Godrun standing near the door, pitcher in hand. He drew himself up so she would not notice his weaknesses and replied, 'He finds wisdom in the guidance I offer him.'

The woman drew nearer, her eyes wide. 'How fine that must be to be so favoured.' She bit her lip. 'He scares me.'

'His bark is loud, but I have never seen him raise a hand to a woman.'

'All these Normans scare me,' she said, wrapping her arms around the pitcher. 'They treat their own women with high regard and kindness, but they look upon English womenfolk as if we are . . . we are nothing more than vessels for their desires.'

Balthar felt his heart go out to the quiet girl, but there was nothing he could say for he had seen the evidence of her accusation with his own eyes.

'Have they harmed you?' he asked gently.

She shook her head, raising her chin with defiance. 'I have resisted,' she said. Yet when he saw the tears fleck her eyes, he knew, as she knew, that it would only be a matter of time before she would be forced to succumb to the demands of the Norman men, if not those of the king himself.

'They bow their heads before the altar and pray to God more

than any Englishman, and yet they allow the Devil to take them too often,' he murmured. 'There are ways to deal with them. A sweet smile followed by a swift retreat works better than a sharp tongue.'

'I fear I am not strong enough, nor clever enough.' She bowed her head. He noticed her hand trembling and understood how hard she fought to keep a brave face in that den of wolves.

Balthar hesitated and then placed a finger under the girl's chin to raise her head so he could look into her blue eyes. She made him think of the days of his youth, and yearn for them. Memories of simpler times and vitality and passionate feelings flooded his mind. 'I will be your protector,' he said, his voice strong. He felt warmed by the relief he saw lighting her face.

But her features darkened just as quickly and she began, 'Your wife—'

'My wife cares only that she has gold brooches and fine food to make her fat. Her tongue is sharper than any Norman sword, but I am still the master of her.' He studied her smooth skin and her shining hair, as bright as the gold that adorned the king's hall, and he saw the vitality that sparkled in her eyes. How different it was from his wife's face, who now reminded him only of winter on the Wessex plains.

He withdrew his fingers, realizing he had begun to caress her. His breath catching, he turned away and raised his head, aloof once more, but he could still feel her eyes upon him.

'Think of this palace as the woods in winter. Wolves wait everywhere,' he began. 'But with a guide who knows the lie of the land, a safe path can be found through it. Stay close to me and you will survive.'

In the depths of the building, William loudly demanded more wine. There was a clatter. Something had been overturned. The visit of his two guests had disturbed him more than he had shown. Balthar immediately began to wonder how he could turn this to his advantage. Godrun hurried back to the door to answer the monarch's call. She paused at the threshold, her smile tentative yet hopeful. He felt excited by the possibilities it held, but it was not the time to examine them. In the hall, the king raged, all semblance of calm now gone. Balthar could not help but think that for all the terrible events they had endured in recent times, the worst still lay ahead.

Chapter Eight

The white dragon banner of the English rebels fluttered against a cerulean sky. As one, the long column of warriors raised their faces to the sun cresting the distant streak of woodland in the east. Their full-throated voices rang out in song of battles won and hearths awaiting. Above the windswept marshes, oystercatchers swooped, their cries joining the jubilant chorus.

Redwald looked along the narrow flint causeway towards the island rising from the wetlands ahead. The marshes reeked of rot and the gnats already danced in clouds, but he cared little. Life was good. Two summers gone he would never have believed he would taste such sweet hope again. His thoughts flew back to his flight from London after the invasion. The Normans had hunted him like a dog across the fields for his close ties to the old king. He spat. Harold had failed them all. How strong he had seemed as he waited for King Edward to die so he could seize the throne, with all his talk of power and what strong men would do to gain the prize their hearts desired. How easily Redwald had been seduced by those words. He felt a pang of self-loathing for his own weakness. He had tethered his days-to-come to Harold in the belief that he would be well rewarded and it had almost cost him his life.

'You saved Hereward, I hear tell.'

Redwald looked back and saw it was the monk. Alric showed a pleasant face, but Redwald could still see the suspicion in his eyes. It had been there from the moment they first met, he did not know why. 'Any man here would have done the same.'

'True.'

'Have you ever saved his life? I hear tell he spent all his days saving yours.'

'My work is saving souls and leading them to God.'

'How hard it must be, then, to find yourself grubbing around in the bloody business of mere men.' Redwald caught himself. He smiled, showing his teeth. 'Forgive me, my words are too sharp. My legs ache and my belly rumbles and it has turned me sour as vinegar.'

The monk peered past him towards the Isle of Ely where the minster tower on the top of the mound rose proud against the sky. 'Hereward speaks warmly of you, and I trust his judgement in most things.'

Redwald heard the lack of commitment in the monk's words, but he kept his smile fixed and said nothing.

'You owe his kin much, I am told,' Alric continued.

'His father, Asketil, took me in when I was lost and alone after my mother and father had died.'

'How did they die?'

'That is a tale of woe for another day.' Redwald bowed his head. 'Asketil's act of kindness saved me, and from that day Hereward became my brother. I would give up my own life for him, as any brother would.'

'That is the right thing to say. Asketil is a hard man?'

'Like a church floor.' Redwald smiled tightly. 'He is quick to anger, and his hands become fists faster than most, but he always treated me with fairness.'

The monk nodded as if this simple comment spoke volumes. 'And yet now he sides with the new king. What would make him abandon his own blood for our enemy?'

Redwald shrugged. 'I do not claim to know Asketil's mind.'

He swatted away a fly, eyeing the other man askance. 'Hereward looks on *you* warmly, Alric, and if for that reason alone, I hope we can be friends.'

'If God is willing. Hereward is a fearsome leader. His anger is great, his vengeance greater. Any man would tremble who faced him. And yet locked inside is a good man.' The monk searched for words, his gaze growing faraway. 'A man who trusts, perhaps, too much when he has decided someone is a friend. It would sound mad that such a fierce man would need to be shielded, were it not true.'

'Then give thanks that he has such as us to watch over him.' He looked away into the hazy distance. 'I have not been a good man, Alric. I have turned my face away from God.' He took a deep breath. 'I sought power, though it cost others hard. I lied, and I stole. I have killed in anger. But the Lord punished me for my crimes and I saw in my darkest days how much I had failed everyone. I would make amends now. I would be a better man. Hereward says he has learned much from your guidance. Will you aid me too?'

The monk's eyes narrowed as he peered deep into the other man's face. 'If a man is honest in his desire to come to God, then I would do all I could to help him.'

'Then I need hear no more.'

Redwald looked towards Ely again, his heart leaping at the end of the long journey. Now he could see the smoke rising from the hearths and hear the cries of the gulls scavenging on the midden heaps. The sky had grown a misty yellow in the early morning light and the settlement appeared to be wreathed in a heavenly glow. The palisade stood firm around the jumble of dwellings clustered tight against the minster and its enclosure.

'We have found a good home, have we not?' This time it was Hengist who had spoken. He walked a pace behind the monk. Sweat had streaked the ash on his face and turned his straggly blond hair into rat's tails. Redwald always felt unsettled by the warrior's pale, staring eyes. He thought he saw a hint of madness there.

'Aye, it is good.'

'More than that,' Hengist chirruped. 'It is a testament to Hereward's cleverness.' He swept an arm across the desolate marsh with its scattered islands rising out of the bogs and water. 'See? Here is a fortress unto itself. Even if the bastard king's men could fight their way through the forest that shields the fens, they would never be able to march upon Ely. They could try a boat at high water, if they want to risk drowning in the strong currents.' He grinned. 'Or they could walk across the causeway where we could pick them off one by one by one.' He clapped his hands and did a little dance.

'A safe haven,' Redwald replied with a nod. That warmed him. He had not felt safe his entire life, but here, perhaps, he might finally find peace. He let his eyes drift over the isle, caught between sky and water. Ely stood to the east overlooking the lethal bog of Grunty Fen which almost split the land into two smaller islands. Could he ever consider it home after the grandeur he had known at King Harold's court?

'Even if the bastard Normans make it to the isle, we are not done for,' Hengist continued, talking to himself now. 'Should an enemy survive the causeway, they would still have to skirt the bog by Haedanham and cross the waters at Wiceford before they could even draw near to Ely.' He smiled. 'Let the Normans build their castles. Here God has provided his own.' After a moment's reflection, Hengist pulled a bone whistle out of his breeches and began to play. Redwald drifted with the tune. Hengist was a rough man, yes, and as mad as a March hare, but the music he played was sweet.

Once they had left the grey flint of the causeway for the isle's sward, the warriors cheered and shook their spears in the air. The air smelled fresher, scented with the hint of woodsmoke and the stews bubbling in the pots on the home-fires. The weariness fled from their legs as they made their way along the mud-baked tracks, their progress only slowed by the biers carrying the dead at the rear of the column.

Guthrinc cracked his knuckles as he strode beside Redwald,

looking the smaller man up and down. 'It is true, then. Only the good die.'

'A tough piece of mutton like you will be around long after I am gone,' Redwald replied, raising one eyebrow.

'Aye, to mop up the tears of joy of your woman, and give her some glee for once in her poor life.'

'Leave him, Guthrinc,' Hereward called back from the front of the column, grinning. 'He would make a prettier head than yours atop a pike.'

'Your face would affright even the ravens,' Kraki the Viking growled, the merest hint of humour flickering in his dark eyes.

Guthrinc threw his head back and laughed, clapping Redwald across the shoulders so hard he almost pitched across the track. 'I will let you buy me ale in the tavern later, apple-cheeks,' he roared, striding off to the front of the column. 'Would you not rather be back with your wife, Hereward?' he called, adding without waiting for a reply, '*We* would rather be back with your wife.' The men laughed and Hereward too.

The gates in the palisade ground open as the warriors neared and more cheering rolled down the green slope from the settlement. Hengist ran a hand through his greasy hair and gaped at the large crowd they could see milling around within the enclosure. 'Is every man and woman in the fens come to see us home?'

'More new faces to join our army,' Redwald exclaimed. 'Word spreads of Hereward's bravery. Soon we will have everyone from Northumbria to Wessex here.' He could scarcely believe how many people he could see gathered beyond the gates. What had started as a trickle of new recruits had become a deluge pouring in from all parts of the land. Every time he thought it had reached its limit, yet more would arrive.

Kraki frowned, wrinkling the jagged scar that ran from above his left eye, across his nose on to his right cheek. 'More strong right arms are good, but still there are far from enough to challenge the king. And soon the Bastard will come for us.' Hereward flashed a black look at the Viking. Kraki shrugged, refusing to be silenced. 'And how will we feed them all, eh? Answer me that. We can scarce feed the men we have now.'

Hereward glanced back once more, his face grim, and this time the Viking nodded and fell silent. 'Every man's belly will soon be full, you have my word,' the Mercian announced. 'We will feast like kings to celebrate the bloody nose we have given to the Normans.'

Redwald could see Kraki was troubled. 'Is this wise?' the younger man whispered. 'I have heard Hereward worry about this with the monks at the church long into the night. He said it would not be Norman iron that defeated us, but starvation and sickness and the betrayal of our own—'

'Quiet,' Kraki snapped. His eyes flashed a warning. 'You heard our leader. This is not the time to talk of such matters.'

Redwald nodded. 'But this will not go away if we close our eyes,' he murmured.

The column of warriors passed through the gates into the throng. The cheering enveloped them, the tumult doubling once word of the great victory rushed through the crowd. At the forge on the main street, Eni the smith downed his hammer and stumbled out into the sun. Penda the carpenter laid his chisel on the newly cut piece of oak and joined him. The rattle of the looms stilled. All the workshops emptied, and the rows of timber halls too, as people streamed past the barns and the stinking livestock pens to the gates.

Redwald saw many unfamiliar faces among those who were clustering around Hereward, reaching out to touch his arm with tentative fingers. Redwald thought his brother looked troubled by the reception. His smiles were forced, his eyes darting.

Amid the crowd, women searched for the men they had feared would never return. Their eyes brightened when they saw the longed-for face, and they snatched a kiss before hauling their husbands back to their homes, and beds. Kraki's woman Acha shoved her way through the throng, her expression sullen beneath her raven-black hair. She raised her chin as she moved through the sea of warriors, ignoring the lascivious glances of the many in Ely who desired her. Kraki's lips parted in a broken-toothed grin when he saw her, and she put on a pleased smile in response, though Redwald saw it fade when the Viking pawed her into an embrace. Instead, she glanced back through the crowd, searching, until her gaze fell on Hereward. Her attention lingered there for a long moment.

As Redwald mulled over what he had seen, Hereward hailed him. 'We must meet later to speak of our plans,' the leader said, hauling the younger man to one side. 'The Normans will not hide away with their tails between their legs for long. They will return with more men—'

'Hereward,' Redwald interrupted, laughing. 'Enjoy this great day. We should do naught but raise our mead-cups until our heads spin. Plans are for another time.'

The other man contrived a smile, but Redwald knew him well enough to see the worry in his eyes. 'You carry the weight of all the English on your shoulders, brother,' he continued in a gentle voice. 'Do not let it break you. One day to seek out a few comforts will give you the strength to go on until the seasons turn. And not just you, but all these men. A good leader knows when to rest as well as run.'

Hereward nodded, his smile becoming more honest. 'Wise words. I expect no less from you, brother. You were always the one with the sharper wits, and I take great comfort that you are here to advise me now.'

'And I always will be.' Redwald gripped the other man's arm and nodded. 'Now . . . ?'

'Now I must seek out Godfrid's father and mother,' Hereward replied, his features darkening as he glanced towards the crowd. His gaze fell upon a grey-haired man and a smaller woman with heavy hips. Their shoulders were hunched as if they already understood the truth. 'They should know their son was a hero, who gave his life for the English in this hard battle we fight. It may give them some small comfort in their grief.'

'Let Guthrinc tell them. He knows them.'

Hereward shook his head. 'It must come from my lips.'

He drew in a deep breath. 'Remember when we were boys, Redwald? Nothing to do but fish and play with wooden swords,' he said with a note of loss. 'What became of those days?' He reflected for a moment, then pushed his way into the milling crowd.

CHAPTER NINE

A storm-cloud of black wings whisked across the clear blue
sky. Hereward jerked his head up, but the birds were
already lost in the glare of the sun. Rooks, he guessed, roosting
in the dense ash-wood to the south. Strangely chilled despite
the summer heat, he glanced back across the bustle of Ely for
human comfort. So many people now congregated there, he felt
sure the settlement could sprawl to the size of Eoferwic within
weeks.

Near the Speaking Mound, boys lumbered with arms filled
with cordwood for the fire where they would roast the meat,
but not this night. He had already decided the feast would be
delayed. New plans and another long road lay ahead of him
before he could rest.

He turned back to the track between the houses. The
herbs growing along the timber walls in the sun scented the
air: coriander and dill, thyme and summer savoury. As he
approached the modest dwelling at the end of the path, he felt
the weight upon his shoulders ease. It still smelled of new wood,
the straw of the thatch golden and thick enough to keep out
the spring rains. The local folk had insisted they should build a
hall grand enough to suit the most powerful thegn, but he had

refused. Until the war was over, comforts were a distraction.

As he neared, the door creaked open and Turfrida emerged from the smoky interior. Like a cat, she was, in both grace and features. Her wide, slanting eyes sparkled with wit and her smile was as knowing as ever. Many men found her cleverness and confidence intimidating. But he had been lured by it from the moment he first glimpsed her at the battle-fair in Bruges five summers gone. She had readied herself for his return. Her dress was of finest linen, dyed amber like the setting sun, hemmed with black and fastened with a silver brooch. With her hot tongs, she had curled the tips of her brown hair, and it folded out from under her white head-dress.

As she made to speak, Hereward embraced her. She smelled sweet from the mysterious unguents she massaged into her skin every night. The kiss lingered, but once it was done she took his hand and led him into the dark home. On the low wooden bed, she snatched off her head-dress, unfastened her brooch and pulled her dress away.

'These days apart have been too long,' he murmured, stripping off his filthy breeches.

'Throw off your burden and let me ease your worries,' she whispered, laughing.

His worries sloughed off him, and for the time of their love-making he thought of nothing but Turfrida. They lay together as their breathing subsided. The room was hot and sweat slicked their bodies.

'Did the stars and moon tell you I would return?' he breathed in her ear. 'Or the rabbits or the igles or the bats?'

She pinched him, feigning a scowl. 'You laugh at my ways, as you always have. One day I may put a curse on you.'

'The dangers of sharing life with a witch.' He pretended to sigh wearily.

She rolled on top of him, nipping with her teeth. 'Some men would be proud to lie with a woman skilled in the mechanical arts.'

After a moment, he spun her over and pinned her down by

her wrists, both of them laughing together. 'I am proud,' he said, 'as you well know. And prouder still that you came back with me to this God-forsaken place and a life of blood and sacrifice.'

Her smile seemed to grow sad. 'I knew what the gods intended for you long before our handfasting. I chose to stand with you then, and I will never wish anything else.' She hesitated, adding, 'Whatever may come to pass.'

'You do not miss Flanders?'

'I miss my father. But you care for me now. And though the king has done his best to break this land in two, this place is close to my heart. And I have been welcomed by all.'

'Even the monks,' he teased.

'They turn their eyes away when I pass by and pretend I am nothing but mist. But they have not called the witch-hunters to burn my flesh with hot rods, and they have not tossed me into the waters, with rocks tied to my arms and legs to drag me down, and for that I must give my thanks.'

'These are English monks. They know their friends and say their prayers to fit.' He threw his arms behind his head and stared up into the smoky gloom of the roof. 'Our English churchmen are afraid of the Norman priests as much as the folk fear the warriors. The king brings his own abbots in, and takes the gold and the food. Our monks know the ways they have held close in their prayers are under threat.'

'And they must work harder to preach their Christian ways,' she said, resting on one elbow. 'There are more heathens now than there were before the Normans set foot upon your land. In fear of death and harsh rule, many turn to the old ways. They will pray to any god, if it will help them live on. Many fear it is—'

'—the End-Times,' Hereward completed. 'I hear that everywhere I go. Sickness and starvation and war and death. I see only a man who can be brought down to his knees and better days ahead.'

She nodded, saying nothing.

Hereward furrowed his brow. 'What do you know? You have seen more visions?'

'I see . . . much. I hear whispers, in the wind, in the streams.'

'Tell me.'

'I feel a shadow in my heart,' she began hesitantly. 'Last night I dreamed of an old woman sitting alone upon a pile of bones and her head shook with her sobs. She was dressed all in black and at first I thought she was a crow, or a raven. Beside her, there was a churn, but it stood empty. And then a great fire swept across the land, and the woman turned to smoke and drifted away.' Her face darkened and she looked towards the hearth, though it was filled only with grey ashes. 'And you were there, husband. You came with the fire, and you laughed as it burned all before you.'

Hereward eased off the bed and stretched, feeling the aches in his muscles from the long hike. The blue-black tattoos on his arms flexed under the gold rings. He padded across the reeds on the compacted earthen floor and poured a wooden cup of ale, sipping it as he reflected on what she had said. 'What does it mean?' he asked, feeling his wife's eyes upon him.

'I worry for you,' she began, choosing her words. 'It means—'

'It means that in these End-Times, if that is what they be, I risk destroying what I try to save.' He knew what her vision foretold and it was something he had always feared since he had first sensed he was not like other men: that if he released that devil he knew lurked deep in the darkest parts of him, he would become like the Devil, bringing hell to Earth. A cure worse than any sickness. Worse than William the Bastard. He drained the cup and turned back to her. 'I can only do what I believe is true. Let God decide how it falls.' He smiled with affection when he saw the concern etched in her face. More than anything he wanted to soothe her worries. 'No harm can come to me when I have you to watch over me, and Alric and Redwald,' he added, softening his voice. He wanted to say, *I can do no harm.*

She seemed pleased by his words for she smiled and climbed

off the bed to wash herself. 'Then all will be well for I will always watch over you.'

'Let us talk no more of End-Times and fire and bones. We shall raise our cups and sing our songs. And if I hear one whinge from Alric I will kick his arse. That monk can find sourness in even the sweetest mead.'

When Turfrida laughed, Hereward felt pleased that he had lightened her mood. He ensured their conversation was light as he dressed in a clean tunic and breeches, and he was content that she had other things on her mind.

'The monks told Brictiva of the new laws the Normans are bringing from their home,' she said, setting her jaw. 'A woman will marry and serve, that is to be our place in William's England. Serve! Love will matter no more. A father will give his daughter as a token with the land he gifts and the husband will own all. There will be no sharing, Hereward.' She narrowed her eyes. 'And we are to be silent when among folk, and submit to the will of our husbands and fathers, as Eve was less than Adam, so says that Christian book.'

Hereward hid his smile. He felt pleased that his wife's fire had not been dimmed by the hardships she had been forced to endure in his company.

'Are women then not to be free?' she pressed. 'Are we to be slaves? Is this right?'

'It is not right, wife, but it is the Norman way, and another sign of how grim life will be if we bow our heads to the Bastard.'

Turfrida clenched one small fist and glared. 'If you do not bring him low, know that the wives of Ely will rise up in your stead and make the heavens shake.'

'That cowardly king would quake if he could hear you,' Hereward said, and they laughed and discussed what celebrations would be made once the Normans fled back across the whale road, and how many new babies would be born nine months later.

Then he held her face in his hands and kissed her before stepping back out into the hot sun. But as he made his way along the track towards the throb of life, he glimpsed a figure skulking in the shadows behind one of the homes. Instinctively, he dropped his hand to his sword hilt. But then Acha eased into the glaring light, her eyes darting around.

'You should not be here,' he said.

'Your words were not so harsh when we lay together in Eoferwic,' she replied, her implacable eyes as black as her hair.

'Those days lie far behind us and I am not the same man now.' Unbidden, his thoughts swept back to their hungry love-making while the snow blanketed the Northumbrian city, and he felt a pang of guilt. He pushed the vision from his mind, but he noted she had not lost any of her beauty in the intervening years.

'Your heart is the same. I know it.' She stepped closer to him, so that her breasts almost brushed his arm.

'You have a man. Kraki. He will protect you—'

She waved a hand as if swatting a fly, her nose wrinkling. 'He stinks, he snores in an ale-sleep every night, and his moods are as dark as the winter sea—'

'And he will not take you back to your home, or show you the life you would have had if you had stayed in the Cymri court.'

She would not meet his gaze. 'You and I are of a kind. You know that. We should share our days and nights.'

'I say again, I have a wife.'

'And I say again, take another. One that befits a leader of men.' Her eyes gleamed with defiance and her lips curled back from her teeth. 'With me beside you, crushing the king will only be the first of the great tales they will tell about you in days to come. Who knows what heights you could reach?'

'I know what it is you want, and I know you will go to any lengths to get it. Once—' He caught the words in his throat and shook his head. 'No matter. This is done. I will be gone from Ely for a while. When I return, let us not speak of this again.'

He pushed past her, though he could feel her cold eyes upon his back as he moved along the track. Yet barely had he gone four spear-lengths when he glimpsed a hulking figure beside the well. It was Kraki, his expression unreadable. Hereward wondered if the Viking had overheard any of the conversation, but when he glanced back, the other man was gone. The rivalry and suspicion that had once lain between them was still close to the surface, and it would be an ill thing for it to rise again.

CHAPTER TEN

The hooded man pushed his way through the crowded street. A beggar, he seemed, shoulders hunched from the burdens of his life. His gait was weak and shambling, his cloak, tunic and breeches filthy with the mud of the road and reeking of sweat and loam. He leaned on a tall willow staff to help him over the sun-baked ruts.

Wincestre throbbed with life. Since the new king had set to building a new world in which to live, many had come from nearby towns to seek a living, the beggar saw as he looked around. In the smithies, the hammers never stilled. The rattling of looms sounded from a hundred doors. Men shouldered bales and dragged sacks, and carpenters sang as they stripped oak logs for new house beams. In the marketplace, merchants competed for attention with ever louder cries while their boys fought with each other in the dust. The earth-walker's head rang with the din of hens squawking in their crates and droves of grunting pigs herded towards Butchers' Row where the blood ran in the street and clouds of black flies droned. Never had he seen so much food, or such wealth.

The beggar wandered the winding streets. Past the remnants of the old stone buildings left by the Roman conquerors he staggered, and up to the gates of the new conqueror's palace. He watched and he listened, missing nothing. What a strange place this was, he thought. Bought with the blood of Englishmen and built on the bones of generations. And now Wincestre filled with folk picking over the remains for their own selfish needs.

In the shade of an apple tree opposite the palace gates, he sat and waited. Every time the gate opened, he lowered his head and watched from under hooded eyes. Finally two men sauntered out. The beggar recognized the Mercian brothers Edwin and Morcar, heads raised as if they still held power over all they saw. Once they had passed, he forced himself up on his staff and limped after them. The two men and their shadow weaved through the crowds. The brothers dawdled in the market, examining the fine Frankish jewellery, delicate glassware from the Rhineland and gleaming Flemish swords, all fresh from the ships on the south coast. Their heads dipped close together in conversation. They deigned to speak to no other.

As the pair sheltered from the heat of the midday sun in the shade between two workshops, the beggar stepped up. 'Alms, sirs?' he enquired, holding out filthy fingers. When Edwin shook his head and held up a stately hand to urge the stranger away, the beggar raised his head and whispered, 'No words of comfort for an old friend?'

The two men jerked, frowning. Hereward eased his hood back a little so they could see his face. 'You will have us all killed!' Edwin hissed, glancing around.

'True. No words of denial will save you from the king's wrath if you are found with such an enemy of the crown,' Hereward whispered with a shrug.

This seemed to drive Morcar to a rage. His cheeks flushed red, but he was forced to stifle his fury for fear of drawing attention. Gritting his teeth, he muttered, 'Do not put us at risk.'

'Not after you have worked so hard to worm your way into the king's favour, or at least keep your heads upon your shoulders.'

'Why are you here?' Edwin demanded. 'No place is more dangerous for you.'

From the depths of his hood, the warrior searched the passing throng. The king's men were everywhere in that town. 'A matter of import. But you are right, this is not the place to talk. The tavern.'

Their faces hardened, but he knew they would not risk a confrontation. Along winding tracks among the houses the brothers forged, casting furtive glances as they went. At that time of day, the alehouse was all but empty. They paid for their drinks and huddled at the back of the long, low hall amid the reek of stale beer and woodsmoke.

Turning up his nose, Edwin nodded at Hereward's beggar's clothes. 'These masks served you well when you were a youth, troubling your neighbours in Barholme. Your true face was always a sign of coming strife. As now.'

Hereward grinned. 'I have travelled from Ely into these dangerous waters because you are needed.'

Edwin and Morcar exchanged a look. 'By you?'

The warrior leaned forward, lowering his voice until it was barely a whisper. 'By the English. You each have many loyal men. Two armies. Bring them together with my own in the east and we will have the numbers to drive the treacherous Normans out.'

Edwin snorted and shook his head. 'And who would lead this army? You? A man made outlaw by his own father? A thief and murderer who cannot contain his own burning anger? You were always as much a threat to those around you as to those you faced.'

Hereward's eyes narrowed. 'I am not the man I was.'

Morcar lowered his head over his ale-cup. 'No matter how big your army, the king can never be defeated.'

'Yes, he defeated you once, in the north—'

'And we were lucky to escape with our lives,' Edwin interjected, eyes blazing.

Hereward leaned forward, hands outstretched. 'You think

69

you are safe here? The king keeps you close where he can watch you. He keeps you well fed and drunk on mead, but a time will come when he will take away your land, and then your heads.'

'Aye, that may well be,' Morcar said, nodding slowly. 'And we will be ready for him to make his move—'

'You will not see it coming,' the warrior insisted. 'I have many plans in place, most of them hidden like serpents in the grass, ready to rise up and bite when the time is right. Only one thing holds me back – too few men. And we can change that here.'

'I have no faith in you,' Edwin said with a shake of his head. He glanced towards the door where two men were arguing in loud voices. 'The north will rise up again soon. Were I to send my men to fight, it would be there. But I have done that once and almost paid the greatest price. No more. Let someone else fight the king. My brother and I will eat his food and enjoy the comforts of his court—'

'While England burns and folk die?' Hereward snapped.

'Folk always die,' Edwin said, rising. He beckoned to Morcar to follow. 'This is not my worry.' As the two nobles made to leave, Edwin turned back and said, 'I have shown you a kindness here for your father's sake. He was always a loyal thegn. But if I see your face here again, I will have you dragged before the king and your miserable life ended.'

Hereward watched the brothers stride out into the bright sunlight. He refused to be perturbed. His army needed to be built into a force that would make the king quake, and nothing – not even two haughty earls – would stand in his way.

CHAPTER ELEVEN

Bubbles broke the surface of the filthy marsh-water. A moment later the young man burst from the stinking surface, gasping and flailing and crying out in panic. Black mud streaked his face and hair and soaked his tunic. Laughter echoed across the wetlands from the slopes of Ely where the callow youths who wished to be warriors waited with their spears and their shields still smelling of fresh paint.

A cloud of flies droned away as Hereward grasped the man's tunic and hauled him out of the stagnant pool. He was still exhausted from the long journey back from Wincestre, but there was work to be done. With a shake of his head, he tossed the man on to the bank where he wheezed and sputtered and coughed up the foul stew. 'Here is your lesson,' he called to the watching group. 'A man is not a fish.'

'You should see Penda kiss a girl,' someone called, making loud popping noises and flapping his arms.

'That's how he fucks,' someone else shouted.

The others all fell about laughing. Hereward offered a hand to the unfortunate recruit, who glowered at his fellows. He wiped the mud from his scowling face and stalked back to his place at the end of a line.

'This is a world of water,' Hereward said as he walked along the front of his audience. He studied the faces, young and not so young, all of them untutored in the ways of battle. Some would not see out the winter, their blood draining into the fenland bogs. But there was no doubting their determination to do whatever they could to repel the invaders. 'If you treat it like the world of solid land that most of you are used to, it will claim your wretched lives.' He plucked up the hollow reed that Penda had dropped, tipped his head back and placed it to his lips. Pointing at the sodden young man, he said, 'This time use those shells on the side of your head. This reed will let you breathe while you lie beneath the water. You will all be eels, waiting to bite the unwary earth-traveller who steps into your home.'

He strode back to the edge of the black water and swept one arm towards the glassy wetlands. Barbs of golden light glinted from the morning sun. 'Now it is hot and bright, but soon the mists and the rains will come. They will be our cloaks, as the night is now. The Normans are used to fields of battle and shield walls and horsemen. Not a place that shifts around them even as they watch. They do not understand this world. But we do. We will be like ghosts. Our foes will not be able to touch us. And they will fear us, as they fear ghosts, as they fear the judgement of God.' He clapped his hands. 'Now come. Show me some of what I said today has entered your thick skulls.'

The new recruits trailed out. Some were eager to show their courage, others wary. From the reed-beds dotted along the edges of the marsh they broke off stems and then one by one they waded out into the still waters. When Hereward raised his right arm, the men turned and waited for his signal. As he lowered it, they sank beneath the surface. The ripples dissipated, and within a moment not a sign remained that any of them had been there. The Mercian nodded and grinned. If he could teach them enough to save even one life, it would be worth it. He picked up a stone and hurled it out into the marsh. With the splash, the new warriors rose up, each one a ghastly, black-streaked apparition that would strike fear into the heart of the bravest Norman.

'Be proud of yourselves, you are now all eels,' he called to the dripping men. 'Once the world-candle has dried your bones, we will begin anew. There is much to learn.'

As the men waded out of the bog, Hereward set off up the slope to where the rest of the newest recruits were at practice. Alric waited for him at the top of the bank, a wry smile on his lips. 'You would make a good preacher,' he said.

'Burn out my eyes now, monk, and be done with it.'

The other man laughed. 'The church coffers would never be so full, with every rich merchant too afraid to leave without dipping his hand into his purse.'

'The church fills its coffers well enough without my aid,' the Mercian replied with a grin. 'Abbots think wine only comes in cups of gold.'

The slopes around Ely's ramparts throbbed with activity. Hereward watched the warriors at work. He was reminded of the battle-fair at Bruges where all the spears-for-hire went in search of well-paid employment for the coming year. Under Hengist's severe gaze, some men dug pits along the edges of the ditches, burying sharpened stakes in the bottom, then covering the hole with dry branches and leaves. He had witnessed the effectiveness of those traps time and again in Flanders. There, the defenders smeared the stakes with shit to kill any survivors with the sickness that came from the filth.

Guthrinc marched along a line of ten men armed with hunting bows. As he dropped his arm, they released a flight of arrows at painted straw targets. A few hit their mark. Most sailed well over. Guthrinc clasped his head in both hands and threw it back in a silent exclamation of exasperation. 'Let us try something easier,' he boomed. 'Like Horsa's barn.' He caught Hereward's eye and shook his head with exaggerated weariness.

Near the wall Kraki bellowed at a row of red-faced, sweating men, each one clutching a borrowed axe. 'Your arms are as weak as babes,' the Viking roared. 'A huscarl can hack a man

73

from shoulder to stern with one blow. The only work your right arms have had is playing with yourselves each night.' Spittle flew from his lips as he thrust his grizzled face a finger's width away from the nose of the nearest man.

Redwald sauntered over from the direction of the gates. Alric stiffened, though Hereward did not know why. If there was some argument between the two, he didn't want to hear it. 'You will have an army to be proud of,' Redwald said, looking around as he arrived.

'Or Guthrinc and Kraki will have broken each man in two and we will be forced to arm the women,' Hereward said.

'No bad thing. I would think twice about facing an English woman in a battle-fury.' He nodded to Alric. 'I would speak with you when your work is done, if you will hear me. There are things in my heart that eat away at me like the wolf, and I would seek the peace only God can give me.'

Alric seemed taken aback by this request. He flushed and said, 'If I can aid you, I will.'

'Good.' Redwald turned back to his brother. 'You have made your plans for our strike against the Norman bastards?'

'Our men crawl through ditches and hide in tree-tops. They see every move the Normans make. We know where their numbers are strong and where their defences are weak.' Hereward turned and gazed out across the wetlands and the thick woods. 'Once Hengist is rested, he will take our three best men one last time. Hengist is a water-rat. He could lie under William the Bastard's nose and not be seen.'

'And then . . . ?'

Hereward grinned. 'And then we will tear through them like a storm of axes.'

'Show mercy in victory,' Alric pressed.

'Did they show mercy at Senlac Ridge? You were there, brother, at Harold Godwinson's side. What mercy did those Normans show our king and the good Englishmen who stood there that day?'

Redwald snatched his head away, his eyes suddenly haunted.

Hereward realized the horrors that his brother had witnessed that day had hollowed him out. He glanced back at Alric, his tone lightening. 'If they give up their arms and agree to leave, I will show mercy. You have my vow.'

CHAPTER TWELVE

When the sun reached its height, the warriors ended their work, collapsing in breathless heaps in front of their hard taskmasters. On weary legs, they trailed back through the gates in search of bread and a cup of ale. The women waited with pitchers of drink. Some of the younger ones smiled and held the eyes of the warriors, making it plain they were offering more than just mead. They tied ribbons round the most favoured fighters, tokens or promises. Once done, they cast cold eyes at the waiting whores who had joined the throng making their way to Ely. There was no food, but a fighting man could find comfort between a pair of thighs whenever he needed.

Hereward and his closest advisors ate no midday meal. They made a show of their abstinence as they wandered past the men sheltering in the shade of the open barns. In his travels through Flanders, the Mercian had seen too many commanders wallowing in luxury while their men grubbed for morsels in the dirt. It had sickened him to see such superior behaviour when he was a spear-for-hire. Now he was leader he would not inflict it on his own men. He knew from experience that they would reward him with loyalty.

A cry rang out from the gates as they sweltered in the lazy heat outside the abbot's hall. New arrivals were requesting entrance. With Alric and Redwald, Hereward made his way down the dusty track to greet those who had answered the call.

When the gates ground open, a huddled crowd of perhaps twenty men, women and children stood there. Their faces were streaked with mud, their tunics and dresses filthy, and they had the wide-eyed, hollow-cheeked appearance of folk who had not eaten in days. A young girl as pale as snow lay in her father's arms, her eyelids fluttering. Some pressed their palms together and whispered their thanks to God. Others threw their arms to the heavens and cried with joy. Hereward felt touched by the hope he saw in those faces as they traipsed past the palisade and into Ely. He heard gruff Northumbrian accents and the lilting tones of Wessex, some of his own Mercians and others with the strange tongues of the borderlands to the west.

The warriors clambered out from the shade to welcome the new arrivals in. The women offered cups of ale. The tradition of English welcome to strangers never would be ignored. But when Hereward peered into the faces of the Ely folk, he saw flickers of doubt. With every new mouth to feed, their meagre supplies diminished further.

'Will we ever have to close the gates?' Redwald wondered as if he could read his brother's thoughts.

'How can we turn the needy away?' Alric whispered. 'And *we* have created this hope that brings them to our door. Can we then deny them?'

'The more strong right arms for our army, the better,' Hereward said. 'We turn no one away. The answer is to find more food.'

Two men, of perhaps eighteen summers, and a woman of the same age broke away from the weary group and came over. Hereward had seen them eyeing him furtively and whispering behind their hands.

'You are the ring-giver,' one of the men said, pointing to the gold bands around Hereward's arms. 'You are the one they tell of? The warrior Hereward?' Pale, he was, with thick red hair and a sweep of freckles across his nose. The other man had darker hair, but the same pallid complexion. Enough similarities lay in their features to suggest they were brothers. The woman was pretty, with the blonde hair of Danish blood. She had done her best to keep herself presentable: her face was clean, her hair combed, and her yellow dress, though raggedy, had once been fine.

'I am Hereward.'

The red-headed man beamed and the other man let out a grunt of relief. The woman's eyes lit up. 'In Leomynstre, we heard the tales of the bear-killer and his army who lured the Normans into their death chambers,' the red-headed one gushed. 'My brother and I, we wished to be a part of this battle-dance, but we feared the tales lied, or were stirred up to create false hope, or . . .'

'I am Edoma,' the woman said with a sweet smile. 'The one whose tongue flaps like a sparrow's wing is Sighard. And that is Madulf. They offered me protection on the long road after the Normans killed my kin. We will do all we can to help.'

Hereward looked around the fresh faces and felt the weight of responsibility. They came to *him*, by name, not to the rebels. Their future days were in his hands now.

'All you have heard is true,' Redwald said with a broad grin.

'We welcome you here to Ely,' Hereward added. 'Go with my brother Redwald and tell him your skills, and we will find a use for each one of you.'

He caught sight of a scowling man at the back of the straggling column. His tunic was filthy and blood smeared his face. His arm was wrapped around the shoulders of a woman, his wife, Hereward guessed, who clutched a dirty cloth to the side of her face as she rested her head on her husband's chest. She trembled with each step she took.

The Mercian pushed his way through to the couple. 'You are wounded,' he noted. 'Go to the minster. The leech will tend to you at the infirmary. Take no heed of his gruff manner. He is hard pressed and may make you wait a while.'

The woman forced a thankful smile. Her husband continued to scowl. Hereward thought how weary he looked, as if his legs would give way at any moment.

Alric leaned in, mystified by the way the woman pressed the cloth to her face. 'What did this? A wolf?'

The man laughed bitterly. 'A wolf. One that walks like a man and speaks with a Norman tongue.'

Hereward's face darkened. He reached out to the cloth, slowly so that he would not alarm the woman. When he saw she would not resist, he gently lifted the material away. The monk uttered an oath, his hand flying to his mouth. The woman's face had been burned, the straight line of the raw wound almost cutting down to the cheekbone. The skin around it was blackened, and he could smell the sweet stench of rot from the exposed flesh. He had seen that kind of wound before, the touch of a poker that had lain long in hot coals.

'Who did this?' he hissed.

'A witch-hunter.' The man choked back tears of anger. 'The churchman and three Norman knights caught us on the road and accused Burwenna of witchery because she had made an offering at a well upon the way. They dragged us to a hut beside a church and demanded a confession.'

'I would not confess,' the woman croaked, 'for I knew they would then take my life. So they burned me with the hot rod, to force the words out of me.'

'And still she resisted,' the man said, his voice breaking. His eyes flecked with tears and he hugged his wife closer to him. 'We escaped them only when they left the hut to meet four more knights who came on horses.'

The witch-hunters followed the Normans the way rats followed a butcher, Hereward knew. As the invaders crushed all resistance with brutal force, the churchmen darted here and there in the confusion, rooting out the heathens with fire and iron. He recalled the churchman who had come close to capturing Turfrida in Flanders and his blood boiled. Was this the same man, the one seen as the cruellest witch-hunter in all

Christendom? If it were, they had business, this cleric and he. 'No one will harm you here,' he said to the couple gently. 'Hurry to the leech now, and know you are safe.'

Once the couple had offered him effusive thanks and set off up the slope to the minster, he cast a cold eye towards Alric. The monk squirmed. 'You know I do not condone the ways of the witch-hunters. They are a breed apart, even among men of God. We fear them as much as the heathens do.'

'You will be judged by their actions, monk, whether you like it or not. Folk see only preachers.'

Chastened, Alric bowed his head. The Mercian softened. 'You keep God well here. All in Ely know that. And the children love you, and they are the harshest judges of all.'

A smile sprang back to the monk's lips. 'I would take you to the Camp of Refuge. High matters have kept you away since our return, but it would be well for you to see your folk.'

Hereward was baffled, but Alric would say no more. They made their way through old Ely and along the new track to the lea on the southern slope of the island. As they passed through a copse to where the woods had been newly cleared, the Mercian came to a halt, caught by the sight of the vast camp sprawling down to the water's edge. It had more than doubled in size since he had last visited.

The sounds of mallets, saws and adzes echoed everywhere. Axes hacked into tree trunks along the edge of the wood and men bellowed warnings as each tree thundered to the ground. The branches were chopped off in quick succession and hempen ropes tied around the trunks to drag them down to the wood-workers. He surveyed the new buildings rising from the ground all around the encampment. Some were little more than shacks, barely high enough for a man to stand upright. Others were clearly constructed to house several families. Many looked as if a strong wind would bring them crashing down. Sods of turf made up for the lack of good straw for the thatch. The dwellings were so tightly packed there was barely space to squeeze among them, and in the narrow tracks and rat-runs, new neighbours forced past each other, stumbling and cursing.

'So many,' he muttered. He estimated almost four thousand now crowded into that camp.

'So many,' Alric repeated.

The air reeked of human filth and piss. As he entered the throng, the clamour rang so loud all around he could barely hear Alric's conversation. In that crowded space, tempers were short. A pockmarked smith threw down his hammer and barked a curse at a gangly youth who had stumbled against a rack of cooling rods. Within moments, fists were flying. The two men rolled around the dusty ground outside the ramshackle smithy. They wrestled furiously as yapping dogs snapped at their tunics. Two red-faced women bellowed at each other, hands on hips – the wives, Hereward guessed – and soon they were pulling each other's hair. Snot-nosed children ran around the brawl, laughing and pointing.

Hereward's features became drawn as he pushed his way further into the Camp of Refuge. Lethargic children with big eyes and too-sharp bones squatted in the dirt outside their homes. Through open doors, he glimpsed sick men and women rolling and moaning on their beds of straw. The stink of vomit and sweat was fierce in the stifling heat. More fights. Broken limbs and untreated wounds. Excrement pooled beside the houses where the children played. And everywhere there were bodies pressed tight and cries for help and calls for alms.

Hereward came to a halt and looked around. Not even in the grimmest parts of Eoferwic had he seen such a miserable sight. 'They say we are the Devil's Army,' he murmured, barely aware of Alric's eyes upon him. 'Then this must be hell.'

'Aye, hell it is.'

He heard the odd note in his friend's voice and looked into the monk's face. The other man stared back. His lips were tight but his eyes held a glint that Hereward knew well. 'I see why you brought me here. There are some who say your heart is too big. I say ours are not big enough.'

The Mercian realized that the men and women had come to a halt and were watching him as if he were, as Alric had suggested, a king come down among common folk. Silence fell on the crowd. He looked around those dour faces and expected to see some hint of accusation, or blame for their predicament. But he glimpsed only blank acceptance, and then, after a moment, a smile or two breaking those solemn visages, flickers of hope like candles in the dark of the night. His name rustled out, and again, and another time, the whispers building until it became like a murmured prayer at matins.

Hereward felt humbled by what he heard in that sound. He glanced down at a blond-haired boy looking up at him. The lad seemed a little frightened by this figure that had so troubled the adults. For a moment, he saw himself at the king's court so long ago, and then, in the rush of emotion that came with recognition, he broke into a reassuring grin. Bending down, he grasped the boy and swung him up on to his shoulders. 'You shall be king for the day,' he called, and those around laughed as he had hoped. 'What shall be your first decree?'

The boy hesitated, unnerved. As the crowd shouted encouragement, he was caught up in the spirit, and threw his arms in the air, calling, 'Bread!' The throng cheered and clapped.

Hereward laughed, tickling the boy beneath his armpits so that he squirmed. 'Bread it shall be,' he cried. 'And more besides.'

He sensed Alric eyeing him uneasily. In that wordless glance he saw a caution that he should not promise what he could not deliver. But as he set off through the Camp of Refuge with the boy still on high, he said quietly to the monk, 'I have not been a good leader. I thought my work was to defeat the Normans by using all my skills as a leader of battle-wolves. And yet I missed the battle beneath my nose. We must win here, in the Camp of Refuge, if we are ever to win the greater fight.'

'Then what should we do?'

Hereward pushed his way through the bodies up the slope to the edge of the camp and then he turned and surveyed the island. 'We need men and women who will fight for food as we fight our foes. And leaders who will send them into battle well armed and with good plans. Look. Ely is rich in beasts of the chase. The soil is good. There are plants in the woods and on the edges of the marshes, and fish, and soon there will be berries and nuts. And with gold we will buy more food from the merchants in the towns. They would rather sell to us than to those Norman bastards.'

'Gold?' Alric enquired.

Hereward nodded, smiling. Already a plan was forming, if he had the time and the wit to make it real. 'Once again you have taught me a lesson, monk. Should I ever forget your true worth, may God strike me dead, for you have made me man not devil. No mouth will go unfed while I am here in Ely, I vow this now. I am not William the Bastard, I am Hereward, I am English, and I will never betray the folk I have called beneath my banner.'

The boy cheered. Hereward put him down and kicked him up the arse to send him on his way. As the lad scurried off, he grunted, 'I hate children.'

CHAPTER THIRTEEN

Gobbets of fat sizzled and spat in the roaring flames. The sweating slave turned the spit and the sticky scent of the roast ox swirled up with the grey woodsmoke. Around the bonfire, the women lifted the hems of their finest dresses and whirled to the harpist's tune with faces bright from the heat. Now the scop had finished spinning his tales, the drunken men bellowed a bawdy song to accompany the wild dance. They clapped and stamped their feet to the beat. All life in Ely had gathered on the green for the feast – old friends and neighbours and new arrivals, warriors and monks and ceorls.

Beyond the circle of light cast by the fire, Hereward clutched his mead-cup and watched the festivities. Alric stood beside him, as sober as always. 'You are thinking of Vadir,' the monk said as he eyed the other man's reflective expression.

'He liked a good feast, and enough ale to drown himself.' Hereward recalled scrabbling out his friend's grave in the hard Flemish soil.

The monk raised his head to look up to the sprinkle of stars across the clear night sky. A bat flitted overhead. 'Do you yearn for the days when every woe could be made well by cutting off its head? Now you battle with enemies who are like the mist. Not enough food to fill the bellies of these folk who rely on you so. Men at your shoulder each with a smile on his face and a sword behind his back. Fear of the king, fear of the End-Times, fear that everything familiar is gone, never to return. Fear everywhere, eating its way into hearts like a sickness so that soon Englishmen will tremble too much to lift a spear. Why, beside that William the Bastard is a half-lame deer.'

Hereward laughed. 'Ah, monk, where would I be without you to show me the dark in the brightest day?'

Alric smiled to himself. 'I would not want you to become soft.'

Lost in his thoughts, the warrior wiped mead from his chin with the back of his hand. He still did not know why he had chosen this bloody path when it would have been easier to cross the whale road and earn good coin with his strong sword-arm. His demons were eased, though, he knew that much.

'Good news from your journey to the south?'

'A hunter bides his time.'

'No, then.'

Hereward shrugged. 'I have more than one dog running.'

'You keep your secrets close.' Alric searched his friend's face for clues. 'To protect us, I would wager.'

'There is nothing to be gained from staring into the dark.'

The monk nodded towards the festivities. 'These folk eat heartily and drink until their legs fail, but not because they are at peace. They would savour the last drops of life because all here know this may be their last feast.' He paused, looking down at his feet. 'At least tell me: how bad is it? You owe me that.'

Hereward tightened his jaw, but he could not deny his friend. 'We are few. The king's men are many,' he began, choosing words that would not dwell on hopelessness. 'William the Bastard has had his hands full since he stole the crown. New laws, new castles, taxes to collect, Norman knights to reward, and not a few restive English folk. But as more and more of our own bow their heads to him, his time is freed. Soon his cold gaze will turn towards the east. And William the Bastard is not a man to do things by halves. When he comes for Ely, the slaughter of the English army at Senlac Ridge will seem as nothing.'

'Are we not growing stronger by the day?' Alric replied, holding out his hands.

'Not fast enough. We need more men, and seasoned fighters at that. We need weapons that can match the Norman sword and crossbow. We need food for that army, and gold, for where there is gold there is power.' He let his gaze linger across the heads of the feasting Ely folk. 'And we need for the English to believe we can win.'

'Your fame is spreading far and wide.'

'Not fast enough.' Hereward swilled down the last of his mead and grinned. 'No one said this fight would be easy. There are paths through the wilderness if only we can find them.'

'If anyone can find them, it is the man who slays bears and tears the throat out of wolves with his own teeth,' Alric baited. He beckoned to Acha who was circling the feast with a pitcher of mead. 'Drink more and ease your troubles,' he added.

Hereward looked away into the gloom as Acha sauntered over. He could feel her gaze heavy on him. 'Let me fill your cup,' she purred. 'You were missed these last few days.' She poured the mead, leaning in closer than she needed.

Before Hereward could respond, she let out a cry of shock. The golden mead splashed on to the mud. Kraki had grabbed her arm and was dragging her away. 'Watch this one,' the Viking slurred drunkenly. 'She has a sting like a wasp.' Acha glowered as she stumbled back towards the fire.

'If he treats that one like a mare to be broken, he will get kicked where it hurts,' Alric said uneasily. Hereward observed Acha's murderous glare and began to worry that a kick would be the least of the dangers lying ahead.

They strolled around the perimeter of the feast. Hereward watched the men slicing hot slabs of beef and wolfing down the meat before they had trudged out of the ashes. 'They eat as though there will be no tomorrow,' he muttered darkly.

'The hunger will pass, God willing,' Alric exclaimed, grabbing his friend's elbow. 'Come, let me show you the fruits of your promise.' He pulled the Mercian through the crowd until he found the red-headed youth and his darker brother, and the girl who had accompanied them to Ely, sprawling on the slope of the Speaking Mound. 'Meet your new Masters of the Larder,' he announced. 'Sighard, Madulf and Edoma.'

Sighard jumped to his feet, wiping his greasy hands on his tunic. 'Alric said it was your idea.'

'What idea?'

The red-headed lad plucked up a sack and held it open for Hereward to see. 'Burdock and rape, from the forest,' he gushed.

Hereward turned up his nose. 'That won't fill many bellies.'

Standing, Edoma pushed back her blonde hair and said shyly, 'We bring back only handfuls so the monks can tell us if they are of use. But we know where they grow now.'

'Not just these plants,' Sighard said with an enthusiastic sweep of his arm. 'We have travelled far and wide around Ely. We know where the boar roam, and the deer. Good land where we can plant barley and wheat . . .'

'If we can buy seed,' Madulf added sullenly. The brown-haired brother remained seated.

'. . . and in the Camp of Refuge, the women are building willow baskets to catch eels,' Sighard continued.

Alric pointed towards the church tower on top of the hill. 'At the minster, we have a barn which we are starting to fill with the food our new Masters of the Larder have found. These three have uncovered skills they did not know they had.'

'Then you deserve the thanks of all here,' Hereward said. He knew the monk was being kind; few others in Ely had the desire to spend their free hours foraging. 'This work is as vital as any we do.'

'I would be fighting,' Madulf growled, drawing himself up. 'That is why we came to Ely.'

'Be careful what you wish for,' Hereward said sternly. 'But if that is what you want, you will get your chance.' He noticed

Edoma was looking past him, distracted. When he followed her gaze, he saw Redwald leaning against the wall of a house, studying the bonfire.

'I think I will see if your brother knows how to dance,' she mused. As she walked away, the two brothers watched her go, scowling. They flashed each other a look and then both hurried after their friend.

'Edoma has won two hearts, it seems,' Alric observed. The youths positioned themselves either side of the girl as she chatted with Redwald.

Hereward grinned. 'They are too young for her. She has a taste for tougher meat. But they will learn.'

For a moment, Alric watched the small group, lost to his thoughts. Then he murmured, 'You trust Redwald?'

The Mercian glanced at the monk, taken aback. 'There is no man I trust more.' He pursed his lips. 'Though if you held a spear to my neck, I would say you could match him,' he added grudgingly. 'Why do you ask?'

Alric shrugged. 'I have not shared the years, like you and he. I know only what I see, and I do not see enough to make a fair judgement. He smiles easily, and he has the face of a boy.' He paused, choosing his words. 'But what hides in his skull I am not sure.'

'You have spent too many days in my company. You start to see enemies everywhere.'

With a sound like a flock of gulls, a crowd of children ran up and circled Alric, tugging at his tunic. 'Your friends have come calling,' Hereward noted. 'I would have thought they'd had a bellyful of you during those dull lessons you preach at the minster.'

'Never,' the children cried.

Laughing, Alric allowed himself to be led away. With a warm smile, Hereward watched the monk go and then turned and walked up the slope towards the church tower silhouetted against the starry sky. He paused at the minster enclosure, listening to the owls hoot and enjoying the night-breeze on his face. Each moment of peace now felt more precious to him than all the gold in the church. Pushing open the creaking gate, he followed the snaking path through the beds of herbs towards the cluster of wood and wattle buildings, the stores, the eating house, the school, the monks' halls. At the church door, he prowled inside, his leather soles whispering on the stone flags. Fat candles flickered around the altar and shadows danced across the walls. He breathed in chill air scented with tallow-smoke and sweet incense. From one of the annexes, he could hear monks chanting in the Roman tongue, the music of their voices echoing up to the rafters.

He found Abbot Thurstan kneeling in prayer beside a shrine. Offerings had been laid before it – bread, a bunch of summer savoury, a cup of mead, a piece of embroidered linen – the silent cries of people filled with worry for the days to come. As Hereward neared, the abbot jerked his head up as if he feared an attack. When he saw it was the Mercian, he nodded and clambered to his feet. He was a tall man, silver-haired and thin as a needle, with gentle ways and an air of quiet reflection that won him many friends. He had more learning than any other man in the fens, Hereward had heard.

'Do you pray for me, Father?' Hereward asked with a wry smile.

Thurstan raised one eyebrow. 'Some would say you need all the aid you can find.'

'There is truth in that.'

The abbot saw his visitor scrutinizing the shrine and said, 'Make an offering. St Etheldreda may look kindly upon a kindred spirit.'

Hereward frowned. 'How so?'

'Etheldreda refused to submit to an unjust king. Egfrith was his name. Though she wished to become a nun, she had been promised to him by his neighbour, her father, King Anna of East Anglia, on the understanding that she remained a maid.'

The Mercian smiled grimly. 'The understanding lasted . . . a day?'

'Egfrith was filled with lust and had no intention of keeping the pact. Etheldreda fled back to Ely where she built this church. She set free all the bondsmen on her land and lived the rest of her days close to God. After she died, those who prayed to her received her aid from heaven, so we are told. And when her body was moved to a greater tomb after many summers, it was as if she had died only that day, though she had lain in wet earth.'

'Then I will make an offering and say a prayer, Father. We are beset by enemies on all sides, and here at home too. If heavenly aid comes my way, I will not turn up my nose.'

Thurstan laughed, but only for a moment. Taking a spill, he began to light the candles along the wall near the shrine. 'We pray for you every day, Hereward,' he said. His face glowed as a flame licked up.

'Your monks still have no ill-feeling towards my men? William the Bastard will punish them like no other for their aid.'

'Only if you fall. No, we made our choice. The king would have come for us sooner or later. A Norman abbot would be here, one with a cold eye and an iron grip. As long as your spears keep the Normans at bay, we can still live as we always did, and we give thanks for that.'

Hereward raised his head to look up into the gloom enveloping the rafters. 'We need more gold, Father.'

'You cannot eat it.'

'We can buy food from the markets to the south. And weapons. And pay spears-for-hire.'

Thurstan shook his head. 'I cannot let you take the church's treasures, Hereward.' He lit the last candle and blew out the spill.

'And I would not ask you for them. You have been good to us and I would not risk our friendship. But I have some thoughts and seek your guidance—'

Before Hereward could press the abbot further, a fearful cry rang out somewhere beyond the church. Another voice picked it up, and then another until a tumult echoed all around.

'We are under attack,' the warrior snarled, unsheathing Brainbiter. He dashed towards the entrance, the abbot close behind.

When he tore open the door and bounded out into the night, he first thought the feast-fire had been stoked too high. Sparks sailed overhead and clouds of smoke wafted across the minster grounds. Then through the fug he glimpsed an amber glow near by. White-faced monks raced around the enclosure, fearful that the fire would spread. Hereward grabbed the nearest one by the shoulders and bellowed, 'Fetch water from the well. Line up your men.'

As he darted towards the burning building, he saw it was already too late. The thatched roof had collapsed inwards, the timber frame nothing but a blackened skeleton swathed in shimmering orange. He threw a hand across his face to shield him from the heat, his suspicions swiftly rising.

Breathless, Alric stumbled up, his jaw dropping when he realized what building was alight. 'The food store,' he gasped. 'Our meagre supplies . . .'

Hereward could hear frantic cries rising up the slope from the feast. Once folk realized their supplies had been further depleted, they would be consumed with despair. And those black thoughts would spread like the plague in that crowded place. It could be the undoing of them.

'We are accursed,' the monk gasped.

'No curse this. No act of God,' the Mercian growled. 'There were lit candles in the store?'

'Of course not.'

'Then men set this fire.'

The monk gaped, turning slowly to look over the thatched roofs of the settlement. 'Who would do such a thing?' He paused, his thoughts racing. 'We have enemies, here, in Ely?'

'Would the hungry men and women of Ely set our store alight? No, this is an attack.' Hereward gritted his teeth. Already he could see the final outcome if this threat were allowed to run its course. 'Our army will not be defeated by cowards who stab us in the back while we look to the greater enemy,' he said in a stony voice. 'At first light we will begin anew, and all within this place will learn that we will suffer no more hands raised against us.'

CHAPTER FOURTEEN

The guard's black eyes glinted in the candlelight. Beside the heavy oak door to King William's hall, he stood like a rod of iron. His face was as cold and hard as his long mail shirt and his helm and his double-edged sword. He was dressed for war, as was every Norman that strode through Wincestre these days. As usual, Balthar the Fox watched from the shadows. What mysteries transpired behind that long-closed door? he wondered. He felt uneasy that there might be a gap in his knowledge. News was his gold, sifted and piled high to achieve the wise counsel that had bought him such a comfortable life.

As he agonized over what he was missing, the door trundled open and the guard stepped aside. Aged men trailed out, their faces ashen. The wavering light carved lines of tension into their features. Each one was a cleric of high regard, Balthar noted, puzzled. There was Ealdred of Eoferwic, with the nose of a falcon and a gaze like winter, and Wulfstan of Worcester, rotund, flushed and sweating. Heads bowed, Bishop William of London, Bishop Giso of Wells, and Abbot Baldwin of St Edmunds Bury followed, their whispers strained. Each one had committed himself to the cause of the new king, almost before the crown had settled upon his head. The future course of England was as much decided by these men as it was by William the Bastard's army. What could have left them looking as if they had peered into the depths of hell?

Once they had passed, he slipped through a side door into the hot night. The mallets had stilled. The fires of the masons and carpenters were nothing more than hot embers. Blissful peace lay across the palace grounds, and it would remain that way until sun-up, when the frantic work of rebuilding would begin again in force.

Squatting behind a heap of fresh stone, he watched the clerics emerge from the hall's main door. Their voices grew louder, their tone now clearly worried, even frightened. He eased out from his hiding place, trying to hear their conversation.

'You are more spider than fox.'

Balthar jumped as he felt a heavy hand grip his shoulder. He whirled, readying his excuses for the king's guards. Instead, he found himself looking into the faces of Edwin and his brother Morcar. The two Mercians reeked of wine and their eyes were dull with drink.

'Spinning your webs,' Edwin, the taller and stronger of the two, continued. 'Always watching and listening and waiting for a fly to fall into your lap.' He hooked his fingers in Balthar's tunic and drew him in.

'I serve the king,' Balthar replied, unafraid.

'You serve yourself,' Morcar snapped.

'And you do not?' Balthar held the horse-faced man's eyes with defiance. 'Some say two great earls . . . two once-powerful men who commanded the respect of the English . . . could have rallied the beaten folk of this land to throw off the yoke of the Normans.'

Edwin raised his fist. Balthar set his jaw. Blows aplenty he had taken in his life; another would matter little. And all there knew that a price would be paid for any harm to one of the king's advisors. The Mercian's hand wavered, then fell to his side. 'We took a stand—' Edwin began.

'And ran at the first sign of trouble,' the Fox replied,

emboldened. 'Some say.' He smiled, knowing it would sting harder than any fist. 'When those who had the power to resist now drink Norman wine, in Norman halls, at the court of a Norman king, can any man blame plain folk for saying, "This is what God intended"? We follow the path of those who once led.'

Edwin thrust Balthar away, snarling, 'And still you spin your webs, with words now. That is not the whole truth, and you know it.'

'This matter is not settled,' Morcar said, shaking his fist. 'Even now, men rise up in the north. And they are not alone—'

Edwin grabbed his brother's arm and spun him round. 'Enough,' he growled.

Balthar tensed. 'You have heard news from the north?'

'Afraid that your web fails you, spider?' Edwin sneered.

'I know the north rises,' Balthar replied indignantly, but his words were drowned by mocking laughter. The two brothers clapped arms around each other and lurched back towards more wine. The Fox felt his cheeks flush. Was this mysterious news the reason for the king's conclave with the clerics? 'If another war is coming, so be it,' he called after the two noblemen. 'But still I see you sitting here drinking the king's wine.' The Mercians came to a halt: his words had hit home once again. But after a moment they staggered on their way without a backward glance.

They would regret treating him so, Balthar silently vowed, but already his thoughts raced towards this new mystery. With a hunger as if his belly had been empty for days, he turned and hurried towards the small house where Godrun lived. He enjoyed their talks each night at this hour more than he could express, though each one always ended dismally, with him trudging back to the cold bed he shared with his wife. But now there might be a double dish of cheer. If Godrun had been serving the king this evening, she could well have overheard the discussions.

He slipped past the guards at the palace gates – they were

used to his comings and goings and paid him no heed. In the moonless dark, he stumbled along the familiar path among the ramshackle, filth-reeking hovels. Drunken song rolled out from some of the open doors, or the mewling of babies. When he passed, he kept to the shadows. He could not afford to be seen heading for a young woman's home, for in Wincestre tongues were like knives.

Yet as he neared he heard cries emanating from Godrun's hut. Fear clutched him. He quickened his pace, his fingers closing on the small, bone-handled knife his father had given him when he came of age. At the door, he heard those cries more clearly. His chest tightened. With trembling fingers, he eased the door open a crack.

Godrun lay on filthy straw beside the cold hearth. She was naked. A grunting Norman noble was atop her, thrusting. The sweating man gripped her wrists to pin her down, but her pale legs were high and splayed wide. Balthar fought against himself, but his gaze was drawn inexorably to that space between her thighs where the aristocrat's cock slid in and out. He felt equally sickened and excited, and though his stomach churned he could not look away for long moments. As he watched, he realized Godrun was not struggling; indeed, she seemed to be writhing in time with her lover. He reeled back a step as if he had been slapped. But then he looked up and saw the girl staring at him. Her eyes were wide and pleading. Balthar held her gaze for a moment, confusion swimming in his head. Then he closed the door and pressed his back against the wall, covering his face.

For the first time in many seasons, he felt adrift. No cunning fox here, he thought with bitterness. He could make no sense of anything, not least the emotions churning inside him. He recognized the Norman, one of the lesser nobles waiting for crumbs from the king's table. Had Godrun played him for a fool, carrying on with this knight while he did what he could to keep her safe? His cheeks burned at the thought, but in sadness not anger.

Like a whipped dog, he slunk around the side of the hut and

covered his ears from the sounds of love-making. When they had subsided, a few moments of silence elapsed before the door rattled. The silhouette of the departing lover swept past along the path.

Balthar drew himself up, taking three long breaths to steady himself. Once he felt able, he crept back around the hovel and slipped inside.

Now dressed, Godrun stood by the hearth. 'I knew you would return,' she said, her voice flat.

Balthar tried to speak, but his throat was too dry.

With a cry, the young woman ran forward and threw her arms around him, burying her face in his chest. He felt surprised by the rush of emotion, and the stifled sobs that followed. His hands fluttered like a bird's wings in the air before he allowed himself to fold his arms around her. He rocked her gently, blinking away his own tears.

'Forgive me.' Her voice rose up, muffled.

'Why?' he asked.

Those wide eyes peered up at him, brimming with tears. 'There is no escape for me from the men here.'

'The men? Not . . . not that one alone?'

'If I did not give myself, I would not be allowed to stay. I know that.' She bit her lip. 'You could never protect me.'

'And . . . and you strove to keep this from me . . . to . . . save my feelings?' She nodded. He closed his eyes, stung by his failings. How could he have been so blind to what was transpiring beneath his nose? In other times, he would have laughed in bitterness at the irony that the Fox had missed so much.

'Do you forgive me?' Her voice was barely a breath as she lowered her face again.

'How could I not? You did what you did to survive. As do we all.' Balthar felt pity for the girl. Yet even then he was distracted by the warm, sexual muskiness rising from her. He felt his cock stiffen within his tunic. It pressed against her belly. When she did not pull back, he felt another confusion of feelings stir within him.

97

'Will you now abandon me?' she asked.

The asking of the question summoned an answer that surprised even him. 'I could never abandon you.' He grabbed her hand and smothered it with kisses. He felt shocked by the rush of feelings for Godrun, though a part of him realized he had been captured by her from the first moment he had laid eyes upon her. The way she looked at him, with respect, even awe, the manner in which she had been so open to his offer of friendship, her innocence, and, yes, the allure of her face and body, all of it had snared him like a rabbit in a trap. No fox here; he was prey, and he relished that feeling as much as the name the king had given him.

At first she jerked her head back in surprise, but then he saw a curious smile spread across her lips. 'How could so great a man look fondly upon a mouse such as I?'

He hugged her to him and kissed the top of her blonde head. 'You will not suffer at the hands of these men again. I will speak to the king himself—'

'And you will tell him I am yours?'

Balthar hesitated. 'In good time.' He hid his fear at the momentousness of his commitment, all the things he was putting at risk: his position with the king, his power and growing wealth. He offered a comforting smile. 'I am the Fox. I will find a way through this, and we will both be well.'

He kissed her on the head once more, dried her eyes, and gabbled arrangements to visit her soon. Out in the stifling night, his head spun with euphoria. This was a beginning, of that there was no doubt, and who knew what wonders lay ahead. His feet all but danced up the path to the palace. Godrun's beautiful face floated before his eyes. He could feel the smoothness of her skin, and all he wanted to do was press his lips upon hers.

But as he neared the lamps gleaming on the palace gates, he felt his exhilaration ebb away. The tranquillity that had reigned there earlier was gone. From the grounds beyond the wall he could hear a hubbub of low voices, the clank of iron, the sound of many feet hurrying across the hard-packed mud and the neighing of horses brought from the stables. He stepped through the gates into a whirl of activity. Warriors swarmed in hauberks and helms as if for battle. Commanders barked orders. Scouts dressed only in tunics for light travelling were mounting their steeds and drawing towards the gates.

Baffled, and growing increasingly concerned, Balthar weaved his way through the throng. Once he had stepped into the relative peace of the hall, he realized his heart was pounding.

By the cold hearth, the king strode among his commanders, disseminating orders in a loud voice. He too was dressed for war, his vast belly straining at his long mail shirt. Yet for all his girth, Balthar saw no softness. Only power. Once the monarch had dispatched the final commander, he turned and caught sight of Balthar hovering by the door.

'The Fox!' he boomed without any humour. 'Where were you hiding, you sly dog? I have been calling for you.'

Balthar stepped forward, bowing and scraping. 'Forgive me, my lord. I—'

'Enough chatter.' A grim smile spread across his lips. 'I have taken your counsel, Fox.'

'My lord?'

'To put the spear to the nest of vipers.'

For a moment, Balthar struggled to comprehend the king's allusion. 'Ah . . . the . . . the uprising in the north?' he stuttered.

'The time for brooding has passed. All hell is breaking loose.' William clenched one gauntleted fist. 'The long-expected invasion by the Danes has come.'

Balthar grew cold. 'How many men?'

'Some two hundred and forty ships sailed past the south and have been raiding the east, each one filled with Sweyn Estrithson's most seasoned warriors.' The king prowled around the hearth, his face darkening. 'A force as large as the one you English faced at Stamford Bridge three summers gone.'

'Harold defeated them—'

'And in that victory your army was torn apart. This time the Northmen will be aided by your own kind. Word reaches me that across Northumbria the folk are rising up in readiness to join Sweyn's men. Edgar the Aetheling, Gospatric and Waltheof have amassed their own army and are also set to join the Danes.'

Balthar blanched, pressing the back of his hand to his mouth. 'A force of that size has never been known. What hope do we have?'

The king lashed out with the back of his hand. Balthar saw stars, and when he came round a moment later he was sprawled on the flagstones. The iron taste of blood filled his mouth.

William loomed over him, his face as fierce as that of a ravening wolf. 'I will not let what I have gained slip through my grasp like that whipped cur, Harold. This land will be mine, though I slaughter every man, woman and child living in it.'

CHAPTER FIFTEEN

Blood spattered on the boards. The kneeling captive wrenched his head back from the fist slammed into his blue-mottled face. Gore caked his nose and dripped from his split lip. He let his head drop, his sweat-soaked hair falling across his features. Both his arms had been yanked up behind his back, tied at the wrists with hempen rope, with the other end thrown over the rafter and pulled taut. His vinegar-reek filled that hot, dusty house. Fear-sweat, Alric thought, sickened by what he was witnessing. The man's rasping breath echoed through the stillness. His name was Jurmin, a weaver who had lived in Ely long before the rebel army came. He had always seemed a good man, the monk thought, diligent, courteous, with a quick wit, and he bowed his head in church without any prompting.

Two men stood in the shadows, spears at the ready in case Jurmin showed any resistance. Hengist prowled in front of the prisoner, his knuckles split. 'Answer me,' Hengist demanded. 'Who else works for the king?'

'I am true,' Jurmin mumbled through his ragged lips. 'I would never risk the lives of my own by helping the Bastard's men.'

'Lies.' Another punch cracked through the dry air.

The captive threw his head back, his eyes filled with tears of pain, or rage, or frustration. 'You take our food to fill the bellies of your men, when we can barely feed our own,' he shouted. 'Is it any wonder some here whisper behind your backs?'

Hengist levelled another blow.

Was this what it had come to? Alric wondered. They had arrived in Ely as saviours, but now stayed on as tormentors. How long before the folk of Ely became sickened by the undercurrents of fear and threat that now rippled among the houses? Since the store had been burned and the threat of starvation loomed larger, Hereward had grown colder than at any time since Alric had known him. At least he had insisted no lives should be taken. But he sat in the church every morning and listened to the tales of his spies, the rumours and the gossip that took on more weight with each telling. Neighbours pointed fingers at neighbours, perhaps in all honesty or perhaps in fear that they themselves would be accused. And Hereward's warriors hauled in men and women to face harsh questions – and worse, if the accusations were great.

Jurmin spat another gobbet of blood on to the boards. The monk winced as he searched the man's battered features. He saw no guilt there, though he knew he could be mistaken. But he had never felt the accusations against the weaver were true. They reeked of petty jealousies against a man who had always caught a woman's eye. No more, he thought, as he studied the man's pulped face.

Unable to bear witness to the brutality any longer, he slipped out into the hot day. No one noticed him go. Shielding his eyes against the glare, he looked out over Ely boiling under the merciless sun. The baked mud tracks among the houses were deserted, the sound of the looms and the hammers barely a whisper in the stillness. It had been this way for days now, this feeling of the world holding its breath. Fearful eyes turned towards the gleaming landscape, watching for an attack they all knew must soon come, waiting, sweating, hungry and tired. Anxious eyes turned to their neighbours, suspecting ones they had once called friend. The relentless heat only made tempers simmer more. The entire settlement felt as though it was on the brink of catching alight. Would that the rains would come to dampen passions.

He glanced up towards the food stores where men in dented helms and rusted hauberks squatted by the doors. These guards were all Northmen, former huscarls and axes-for-hire, the fiercest warriors that Hereward had at his disposal. Though they had lost only a little of their supplies with the burning of the store, every morsel was precious. No one would now dare venture near the provisions with those cold Viking gazes levelled at them.

Alric shivered, despite the heat. His neck prickled at the mounting sensation that this terrible waiting was about to end. What came after would undoubtedly be worse still.

Wiping the sweat from his brow, he hurried down the winding path, through the gates, and under the cool shade of the ash trees to the edge of the vast expanse of marsh. Fat flies buzzed over the brown pools of water. The air reeked of rotting vegetation. A few men gathered around the small jetty of iron-hard timbers reaching out from the isle's bank. They were laughing, a surprising sound in the grim mood of the last few days.

As he neared, he glimpsed a boat moored at the end of the short pier. It was one of those strange craft that he had seen only the fenlanders use, a seemingly unstable circular design with cured hide stretched over a willow frame. But the local folk skimmed across the surface of the marsh upon them, propelled by a long ash pole.

Hereward stood at the centre of the group of men, more at ease than Alric had seen him since the night of the feast. When the group broke up, two of the men heaved a bale between them and set off up the path. Hereward strolled over, cracking his knuckles.

'The Normans swagger, showing off their strength with ships to stop supplies reaching us,' the Mercian said, grinning. 'But these smaller vessels can speed through William's sail-wall, under the noses of his men, without being noticed.'

The monk pointed at the boat. 'How much can they carry? One ham-hock?'

'We take what we can get.'

'It is good. Forgive me. My mood is dark. Any food helps ease the worries of the folk here, and if we must send out a fleet of those strange boats to fill bellies, so be it.'

'This battle will be long and hard, and like all battles there will be times when the tide turns—'

'And we fear we might drown?' Alric felt all his worries rush up through him, and he could not contain them any more. He reached out his arms, pleading to his friend. 'Turn back from this madness. We are making our allies into our enemies. When the folk of Ely start to fear us as much as they fear William's men, then we are in a deal of trouble.'

'We are a long way off being feared as much as the Bastard's invaders,' Hereward snapped, his eyes narrowing. 'Have we slaughtered women and children? Have we burned villages to the ground? No, we cuff ears, as we would with unruly children.'

'Cuff ears?' Alric exclaimed. 'I have just watched the weaver kneeling in a pool of his own blood.'

Hereward glowered, but only for a moment. He sucked in a deep breath, softening, and said, 'You are a godly man, a good man, and you see only heaven and hell around you. But there is a long road we must all travel between the two. Would I wish harm upon these folk who have taken us in and shown us kindness? No, never. Nor would I wish to see them harmed by their own failings. I know some grow to hate me. I care little. My work here is to give them back what has been stolen from them by the Normans – all the riches of England from the years gone by, still there for days yet to come.'

'There must be an easier way.'

'There is no easy way for anything in this life. It is a hard road with death at the end, but we do what we can. Come, let us break some bread.' He held out an arm to guide Alric back up the slope.

The monk shook his head. 'I am not hungry.'

Hereward held his gaze for a moment, perhaps seeing the gulf that had appeared between them. Then he nodded and repeated, 'You are a good man, monk,' before climbing up the track after the others.

Alric sat on the end of the jetty and dangled his legs over the edge. He muttered a prayer for his friend and asked God to guide that lost soul to better days. He worried about the Mercian, as he had for so long now. Hereward's demons were fierce, his suffering great. He deserved some respite from his struggles.

Once he had found some peace in his own soul, Alric wandered back up the track towards Ely. Hereward needed his counsel, he saw that now, and he had been remiss in allowing less level-headed advisors to whisper in his friend's ear. As he neared the ramparts, he glanced along the wooden palisade and felt surprised to see no sentries on duty. He shrugged. Who would wish to stand out there in the midday heat? he thought. Though he would not care to be one of those guards if Hereward discovered their absence.

The gate stood ajar and he eased inside the fence.

The steady *chok* of someone cutting wood echoed from the direction of the minster. A dog barked. The smell of bread baking in a clay oven drifted through the open door of one of the houses. Ely sweltered under summer's blanket, but the monk felt no peace in the stillness. Unable to decide what troubled him, he wrinkled his brow and looked around. Two men, barely more than shadows in the glaring light, moved past a gap between two dwellings. The hairs at the nape of his neck prickled, though he was still unsure what it was he had seen.

He wiped the sweat from his brow, and, leaving the path, made his way through the jumble of houses. Easing past heaps of rotting waste and piles of shavings from the wood-workers, he stepped on to the back track. The two men were entering a small hut near the palisade. Only glimpsing their backs, Alric felt unsure of their names. They were not guards, though, or

Hereward's men, he knew that, and so the spears they gripped as they slipped through the door troubled him.

For an instant, he frowned. He should warn Hereward, or Guthrinc, or one of the other leaders, but then he might be consigning more innocent souls to a savage beating. Setting his jaw, he strode down the track with determination to investigate this matter for himself. At the hut door, he paused and listened. Low voices murmured within, the words unclear. Alric pressed his ear to the crack. The rough wood grated against his cheek.

The blow came from nowhere. As fire flared through his head, he crashed on to the hard-baked track. Groaning, he rolled on to his back. Two figures loomed over him, silhouetted against the silver sun. Hands grabbed his tunic. Before he could call out he was dragged into the smoky, dark hut.

A ruddy glow from the embers in the hearth lit the faces of the four men clustered around him.

'It is the monk, Hereward's man,' one of them growled.

A large figure stepped forward, shaking his spear at Alric. He had shaggy black hair and a mass of scar tissue running the length of his right arm from a wolf attack. The monk recognized him now. His name was Saba, a leatherworker who had come to Ely from Earith when the Normans had started to terrorize the local folk. He was a sullen man with a temper made worse whenever he had drunk a skinful of ale.

'I mean you no harm,' Alric protested.

Saba's humourless laugh cut him dead. 'One word from you of our meet here is harm enough.'

The monk took stock of the spears and the fierce expressions, his blood growing cold. 'What do you want?' he asked in a quiet voice.

Saba bent down until his face was only a hand's-width from Alric's nose. 'Blood, that is what we want. The blood of your master. By the end of this day, Ely will be free and Hereward will be dead.'

CHAPTER SIXTEEN

The icy winds blew across the great black ocean. High over-head, white gulls wheeled against a slate sky, calling out in the voices of children. Harald Redteeth crunched across the pebbles on the shore. Ivar, cold and grey and silent and dead, wandered four paces at his back. His father walked at his side, furs wrapped over his gleaming hauberk, his hair and beard wild in celebration of his ancestors. He was telling Harald of Ragnarok and of the end of the world in flames – a tale of the last days of the gods and men that the Viking had heard once long before, as a boy sitting by the fire while the sun set over the snow-blasted mountains in a blaze of scarlet and gold. This second hearing stirred him just as much.

His father's voice croaked as if he had not spoken in many a day:

> 'Brothers will fight and kill each other,
> sisters' children will defile kinship.
> It is harsh in the world, whoredom rife
> – an axe age, a sword age
> – shields are riven –
> A wind age, a wolf age –

before the world goes headlong.
No man will have mercy on another.'

Harald nodded, understanding. 'I will have no mercy.'

The gulls called 'mercy' in the tongue of his ancestors. *'Eir, eir.'*

He turned to look at his father, but he could no longer see his face. Shadows swallowed it, and all of them, and the world.

No longer was it cold, but hot and sticky and reeking of sour sweat. The dark still closed around him, but he could feel the rough straw under his back and the stinging of his wounds. He felt overwhelmed by a deep yearning to return to the shores of the great black ocean and walk with his father a while longer. He ached for the comfort of those simpler times. The old man's stories of the traditions of his kind summoned a warm sense of belonging to something greater than himself. *Defend the old ways unto death*, his father had insisted. *Without them you are nothing.* And he had kept them in his heart always, though wave upon wave of Christian men broke upon the rocks of his northern homeland.

He squinted, but the gloom of the dusty hut crushed down still. From the corner of his eye, he glimpsed the red embers in the hearth, twin eyes watching him with hunger, waiting for him to loosen his grip on life. How many winters had he lain there? Ten? Or more? He recalled the fierce cold that had left him shaking and his teeth rattling. Then the burning heat that had slicked him in sweat from head to toe. His skin still felt seared where the flames had touched it on that night of the battle, and his side was afire from where the English spear had stabbed him.

Once again he had failed to slay Hereward. He could not stumble away from life while his vow remained unfulfilled and Ivar unavenged, though they whittled him down limb by limb. Honour demanded that he did not die, and honour was all, and if Death came for him, he would clamp his hands around its throat and squeeze until he had crushed it.

Time passed.

He swam in a sea of memories of the old days, of the blood-sacrifices to Woden in the grove on the hillside, and the mead-cups raised in oath. Of battle! And in his delirium, he felt that he rose, or his spirit did, and he padded from that hut and through the twilit enclosure, watching the glowering Normans as they still counted their dead, while they ran the stones along the edges of their blades. They were a proud race, but the English had whipped them. The invaders would not take that, Harald Redteeth saw. The Normans understood honour too, for some of his own blood flowed in their veins.

And his shade drifted on, to the great hall that stood in the shadow of the keep, and to William de Warenne and Ivo Taillebois, sitting by the hearth, drinking blood-red wine. He hovered there in the shadows, listening.

'I miss my home,' William muttered, peering with dismal eyes into the low flame. 'This God-forsaken place of rain and mist and marsh. Is the land we have claimed worth this hardship?'

'It is worth it if the king says it is,' the Butcher grunted. 'He has lusted after this place for so many years now, he will never loosen his grip on it. If the English understood that, they would not waste their breath fighting.'

'And in the meantime they carve through our numbers and we can do naught but take their spears. Is this the Norman way?'

Taillebois drained his cup. 'They are cunning, these English. We never gave them the respect they deserved. We thought them slow and ale-addled, with mud for wits. We will not make that mistake again.'

'You believe our plan will work?'

Ivo nodded.

'You have chosen wisely?'

The other man nodded again.

'Two prongs to our attack?'

The Butcher smiled.

'Then let us hope there will be a quick end to this.'

Though it was still warm, the Butcher tossed another log into the hearth, sending the golden sparks swirling upwards. 'It will be quick or it will be slow. It matters little as long as we have an end. And there will be one. We have our eyes and ears within the camp at Ely. They send back word of everything those bastard English do. And soon we will cut the heart out of that Devil's Army. The rest will be easy.'

'Without their leader—'

'They will fall apart. Hereward has given them shape and fire. Once we have his head upon a spike, the rest will come meek as sheep. We will fall on them like wolves. Never will there have been a slaughter like it. And then none of these English will dare raise their faces to us again.'

All this Harald heard as his spirit floated in the shadows on the edge of the hall. Though ghosts were silent, he must have made some noise for William and Taillebois wrenched their heads towards him. What they saw, he did not know, but the expressions on their faces suggested it was some hellish thing. But then his wounds called to him, and he found himself back upon his dirty straw, every fibre of him on fire. He sweated and he moaned, and then he drifted back into the dark.

And as he receded from the light, only one thought glowed in the depths of his skull: that for the first time he felt pity for that Devil's Army, and for Hereward.

CHAPTER SEVENTEEN

Smoke swirled up into the dark. The slender shoots and green leaves crackled and crisped brown in the flames as Turfrida hunched over the hearth. She inhaled the sour fumes and then threw her head back, her eyes wide and dark. Sweat glistened on her forehead. Hereward glowered from the other side of the fire. The orange glow lit lines of worry in his face.

From the rafters, mouse and bird skulls and iron trinkets hung. They clinked in the breeze as if brushed by invisible fingers. The Mercian raised his head to watch the stirring. Were these the spirits with which his wife communicated?

'Tell me,' he murmured, 'what do you see?'

Her eyes rolled back so that he could see only white. The foul-smelling smoke from the plants she had selected in the woods that day swept her to another place, he knew, where the birds and the beasts of fields spoke to her.

More ravens? More death? Defeat? Should any other dare suggest only failure lay ahead, he would deny it to the heavens. But if that claim were made by Turfrida, he knew it would tear the heart out of him. He watched the tremors run through her features, and thought of his mother, beaten to death by his father's hands. He would never see his wife hurt, or any woman.

She had become a strength to him, like any spear-brother, and he could no longer imagine life without her counsel. That, too, surprised him. Turfrida, Alric and Redwald: his three lights in the dark of this bitter war.

'I see . . .' Rustling like old parchment, her voice drained away until he felt she had forgotten he was there. He studied the line of her high cheekbones. Her cheeks seemed hollower, her eyes darker ringed, since she had begun her ritual. A shadow crossed her face and she continued in a soft, rolling tone, 'Fire . . . a wall of flames . . . and you stand against it, with your sword raised high. And there is fire in your eyes too. And everywhere lie the bones of men, English and Norman.'

He flinched as she spoke. This was a vision he had dreamed himself. He tried to recall if he had ever told it to her. How long had it haunted him now, this fear that he would start as saviour and end as destroyer, a pattern that had repeated time and again since the days of his childhood? 'I need no portents of days yet to come,' he said as gently as he could muster. 'Tell me of here . . . now . . . in Ely. Is this course the right one? Or do I risk losing the few allies we have in this battle?'

'I hear whispers only,' she croaked, cocking her head on one side as if listening. Her fingers fluttered to the necklace of small bones around her neck that she always wore under her dress. 'My ancestors speak to me,' she murmured, distracted. She raised part of a finger-bone. 'My grandmother calls out. And her mother before her, and her mother too. My own mother is here, and when I die, my bone will join them and I will speak wise words to my daughter, should we have one.'

'What do they say?' he pressed. In his experience, these spirits often talked a great deal and said nothing.

'They speak of the Normans . . .'

'An attack?'

She shook her head. 'They make their plans and bide their time.'

Hereward gritted his teeth. Would that the spirits told him

something tangible, that would put his mind at rest or give him guidance.

'A man will ride here, to the fens,' Turfrida continued. 'A man who wears the cloth of God, but carries a sword.'

'A Norman priest.' He spat in the fire. 'Their churchmen cannot decide if they should pray or kill.'

'The threat is growing, husband. A tide of blood washing across these fens.' She held her hands over the fire until he feared she would burn. Not once did she waver. She was stronger than any woman.

Hereward peered into the flames, feeling both a sense of urgency and frustration. 'Then I must turn my gaze outwards once again.'

Turfrida flopped back from the fire, seeming weakened. Her breathing was shallow and sweat now stained her amber dress. The Mercian jumped to his feet and hurried to her, helping her up and holding her in his arms. 'You have done enough,' he murmured. 'You must rest now. I would not see you made ill by my demands.'

'I worry for you, husband,' she muttered. 'So many threats all around. I would keep you safe.'

'And you do.' He held her face in his hands and kissed her. She felt too hot. 'Lie down a while,' he murmured, 'and drink a little. I will not be gone long.' She nodded, forcing a wan smile. She looked so troubled that he did not want to leave her, but he could not ignore the burden of his leadership. With reluctance, he stepped out into the warm evening. The moon was bright and the stars gleamed against the blue-black sky. It was a good night. He could have been drinking mead with friends in the tavern in Barholme, or walking in the woods with Turfrida as they had done many a night in Flanders. And yet here he was, despised and feared by allies and enemies alike. He shrugged, trying to put such thoughts from his mind, though they came to him too often these days.

Three boys and a girl ran past chasing a moth. They laughed, the boys tumbling as the girl tripped each one in turn. Outside

113

his home, old Offa sat on a log, swilling down his ale. He looked drunk already, his eyes slow and his belly wobbling under his tunic with every movement. He nodded and grinned as Hereward passed. From open doors echoed the sound of wives scolding their husbands, or singing lullabies to their babies, or men bellowing the bawdy songs they usually reserved for the tavern. A good night, he thought, and good people, who deserved more than he could give them.

In the minster enclosure, the refectory loomed up, a scruffy timber-framed building with a thatch that was bare in parts and would let the rains in during the heavy storms. The door was open and the hearth-fire cast a light across the baked track. The rebels had come to call it home. Every day they sat cheek by jowl with the monks, raucous conversation in conflict with quiet reflection, their armoury of looted Norman double-edged swords, axes, spears, shields, helms and hauberks looming over the sober clerics. Two walls had been given over to this weaponry; the other two were lined with tapestries, which, though not grand, had been executed with some artistry. Hereward remembered the tapestries in his father's hall, ones that had comforted the Normans who occupied it until he had burned the place to the ground.

He bowed his head to enter the smoky atmosphere. Straw crackled under his shoes as he strode in. A table ran the length of the hall, chunks of bread and empty stew-bowls scattered among pools of ale. Five men sat on benches at the far end, waiting for him. Hereward glimpsed Kraki first, little more than wild hair and beard and scars in the half-light. He glowered, but then the Viking always glowered, and Hereward could not tell if he simmered with jealousy over his woman's changeable affections or if he simply brooded.

Guthrinc, now, there was a man who laughed enough for two. He laughed when he was spearing Normans and when he was gnawing a goose leg, and probably when he was tupping women too, for all Hereward knew. He was taunting Kraki, seemingly caring little that he was poking a bear with a stick.

114

But then he towered over the squat Viking as he towered over all men. Redwald was smiling at Guthrinc's jokes. He flashed a shy look when he saw Hereward approach. Hengist sipped his mead, his pale eyes darting around. Sour, he seemed, Hereward thought, still consumed by the murders of his folk. That, or mad, as the other warriors said. The wounds on his knuckles from the beatings he had dealt still looked raw.

The abbot sat at the end of the table. Hereward had seen some dour monks in his time, but Thurstan seemed at ease with the other men's horseplay. A faint smile ghosted his lips. He would give wise counsel.

'You are late,' Kraki grunted. 'Your wife offers you too much comfort.'

'There speaks a man who is not getting enough,' Guthrinc said, making his right forearm erect. Kraki raised his chin imperiously, refusing to be baited.

'With a woman like Acha, it's a wonder he ever leaves his home,' Hengist muttered.

Hereward sat on the bench, resting his arms on the table. 'Where is Alric?' he enquired.

'Perhaps he plays with the children,' Redwald replied with a grin. 'He is more at home with the young ones than with these grave matters.'

Hereward's brow furrowed. 'It is not like the monk to miss our battle-meet.'

'If he comes, he comes.' Redwald shrugged. 'You have enough wise heads here already. And Guthrinc.'

The big man feigned disdain.

'I would value Alric's skill with children during these talks,' Hereward said wryly. Once the abbot had finished laughing, the Mercian turned to Hengist, his features darkening. 'What of Jurmin? Has he had dealings with the Normans?'

'He keeps his lips sealed,' the rat-faced man replied.

'Because he knows nothing?' Guthrinc enquired. 'Or because he knows too much?'

'Folk dare not speak, even if they are true. They are afraid of saying the wrong thing.' Hengist poured himself more mead, swilling the amber liquid around the wooden cup as he peered into its depths. 'They are afraid of the Normans, they are afraid of us.'

'How many enemies do we have within Ely?' Hereward asked.

Hengist shrugged. 'One. Ten. An army. There is no way to tell. Strangers turn up at the gates every day. They could all stand with the Normans, for all I know. Do we send them away when they offer their right arms to our cause?'

'We need them,' Guthrinc said. 'Only by swelling our numbers will we drive the enemy back.'

'But if we are allowing our foes to creep in through the gate,' Redwald began, 'we are—'

Kraki leaned forward, slamming his mead-cup on the table. 'We should be plotting against the Normans.'

'My friend has a harsh voice, but he speaks true,' Guthrinc added. 'The more we turn our eyes inward, the more we leave those devils to build their plans in the shadows. Give them time to plot and scheme and we risk our own doom.'

'We should harry them,' Kraki boomed. 'Cut them down, man by man, rout and chase and tear them to pieces, so they get no time to think.'

'More men will come soon,' Guthrinc continued, nodding. 'And more after that. You know the king will not turn away. Better to strike now, while their numbers are few.'

Hereward looked around the sombre faces. 'How?' he asked. 'When our own men starve and they are so weak they can barely walk from one end of Ely to the other. We need more food.' He looked to the abbot, but Thurstan simply held out his hands in bafflement.

Redwald rose from the bench and stretched his legs as he strode to the edge of the shadows that lay beyond the firelight. 'It is true that we must keep our eyes on our foes. But what good will it be if we then get a spear in our backs? We have enemies all around, and the ones within Ely are nearer and as such more dangerous.'

Hereward squinted to try to read his brother's expression. 'Then you say we continue down this path of crushing the folk of Ely to see who squeals like a pig? They have offered us shelter. They showed faith in our words. To act so harshly only turns them against us.'

'We must be cruel to be kind in days yet to come,' Redwald implored. 'If we are soft now, they will suffer more in times ahead.'

Kraki grunted. Guthrinc nodded thoughtfully. Hengist gulped more mead.

'Alric thinks we harm only ourselves by being so hard on these folk. He tells me we should step back from treating our friends like enemies—'

'And see more stores burned down? The monk is not here to put his shoulder behind his words.' Redwald paused, realizing he might have overstepped a mark by interrupting Hereward, and when he began again it was with a pleasant smile, his arms outstretched in a genial manner. 'Alric is a man of God, not a man of war. In times of peace, he will keep us all on the path to heaven. But these days we need men who have struck with iron and tasted blood on the wind. Their word counts for more. Do you not agree, Father?'

After a moment's thought, the abbot nodded. 'I know little of battle and the plots and plans required to win them. But I do know that the Normans must never be allowed to reach Ely, for the price will be terrible indeed. That should be our sole guide when discussing our actions: how do we break the king's ring of iron?'

'Abbot Thurstan speaks wise words, as we all knew he would,' Redwald said. 'Crush the troublemakers here in Ely and our eyes can once again be turned beyond our ramparts. Crush them in a way that puts the fear of God in all here and keeps their heads down while we do our work. We can beg for their forgiveness when the war is won.'

Guthrinc eyed Redwald askance. 'You learned much at the right hand of Harold Godwinson.'

'He was a great man,' Redwald agreed.

'He was a hard man.' Guthrinc stroked his chin, giving nothing away of his innermost thoughts.

Hereward simmered as he listened to the counsel. Alric had been right. The days when he could solve all his problems with Brainbiter now seemed simpler times. 'How have we been brought down to this? What songs the scops will sing of us in days to come: how the great heroes of England brought naught but fear to their own.'

The men around the table fell silent, watching him from under their brows.

After a moment, Hereward clenched his fist. 'Then we have no choice. We must be divided, though it weakens us. From tomorrow morn, half our army will harry the Normans out in the fens. The rest will crush our enemies here in Ely.' Doubt lit the faces of the others round the table. No one there believed they had the resources or the strength to win on two fronts, he knew. 'This is not the path I would have chosen for us, but it is the one we face. Stand or fall, the coming days will decide our fate.'

Chapter Eighteen

The embers in the hearth glimmered away in the dark. Alric wrenched his bruised head up from the packed-earth floor. Silent shapes were hunched around the fire. The four men squatted, gripping their spears to balance themselves. The monk strained at the bonds fastening his hands behind his back, but the rope had been tied too tightly. His wrists burned and his muscles ached, but that pain was nothing compared with the agony of dread in his heart.

The waiting had been unbearable. Every time the door had opened, he had seen the shadows lengthening, knowing that when the light finally faded, Hereward's life would go with it, and the hopes of all the folk in Ely. Time and again, he had pleaded with these traitors to turn away from their path of betrayal. The Norman word could not be trusted, he pressed, whether they had promised riches or survival once the king's forces overran the settlement. They only laughed at him. When he protested further, they cuffed him with the shafts of their spears or kicked him in the ribs until fire flared through him. Whispered prayers had only brought blows to the face that left blood caking his nose and his lips split. And when he had tried to reason with them, urging them to recall what terrors the king had already unleashed upon England, he felt the sharpness of the spear-tips.

They would not be deterred, he could see that now. He wanted to believe they were weak, or consumed by greed, but as he watched the cast of their drawn features when they prowled around the hearth, he realized they were only scared.

Saba opened the door a crack. Alric peered out and saw moon-shadows thrown across the grey path leading to the hut. It was bright out, not a good night for murder. Saba appeared to be considering this, for he looked up at the moon and stars and then bowed his head in a long moment of reflection. When he turned back to the others, he nodded. 'We can wait no longer.'

The men grunted, keen to get this business done.

'When we have struck, send the fire-boats out to warn the king's men. They wait for our beacon.'

'You will be punished, in this world and the next,' the monk called out.

Saba cast a murderous glare as if seeing him for the first time. Alric stiffened, though a part of him knew there could be no other outcome but death once they had allowed him to see their faces. 'You will be found out,' he said, maintaining a brave front.

'The folk will thank us in the end. Hereward only drags out our misery. We starve, slowly. And when the king's men come, do you think there will be a man, woman or child still standing in Ely when we have turned our faces away from them? Better to bow our heads now and plead for mercy. Then at least there is some hope.'

The monk sensed that Saba was still trying to justify his actions to himself. 'You must have faith,' he pressed. 'I know all of you. You are good men. You care for kin and aid friends and strangers alike. You work hard. But the stain of this blood will never be washed away—'

'This world has been turned on its head,' Saba snapped, cutting in, clearly stung by Alric's words. He shook his spear at the monk. 'Right or wrong, who can tell which is which? None

120

of us know our places any more. You, monk, you live your days in a land of milk and honey. The rest of us must fight to live. Do not judge me.' He pointed his spear at one of the other men, a new arrival in Ely. He was squat with broad shoulders and a wind-chapped face like a seaman's. His speech had the thick tone of Northumbria. 'If he cries out, kill him now and be quick about it. But he will want to hold on to life like any man so he will be silent. But leave a good time before you end his days so his screams do not draw men out from their hearthsides. Once Hereward is dead, burn this hut with his body in it and none will be the wiser.'

The Northumbrian man nodded, squatting back by the fire.

'Three of you,' Alric said with contempt, trying another approach. 'Would you give up your lives so easily? I have seen Hereward kill more than that number without taking a breath.'

Saba eyed him for a moment, and seemed about to speak. But then he kicked out and Alric's wits spun away. When he came round the other three plotters were gone. His remaining captor was sharpening the edge of his knife with a stone, each slow, steady stroke reverberating through the hut.

CHAPTER NINETEEN

The full moon glowed high over Ely. The wetlands gleamed silver, but in the town bands of deep shadow carved through the tracks among the houses. As Hereward stepped out of the refectory, he looked up to watch the bats flit by. No breeze stirred the ash trees and the oaks on the slopes of the isle. In their crowded homes, folk sweated under the stifling heat still blanketing the fens. Even the oppressive summer temperatures seemed to be working against him.

'There is no path worth the walking that is an easy one.' At the comforting words he turned and glimpsed Thurstan, hands clasped in front of him in the shadows at the corner of the refectory. The abbot gave a reassuring smile. 'If any man could win this fight, it is you, Hereward.' The cleric was a man of few words and when he did choose to speak each one carried weight. The Mercian felt touched by the support, but before he could respond, Thurstan had slipped away into the dark towards the comfort of his own hearth.

Redwald burst out of the refectory, his cheeks flushed. 'To the tavern?' he enquired, rubbing his hands together. 'Let us drink as brothers and make a mead-oath to put iron in our hearts for the coming battle.'

'I would find Alric. It is unlike him to miss our gathering.'

Redwald snorted. 'His mind has wandered from our struggle. He cares more for the poor and hungry here in Ely these days. Leave him to his ministering.'

'I would speak with him about these things we have discussed this evening.'

'You do not need his counsel,' the other man said cheerily. 'Can he see things more clearly than me?'

Hereward's attention was caught by a fleeting movement down the slope near the palisade. He narrowed his eyes, searching the pooling shadows. His vision had been honed by dark fenland nights as a youth, creeping through the reed-beds to steal the fish from lines or fowl from snares. 'Still, it is not like him to be missing,' he murmured, distracted.

'My tongue moves too fast, as always. I see you are worried about him,' Redwald said. 'I will find him and bring him to you.'

Hereward continued to scour the dark. He knew the rhythms of Ely. At this time, most would be by their hearths, with their kin. The evening meal would have been consumed, such as it was, the bowls stacked by the door, and man, woman and child would be readying themselves for sleep in preparation for another hard day tomorrow. Any folk still out would not raise their pace above an amble as they moved to the homes of friends or the tavern. The hairs on his neck prickled. 'Take care,' he said to his brother, 'and if you see aught that is strange, find me.'

Redwald shook his head, laughing quietly at his brother's unease, and set off towards the monk's tiny hut. Hereward continued to watch the quiet settlement. Men guarded the new food store at the minster and the look-outs by the causeway would have long since raised the alarm if the king's men were attacking. With a shrug, he walked out of the minster gate on to the main track leading down to the gates.

Barely had he taken five steps when he glimpsed more rapid movement, this time between two of the older dwellings. A man running, light-footed so no sound carried. The Mercian's fingers slipped unconsciously to the hilt of his sword.

He prowled down the track, trying to discern the look-outs at the palisade. The moonlight illuminated an empty platform where the man should have been. His skin tingled. He slipped out of the silvery light into the shadow of a building and cocked his head to listen for even the slightest sound, urgent voices, the clink of iron. The Camp of Refuge bubbled like a cauldron of stew. Tempers grew hot among the mass of bodies. And across Ely resentment simmered too. All this he knew from Alric, who kept both ears open as he immersed himself in his daily business.

As he weighed whether he should call Kraki to raise some men, movement erupted all around. Figures flitted everywhere he looked. He counted ten ... fifteen ... more. Querying whispers broke the stillness as they called to each other. Footsteps now, rattling out from the sun-baked tracks; they were taking less care as they drew closer to the time when they would act. A torch crackled into life near the palisade, and another only three houses away. This was more than simple argument.

Hereward decided to call for Kraki. But as he took a step back up the slope, a hard rod slammed across his shoulders, and another an instant later across the back of his knees. He crashed down on to the dusty track.

'Here,' a harsh, low voice called. 'We have him.'

The warrior rolled on to his back. Two men loomed over him with spears ready to thrust into his chest. No Normans these, as he had feared, but good Ely men. Running footsteps drew nearer, voices picking up the call.

We have him. The words seared through his mind, telling him all that he needed to know. He lashed his right foot into the knee of one of his attackers. The man howled in pain, stumbling into his companion. Both fell off balance. As they struggled to bring their weapons down, Hereward rolled to one side. The tip of a spear crunched into the dirt where he had been lying.

Jumping up, he seized the spear from his attacker and whipped the shaft into the faces of both men. He heard the crack of noses breaking. The blow was hard enough to stun. He darted away between the homes and did not look back. Weaving among the wooden dwellings, he picked an erratic route to the edge of the settlement and crouched down in the shadow against a wattle wall to gather his thoughts.

When he peered around the corner of the house, he discerned torches dancing among the homes. An uprising, could it be? Not even if all the folk of Ely took up arms could they defeat the army he had amassed. What, then? After a moment's reflection, the truth settled on him like ice on a winter pond. These men were moving as if time was of the essence. They had no need to defeat an entire army if they could simply cut off its head.

He felt a knife turn in his gut as he understood how this thing could play out. No time remained to alert Kraki or any of the other leaders of the rebel army, or to strike back at the men now searching the byways of Ely for him. No time at all. And he could not risk a single cry of alarm. He had to remain silent. Along the narrow, shadowed tracks among the houses he raced, keeping low as he swept past rubbish heaps and wells. When the sound of searching men drew near, he would halt, crouching low in the dark when his every instinct told him to run to his destination as fast as his legs would carry him. Torches flared at the end of paths as he pressed himself back against warm wattle walls.

Over the thatched roofs he hurled a large stone. As footsteps ran towards where the stone had fallen, Hereward darted across the main track, near as bright as day in the moonlight. Once he had crossed into the other jumble of houses, he found the familiar paths and careered with a prayer in his heart, and only one thought in his mind.

As he reached his own home, his fears were confirmed. The door hung open, the amber light from the hearth playing out across the track. Cries echoed from within. Three men lurched out into the night, dragging Turfrida among them. She was struggling like a wildcat, spitting and cursing in her Flemish tongue. One of the men stepped back and jabbed the tip of his spear between Turfrida's shoulder blades. 'Where is he?' he growled.

Hereward drew Brainbiter from its sheath. He recognized the man with the spear: Saba the leatherworker. Turfrida yanked her head around and spat in her captor's face.

The Mercian grinned, despite the fear as cold as a stone in his chest. Though his wife had been raised as the daughter of a castellan, she had a warrior's heart and a tongue as sharp as any flint-eyed fieldworker. Before Saba could punish her, Hereward stepped out from the shadows where he could be seen.

'Leave her,' he snarled.

The three men froze. Their faces drained of blood. Eyes flickered towards his blade and then his unwavering stare. Saba was the first to react, calling, 'Put down your sword and step forward or we will kill her.' He raised the tip of his spear to Turfrida's neck.

'Harm her and you will be in hell afore she cries out.'

'No, they want only you, my husband,' she cried. 'Flee now.'

His eyes fastened upon Turfrida's, and he saw the pleading there. He knew she spoke the truth. With a curse, he sheathed his blade and dashed away.

Blood thundered through his head. As the night swallowed him, Hereward muttered a vow. If Turfrida's life were stolen, every man who had risen up would be engulfed in a wave of blood the likes of which had never been known.

CHAPTER TWENTY

Only a few red embers glowed in the hearth. Stifling darkness closed in around Alric as he lay on his side by the wall. He could barely see his captor squatting by the fire, but he could hear the rasp of his breath. The sweltering heat choked him and his wrists were chafed raw from his bonds, but he forced himself to keep a clear head.

'There is still time to turn back from this course,' he croaked, his throat so dry he could barely swallow. 'Save your soul.' The man did not answer, did not even acknowledge Alric was there. Perhaps in that brute's eyes the monk was already dead.

Alric laid his cheek against the hard earth and murmured a prayer that, when the time came, he would face his death as a warrior, with a song in his heart and the light of heaven in his head. Though he had fought through many sadnesses, he could say that he had lived a good life. He grimaced in the dark. For the first time, he was hoping that the Mercian would unleash his devil when those cowardly foes came for him. If only they knew what terror they truly faced.

He heard his captor stand up. Here it was, the moment of his final judgement. The man hawked up phlegm and spat it into the hearth. A sizzle. The clink of the spear-tip against the stones surrounding the ashes and the embers. A deep breath, loud in the stillness. *Calming himself*, Alric thought, *so he will thrust the shaft down straight and true.* Alric felt the bonds at his wrists cut; a small mercy, perhaps. As the last of the embers began to fade, a deep and abiding darkness descended. The monk screwed up his eyes and began to utter a prayer in as loud a voice as he could manage.

The crash at the door jolted him out of his reverie. A howl like that of a wolf was met by a bear-like roar. The monk strained his head up. He squinted into the gloom, but all he could discern was grey shapes tearing at each other like wild beasts in the midnight dark of the forest. The brawling bodies thundered against the wattle walls. The very rafters shook. A rain of dust and droppings fell on Alric's face and he coughed and spluttered. Yells and curses rang out. One of the fighters sprawled across the floor, his breath rushing from his lungs. He clambered to his feet as some object – the spear? – clattered against the wall. Alric could not make any sense of the fight, who was winning or losing.

Another battle-roar. The singing of iron drawn from a scabbard. A trail of glittering sparks. Alric blinked away the after-glow.

A flurry of sudden movement sped across his line of vision, punctuated by a sharp cry.

'Stuck you, you bastard.' That was the gruff voice of his captor, he was sure. Was the other man dead?

Then, just as fast, the silhouette of the wounded grey figure lunged. An agonized cry tore from the throat of the man who had been on the brink of murdering the monk. Alric heard the tap of the man's heels as he staggered back. Viscous liquid spattered across the floor. *Blood.* The other figure did not relent. The slaughterhouse sound of a blade furiously plunging into meat over and over again filled the hut. Gore splashed all around as the dying man's cries grew strangled and then ebbed away.

Relief flooded Alric. Surely only one man could have slaughtered so brutally. 'Hereward,' he called.

The figure fell to its knees beside him. A face pushed close enough so the thin light could illuminate the contours. Pale features loomed up, the eyes still pools of shadow.

'Redwald?' he gasped.

'I am dying,' his saviour croaked, and toppled forward. The monk grabbed him. The tunic was wet, the sticky blood flowing too fast over Alric's fingers. Redwald quivered from the pain of his wound. 'I am growing cold,' he said, clutching at his side.

The monk dragged him out into the moonlight and tore his tunic open. Though he was not a leech, Alric thought the ragged gash in the warrior's side looked mortal. Redwald glanced down at his injury and shuddered. It was as bad as he had feared. While Alric tried to stem the flow of blood, Redwald closed his eyes. When he looked up once more, he seemed to have reached some decision.

'You must hear my confession. Will you do so?' he whispered, his voice trembling with dread.

Alric nodded.

'Then hear now, how I murdered my own father and mother, killed my own wife, and slew my brother Hereward's love.'

CHAPTER TWENTY-ONE

A dark stream of blood flowed down the silvery moonlit track. Hereward wiped his stained blade on the tunic of the fallen man, then dragged the body into the rubbish-stinking narrow space between two buildings. The rats would soon be feeding. With the dark bulk of the minister church at his back, he crept to the Speaking Mound where the fires were set alight in midwinter and where the girls danced on the first day of spring. Lying on his belly, he looked out over Ely. All was quiet. For the men hunting him, stealth was the preferred strategy, it seemed, and his too. Better that than raise the alarm and risk the deaths of innocent people. At least these cowards would not harm Turfrida while she might be of use in breaking his spirit. If they only knew they had forfeited their lives the moment they had threatened her. He squinted until he could glimpse the outline of Alwyne's grain barn where he had seen his wife taken. Soon now, he silently vowed.

He looked back at the church tower and imagined Kraki, Guthrinc and Hengist drunk in the refectory. For a moment he hesitated, wavering, and then he darted across the track into the shadows. Weaving through the rows of houses, he caught sight of a heavy-set man hunched over his spear. Hereward crouched behind a pile of firewood and waited. When his prey neared, the Mercian flicked a stone along the ground. At the rattling sound, the man halted, turning slowly as he surveyed the quiet homes.

Hereward eased out of his hiding place. In one fluid movement, he drew his blade and swept it in a horizontal arc. The head spun to the track and bounced a little way down the slope, coming to rest against the door of a weaver's workshop. The body crumpled, the hands still grasping the spear. Sheathing his blade, Hereward dragged the remains out of sight. In an instant, he had moved on, leaving only a splatter of blood to mark his passing.

The next man died with Brainbiter thrust up under his ribs, one hand clamped on his mouth to stifle his gurgles.

Hereward crouched by a reeking rubbish heap, listening for the sound of footfalls. When men searched in twos or threes, he lay still, watching them from under hooded brows until they had gone. But the stragglers, the lone searchers, they were easy targets. One by one, he whittled his foes down.

Once he had reduced the numbers a little, he circled the settlement until he could see the grain barn, the wooden roof dappled with lichen. It would be near empty after the long weeks of want. He imagined the cowards huddled inside – ten? twenty of them? – their spears jabbing towards his wife, and he shook with rage. How easy it would be to lead Kraki and a few others down there and put all the traitors to the axe. But a direct assault would likely result in his Turfrida's death. He could take no risks.

As he weighed what few options he had, he spied a boy of barely ten summers. The lad was peering all around and calling out in a faint, reedy voice. When the boy neared, Hereward realized it was his own name that sang out into the hot night. He peered into the surrounding shadows in case it was a trap, and then stepped out into the moonlight. The boy recoiled, his hand flying to his mouth. Spattered with blood, Hereward knew he must look a fearsome sight. He crouched down to the boy's level and put on a warm smile. 'I am here.'

The boy swallowed noisily, then stuttered, 'You must come to Alwyne's barn now or your wife will die.' He dashed away the moment he had uttered his final word.

Hereward grimaced. Cowards indeed to send a frightened child to deliver such a message. But then the weight of this terrible dilemma crushed down upon his shoulders and his hands slumped to his side. Stay and fight and see his wife die? Give himself up and doom all those who had joined him in the rebellion? His head gave him one answer, his heart a stronger one. Either choice would damn him.

'Let me aid you.'

The woman's voice floated out from the shadows. He turned to see Acha waiting there, her raven-black hair gleaming in the moonlight.

'You have come to gloat at my misfortune?' he hissed. 'This is not the time.'

'You wrong me,' she snapped. 'This is not how I would win you.' Her eyes flashed as they had that first time he had met her in Earl Tostig's hall in Eoferwic. 'As I went to look for Kraki, I saw your wife dragged into that barn. I heard what those men said. They will not rest until you are dead and the king has this place in his grip.'

He peered into her face, and for once saw none of her manipulation. 'Very well. I will take your offer of aid, but know there will be danger.'

'You know I am not some scared girl.'

He nodded: as if he could ever see her that way. 'We must not wait—' His words died in his throat as the sound of shuffling footsteps approached. He pressed a finger to his lips and pulled Acha back into the shadows. A moment later, Alric emerged with his arm supporting a wounded man who could barely walk. The monk's face was drawn, haunted even, and battered and bloodied too, but the other man was as white as snow, a stark contrast to the dark stain soaking through his ragged tunic.

Shock flooded Hereward when he realized it was Redwald. He ran out and his brother all but fell into his arms.

'He saved my life,' Alric gasped.

Hereward lowered Redwald to the ground and pulled aside the torn tunic. 'He has lost much blood,' he murmured as he pressed the skin around the spear-gash, 'but the wound is not deep. Get him to the leech to staunch the flow and he will yet live.'

Alric gulped with relief. 'Praise God,' he muttered. Hereward heard a curious tone in his friend's voice, one that sounded as though he wasn't praising God at all, but he pushed it aside. Redwald's eyelids fluttered and he managed a faint smile. 'I have been blessed,' he croaked.

As Hereward rose, Alric grabbed his arm and said, 'There is more at stake here. I overheard my captors planning to alert the king's men . . . with beacons . . . fire-boats. While your eyes are turned to the battle here, the Normans will attack. We will be routed.'

Hereward cursed. This plan had been well made and he was now caught betwixt hammer and anvil. Sickened, he looked with desperation towards the barn, torn by his agonizing dilemma.

'Go,' Acha whispered. 'I will do all I can to keep your wife safe until you can act.'

'Nothing can be done.'

Her breath bloomed against his ear. 'You do not know the smallest part of what I can do. Trust me.'

Once he had reluctantly nodded, Hereward watched Acha hurry towards the barn and then turned back to the monk. 'Take Redwald to the tavern first. Someone else will carry him to the leech. You must find Guthrinc, or Kraki, or Hengist and send them to me at the wharf. We must stop those fire-boats sailing. But tell them to keep as quiet as mice.'

Redwald groaned as Alric hauled him to his feet. 'Nothing will stop me,' Alric vowed, adding with a sympathetic tone, 'God will watch over Turfrida, my friend. Trust in Him.'

Hereward shook his sword. 'I trust in this. By the end of this night, it will have drunk deep. Let that be my oath.' And then he was running down the slope towards the gate.

As he neared, a man burst from hiding, hesitant behind his shield. His spear wavered. Hereward barely saw him through the haze of his rage. The attacker was slow and clumsy and he prodded with his spear as if he were herding pigs. The Mercian hacked through the haft. As the weapon splintered apart, he hurled himself against the shield. His foe stumbled on to his back with a gasp, and Hereward drove the sword into his chest.

Wrenching open the gate, he ran down the winding path to the waterside. In the bright moonlight, the wetlands were aglow. Pools of silver lay among the silhouetted trees. He peered out across the mere and discerned two of the small, circular boats. Their occupants were hunched over, pushing through the water with their long staffs. Each vessel appeared to be towing a second, empty boat. His heart sank. Already adrift and too far out for him to reach. At least they had not yet lit the beacons.

As he ranged along the shore looking for another boat, he saw that the vessels that had been moored there had all been scuttled. Their enemies had taken no chances.

A voice hailed from the direction of the town. Guthrinc and Hengist were lurching drunkenly down the track. Hengist grasped his spear, though he was in no fit state to use it, but when Hereward saw that Guthrinc carried his bow, he raced up and snatched it off him.

'Steady,' the towering man cautioned.

'You could not hit a barn if you were a spear's-length from it. Now still your tongue.' Plucking an arrow from Guthrinc's leather quiver, Hereward flexed the bow. He gritted his teeth. Long hours had he spent practising in front of targets since his failure to master the weapon in Flanders had cost his friend Vadir his life. No one else would suffer for his failings. He drew the bowstring taut and let fly the shaft. It whisked harmlessly between the two boats and splashed in the water.

'Hrrrm,' Guthrinc grunted, critically. 'You would do better aiming at your barn.'

Hereward ignored him, notching another arrow. He steadied himself, putting his rage to one side as best he could.

A golden flame flickered to life in one of the boats, and then in the other. The men were leaning back towards the tow-boats, to set their contents alight, the Mercian guessed. He drew the bowstring, fixing his eye upon the glow. The shaft whistled across the mere. A cry rang out and the left-hand light fell as the man pitched forward, wounded or dead. With a roar, the tow-boat erupted in flames. Hereward shouted a curse. He guessed the falling man had upended a bowl of oil that had been intended to be used for the beacon. The flames swirled up high.

'Ah,' Guthrinc said, fingering his chin and nodding, 'you made the light brighter to draw the enemy to it. That was your plan all along, yes?'

Hereward cursed once more.

With fleet fingers, he notched another shaft and let it fly. This time the second man pitched over the side of the boat, taking the light with him. Hereward grunted, handing the bow back to his companion. He watched as the first boat was consumed by the fire. The blackening wood and hide disappeared with a sizzle beneath the dark surface.

'Let us hope we caught them in time,' Hengist muttered, already sobering, 'or else we will be overrun by Normans while our backs are turned.'

Hereward was already starting back up the path. He beckoned furiously for the other two men to follow him, calling, 'This is only the start of it. Now we have a true fight on our hands.'

CHAPTER TWENTY-TWO

The dark bulk of the barn loomed up against the starry sky. Hereward crouched in the shadows with a good view of the door. He prayed that Acha's silver tongue had kept his wife alive. Guthrinc leaned over his shoulder, his breath reeking of ale. 'I can see them now,' he murmured, 'slumped inside, stewing in their own fear-sweat. They must have planned to capture you quickly and with ease, and never thought more than a few steps beyond that.'

'And they would have. Fate smiled on me.'

'Warriors make their own luck.' Guthrinc settled back. 'Now what do we do? This is a fine game of merels where no one can make a move without losing.'

'They must pray that the Normans will come and save their cowardly necks,' Hengist spat. 'They will sit it out for as long as they can.'

Hereward turned to Hengist and whispered, 'Find Kraki. Set look-outs along the shore to watch for any sign of the Normans approaching by boat, and at the causeway. Wake the rest of the men, and arm them, but do it quietly and make them wait within their homes for the order. Do nothing that might frighten our enemies more.' He cocked one ear, half-expecting to hear the steady clank of Norman swords upon shields approaching out of the dark. 'Time is short. Make haste.'

Without a word, Hengist scrambled back along the side of the house and disappeared into the night.

'An army, hiding by their hearths,' Guthrinc said sardonically. 'These battle-plans of yours never fail to surprise. No wonder the Normans are always wrong-footed.'

'By the end of this night, you will wish you were hiding by your hearth, you mead-addled ox.' Hereward stared at the barn, feeling nagging doubt. For all he knew, there might be more English waiting to rise up. Had he allowed himself to be fooled by the cheers, whereas in truth he and his army were not wanted there? Perhaps *they* were the enemy and the Normans seen as the saviours of a suffering people.

'And there is more mead still to drink while we waste time here,' Guthrinc said. 'So enlighten me. What course will you take?'

Hereward stood. 'I will walk in.'

The other man raised an eyebrow. 'Ah. Your wife has taught you some of her witch-ways. Iron cannot touch you. Swords and axes break, spears fall apart.'

'They want me. There is no gain to them in harming Turfrida. They will set her free.'

Guthrinc's voice grew more serious. 'And you will deny the English a leader, and thereby let the king win?'

'Not if you plough your furrow without falling over those big feet.'

Guthrinc narrowed his eyes. 'What are you planning?'

Once he had listened to the scheme, Guthrinc pursed his lips in doubt, then shrugged. 'It is your neck. Do not expect me to wait around to bury you.' He strode off among the houses. When Hereward heard him making his way back, he steeled himself and darted to the barn. He listened to the low drone of voices coming through the timber, and then wrenched the door open.

Spears bristled. Harsh voices called out his name, some in

shock, and some, he was pleased to hear, in fear. A church candle was set on the ground. Shadows danced across the walls so that at first he thought an army waited there. But as he scanned the scowling faces, he saw that it was only about twenty men, still too many for him to defeat alone, but perhaps not so many that his plan would fail. At the back, he glimpsed Turfrida. Hereward felt his rage flicker to life once more when he saw Saba gripping her arm.

'Take your hand off her,' he snarled.

Saba snatched his fingers away as if he had been burned, but another man's spear leapt to Turfrida's neck. Beside her, the Mercian discerned Acha, her pale face floating in the gloom like that of a ghost. She had given herself up to this wolves' lair as she had promised. He looked at her with new eyes, and she nodded in turn.

'Kill him,' Saba growled.

Hereward drew his blade. Hunched over their spears, the men circled him, looking for a way through his defences.

'Throw down your sword or your woman dies,' Saba snapped. 'You are no fool. Do not defy us.'

'My love, why did you come here?' Turfrida called. Her eyes glistened in the candlelight.

'No man of honour would see a woman die in his place.' He let his gaze drift across the gathered men, accusing each in turn with his cold stare. When his eyes fell upon Turfrida, he smiled, softening. 'I could never turn my back upon you, whatever the cost.'

'But you would put the lives of all in Ely at risk by taking this foolhardy stand against our king?' Saba said, jabbing a finger at the warrior. '*My* wife's life. My children's lives. We starve here. We fall ill from the sickness. We suffer each day. And when the Normans come, and you are put to the sword, all of us will pay with our lives.' Saba's voice cracked with emotion.

Hereward tried to stay calm. 'All I asked of you . . . of all here . . . is courage. If we show our defiance with one face . . . if we speak with one voice . . . there is not an army in all the world

138

that could defeat us. Your neighbours have heard my call. The boys you played with as a child, now men. The women who share their bread with your kin. And by your actions this night, you have placed a Norman sword at the throat of each and every one of them.'

The words must have stung Saba hard, for he shook his fist and roared, 'There has been only suffering since you arrived. Our food is taken to feed your men. There is no peace in our home, and the air stinks of shit all day and all night.'

'And where is Dunnere's daughter?' another man called. An angry murmur ran through the band.

Hereward flinched.

'Aye,' Saba snapped. 'Where is she? We searched high and low for that girl. No one hereabouts saw her leave. I'll tell you where she is. One of your men had his way with her, then killed her and dumped her poor body in the deepest bog. Everyone in Ely knows it's true.'

'None of my men would do such a thing,' Hereward said. He hoped his voice stayed steady.

'Dunnere's been a broken man ever since,' Saba continued. 'Yet another misery you have heaped upon us.' He turned to his men and urged, 'Kill him, for Dunnere and his daughter.'

As the spears stabbed towards him, Hereward yelled Guthrinc's name.

What sounded like the bellow of a wild beast resounded. As the rebels whirled, Guthrinc crashed into the barn, waving a burning brand in one hand and an axe in the other. Before any man could react, he thrust the torch into the chest of the nearest rebel. The tunic caught alight in an instant and flames surged up the torso. As his screams ripped through the barn, the dying man crashed against another rebel, and then another, setting both on fire. Within moments, the barn was filled with confusion, yells and howls as Saba's men scattered in terror. Guthrinc carved through it, wielding the axe and the brand in equal measure. Hereward joined him, hacking into the chaos with his sword.

At the destruction of his plans, Saba had become enraged. Hereward saw his brief advantage begin to slip away. 'Kill the woman,' the leatherworker yelled, spittle spraying from his mouth in anger. The leader of those cowards knew his only hope was to lure his hated enemy into risking his neck to try to save his wife. And Hereward knew he had no choice but to do so.

Saba's man whirled his spear towards Turfrida's neck. Desperation gripped Hereward. His own life meant nothing now. As he prepared to throw himself forward, Acha lunged from the gloom. In her hand, a knife glinted in the candlelight. The spearman fell in a gush of crimson, and Hereward ran to his wife's side. For one moment, his eyes locked upon Acha's unreadable stare. He prayed there would be time for thanks later.

Roaring like a bull, Guthrinc tore through the rebels. Smoke swept around the barn from the twitching bodies burning on the ground. Snatching Turfrida's wrist, Hereward yelled to her, 'Stay near to me.' He hacked a path to the door and as he dragged Turfrida into the shadows among the dwellings, he looked back and saw three figures pile on Guthrinc. They crushed him to the ground, raining blows upon him.

'Save him,' Turfrida cried, her voice breaking.

Hereward did not slow. 'He has a thick skull, and it is me they want dead. We must get you to safety first, then we shall see how brave they are.'

From behind them came the drumming of feet: the chase was on, the prey sighted. As they broke out from the edge of Ely, Hereward looked to the Camp of Refuge. There, among the mad jumble of closely packed dwellings, he and Turfrida could lose themselves.

Sweat flew from his brow as he ran across the turf towards the new camp. Turfrida stumbled to keep up. At his back, the moon illuminated four pursuers armed with spears.

Across the open space they raced, and into the camp. The warm breeze filled with the stink of shit and rotting rubbish.

Hereward weaved among the huts. The narrow path would hinder his enemies, already hampered by their unwieldy weapons. Yet as they reached a clearing, Turfrida stumbled and fell, dragging Hereward down with her.

Snarling, Hereward rolled on to his back, only to look along the shafts of three spears. The iron tips wavered a hand's-width from his face. A foot ground down on his right wrist, forcing him to relinquish his sword. It was kicked away into the dark.

'You are done,' Saba growled breathlessly, 'and this foolish war with our new masters is over.'

'When William the Bastard tightens his grip on this land, you will regret every word you uttered this night.'

Saba sneered and drew back his spear to strike. Hereward felt proud that Turfrida did not plead for his life or cry.

From the dark, a stone crashed against the back of Saba's head. He cursed, his hand flying to where the missile had struck, and when he withdrew his fingers blood stained them. In a rage, he spun round to confront his attacker. Only a boy stood there, the lad Hereward had carried aloft only eight days before. 'Bad men,' the boy called, his voice high and indignant. 'Leave him be.'

Saba looked as if he had been slapped. Other figures emerged from the night on all sides, gaunt-faced women and men, each one condemning him with their cold stares. The leader of the uprising turned slowly, reading the silent communication in those faces.

'He is the enemy here,' he insisted, pointing at Hereward.

The crowd advanced in silence. A torch flared to life, and then another, catching the begrimed, frightened faces of Saba and three other spearmen in their flickering light. Hereward looked around at the dark expressions of the men and women surrounding him, not yet understanding what he was seeing there.

'He is the enemy,' Saba repeated, his voice growing shrill. 'He has taken food from the mouths of the folk of Ely—'

'To feed us,' someone interjected, their voice hard.

'He will bring the wrath of the king down upon all of us, those who lived here before, and you as well,' Saba shouted. 'Better to throw ourselves upon William's mercy. Save your necks. Join me.'

Sensing the mood of the crowd, the other three men lowered their spears. Hereward clambered slowly upright, holding out a hand to help Turfrida to her feet. He held her in his arms, near overcome with relief that she had survived.

'You are fools, all of you,' Saba raged. His spear shifted from side to side to keep the crowd at bay. Hereward watched the leatherworker's gaze alight upon his two captives. He scowled with determination, recognizing, perhaps, one last chance to seize victory. Pushing Turfrida aside, the Mercian turned, looking for his blade, but it was lost somewhere in the dark.

Saba saw this too and grinned. He thrust his spear towards Hereward's chest.

The tip never reached its mark. Hands grabbed the shaft to hold its progress. And then the crowd lunged forward as one, grabbing hold of Saba and dragging him down into the sea of bodies. Hereward heard the sound of punches and kicks raining down on the leader of the uprising. He cried out only once before his voice was stilled.

The other three men threw down their spears, but the men and women of the Camp of Refuge grabbed them with no less force, dragging them away among the homes. And then the folk swarmed around Hereward, demanding to know if he was well. He looked into their faces, barely comprehending what he saw there. Never had he felt such belief in his abilities before, nor such hope in the freedom he promised.

'Here is your true army,' Turfrida whispered in his ear, 'and this one is not sent by the Devil.'

CHAPTER TWENTY-THREE

The pitiless sun beat down upon the crowd gathered on the green. Like a spear, the shadow of the church tower stabbed through the heart of the solemn assembly. No one spoke. Beyond the palisade, the wetlands shimmered in a heat haze. Flies buzzed above the stagnant pools, and bees droned lazily among the beds of herbs and vegetables.

Hereward raised his head to look out across the folk of Ely. It seemed that everyone who lived there had ventured out into that fiery morning to witness the judgement upon the failed uprising. He saw the grim faces of the ones who had long called that place home, still coming to terms with the deaths of men they had known since they were children. And, too, he saw the unforgiving eyes of those who had made their way up from the Camp of Refuge. To his left, at the foot of the path to the minster, stood Thurstan and the monks. Doubt was etched into those features, he could see. When his bloody ire was directed at Normans who would plunder the Church's gold and steal their freedoms, his brutal ways could be tolerated. But last night he had slaughtered good men who had bowed their heads before the altar every Sunday and feast day, men whom the monks knew as their own.

His heart heavy, he looked down at Saba who knelt in front of him. Blood was caked around his nose and mouth. Blue bruises dappled his cheeks and forehead. The leader of the uprising hung his head so that his lank, greasy hair fell across his face. Hereward couldn't tell if it was to hide his shame or his fear.

'Last night the fate of England hung by a thread,' he began. His commanding voice carried out through the hot, still air. 'We looked beyond the ramparts for our many enemies abroad, never thinking to look amongst our own.' He chose his words carefully, subtly reinforcing the notion that he was one of them, not an outsider who had seized control of their birthplace. 'These men . . .' He nodded to Saba who still did not look up, and to the knot of prisoners, heads bowed in a circle of spears. '. . . These Ely men. You know them. You buy their wares, and ask after their kin, and laugh and share riddles and feasts. They are as familiar as the church tower that shows God watches over this place.' He looked up to the heavens as if seeking divine inspiration, knowing that every word, every action, could decide the future of the rebellion there in Ely.

'But have no doubt, these men, your neighbours, your friends, pressed the tip of a spear against all your throats last night, and held your lives in the balance,' he continued. 'For their own ends, they were prepared to give you up to the Maker. They cared not for your long friendships, or for your wives or your children. They cared less for the hopes in your hearts . . . hopes of a life free from the king's grasping hands around your necks. Have no doubt they would have given you up to our enemies in the blink of an eye, to save their own skins.'

For the first time, Saba's eyes darted up, the stare hate-filled. That look denied Hereward's account, but he knew the leather-worker could say nothing without risking another beating.

Hereward let his gaze wander over the rapt faces of the throng. They were scared; they yearned for a strong leader, a protector, in these turbulent times, and they wanted to believe every word he uttered. He felt a pang of guilt for the harsh light he had cast on the events of the previous night – none of it could ever be as simple as he made out – but he needed these people as much as they needed him.

'We cannot afford to have enemies behind us as well as at our front,' he continued, his voice growing louder. 'It will not be Norman swords that prove our undoing, but the blade in the back from folk we thought friends. No more can we carry on this way. Not if we wish to live, if we want to taste the sweet mead of victory against the bastard who has stolen the crown, and would steal what little we still call our own.'

No one moved. It seemed as if they were statues, oblivious to the hot sun. Hands shielded eyes, casting faces into shadow, so that he found it hard to read their expressions. No breeze stirred the branches of the ash trees and oaks around the isle. Even the birdsong was muted.

'No more,' he repeated, loudly. 'Do you stand with me this day?'

At first there was only that abiding silence. Then a murmur rippled out through the crowd. It was not enough.

'Do you stand with these men – my army – no, *your* army – who have vowed to give their lives to keep you safe?' His voice grew louder still, heavy with passion. The murmur came back, growing to a cry of assent. 'Do we stand as one army, warriors and folk together, ready to fight for Ely, for the English? Are we together, now and always, in this war?'

The cry became a cheer. Faces lit with passion, and hope. He steeled himself. Through the last hours of darkness long and hard had he weighed his actions, hours which seemed to stretch on into eternity. In the end, he had accepted his only possible course if victory was to be theirs.

'From this day on, every new face that wanders up to the gates of Ely will be taken up to the church before they have uttered one word. And there they will be made to swear over the sacred shrine of St Etheldreda that they are true. She will see into their hearts and, if they lie, God will strike them blind.' He watched shadows cross those bright faces as the fear of the Lord filled them. He pointed to the heavens. 'God will pass judgement upon them, not men.' He looked past the crowd to where Abbot Thurstan stood, hands pressed together as if in prayer. The cleric nodded in agreement. 'And now we must pass judgement on those among us who risked the lives of all here by standing with the king,' he continued, looking down at Saba. The leader of the uprising turned his face towards the ground.

Before Hereward could continue, a disturbance churned the crowd. A woman with a weathered face forced her way out of the throng, her arms around the shoulders of two boys. Their pink cheeks were streaked with tears. It was Saba's wife, Arild, and their two sons.

'Let him be,' she cried, her voice carrying across Ely. 'Have mercy. He is no more than a fool.' She glared at her husband. 'Fool,' she repeated, shouting at Saba. 'These spears keep us safe—'

'These spears drive us towards the grave,' he growled, not meeting her fierce gaze.

'Be silent,' Arild yelled, her voice breaking. She turned her attention back to Hereward and reached out with imploring hands. 'Let him come home, I beg you. These boys need their father. I need a husband who will keep us all fed. Saba is . . . is a good man.' She choked on the words, sobbing silently for a moment. When she had wiped her eyes with the back of her hand, she continued, 'He wanted only to keep his kin safe. Now he has learned a hard lesson and he will never cause trouble here in Ely again. He will keep his head bowed, and work hard and give praise to the aid you and all your army have given us. Do not punish him.' She choked again. 'Do not take his hand so he cannot work, or his eyes.'

Hereward could see her words had moved many in the crowd. They nodded, sympathetic to the woman's plight, and they looked from her to Saba as if he were an unruly child who needed chastisement. The Mercian felt pity too, for Arild had done no wrong. She should not suffer for her husband's crimes. He raised his eyes to the clear blue sky. This notion was not

146

new. He had turned it over in the hours after he had kissed Turfrida in the safety of their home, and made his way down to the shore for the long vigil to watch for any Norman response to the fire-boats.

'I hear your plea, Arild,' he said, looking back to the woman, 'and I know your sorrow.' He could feel his turbulent feelings tugging at him and he pushed them down farther.

Blinking away her tears, Saba's wife managed a weak smile. She hugged her boys close.

'You speak true, your husband is a fool,' Hereward continued, his voice lowering, becoming more intimate as he spoke to Arild alone. 'He let his fears guide him. He had no faith in the rightness of this fight, and he wanted only to keep you – and all here – safe.'

The woman nodded and looked to her husband. The Mercian had no doubt that the man was contrite, now he had been defeated. He turned his gaze back to the gathering. 'Aye, a fool. And yet he risked the life of every man, woman and child here. If we had not brought him low, this morning Ely would be over-run with Normans and the streets would be rivers of blood. Your blood.' Hereward drew his sword and pointed it at the man kneeling in front of him. 'This man . . . Saba . . . is as much an enemy as the Normans. Would we let one of those bastards roam freely within the ramparts, never knowing when they might turn against us, a snake in our midst?'

From the corner of his eye, he saw Arild's face fall. Her lips began to mouth, 'No.'

'Saba made his choice,' Hereward continued, his rising voice demanding the attention of the crowd so they would not look at the woman. 'He stood with our foes, not with his friends. He is no more a man of Ely. He has no home. And he can no longer be allowed to stay here.'

'Outlaw, then,' someone called.

Hereward shook his head. 'He is our enemy in this war, by his own choosing, and he must be dealt with like any enemy. His life must be the only price that can be paid for this crime.'

147

His voice rose to a shout. 'Death, I say.' He raised Brainbiter high, the blade burning in the sunlight.

Arild screamed in anguish and threw herself towards Hereward, the look of devastation upon her face cutting him to the quick. When he did not flinch, she clutched her sons to her and pressed them against her breast so they would not see. Saba looked up, squinting into the sun. His face was contorted more by disbelief than fear.

'Do you think me a weak enemy?' Hereward said, peering down at his prisoner. And then he felt all his emotions rush up and he struggled to keep his face calm. His conflicting thoughts had almost torn him apart. He could not ignore the pain and disappointment he would cause Alric and Turfrida, but that was the burden he would have to bear, however heavily it weighed upon his soul. 'Do you think you can come for me with spears, and come for my wife, and threaten all that we have built here? And that I would smile and send you away as if it were a game?' He looked into the crowd so that they knew he spoke to them as much as to Saba. 'I am not weak. I will meet threat with threat, and if you try to take my life, or the lives of anyone here, I will take your life.'

He felt his heart fall. The war against the Normans would only get harder. If he were merciful now, then when the harvest failed, or the sickness came, or the bodies piled up at the ramparts, another Saba would arise and that time more men would follow him. Fear was his greatest weapon, and with it he would ensure no more enemies stood at his back threatening all that he hoped to achieve. And if he were despised by all within Ely, that was a price he would gladly bear. Freedom from William's yoke for all these men and women, for all England, was a prize worth any sacrifice, any heart-pain. He was worthless. His purpose was all.

Arild's screams tore out. She lashed her hair like a mad-woman and tried to throw herself towards him again. But Kraki stepped forward and grabbed her wrists to restrain her. He held her fast though she squirmed and wrenched and tried to claw like a wildcat. Yet he was not without tenderness as he leaned in and whispered words of comfort in her ear.

Hereward slowly moved his gaze across the folk of Ely. Now he saw that fear amid the beads of sweat, in staring eyes and fixed mouths and furrowed brows. No one could look away from him. They all doubted he would do what he said. They thought of the hundred court, and accusations of murder, and justice, but here in Ely, cut off from the world by water and wood, he would make his own laws. It was the only way victory could be assured.

He saw Abbot Thurstan, his face darkening. He saw Guthrinc, his narrowing eyes revealing a flicker of doubt that this course was the correct one. And he saw Alric, and the monk's devastated stare, and he could not bear to linger upon that sight. He turned to his left and gave a sharp nod.

From the edge of the crowd, Hengist stepped forward, his face like stone. He carried an axe, and beside him walked two men – new arrivals both, keen to be accepted – who could find the stomach for what was to come. They each hooked a hand under Saba's armpit, and though he raged and spat and sobbed, they dragged him with ease to the Speaking Mound on the green where all could see. Arild's wails spiralled high, and then her voice cracked and she swooned in Kraki's grasp. God had administered his mercy.

The Mercian turned to the quaking band of prisoners who had followed Saba. They looked as if all blood had drained from them. 'By rights, you all should die this day for the part you played,' he said loudly above Saba's keening cries. 'But if you swear an oath to follow me under the sight of God, and that never again will you stand with the enemy, then you will be spared.'

The man gabbled their oaths, fighting to be heard above each other.

Hereward nodded. 'So be it.' He knew something had changed this day, and that this war – and his life – would never be the same again, though he was not sure what it was. He nodded again, and Hengist raised the glinting axe high over his head. 'Let this bring an end to it,' he announced. 'From this day, we are as one, for ever more. Let the Normans fear us now, for we are hungry battle-wolves and we will not rest until we have claimed victory.' His voice rang out across Ely, then, as the words died away, a terrible silence hung in the air. All faces turned to Hengist, and Saba.

The axe came down.

CHAPTER TWENTY-FOUR

21 November 1069

The world was burning. A pall of smoke hung over the Northumbrian countryside, obscuring even the sun, if day it still was. As Balthar turned slowly, all he could see was the black cloud stretching from horizon to horizon and walls of flame beneath it. *Hell*, he thought. Every village, barn, hall and hut they had passed, aflame. All the grain stored for the coming winter turned to ashes. Every cow, sheep, pig and hen slaughtered, their carcasses tossed into the conflagration. Even the fields themselves had been salted so that they could support no life. Only a wasteland remained.

Never would he have thought he would be amid such horror, so far from the comforts of the court where he practised his wiles.

'Do you like my works, Fox?' King William enquired, grinning. His horse looked like a pony under his bulk. A mountain of iron, he seemed, his hauberk straining across his girth, his helm proudly marked with the dents and scratches of a hundred battles. His sword and axe hung at his side, both of them notched and stained with blood. At his back, his army brooded, row upon row of seasoned men.

'Your wrath is mighty indeed,' Balthar replied. He forced a smile though he was filled with a terrible dread. Never had he witnessed so much carnage, never had he expected this degree of brutality when the king had promised to put down the rebellion sweeping across England. He clenched his legs against the flanks of his horse to stop them trembling. 'Surely no man would dare turn against you after this.'

'Let this be a lesson to you, Fox. No one heeds a whisper.' Red-edged flakes of charred wood settled on his shoulder and he brushed them away with the back of his hand, seemingly oblivious to the plumes of stinging smoke that swirled around him.

'Your voice will carry to the walls of Eoferwic, my lord, and far beyond into St Cuthbert's Land.'

The road had been hard and bloody and he was sick of it. Once out of Wincestre, they had passed through a land grown restive. The king had been right to move, Balthar knew that. But no one, not even his closest advisors, had predicted the harshness of his response. His judgement had been swift, his army plunging like a spear into the heart of his foes. He had pushed north to Axholme, where King Sweyn's Danes had been making their plans. Once the Northmen had been driven back across the Humbre, William had left the Counts of Mortain and Eu at Lindesege to keep the ground he had won and turned his attention to the west. The king's fire had seemed unquenchable even then. While hardened fighting men flagged from the pace, William had pushed westwards, knowing he had only a short time to quell the spreading uprisings. The Welsh princes and Edric the Wild were no match for him. With barely a pause for breath, he had turned back to the east. In Snotingeham, they had received a message that the Danes planned to retake Eoferwic. The king had no choice but to head to the cold north. Fierce Danish warriors had driven them back from the Aire Gap, and for the first time he had doubted the king's ability to crush all who stood against him. But that night he had seen the determination burning in William's face, and the next morning the army had skirted the river's edge until they found a place where they could chance a crossing. Fifty men had been lost in the surging, freezing waters, but that seemed only to drive the king to greater resolve. And as he rode on towards Eoferwic, the slaughter had begun.

Balthar turned his attention back to the dismal cluster of houses and barns ahead. The land here was flat and poor. Starvation would always be looking over the shoulder of the poor souls who tried to eke out a living in this hard place. Leaving their horses, the Norman warriors strode into the village, burning brands held aloft. Balthar's chest tightened as he watched them torch the thatched roofs. This sight repeated, every hour, every day, like a nightmare from which he could never escape. How many times had he witnessed it since they had ridden north from Wincestre? The first time he had vomited down the flanks of his steed. How the king had laughed. Now he knew exactly what to expect. If only he could tear his eyes away – but the king would curse his weakness, deeming it a sign of infidelity. And now, after all he had seen, he could not afford to fall from the king's favour.

And so he watched.

In the cold wind, the flames roared. As the local men scrambled out of their meagre homes, armed only with cudgels or stones, the warriors hacked them down, in front of their wives, in front of their children. The women screamed and cried and raked jagged, dirty fingernails. Leather gauntlets cracked into their faces, breaking noses, splitting lips. If they tried to rise from the ground, the warriors struck them again, and again, until they lay prostrate in the growing pools of blood spilling from their menfolk.

Even victory would not be enough for the king, Balthar could see that now. He had decreed that no males would be allowed to survive. From the Humbre to the Tees, the land would be laid waste. No more proud Northumbria. All food would be destroyed, so if any fled the coming judgement they would starve in the bitter winter: a slow death, the Fox knew, worse than any bloody ending on the tip of a spear. What manner of man could inflict such horrors?

And yet William smote the north with no anger, no glee, no contempt. He did it as if he were killing rats in a barn.

Roofs collapsed inward with a gush of golden sparks. A whirlwind of fire swept through the barn. So loud was the squealing of the pigs, it drowned out the roar of the conflagration and the howling of the grieving women, until one voice by one, by one, it died away. Then only sobbing drifted out into the day-turned-night.

Balthar screwed up his eyes, trying to force his thoughts back to that last night in Wincestre. When William had told him of the plans to ride north, he had raced back to Godrun. His wife, his sons, they barely entered his mind. Only Godrun, so beautiful, little more than a child. And he had begged her to lie with him, though she still smelled of the sweat and seed of the Normans who had commanded her body. He recalled the softness of her skin, not leathered and lined like that of his wife, and he remembered her eyes showing him a time long gone. A pact had been sealed that night. He would save her, and together they would find what had been lost in his own life. Godrun was all that mattered to him. If he could endure these days of horror, he could return to her and all would be well; he had to keep reminding himself that.

But then he opened his eyes and saw only butchery.

'I could never allow the Danes to build a new kingdom in the north, a place where that bastard Edgar the Aetheling could plot against me,' the king said, letting his gaze wander over the burning village. 'The north has always been a thorn in the side of the kings of this land, but never again will these unruly folk dare threaten me. No, this will be a land of ghosts.' He swept one arm out across his men. 'Ivo the Butcher whines like a child about a few mud-spattered wild men of the woods, but here is the true Devil's Army.' He threw his head back and roared with laughter.

Mad, Balthar thought, hoping his accusation did not show on his face. *And drunk on blood.* And he was not the only one to think such treasonous thoughts. When he glanced back, he saw eyes darting and shadows crossing the faces of some of the king's closest knights. But they would not speak out. No one would.

Through the mantle of smoke, a boy wandered out from the blazing village. He looked no more than five years old, his blond hair a tousled mass. He was bawling, his arms outstretched towards the king and the waiting army.

'Have mercy,' Balthar pleaded, his hand flying to his mouth when he realized the involuntary plea had crept out.

The king eyed him coldly. 'I said all males would die. He is a male, is he not?'

Balthar swallowed, no words coming. He felt sickened by his own cowardice. William nodded as if the Fox had agreed with him. With his knees, he urged his horse forward until he was beside the child. The boy reached up his arms, howling. Drawing his sword, the king raised it above his head.

'I spoke in error, Fox. I should have asked whether you like *your* works, for this . . .' He held out his left arm and looked from burning horizon to burning horizon, '. . . all this came at your urging.'

'I did not mean—'

'You should watch your tongue, Fox. Your words have more power than even you realize.'

Balthar bowed his head, his guts in turmoil. How could he have foreseen the repercussions of what he had said? His thoughts had been only for love, and Godrun, and the chance she presented for him to build a new life. He raised his eyes to see William grinning at him as if the king could read his thoughts.

The sword swept down.

'Now,' William the Bastard bellowed, turning back to his waiting army, 'let us ride for Eoferwic. The blood that has been spilled these days will be as nothing to what lies ahead.'

CHAPTER TWENTY-FIVE

The cry echoed through the stark ash trees. Alric jerked upright on the back of his dun pony. His thoughts had been drifting to take his mind off the bitter cold and he had dreamed of his hearth-fire at the monastery in Jarrow. His breath clouded in the sharp morning air as he looked around for Sighard who had been scouting ahead. His hands were red raw from the cold, and he could barely feel his fingers.

'Where are you?' he called, his frozen lips struggling to form the words. The only sound was the wind moaning through the high branches.

The snows had come early to the fens that year. Barely, it seemed, had the meagre harvest been stored in the barns and an ox been slaughtered by the Northmen among the Ely folk to mark the Blod-Monath, when fat white flakes swept in to coat the trees and grasses of the isle and lie in drifts among the reed-beds. Yet even in the harshest weather they had to venture along the secret trade routes through the dangerous countryside to bring back food, or salt or flax or antler.

The monk turned to Madulf who leaned over the neck of his steed. His face was contorted with concern for his brother and Alric could see it was all the man could do to restrain himself from riding hard to investigate the cry. Beyond him, Redwald was stooped upon his horse's back, as pale as death, his face still drawn from the pain he had suffered recovering from his wound. His hand gripped the hilt of the sword he had stolen from a dead Norman on one of the English raids.

The three men slid off their mounts and crunched into the calf-deep snow. Keeping low, they crept between the trees until they glimpsed Sighard standing by the side of a frozen lake that glittered with hoar-frost. He was alone. He threw his hood back, his wind-chapped face pink, and he waved. 'Here,' he called. 'Come see.'

Madulf stomped past Alric, glowering. 'You gave me a fright,' he barked. 'Have you no thought for anyone but yourself?'

Sighard beckoned furiously.

'He has likely found a bush in the shape of a pig, or a lame bird,' Madulf muttered, setting off in a run.

Alric followed, Redwald limping behind, to the edge of the frozen pool where the yellow reeds swayed in the bitter wind. Beyond the cover of the trees, the world was leached of colour, like old bones. Sighard squatted on the rock-hard mud bank to examine a dark shape in the mere in front of him. Alric ground to a halt, his breath catching in his throat.

The body of a man lay in the shallows, the bottom half frozen fast in the water. His beard and hair were frosted, his head flung back and his rigid arms reaching out across the ice as if he had been bathing in the sun when his soul fled. His skin had already blackened and the birds had taken his eyes. Yet the wolves had not consumed his flesh so he could not have been long dead, Alric surmised. There was a black gash across his neck – from the hack of a sword-blade by the looks of it – and more black stains on his tunic from stab wounds.

'It is Eni,' Redwald murmured. The four men stared at the ravaged face of the scout whom they had all last seen swearing a drunken mead-oath in the tavern three days gone. He was to roam the hidden trade path, watching for the king's spies. None of the Bastard's men would bring him low, he had vowed.

As silent as a shadow, he would flit along the old tracks, and he would return with any news of the invaders' movements so other paths could be taken.

Alric looked deep into those hollow eye sockets.

As one, the four men spun round, searching among the black boles of the ash trees for any sign of movement. The wind howled across the ice and lashed the trees. An iron-clad army could march beneath that roar and they would never hear it.

'Fool. Why did you draw us out into the open?' Madulf snapped at his brother. 'You are doing the king's work for him.'

'You growl like a hungry dog, always,' Sighard laughed, striding back through the reeds into the cover of the trees. 'Do you think the king's men will sit here, in this weather, waiting in case we ever took this way to the market? Why, we might not have come here till spring.'

The monk grew taut, eyeing the grinning young man. Sighard seemed uncommonly cheery for one who had discovered a comrade slaughtered and half-frozen in a lake. 'How many scouts have we now lost since the leaves fell?' he muttered.

'Five,' Redwald replied, pushing his way through the reeds.

'And the king's ships have been blessed with great luck in blocking our supplies, though our boats come in at different times and along different courses.'

Redwald glanced back. 'What say you?'

'When Hereward took Saba's head, he made every good man and woman in Ely afraid of him. No weavers or smiths or millers will raise spears against his rule from now on,' the monk began, suspicion hardening in his chest even as he spoke.

'But the king could still have eyes and ears in Ely, even one man whispering our plans into Norman ears, is that it?'

At a fleeting, unguarded look from the other man, Alric regretted giving voice to his doubts. He flinched as blood-soaked visions jerked into his mind. Redwald's mother, her throat slit. His father, drowned in a pool. Hereward's first love, Tidhild, and Redwald's own wife, heavy with child, both stabbed to death. He screwed up his eyes to force the pictures away, and when he opened them, Redwald was smiling as if he could read those thoughts. The monk shuddered. Never would he have guessed what devil lay behind that innocent face. He lowered his head, pretending to watch his step on the frozen ground, but he scrutinized the other man from under his brow.

Neither of them had mentioned that grim confession when Redwald had thought he was dying. Yet Alric had found cold eyes upon him time and again, and he knew that Hereward's brother rued his decision to give voice to his darkest secrets. The monk clenched his fist. If only his compact with God allowed him to reveal the bloody contents of that confession. But no, he would have to carry its burden upon his own soul. At least Redwald had sobbed with remorse as he spoke of his crimes, and in those cries Alric had heard an honest desire to expunge the stains from his soul. That allowed him to sleep at night. Every man carried some blackness within, and all deserved a chance to wipe it away and start anew. Perhaps Redwald's rapid healing from his spear-wound was a sign that God had accepted his confession.

In the trees, their horses steamed and stamped their hooves. Sighard and Madulf were still bickering. 'It would do no harm to choose another road to complete our journey,' Redwald murmured. 'Take no chances and trust no one is the best way to keep breathing.'

Alric clambered on to his pony and dug in his heels to urge it to follow the other horses off the track into the trees. The empty baskets strapped across its back, waiting to be filled with provisions, rattled and strained at their leather straps.

'There is another track not far away,' Redwald called back. 'Few know of it. The going will be hard, but it will serve us well.'

Alric watched the rise and fall of the other man's shoulders as he rode. Even if he could break the sacred trust of the confession, how could he ever tell Hereward that the man he called brother had killed his woman. The warrior would be shattered to learn that terrible truth, for he held Redwald in the highest esteem.

The new track was barely wide enough for a horse. It snaked through the woods, seemingly leading nowhere. In the snow, Alric would never have recognized it was there, but Redwald, with his keen eye and his youthful memories of this place, found it in a moment.

'Hot mead in the tavern when we reach Grentabrige,' Sighard announced brightly as they trotted along. 'I would drive this winter ache from my bones.'

'No time for your drunkenness,' Madulf grumbled. 'We have work to do. And that town will be swarming with the king's men now he has built his castle. One wrong word and you will be kicking your last on a gibbet.'

Ahead, Redwald bowed his head, and Alric had the strangest feeling he was smiling to himself. 'And which of you will be hurrying home to whisper honeyed words to the fair Edoma?' he asked in his melodic voice, without looking back. 'Both of you, perhaps?'

The two brothers fell silent. The monk realized Redwald was teasing them. Alric had himself caught sight of Sighard and Madulf playing the harp and singing to the pretty woman who had accompanied them when they had arrived at Ely's gates, but he had paid it little heed. Redwald missed nothing, though. He was like a hawk.

The wind cut right through them as they followed their circuitous route through the wild landscape. Red, raw fingers clutched woollen cloaks around them. Their steaming breath mingled with that of their mounts in the frozen air. The rolling rhythm of the horses dulled their thoughts as the cold seemed to fill them up from within. Snow-blanketed woods merged into the colourless sky, and in that half-aching, half-dreaming state, Alric fancied they truly were living in the End-Times, as the wise women prophesied.

Out of the banks of folding white, the ramparts and palisade of Grentabrige coalesced, and rising above it the tall tower of the new castle perched atop a hill. When he saw that sight, Alric somehow felt colder still. From the ice-locked banks of the

River Granta that flowed through the town, geese took wing, their honking carrying far over the chill world as they soared above the rooftops. The four travellers pulled their hoods low over their eyes and kept their heads down and their shoulders hunched, better to resemble the English who had been broken on the Norman mill. They were not alone. Despite the harsh weather, thin trails of men and women, on foot, or horse, or cart, were making their way through the snows on the river floodplain towards the gates.

He closed his eyes and prayed that they would all escape with their lives.

CHAPTER TWENTY-SIX

The grim guards upon the wall looked down on the desperate souls passing through the gates of Grentabrige. Alric, Redwald, Sighard and Madulf turned their faces away as they merged into the throng. Once inside, their nostrils wrinkled at the reek of woodsmoke, excrement and wet straw. Though his skin pricked with apprehension, Alric looked around the rutted street and marvelled. Not since Eoferwic had he seen a town so large and lively. Folk milled along the rows of workshops. Merchants clogged the way with their snorting oxen and fat pigs as they herded them towards the market. The monk's ears ached from the thunder of hammers and looms, and the conversations delivered at a bellow to be heard above the din.

Redwald slowed his horse so that he trotted alongside Alric's pony. His words emerged from the shadows of his hood. 'What is this?' he hissed. 'Is there now a new garrison here in Grentabrige?'

Alric saw immediately what he meant. Wrapped in thick, black cloaks against the cold, Norman soldiers seemed to be gathered everywhere in twos or threes. They murmured to each other in their guttural tongue, ignoring the stream of shivering

English who passed by them as if they were no more than rats scurrying from the mill.

'We must take care,' Redwald whispered. 'One wrong word could easily reach their ears.'

Alric cast a surreptitious glance back at Sighard. The young man was laughing loudly at his brother's complaining. Neither seemed to have noticed the quiet sentinels along the street.

'Fools,' Redwald muttered. 'They will be the death of us. We should not have brought them.'

'Two of us would not have been able to carry all the provisions we need,' Alric replied. 'And they have proved themselves to be more than able in keeping the barns and our bellies full.'

'Still,' Redwald murmured, showing no sign that he was speaking, 'I would have left them back in Ely.'

The market was noisy and congested. The snow had turned to stinking brown slush underfoot. Alric thought his toes would never be warm again. Once they had broken the ice on the water troughs, they tied up their horses. Before they divided to purchase their wares, Redwald cautioned the two brothers to act as if a Norman stood at their shoulders at all times. Whether they heeded this warning, Alric could not be sure.

'My brother will be keen to know what we have seen here,' Redwald whispered as he helped Alric carry the baskets into the crowd.

'Will this change his plans?'

Redwald shrugged. 'These days he keeps his thoughts to himself. I know him better than all, and even I cannot tell what passes through his head.'

'He has been much changed since the summer,' Alric agreed.

'For the worse. He should heed his friends. Throw off his burdens and share his woes. Only his woman—' He caught himself. 'Only Turfrida knows his heart, and what wisdom can she give on war? In this time of growing threat, he should have his wisest friends around him. He needs to hear strong voices.'

'Will he make his move when the thaw comes?'

'How can he?' Redwald said with a note of bitterness. 'Our

numbers have swollen, but not yet enough to mount a real challenge.'

A thin-faced man with a fledged sparrowhawk upon his gauntlet called to them, 'Only twenty-four pennies. And a small price to pay for this winged wonder. No prey can escape his sight.' He turned up his nose when Alric waved him away.

Redwald grunted. He seemed barely able to contain his grievance. 'This path of his will be the end of us if we do not take care. He waits, and he waits,' he said under his breath. 'Only by joining with the uprising in the north can we truly be sure that we will have a force to be feared.'

The monk shrugged. 'The news from the north is not good. And if the king is attacking there as they claim, how long before his wrath turns east?'

'My advice would be to strike now, strike quickly,' Redwald whispered. 'While William's back is turned.' He fell silent for a moment, then added in a voice so quiet Alric could barely hear it, 'Make him fight two armies on two fronts. Tear his own army apart and wear down his men, as King Harold's army was worn down by his battle in the north when the Bastard sailed to our shores.' He pretended to adjust his grip on the basket as two Normans strode by. Once they had gone, he continued, 'My brother should be made to listen to his friends, for his own good, and ours.'

'I will speak with him when we return,' the monk whispered in reply.

Once they had bought the salt and flax they needed, they heaved the baskets back towards the horses. As they were strapping the laden panniers across the back of Alric's beast, angry yells rang out from the other side of the market. Alric and Redwald kept their heads down until they heard a voice that was unmistakably Madulf's shouting, 'Leave him be.'

Redwald cursed under his breath. He dropped his head and walked without any show of urgency towards the source of the disturbance. Alric followed in his wake. A silent crowd had gathered in a wide circle on the far side of the bustling market.

Redwald and Alric pushed their way through the wall of bodies to the front. In the centre of the circle stood Sighard, his arms gripped by two Norman soldiers. The young man kept calm. He knew that to resist would only result in drawn swords, or worse. Madulf's face was flushed with anger, but he too kept his hands by his sides. His eyes darted towards Redwald and Alric and then quickly moved away.

A man prowled in front of Sighard, a priest by the look of his *pillicia*, Alric noted. The long woollen tunic was brown, free of any adornment, but the material was thick and likely fur-lined to keep out the cold. The monk studied the churchman's dark eyes and cold face, the long black moustache, and the black hair that had been shaved at the back of the skull in the Norman military style. These priests of William's were hard to tell apart from his warriors – and just as cruel and brutal, he had heard tell. Where was the love of God in men like that?

'What means the woman to you?' the cleric asked in heavily accented English.

'I do not know her,' Sighard replied. He pushed his chin up in defiance, then saw the priest's icy stare and let it drop again.

'She is a witch. And now she is free to weave her spells and curse her neighbours, because of you.' The priest thrust his face close to Sighard's, so that their noses were almost touching.

'I saw only a man threatening a woman,' Sighard replied, his voice steady. 'How could I know she was a witch?'

'The Devil's own always lie. You aided her escape, did you not?'

Alric held his breath. If the priest gave the order for the soldiers to take Sighard away, it would be the end of him. He would be forced to hold an iron rod that had been heated in the fires until it glowed red, or he would be weighed down with rocks and thrown into the freezing waters of the river. In his agony, he would confess to anything, and then his life would be forfeit.

'He cannot help himself when he sees a woman in need. He is like a lovesick fool,' Madulf interrupted, his voice wavering.

The churchman looked back at Madulf, and once he had decided the other brother was no threat, he returned his attention to Sighard. 'I do not believe that you can be trusted. You must take the witch's place, until I can be sure—'

'Wait.' Alric stepped forward. 'I am a man of God, like you, a monk, from the monastery in Jarrow in the north. My name is Alric.'

'You are far from your home,' the priest said, his eyes narrowing with suspicion.

'As are you.' The monk swallowed to steady his nerve. The crowd blurred into the background around him as he focused on the words he would have to spin to save all their lives. He ignored the searching gaze of the Norman soldiers and enquired, 'What is your name?'

The priest hesitated, puzzled by this interruption. 'I am called Emeric. I have been directed by the Pope himself to hunt witches. My travels have taken me across Europe. And I have done God's work everywhere I went. The Devil has fewer servants now.'

Alric forced a smile which he hoped was charming. 'And now you are in England.'

'You have many witches here,' Emeric snapped. 'Away from London, they lurk in every town and village. Brother, your English Church has failed in its duty, but now I am here to do your work for you.'

'And we are grateful for all the aid you give,' Alric said with a slight bow. 'But this man is not another burden for you.'

The priest looked to Sighard and then back to the monk, frowning. 'You stand by him?'

'He is a fool where women are concerned, as his brother says. But more than that, he is my servant this day.' The monk pressed his hands together as if in prayer. 'As you say, I am far from home and this land is strange to me. I travel to Yernemuth where I must seek passage to Flanders and without this man to guide me I will never find my way. In this hard winter, that could cost my life. I beg a kindness, brother. Let me take my guide, and you have my word that I will chastise him for what he has done.'

Emeric studied Alric's face. The monk wanted to squirm. He felt the priest was weighing his every word and once he had been found wanting the soldiers would drag him away too. After a moment, the Norman churchman replied, 'Yernemuth, you say? Once these snows clear, I would travel north myself. I hear these wild fenlands are filled with witches.'

Alric only smiled. Despite the cold, he could feel the sweat trickling down his back.

Emeric turned to Sighard and barked, 'Go to your master. But if we meet again, know you will be forced to confess before the eyes of God.'

Sighard wrenched his arms free from the soldiers, and all but ran past Alric and into the crowd. Madulf followed him. Redwald was nowhere to be seen. Alric gave a pleasant smile and a nod, and turned away before Emeric could question him further. But he could feel the priest's lowering gaze upon his back as he pushed into the crowd, and he knew that he had had a lucky escape.

Chapter Twenty-Seven

Splashes of blood scarred the virgin snow. Almost black in that white world, more gore puddled around the body of the mercenary. A gleaming helm protruded from a drift, a broken spear beside it. The wind howled through the stark branches of the wood as a shadow swept across the fallen warrior, and came back.

'The Devil will take your soul,' the voice screeched. 'I am a man of God.'

Hereward threw his head back and laughed. He was wrapped in furs greased with lamb fat to keep out the bitter cold, but his blond hair lashed in the gale. All around, his men bellowed their humour, their ash-streaked faces grinning death's-heads. Hengist did a little dance.

The upended churchman swung back again, his face crimson with embarrassed fury, his grey-streaked hair sweeping the snow with each pass. He was suspended from the branch of an oak by a rope strapped around his ankles, his hands tied behind his back. Whenever his swinging began to slow, Hengist darted in to give him a shove.

'Would you enjoy this more if we tied the rope to your neck?' Hereward taunted.

The cleric changed his manner, pursing his lips as he put on a sorrowful expression. 'Have pity on me. I am but a poor traveller doing God's work in this cold land. I have not had a full belly for many a day.'

'He is sorely lacking in bread, indeed, but he has plenty of gold to chew on,' Guthrinc called from where he squatted next to the oak, searching through the sack the churchman had been carrying. He raised a glinting gold chalice over his head. 'He has a *goldhord* here that would please a king. Plate, cups, chain and other adornments.'

'That belongs to God,' the cleric spat.

'And you were keeping it safe for him,' Hereward nodded with a wry smile. 'This gold will buy much food for the hungry folk of Ely. As a good Christian man, your heart must be warmed to know your toils will mean none starve in this harsh winter.'

'You think yourselves brave warriors. You are nothing more than thieves and murderers.' Spittle flew from the churchman's mouth.

Hereward laughed again. 'You call me thief. While we fought, you bowed your head to William the Bastard like a whipped cur, forsaking all those who prayed in your church. But now you fear you may not be as well rewarded as you once thought.'

The cleric closed his eyes and intoned a prayer, trying to drown out the Mercian's words.

'Now the king sends in his own Norman churchmen to take your place, and seize the riches you have heaped up behind your altar,' Hereward continued. 'And so you fled. And to aid your flight you stole from God, and from the folk who paid for this gold with their hard labours. But you made the mistake of passing through the fens in your search for a place to hide. This is my land, and here not even a spear-for-hire can keep you safe.' He nodded towards the dead Northman. 'God set justice upon you.'

'Blasphemy,' the cleric yelled. 'You would dare speak for the Lord?'

'Why not? All churchmen seem to do so without fault.' The warrior gave a lupine smile, then nodded to Guthrinc and said, 'A good day's work. Take it. We will put it to good use when we return.'

Hengist giggled, giving the churchman another shove. 'You mean to leave me here?' the prisoner cried, wrenching his head up to look at his captors as he swung. 'I will freeze to death.'

'Shout louder. Your friends the Normans are near by searching for us. They will cut you loose.' Hereward walked around the dangling churchman.

The prisoner's face turned the colour of the snow. He knew what the king's men would do if they found he had been stealing the gold they considered their own. Through gritted teeth, he growled, 'I will see you hunted down and brought to justice for this.'

'This man of God has balls.' Kraki traced the cleric's path through the air with the tip of his spear.

'You need some of those, Hengist,' Guthrinc said, slinging the sack over his shoulder. He pointed at the prisoner. 'Cut his off.'

The churchman cried out. The warriors jeered.

'Do not torment him,' Hereward said with a laugh. 'He has already sold his soul to William the Bastard. He will pay soon enough.'

The cleric's angry shouts rang out at their backs as they moved away through the trees towards the edge of the frozen marsh. Large flakes began to drift down, filling their footprints.

'This gold has warmed my heart better than any home-fire,' Guthrinc said cheerily.

'Still, it is not enough,' Hereward replied, searching the colourless landscape for Norman scouts. 'If we are to build an army that will crush William's men as they crushed King Harold's warriors, we need the kind of gold that would fill the royal coffers.'

'That is a lot of fleeing churchmen to rob,' Guthrinc hummed.

'You have a plan?' Kraki looked like a bear in the depths of his furs and his hauberk, fire flickering in the shadows of his helm's eyelets.

'Gold to buy food to fill an army's belly and to bribe folk to keep our paths hidden? Aye, plans I have. And I have listened to the words of Abbot Thurstan himself to be sure they are good. But I need an army to make them bear fruit.'

'You need an army to gain an army,' Guthrinc replied. 'Now there is a riddle to tax even the sharpest mind.'

Hereward did not reply. He had wrestled with the problem since the long, hot summer months without finding the answer he needed. Yet the success of the rebellion depended on that very solution. Gold would buy them victory. Without that, they were merely fleas nipping at the hide of the dog.

Beneath chalk skies, in the face of the blizzard's teeth, they loped along the old narrow tracks and the hidden byways. On the banks of the Old Ouse where the water flowed black and slow between the ice-choked river-edges, they crouched among the sedges and the reeds and watched a group of ten Normans on horseback trek in the direction of Earith. The king's men kept their heads down in the cruel wind, their black cloaks pulled tightly around them.

'Call me thick-headed, but there seems more of those bastards each day, and they wend ever closer to Ely,' Guthrinc muttered, pressing aside the reeds to get a better look.

'Have their numbers swollen?' Kraki growled, casting an inquisitive glance towards Hereward as if the leader had been keeping secrets from him.

The Mercian narrowed his eyes, watching the Normans until they disappeared into the swirling snow. 'If so, then it is done by stealth.'

'Unless they realize we have eyes and ears among their own and are holding their tongues,' Guthrinc said. 'What does this mean? The king is sly, and at his most dangerous when he appears to be doing nothing.'

Eager to feel the heat of their home-fires, the English ran the final miles south across the frozen marsh to the edge of

Hempsals Fen. There the flint of the narrow causeway leading home glittered like shards of ice. No crowd greeted their return as they passed through the gates of Ely. The folk all huddled around their hearths for warmth, listening to the bubbling of the tangy stews that sweetened the cold air of the settlement. But as the cheers of the returning warriors rang out across the thatched roofs, Acha emerged, swaddled in a thick cloak of grey. Her dark eyes fixed upon Hereward's for a long moment, and they both acknowledged the strange, unfathomable bond that had arisen between them since the summer uprising. With a curt nod, Hereward moved on, knowing it was unwise to dwell too much on the meaning of those feelings. He kept his gaze on the snowy path, fighting the urge to look back to see if Kraki had observed that fleeting look.

Near the track to his dwelling, a bear waited. It was only as he neared that Hereward realized it was a man, wrapped in thick furs, his wild hair almost obscuring his ruddy, wind-chapped face. He didn't move, and so much snow had fallen on him it looked as if he had been there for days. As he peered into the face, the Mercian was shocked to see it was Dunnere the miller. Not for long months had Hereward seen him. Since his daughter had vanished, he had kept to the confines of his dusty mill and only those who fetched the sacks from his door had seen him. Through all that time, it seemed he had not cut his hair, nor, from the smell of him, bathed. His nose had the broken veins of a man who drank too much ale and the skin under his eyes sagged down like melted wax.

'Dunnere. It is good to see you,' Hereward began.

'I request a boon,' the miller said, ignoring all pleasantries. 'Only you and your men can help me now.'

'Your daughter.' The long-missing girl could be the only thing on the man's mind.

Dunnere nodded. 'All my days are grey.' He choked on the words for a moment before mumbling, 'I pray for word that she is safe. Even that she has run off with some wild lad, and is afraid to tell me she is with child. Anything.' A juddering breath racked him. 'Sometimes I even pray that her body will be washed up. At least then I could give her a Christian burial and put aside this endless worry that blights my life. And then I curse myself and wish *I* were dead for thinking such a thing.'

Hereward rested a comforting hand on the man's shoulder. 'You must have strength—'

'Have strength, you say? If I did not have strength I would long since have thrown myself into Dedman's Bog.' He bowed his head, steadying himself. 'Some say that she could only have had her virtue taken by one of your men . . . and then her life. I do not believe such a thing.'

'What would you have me do?'

'When your scouts are out across the fens, have them ask after her. If she yet lives, someone must have seen her. Just to know that she . . .' He covered his face with his hands as a silent sob ran through him.

'I will do as you ask,' Hereward soothed, knowing that he could do no such thing. More than anything he wanted to bring comfort to this good man, but it was beyond him. 'Do not lose faith,' he whispered. 'In my heart, I am sure there is an honest answer to this mystery, and you and your daughter will be reunited.'

The miller pumped Hereward's hand, seeming pathetically grateful for these miserable few words of comfort. 'You are a good man,' Dunnere said, wiping the snot from his nose with the back of his hand. 'It warms my heart to know I do not stand alone in my suffering.'

Hereward watched him stumble away through the drifts, feeling his spirits fall lower still. *A good man*, he thought bitterly, and spat into the snow.

Before he could move onwards, Hengist hurried up and lurched into his path. Hereward felt troubled by the odd gleam that now seemed to have settled in the other man's eyes. 'Brunloc tells me ten more men left while we were gone,' Hengist said, pulling his cloak tighter.

'This winter is hard. We knew some would not stay the course.'

'Aye, but this is more than we expected. And the numbers grow greater by the week. A trickle now, soon a flood if things stay as we are.' He stamped the snow off his shoes. 'Soon we might have no army to speak of.'

'Most will not risk travel in this harsh weather. The true test will come in the spring. Till then we will find some way to put fire in their hearts.' He nodded and walked on, hoping Hengist would take some encouragement from his words. But the other man had spoken the truth. They were losing warriors faster than they could bear. If the flow was not stemmed by the spring, the uprising would die, and the hopes of the English with it.

He put aside his grim mood and strode forward. As he neared his door, it flew open. Turfrida stood framed in the golden glow from the fire. He paused, feeling uneasy at the urgency of her appearance, and as his eyes grew accustomed to the light, he saw she did not smile and her gaze was questioning. Fear filled him, fear that had haunted him every day since Turfrida's life had been threatened during the uprising, a dread that she might be the one to pay the price for his own bloody war.

'What is wrong?' he whispered.

He felt relief as her face softened. She smiled, though still a little uncertainly. 'Husband, I have news,' she announced, holding her arms out to him. 'I am with child.'

Chapter Twenty-Eight

Frost glittered in the dead man's eyebrows. The falling snow settled in the hollows of his eye sockets and drifted across the bodies of the five other Norman soldiers lying around the edge of the frozen marsh. Harald Redteeth knelt beside the fallen warrior, listening to the voices of the *alfar* in the howling wind. They called to the souls of these brave dead to join them in the world beneath the seas and the lakes and the hills. The Viking muttered a silent prayer, urging those shades on to Valhalla instead. These Normans were true warriors, even if they followed the orders of fools.

Not so long gone he had himself almost joined the ranks of the *Einherjar* in that vast hall of fallen warriors. But Woden had seen fit to turn him back at the very doors. And he knew why. He still had work to do, blood-work, and like his friend Ivar the Dead who breathed cold breath upon his neck day and night, he would never be allowed to rest until it was done. He stood, feeling the aches that still lingered from his now-healed wounds. Pink scars now covered more of his torso than the skin with which he was born, but each one served as a reminder of who he was.

'Speak clearly. What happened here?'

The gruff voice of Ivo Taillebois snatched him from his reverie. He turned and crunched across the snow to the small group of men surrounding the ceorl who had witnessed the attack. He wore thick furs reeking of grease. His wide eyes had the faraway look of a man still gripped by the horror that he had seen. Flanked by three Norman warriors, Taillebois looked like a raven in his black cloak and breeches, his fist snarled in the front of the ceorl's furs.

'Tell me,' he demanded again. His other gauntleted hand moved to his sword hilt.

'He has had the wits scared out of him.' William de Warenne leaned over the neck of his horse, shivering inside his lilac cloak.

Harald ignored them, drawn as always to the silent member of the group, the old man Asketil Tokesune, Hereward's father. He supported himself on his long staff, his filthy cloak so ragged it surely could not keep out the winter's blades. His skin was as pale as snow, his pebble eyes as black as the waters beneath the ice. The others treated him like a simple child, but Harald saw the truth.

The Butcher shook the ceorl so roughly his teeth rattled. As the sword half-slid from its scabbard, the man came to his senses. 'Ghosts, they are,' he gasped. 'Not men.'

Taillebois hawked phlegm and spat on the snow.

'They have the faces of death,' the ceorl continued, 'white skulls, fresh from the grave. They came with the snow.' He placed his hand upon his heart. 'I . . . hunted fowl. I swear before God, may He strike me dead: this land was empty until your battle-wolves came by. When the wind changed, he was there . . . Hereward . . . stepped forth from hell with his sword Brainbiter. His men, his dead men, struck with spear and axe. Your soldiers fell without even a cry. What hope did they have? Barely had a prayer escaped my lips when the dead men were gone, into the snow and away.' He fluttered a hand towards the heavens. 'God help me that I had seen such things.'

William pulled his cloak tighter, his teeth chattering. 'This is not good enough,' he said to the Norman commander. 'We kill

176

one of theirs, they slay five of ours. Be like a sly fox, the king said. Aye, so sly we barely move. Where are our fangs?'

'We have our eyes and ears among them,' Taillebois growled. 'Soon we will hear news we can use to bring them to their knees.'

The nobleman snorted. 'Soon?' he sneered. 'How soon? If Hereward's head is not on a stick by the summer, the king will fall upon us as he has done upon the north.'

'You already know all you need.' Asketil's voice was almost lost beneath the wind's whine.

'Save your breath, old man,' the Butcher said, thrusting the ceorl away from him. 'When we need to hear your words, we will—'

'Wait,' William interjected. 'What say you?'

Harald watched Asketil's face darken, the lips pulling back from his yellow, chipped teeth. Hatred lay there, of a kind he had never seen between father and son. He felt his distaste for the old man rise.

'You do not know my son as I know him,' Asketil replied, looking up at the Norman noble. 'The ceorl speaks true. He is no man. He is a beast who puts on the face of a man. Show his true face and none would follow him. Find the beast inside him and he will return to the wild and leave this uprising behind.'

Taillebois gave a dismissive laugh. 'Men like that would die before they walked away.'

'Hereward is not a man of honour. He cares only for himself. His mother's blood stains his hands. And, aye, he would see me dead too.' Harald watched Asketil's knuckles whiten as he grasped his staff tighter. 'He has been tamed by the two who are closest to him. Your eyes and ears in his camp have already learned this. You know.'

The Butcher's brow furrowed in thought. He pushed his way through his warriors to stand before the old man. 'The monk?'

'And his wife. The witch. Between them, they have shackled the devil inside him. But those chains are weak. Without their guiding words, he will return to the Hereward of old.'

177

William clapped his hands, grinning. 'Take the monk—'

'No,' Asketil said, shaking his staff. 'The woman.'

The nobleman's grin faded.

'She is his true weakness,' the old man continued. 'For all his fierceness, he is still the child running to his mother, wishing to protect her. All women are his weakness.'

'Take his wife?' William mused, unsure.

Asketil stamped his staff upon the hard ground. 'Take his woman. Cut out her heart.'

The nobleman winced, reeling back on his mount.

Harald stepped forward. 'There is no honour in making a woman suffer,' he snapped.

Asketil turned on him, sneering. 'You are as weak as Hereward.'

Harald smiled in reply. He saw Grim, his axe, slicing through the old man's neck, the head falling to the snow, the blood gushing out.

'You heard from your eyes and ears what happened when his wife was taken by Saba and those others. Hereward threw aside all reason for her.' The old man looked from William to Taillebois. 'There is too much at stake here for soft hearts and soft heads. If a woman's death makes you cringe, then think of her not as wife but as witch. She can be tried and tested and found wanting under God's eyes.'

The Butcher nodded thoughtfully. 'A witch. Aye.'

'Are we not men who fight and die as men?' Harald kept his voice calm, but in his head he heard his father telling him the rules of life by the winter fire: honour, and blood, and the road to Valhalla. These Christian men would have called his own mother witch, and half the women in his village. 'A victory like this has no value.'

As fast as a snake, Taillebois drew his sword and thrust the tip against Harald's neck. Harald held his eyes steady, unflinching. 'You take orders from us. You do not speak out,' the Butcher snarled. He glanced at William. 'It would be easier to lure the woman out of the camp than the monk. Once we have her, Hereward will do our bidding.'

After a moment, William nodded. 'The king was right. The cunning fox keeps his belly full. Once he sees his wife in agony, Hereward will say whatever we want to free her. He will end the uprising himself.'

Grinning, Taillebois sheathed his sword. 'Then it is agreed. We take the witch.'

Now forgotten, Harald watched the Butcher climb back on to his horse, but it was the old man who drew his gaze. The frailty in Asketil's face had drained away. His eyes now blazed with an uncanny fire and he bared his teeth like a wolf ready to tear out the throat of a lamb.

CHAPTER TWENTY-NINE

The body lay at the side of the road. The skin was black, the belly bloated, and ravens had taken the eyes. As he rode towards the corpse, Balthar scarcely gave it a second glance, so many had he seen on the journey. They lined the roads like markers to hell. The stink of human rot hung everywhere in the north, and even the nosegay stuffed with herbs and spices could not bring him respite. He coughed and gagged, his eyes darting towards his shadow riding in silence at his side. Faramond was a dour Norman knight who barely acknowledged his charge. But Balthar was glad of his companionship. No man should venture abroad alone in such a tormented place.

As they neared the body, undulating shadows rushed away into the growing dark. The knight grunted. 'Some say there are more rats in Northumbria than men these days.'

'Oh, to be in the south once again,' the Fox sighed, thinking of Godrun. How distant her beauty and her tenderness seemed amid those grim surroundings. 'Have you heard word when we return home?' he ventured hopefully.

'When the king's work is done.'

Balthar sighed. And when would that be? Eoferwic was already William's. In the days leading up to Christmas, they had ridden through a blasted land into a burnt city – a mere shadow of its former glory – with hungry, desperate folk proclaiming their saviour, the king. Their voices had been raised more out of fear than hope, he knew. They had seen the thick black clouds of carrion birds following the Norman army. But Eoferwic was only one stopping point on the long road of William's bloody obsession. He would not be satisfied until no man was left standing between here and the Tees in the far north.

His breath clouded in the chill, and he shivered. As he looked up at the rising moon in the clear sky, he felt the sting of snowflakes in the wind. It had been a hard winter and it would get harder still, he was sure of it. He closed his eyes and dreamed of the warm fires in the hall the king now occupied in the ruined town. When he opened them a moment later, he glimpsed movement across the river plain outside Eoferwic.

'What is that?' he asked, squinting into the growing gloom and pointing. 'One of the king's war-bands?' He flinched at the cold-blooded brutality of William, who had divided his army into smaller groups and each day sent them out to slaughter men, salt fields and burn any homes or barns in parts they had not yet devastated.

Faramond followed his gaze, and shook his head. Though he did not reply, Balthar saw the knight's hand slip to the hilt of his sword.

They rode on, faster now. As they neared Eoferwic and the reek of wet charred wood that hung over the town, he heard cries carried on the wind. The winter chill seemed to bite even deeper into his bones when he saw that what he had taken to be a war-band was a large crowd of women and children, stumbling across the reed-beds and scrubby grassland towards the gates.

'Do not speak to them,' Faramond warned, his gaze as bitter as that wind. 'Do not meet their eyes. And if they dare reach out to you, strike them with your cudgel.'

'They are poor, hungry souls,' Balthar protested.

'They are already dead.'

181

As they drew towards the gates, the starving beggars noticed them and as one they turned and surged across the road, their cries like those of gulls at sunset. Little more than rags were their dresses, torn and filthy, and many had wrapped themselves in blankets and sack-cloth against the biting cold. They looked like spectres, he thought, with ashen skin and hollow cheeks and eyes fallen deep into shadow, and they reached out with thin, clutching hands as if they wished to draw him back to the grave with them. The children were worse. He could not even look at them.

Faramond shouted for them to clear the path, but only when he drew his sword and beat it against his shield did they cower away. Yet Balthar felt only pity for them. This wandering mob roamed the countryside in search of any morsel that might allow them to live to see another day. But there was nothing, anywhere. And when he looked into their devastated eyes, he saw they knew it.

Overcome with compassion, he looked down at a hooded woman holding out a trembling hand towards him. But as the dancing light from the gate torches illuminated her face, he recoiled in horror. Her nose and lips had blackened, and the rest of her face was swollen and purple like an overripe fruit. Glancing around, he saw the tell-tale signs on too many other women. Ravaged faces, opened sores, black fingertips, blood caking their ears and nostrils.

'The sickness,' he cried, his voice breaking. 'They carry the sickness with them.'

Faramond cursed loudly. 'Ride hard,' he ordered, 'and let none touch you.' He jabbed his heels into his horse's flanks and it lurched forward. Too slow to move out of the way, a woman fell beneath the hooves, screaming.

Terror gripped Balthar. He drove his steed forward in the knight's wake, half-glimpsing the ragged shapes stumbling into his path, hearing the shrieks rise up around him as his mount ground flesh and bone into the frozen earth. Those ruined faces flashed by as if in a fever-dream. Fingers scrabbled at his cloak, his legs. He whimpered a prayer. Lord, let him live and he would be a godly man. Let him live to be with Godrun.

Eoferwic's gates ground open. The mob fell behind, but still the two riders did not slow. Across the ramparts they thundered and on to the rattling bridge across the moat. Only when Balthar heard the gates trundle shut behind him did he bring his horse to a halt. He blinked away tears of fear and looked around. Seemingly unmoved, Faramond loomed over one of the king's men who was hauling the oak bar across the gates.

'Pestilence is abroad,' he was saying. 'Let no stranger enter. And if it is one of our own, look into his face for the signs.' He crossed himself. 'All four horsemen are now at large. Our time must be short. Confess your sins and be ready.' The knight caught Balthar's eye as he dismounted and, almost as an after-thought, he muttered, 'Take care,' before striding off into the night-dark streets.

Still shaking, Balthar clambered down from his steed and all but ran towards the new hall that had once belonged to the Earl of Northumbria. He called for wine, and swilled down the first cup in one draught before staggering to the fire blazing in the hearth. As the warmth began to seep into his frozen bones, he glanced around and saw the remnants of the feast for the Nativity of the Christ on the long table: venison, goose, boar and beef, and honey-cakes and mead too. Even those scraps would have fed the starving mob at the gates for a week or more. He sagged on to the stool and covered his face. How had his world come to this? The promise of Wincestre seemed so far away. Those ravaged faces beyond the gate haunted him, and the bodies that littered every corner of that land. All the monstrous sights he had witnessed since he had ridden north with the king would be seared into his mind for ever more, yes, and the part he had played in such carnage, however small.

'You are weary, Fox? Eat. Drink. This is a time for feasting in praise of the birth of our Lord.'

At the king's voice, Balthar jerked upright. He felt too worn down to play the complex games that would keep him on the monarch's good side. But as he peered into the gloom at the edge of the hall, he saw that William stared into the middle distance, his thoughts elsewhere. He swayed, drunk from his day of celebration. Ale slopped from the cup in his hand. Balthar thought he looked in a morose mood, his mouth turned down and forehead creased. 'Lord, I would not have come here had I known—'

The king flapped his hand to silence the apology. 'How went it today?' he muttered.

'I met with the thegns, lord. They follow only you and will offer any tribute you see fit to demand.'

William shrugged, uninterested. 'You must think me a cruel man, Fox,' he said, wandering towards the hearth.

'My lord—'

'I have seen the way you look at me,' the monarch snapped. His eyes blazed, but only for a moment, and once his melancholy mood had returned, he put one foot on a stool and peered into the flames. 'One day, what I have done here in the north will be seen as a great victory. All the deaths will be forgotten. All that will be remembered is that William sealed his hold upon the English crown.' He took a swig of his ale, adding in a slurred voice, 'This is war, Fox, and war is never won by heroes, only by those who kill faster and better than the next man.'

'You are winning a great victory, my king.'

The flames reflected in William's dark eyes. For a long moment, only the crackling of the logs echoed through the gloom of the hall. 'Fighting to win is all I have known,' he murmured. He seemed to be speaking only to himself. 'Seven summers. That was all I had seen when I became Duke of Normandy. Seven summers, and then the blood-letting began. My father, he was barely a man himself when I was born, and my mother . . .' The words died in his throat. He sipped more mead to moisten his throat and continued, 'My father killed his own brother to become duke before me. And then he himself was murdered, while on a pilgrimage to the Holy Land. Poisoned.'

Balthar sat back upon a stool, his attention piqued. The king's guard was down. Would he reveal something that could be used in times to come? He scrutinized his master, watching every thought and emotion reveal itself in the subtle play of shadow and light. 'Your childhood was hard,' he said gently, encouraging the king to continue.

'My childhood was good. It forged me.' He drained his cup and tossed it aside, but his gaze never left the flames. 'There is no play for a child who is a duke. No, not when every high family in Normandy wanted the power that came with that title. My life hung by a thread, always. Yet there was one man who showed me kindness, my guardian, Osbern. He would sit me on his knee and sing me songs. And sometimes he would tell me tales from the hot lands to the east, where my father died. Every night he would sleep beside me with one eye open, and when they came for me with knives or axes, as they often did, he would put a hand over my mouth to stop me calling out, and he would pick me up in his arms. Then we would sneak out of a hidden door and down into the village, to hide in a peasant's house until the danger had passed. Osbern kept me alive, and he taught me what I needed to do to go on living when I was grown.'

'Then he taught you how to be a good king, my lord,' Balthar said with a nod.

'Not in the way you think, Fox. One night I woke in the throes of a dream. It was summer, the room was hot. I remember now how I was soaked with sweat, and the bed was soaked too.' He smiled. 'Yet it was sticky. I called out to Osbern and rolled over. There was no ear for me to whisper in as I did most nights. His head had been cut off and set upon a stool the other side of the sleeping chamber. Watching me . . .' His brow furrowed as he reflected on this. 'How soundly I must have slept. His throat slit, his head sawn off, and never did I murmur.'

'And they left his head there to frighten you?' Balthar said, aghast.

William nodded, tapping the side of his head. 'Clever. Why kill a boy when you can make him dance? So, yes, Fox, Osbern

185

taught me how to be a king. For he was weak, and he died. And I learned that night that I would never be weak.'

'You are strong indeed, my lord.'

William chuckled silently, though Balthar saw no humour in his words. The king eyed him for a moment before enquiring, 'You would consider yourself a hero, would you not, Fox? In your own world? An Englishman who rose from humble beginnings to stand alongside a king.'

'I am but your servant.'

'But you would rather be back in Wincestre with that serving girl who brings me my wine.'

Balthar flinched.

The king laughed at his reaction. 'Do you think that anything in my court passes beneath my notice?' He tapped the corner of his eye. 'I see like a hawk. Fox, you are as white as snow,' he added, laughing. 'Steady yourself. She is a pretty child. Many of my men have had their way with her.' His face hardened as he said these words and Balthar knew he was driving home a spear. 'You have a wife, and this girl is young and . . . once . . . was pure,' he added. 'So do not judge me, Fox. We are alike, you and I, yes? We both take what we want without a thought for others. We both do what we must to satisfy our desires.'

Balthar felt a chill run deep inside him. As he watched the flames leaping in the king's dark eyes, he began to wonder if William had in some way intended Godrun to seduce him. At that moment, he felt as if he had fallen into deep water. Before he could consider the matter further, the king walked away. On the edge of the shadows, he turned back and said in a flat voice, 'For the next ten days, my men shall ride out to harry the last of the bastards who live on. And once this land is cold and dead, we shall push north to the Tees, and then south-west to Cestre. Peace will come, Fox, heed my words, if I have to leave behind the head of every man in England to show my will.'

Chapter Thirty

Alric's breath steamed in the bitter cold of the church. Along the wall he crept, relieved that the suffocating gloom of that grey day had filled the nave with dense shadows. Guilt tightened his chest, but he had to see. By the altar, two fat candles glowed. The abbot knelt in prayer, and beside him another figure was hunched in supplication. Alric squinted to be sure. It was Redwald, just as Alric had been told by one of the other monks of Ely. Hereward's brother sought absolution from some unnamed sins, they had said, and he had committed to long hours of prayer each day. The monk cocked his head, listening to the drone of the whispered voices. Though they were kin in name only, Hereward and Redwald had much in common, he decided. Each one battled to contain the devil he carried within him. He murmured a quiet prayer that Redwald would be as successful as his brother in finding the road to God. He listened a while longer until he felt too much discomfort at intruding on such a private moment and then he edged back towards the door.

Outside, he looked up at the lowering grey clouds. It was the last gasp of the cold weather. Soon spring's promise would be with them. He felt relieved. That winter had been harder than most and there were times when he had thought they would not survive it. But God had watched over them as they clung together through desertions and hunger and want. Other threats waited, he knew that. Not the least, the certainty that the king's men would at last launch their attack. Ivo the Butcher's eyes and ears within Ely must surely have told him how weak the English were. Only the bitter weather would have kept them at bay.

He pulled his threadbare cloak around him against the northerly wind cutting across the flat lands and hurried to the nearest hall. How long had the English and the Normans been circling each other like wounded dogs, watching for weaknesses, waiting for an opening to attack, but never quite finding the right moment? It seemed like forever.

In the hall, he threw off his cloak and warmed his hands over the hearth. He smiled as he looked to the far end where the children sat in a semicircle, rapt, listening to Acha tell a tale of dragons from her home in the west. Though her nature was often severe, she had surprised him with the gentleness she had shown once she had begun to help with the children's lessons. Beside her, Edoma looked up from her embroidery, and, after a moment's hesitation, came over.

'Have you seen Madulf?' she breathed, a note of worry in her voice.

'Is he not with Sighard at the bake-house?'

'No, I have searched everywhere for him.' Alric smiled as he watched her bite her lip. It seemed she had made her choice of the two young men who had been bidding for her affection. He felt surprised, though, that it was not the sunnier Sighard.

'I am sure he is well. He is likely away learning to use his spear like a warrior now that Hereward has said he is ready to fight.'

She frowned. 'Perhaps. But this is not the first time. I have seen him creep away at all hours, but he denies it when I ask him where he has been. Do you think he has a secret love?'

Alric felt another tug of suspicion. He was starting to see the king's spies everywhere. 'Do not worry so,' he said, putting on a smile. 'But I will speak with him, if it helps.'

As he tried to recall if he had seen anything troubling in Madulf's behaviour, the door crashed open. Kraki stood in the entrance, glowering. He swayed and his scarred face was flushed. *Drunk*, Alric thought. The Viking lurched in, jabbing a trembling finger towards Acha. 'I would have words,' he growled.

The raven-haired woman flushed, but her eyes grew cold. The children looked round uneasily at the intrusion. 'If you have a grievance, take it elsewhere,' Alric hissed. 'You are frightening the young ones.'

'Away, monk,' Kraki snapped. 'My anger is hot and if you get in my way you are likely to feel the full force of it.'

Acha sauntered across the room, her head held up in defiance. 'What is it you want?' she asked in a wintry voice.

'You bring shame on me with everything you do,' Kraki raged, spittle flying.

'You bring shame upon yourself with your actions,' Acha replied, seemingly unconcerned that she was driving the Viking to greater heights of anger. 'You drink, you sweat, you stink like a pig, and now you speak to me like this, here, in front of these children.'

Kraki's bloodshot eyes bulged. When Alric stepped forward to block his path, the Viking thrust him aside with such force that he spun across the floor. Dazed, the monk looked up to see Edoma fleeing from the hall. The warrior's temper was as terrifying and unpredictable as a summer storm.

'I saw you sneaking out of Hereward's house at first light,' Kraki snarled, advancing on Acha.

'Your jealousy has eaten away at your wits,' she spat. 'His wife was ill with the child-sickness and I—'

'You said you would help her so you could be close to Hereward,' the Viking accused, his voice cracking with emotion. 'This is not new. Since we came to Ely, you have not been able

189

to take your eyes off him. You are a faithless whore.' He spat. 'You are mine, not his.'

Acha's dark eyes narrowed, and for a moment Alric was more afraid of her than of Kraki. 'I belong to no one,' she said, forming each word as if it were a pebble in her mouth.

'So haughty,' Kraki sneered. 'You think yourself better than all here. Whatever you were among the Cymri before you were captured, here you are nothing.'

Her lips pulled back from her teeth, and Alric feared she was about to fly at the Viking. Bristling, Kraki took a step towards her just as a blast of cold air blew from the direction of the door.

'Leave her be.'

Alric jerked round to see Hereward looming in the doorway. Guthrinc and Hengist pressed behind him, and Edoma was there too.

Kraki roared like a wounded bear. Never would he have struck a woman, Alric was sure of that, but here was an opportunity to vent his rage. All reason lost, he hurled himself at Hereward and the two men crashed together like stags in the wood. The children wailed and pressed against the far wall. The others could only gape as fists hammered flesh with enough force to shatter wood.

At first Hereward tried to pull away, shouting at the other man to calm down, but Kraki was lost to his rage. So furious was his attack it was all the Mercian could do to defend himself. The two warriors sprawled across the cold floor, locked in a battle that Alric feared could only end in death. With a roar, the Viking smashed his forehead into Hereward's face. Blood spattered.

Alric swallowed. Until then he could see that Hereward had been holding back. But now his eyes clouded and his lips pulled away from his blood-stained teeth, and the monk knew that his devil had been unleashed. The Mercian grabbed the other man's ears and hammered his head against the floor until it seemed his skull would shatter. Kraki lashed out with jagged nails, raking them across Hereward's face.

190

Snarling and grunting like beasts, they thrashed across the boards until Kraki's head slammed against the hearth-stones, stunning him. Hereward's eyes were glazed. Alric could see that all the warrior wanted to do was kill this thing that had threatened his life. Snatching one of the stones that edged the fire, Hereward swung it up, ready to dash out the Viking's brains.

Alric cried out. He wrenched the spear from Hengist's hand and rammed the tip against his friend's neck. 'Stay your hand,' he yelled, 'or as God is my witness I will end your days.'

The stone wavered. After a moment Hereward blinked, his eyes beginning to clear. The rock slipped from his fingers and clattered on to the floor. With a snarl, he swatted away the spear and clambered to his feet, muttering, 'This is madness.'

Shaking his head, Kraki surfaced from his daze. The two men glared at each other for a moment, but the fire had gone out of the Viking too. Hereward paced away, wiping the blood from his nose with the back of his hand.

'If we do not soon turn our spears towards the enemy, we will end up killing each other,' Alric implored, his voice trembling with the shock of what he had done.

Hereward eyed him, then nodded. 'You are the wisest one here,' he sighed. 'We have started to eat ourselves. This must end now.' He turned to Kraki. The Viking swayed on his feet, ignoring the blood trickling down his face from a gash on his forehead. 'You and I have never been friends,' Hereward continued, 'but we have shared the trust that only battle-brothers know. That bond still holds, even now.'

Kraki grunted, watching the Mercian from under lowered brows.

'Turfrida is my wife, and I need no other woman.' Hereward looked from the Viking to Acha, and Alric thought he seemed to be speaking to both of them. 'Even if that were not true, I would never come between a battle-brother and the woman he has chosen. Never.'

Acha lowered her gaze, and in that unguarded look Alric felt he saw hurt, but it passed too quickly for him to be sure.

191

Hereward turned to the others and said, 'Leave us now. Kraki, Acha and I, we must talk and put this thing to rest once and for all.'

Alric trailed out into the cold afternoon. While Edoma took the children back to their homes, he watched the hall from the church doorway, his hands growing raw in the cold. When the thin, grey light began to fade, the three figures stepped out. Kraki and Acha walked towards the track that led to the settlement, but together, the monk noted. Hereward saw him and came over.

'We have reached an understanding,' he said wearily. 'In this, I have failed as a leader. I saw this danger approaching like sails on the horizon, but I did nothing.'

'All is well now?'

'As well as can be.'

'She has feelings for you,' the monk said, shuffling his feet to warm them.

Hereward nodded, looking down. 'But now she will keep them locked away. We all pay a price to win this war, and that is hers. It has been agreed.' He sucked in a deep draught of the cold air. 'You spoke true in the hall. There must be a change. We have sat around too long, gnawing at our wounds, and watching our hopes slowly fade. A few Norman deaths here and there only serves to enrage them. We must ready ourselves for war.'

'How, with only the small numbers we have here? And most of them are untested.'

Hereward looked into the growing gloom. 'There will come a time when we have to risk all.'

Alric's face crumpled. 'It will be a slaughter.'

Before Hereward could reply, a figure ran through the gate into the minster enclosure. Alric squinted and saw it was one of the scouts. He waved an arm furiously. Hereward strode over and bowed his head to listen to the man's anxious gabble. When he returned, the Mercian's face had lightened.

'I was afraid he had word of an attack by the king's men,'

Alric said. 'Can it truly be good news? After this winter, we deserve some.'

'Neither good nor bad, yet,' Hereward replied, his brow knit in thought, 'but fate has given us a chance, and I am ready to seize it with both hands.'

Chapter Thirty-One

Snow engulfed the hooded rider. His horse staggered into the face of the furious blizzard as the blasting wind wrenched at his cloak. Night had fallen and the trail of hoofprints filled as fast as it was made. Balthar squinted past the stinging flakes, but he could see no more than a spear's-length ahead. The bitter cold reached deep into his bones and his belly growled with hunger. And now he felt fear grip his spine. How long before he succumbed to the warm-sleep, or his steed plunged him into a ravine? The mountains were treacherous even in clear weather and daylight. He dug his knees into the horse's flanks, trying to turn it around. But the beast writhed and threw its head back as it started to become panicked now the drifts had reached halfway up its legs.

Balthar looked all around. He could see no sign of William's vast army anywhere. The last thing he remembered was his shadow, Faramond the knight, riding beside him as the snow-storm began. In the warm depths of his cloak, his eyelids had begun to droop as the bitter cold descended. When he had next looked up, he was alone. For all he knew, the army could be close enough for him to ride back in moments, but he had no sense of the direction from which he had come. He called out for help until his throat was raw, but the howling wind stole his words.

If only he had taken more care. But exhaustion had hollowed him out and he wished only to rest. William's campaign across Northumbria to the banks of the Tees had been relentless. They had left behind a land soaked in gore and covered with corpses where the carrion birds blocked the sun as they flocked. But still that was not enough to satiate the king's blood-lust. Barely had the last victim fallen, than the king had turned his entire army around and pushed south-west towards Cestre where the last and perhaps weakest of the northern uprisings still simmered. He had held out hope that Balthar could be back in Wincestre with Godrun before the buds on the trees had started to open. He choked back a sob, afraid that he might never see her beautiful face again.

Digging his heels into the horse only drove it into a frenzy. As it fought its way through the growing drifts, its leg plunged into some hidden crevice and it slid to one side. Balthar heard the bone snap even above the gale. Convulsing, the beast went down. Thrown from its back, Balthar crashed into the deep snow, slamming against the rocks hidden beneath. He shook off his daze and scrambled to his feet only to see the poor creature lying on its side, eyes rolling wildly, breath steaming in the cold. Had he had a weapon, he would have put it out of its misery, but nothing could be done.

He buried his face in his hands. Why was God punishing him so? He had done no wrong. Wiping the snot from his top lip, he tried to summon what resolve remained and hauled himself away through the drifts. His only hope lay in finding his way back to the king's army, he knew that. But if he could at least reach shelter until the snowstorm passed, he might stand a better chance of finding their track over the high land. The thought sounded desperate even as it passed through his mind, but he pushed it aside. He lurched on, the wind dragging him this way and that. All feeling had gone from his hands and feet. Through the snow he waded, until it seemed that he had always been lost in that freezing world. He skidded down a slope, stumbled and fell, picked himself up and trudged on, bent near double into the gale. Just when he began to feel the cold was about to steal his meagre life, he glimpsed what could be the dark bulk of houses through the blizzard. His heart thumped. He pushed aside his fears that his suffering had addled his mind and staggered on. When a huddle of huts and small thatched houses appeared, he almost cried out in joy. Hill farmers, he thought, scratching a bare existence from that poor land. But it would be shelter, and warmth. He dragged up the last of his strength and threw himself forward.

As he neared the hamlet, the wind fell away and the storm swept off into the east. The last white flakes drifted down. After the fury of the gale, the silence and stillness soothed him. Lit by a waxing moon, he crunched through the knee-deep snow to the nearest home. The houses were humble, small and low, the timber weathered. Leaning against the door, he sucked in a deep breath of the freezing air to calm himself and then knocked gently so as not to frighten whoever lived there. When no reply came, he eased open the door, half-expecting an anxious farmer armed with a cudgel.

Inside, only a few embers glowed in the hearth, despite the bitter cold. Nothing stirred. As his eyes adjusted to the gloom, he peered around. An old, dented cooking pot hung over the fire. A few chipped pots and wooden bowls were scattered around, next to a rusty knife and a serving spoon. A bed of filthy straw lay against one wall. Poor by any standards.

As Balthar hovered on the threshold, a whimper rustled out from the dark at the far end of the hut. Whoever was there was scared of this stranger creeping in in the middle of the night, he realized, and who could blame them? 'I mean no harm,' he called in a loud whisper. 'I seek only shelter and warmth.'

'Go away.'

It was a woman's voice, weak and husky. He stepped a few paces into the hut and squinted. A woman in little more than rags with a long, haggard face crouched with her arms around two boys. Scrawny, they were, barely more than skin and bone, with swollen bellies and eyes bulging in faces that were almost skulls. The mother's skin looked ashen in the gloom. Her cheeks were hollow and her eyes settled deep into pools of shadow. But he breathed easier when he saw no sign of the pestilence on them.

'Please.' He held out both his hands. 'Have pity.'

The woman cowered, hugging her children closer as if he were about to attack her. 'Are you with the king's army?' she whispered in a tremulous voice.

'No,' he insisted, afraid of reprisal for the atrocities the king had committed across the north. Surely all now knew William saw them as men saw vermin. 'I am not one of the king's men. I am but a lonely earth-walker caught up in this foul storm.'

This seemed to please her. After a moment, she beckoned for him to enter. He closed the door and almost fell upon the hearth in his eagerness to warm himself. 'Thank God for your kindness,' he gushed. 'I thought I would die.'

'No man should travel over the hills at night in this weather,' she said. 'It is madness.'

'It is.' He bowed his head. 'I . . . I was running away from the army. The things they have done . . .'

'They have blighted this land for ever more.'

'But you survive here, and that is good,' he said, looking up and smiling. His eyes flickered towards the cook-pot. 'Food is scarce, I know, but could you spare a crumb . . . anything? My belly has not been full all this day.'

Her face darkened. 'We have no food here,' she snarled.

'But—'

'No food,' she snapped. After a moment, she looked down. 'We ate the dogs first, and then the horses. Now . . . now we hunt each day. But this winter is harsh . . .' Her voice trailed away as she stared with dread into the dark.

He nodded, understanding the horrors that must haunt them in that place. If he could not find food to assuage his hunger, he could at least rest in the warmth until daybreak. 'Will you let me stay by the fire? I will pay you good coin.' He pulled a silver penny from the leather pouch beneath his cloak and showed it to her. Her eyes gleamed hungrily. With that, she could buy half a sack of corn or a good few hens at the market.

She clawed her way forwards on all fours like a dog and then rose up in front of him, snatching the penny from his fingers. 'Stay,' she insisted. 'And if you have more than one penny in your bag, my neighbours might have one last crust hidden away that you could gnaw on.'

Balthar felt his belly growl at the prospect of even a hunk of dry bread. 'Ask them, good wife,' he said. 'Aid me here and I will see you all well rewarded.'

The woman whispered in her boys' ears, no doubt urging them to watch him so he did not steal any of their pitiful possessions, and then hurried out into the night. Relieved, Balthar knelt by the hearth and rubbed his hands above the hot coals. As life came back into his frozen fingers, he muttered a prayer of thanks. God had smiled on him. In the storm, he could have passed a few spear-throws to the left or right and not seen the hamlet at all. By now, he would have been frozen in a drift somewhere, his body undiscovered until the spring, if the wolves had not devoured it first.

The boys crawled to the shadows at the back of the hut, too weak to stand. How terrible was their plight. He felt pity for these folk. In Wincestre, he had been sheltered from so much hardship, but now, after all the horrors he had witnessed, he would never be that same man.

The boys forgotten, he tapped the iron cook-pot. It swung gently on its chain and a protruding bone rattled. So hungry did he feel, he wondered if there were perhaps a morsel of meat still attached that he could suck off. The silver penny would more than pay for what little he would find. He peered into the pot, but the bone had been picked clean. The juices had all been drunk and the vessel was dry. He shrugged, disappointed. A few more bones rattled around in the bottom. He dipped his hand in and felt around, pulling each one out in turn to examine it, but all were dry. Finally, his fingers closed around a curved bone and he drew it up.

Ice-water sluiced through him as he realized what he was seeing. A skull. A human skull, so small it could nestle in the palm of his hand.

In his shock, he flung the tiny thing across the hut and it rattled on the cold mud floor. Sickened, he scrabbled away from the hearth and clutched the back of his hand to his mouth. What vision of hell was this?

Before he could contemplate the true horror of his discovery, he felt a blast of cold air. The door hung open. The woman was there, and not alone. Hollow-eyed, gaunt faces loomed in the dark behind her. They seemed to hang on the threshold for a moment as if contemplating what they were about to do, and then they surged inside.

Balthar cried out, trying to scramble to his feet, but they swarmed as swiftly as rats. Though he wrenched himself from side to side, hands gripped his arms and legs and pinned him down. 'Please, God, have mercy,' he shrieked.

A man loomed over him, staring eyes gleaming with madness. His lips pulled back from his yellowing teeth in an eager grin and he feverishly ripped open Balthar's cloak. The other men and women pressed in, and he gagged at the sour reek rolling off them. In their trembling hands he glimpsed a smith's hammer and a chisel, a billhook. Most held knives. All his thoughts rushed away in terror at the fate awaiting him. Like a madman himself, he fought, screaming until his throat was raw, but their hunger gave them greater strength.

A fist crunched against his face to still his struggles so they could more easily go about their business. Dazed, he muttered through split lips, 'Let me live. Please, God, let me live.'

The man swung his knife up.

A crash thundered through the hut. The heads of his captors jerked round. Balthar found his eyes gripped by that suspended blade as all his other senses fell away. He thought he half-heard the roar of some wild beast, and the shrieks of frightened birds.

The knife whisked away as a storm of frantic movement broke around him. He gaped, bewildered. In the thin glow from the embers, the looming shapes of his captors whirled about. Shouts and snarls echoed, then a cry of agony, cut short.

A hand shook him roughly from his stupor. 'Run,' a voice commanded. He stared into a familiar face and realized it was Faramond the knight. The Norman warrior flew away, his sword hacking in an arc. Blood sprayed. Balthar clawed himself up to his feet in a panic. Amid the din, his senses spun. Putting his head down, he lashed out blindly and hurled himself between the flailing bodies.

Once through the press he turned, his back set against the wall, to see Faramond thrust his blade through the heart of a man. Two more bodies lay on the floor, leaking gore. But the starving villagers flew at the knight like a pack of wolves, clawing at his face as they leapt on top of him. He crashed down under the ferocity of the attack and his attackers fell on him like rats.

Balthar scuttled crabwise to the doorway and lurched out into the bitter night. On the threshold, he glanced back, despite himself. Under the churning pile of bodies, Faramond's pinned head was turned towards him. His eyes widened in silent pleading. The billhook and the knives ripped down and Balthar turned and ran. There was nothing he could do, he told himself. Sickening screams echoed out into the snow-covered hills, but the Fox refused to hear them. Only when silence fell once more did he suck in a juddering breath. Yet he could not allow himself to think of what was happening in that lonely hut at that moment.

Blinking away tears of fear, he ran to where Faramond's horse waited, snorting in the cold. He clambered on to its back and urged it along the deep tracks in the snow. When the village had disappeared into the dark behind him, he began to shake, and then cry. The knight must have come to look for him when it was discovered he was missing, and Balthar had abandoned him to a terrible fate. As he followed the trail back towards the Norman forces, he shook his head to dispel the shock of how close he had come to death. But he doubted his guilt would ever fade. Never more could he pretend he was the man he had believed himself to be. The dawn would not come soon enough.

CHAPTER THIRTY-TWO

3 March 1070

Flames flickered beyond the night-dark trees where the four men were crawling on their bellies like snakes. There, on the edge of the wetlands, the spring breeze brought the tangy scent of the nearby ocean. Every now and then, the sound of waves crashing against the salt marsh broke through the rustle of leaves and the dim crackle of the fire.

'Wait here,' Hengist whispered, his eyes unnervingly wide and fixed. As he crawled off through the sprouting bracken and long grass in the direction of the bonfire, Redwald, Sighard and Madulf exchanged doubting looks.

'Can we trust him? He is lighter in the head with each passing day,' Madulf grumbled. 'While enemies creep up on us, he could be away whispering to the rabbits.'

'Leave him be,' Sighard replied, throwing a friendly punch at his brother's arm. 'Watching the Normans slaughter kin could send any man away with the ravens.'

Madulf only scowled.

'There is no better scout than Hengist,' Redwald murmured, his attention fixed on the bonfire. He could hear shouts, and singing. If it was a camp, as the scout had claimed, it was a large one. 'If Hereward trusts him, then so do we.'

'Trust,' Madulf grumbled. 'I cannot even trust my own brother.'

'How say you?' Sighard replied, indignant.

'I saw you creeping out from Edoma's hut before dawn,' his brother replied, sullen.

''Twas not me.'

'Lies.'

'Hush,' Redwald insisted, irritated by their constant chatter so close to danger. 'Edoma is a woman of honour. She would not waste her time with either of you squeaking piglets.'

Silence fell as they waited for mad Hengist to return with news that it was safe to advance. After a moment, Madulf whispered, 'We have heard tell that Hereward believes the Normans have eyes and ears within the camp. And that you are charged with deciding who is true and who is the hidden enemy.'

'I said, still your tongue.'

'Is it true?' Madulf insisted. Redwald heard a jarring note in the young man's voice.

A cry rang out from deep in the woods ahead.

'Hengist,' Sighard exclaimed.

Before Redwald could urge caution, the two brothers had snatched up their spears and shields and were racing through the undergrowth. Redwald cursed under his breath. He hesitated for one moment, wondering if he should abandon them to their fate. Then he grabbed his own spear and shield and jumped to his feet. He kept low, his shield high, his weapon levelled. The sounds of revelry from the camp had been snuffed out. Only the breeze moaned through the branches. Ahead the flames licked up. He could smell woodsmoke and the rich aroma of roast boar.

Redwald searched the trees on all sides. It was as black as pitch. Ahead lay a clearing lit by some silvery light. He paused and listened. No hint of a footstep reached his ears. Once again he cursed Madulf and Sighard. Those foolish children.

He would not give up his life for them or for mad Hengist. Determination filled him and he began to edge back the way he had come.

Something moved away in the gloom and he halted once more. He felt his heart beat faster. Was it one of the two brothers? Or Hengist returning? He could smell the fresh paint on his shield as he peered over the lip. His body felt as heavy as stone.

A silhouette whisked past the clearing. A branch cracked away to his right. The whispers of subtle movement rose up all around and gathered pace until a rumble of footsteps was rushing towards him. A torch flared in the dark, and another.

Redwald whirled and crashed through the bracken. Barely had he taken ten paces when a figure loomed up on the edge of his vision. A blow crashed against the side of his helm and he saw stars. A moment later he found himself lying on his back looking up through the bracken fronds. His head throbbed with the thrum of blood. A dark shape hovered over him. He felt for his spear, but it was lost in the ferns.

A torch swept near. The orange glow lit the fierce face of a Dane, his body heavy with mail and furs. He snarled something in a language Redwald did not understand as he drew back a glinting axe.

Redwald threw an arm across his face and cried out.

CHAPTER THIRTY-THREE

The raven banner fluttered in the chill morning breeze. Under the standard's protection, the camp stretched from the edge of the dense woods across the misty salt marshes to the white-topped waves of the grey sea. Tents billowed and flapped and guy-ropes cracked. Next to every entrance, shields brightly painted in red, blue and amber rested against spears and axes. Bleary-eyed warriors squatted around the embers of the night's fires, picking over greasy waterfowl bones and the sticky remnants of roast boar.

Hereward shielded his eyes against the glare of the rising sun and studied the army and beyond it the ships moored along the coast. So many, more than he had ever anticipated. He saw from the scars and the stumps and the missing eyes and the notched weapons that these were the fiercest warriors the far north had to offer. A den of wolves, ready to fall on any fresh meat that came their way. He inhaled a deep draught of the salty air, still sharp with the last cold of winter, and strode down the incline. As his cloak flapped behind him, he could only think that the sound reminded him of the wings of ravens waiting to pick over his bones. Kraki walked at his right shoulder, Guthrinc at his left, a fearsome sight even for these battle-hardened Danes, he hoped.

As they licked their lips and wiped their fingers on their matted furs, the warriors glanced towards him with narrowing eyes. Hereward searched among the tents until he saw Hengist, beckoning. The way had been prepared. Now they had only to hope that they were not opening the gates to hell.

Guthrinc hummed to himself as he looked around. 'How many riches you bring to my life, Hereward,' he murmured, his tone wry. 'And now the chance for a spear in my back.'

Kraki glowered at any man who dared meet his eye. 'They care as much for us as a dog cares for his fleas. We are no threat, and they know it.' Yet Hereward saw his hand never strayed from his axe.

'Keep your heads high,' the Mercian whispered. 'Remember: they sent Hengist back to tell us they would talk.'

'Aye, but what about the other three?' Kraki growled. 'Their heads might be food for the ravens.'

'Ah, such good cheer flows from your lips,' Guthrinc said, smiling at the Danes he passed.

'I know fighting men, unlike you, mud-crawler,' the Viking replied.

Hereward heard the clank of chainmail as warrior after warrior stood up to watch him go by, but he did not look back. As they neared the centre of the camp, he saw Redwald, Madulf and Sighard, still among the living, dipping hard bread into bowls of grey slop. Redwald had a bruise on his forehead and a gash on his right cheek, but the other two looked hale and hearty. Hereward ignored them, his gaze fixed on the largest tent, which had been dyed blood-red, but Guthrinc called to them, 'What torments you suffer. Warm food! A full belly! I am glad I risked my neck to save you.'

Hengist waited by the entrance to the red tent. 'Here, now,' he called to whoever waited inside, 'Hereward of the English, ring-giver, battle-wolf, spiller of Norman blood.'

Hereward came to a halt by the glowing coals of the tent's fire.

A thin trail of smoke wafted up to the pale blue sky, fragrant with the scent of the smouldering greeting-herbs that had been tossed on to the embers. A good omen. After a moment, the flaps of the tent were thrown aside and two helmed Danes stepped out – huscarls, Hereward guessed – followed by a third man. Though he seemed around his fiftieth summer, he stood as tall and broad-shouldered as Hereward, his eyes burning with vitality. His black hair was long and wild, as was his beard. Under his thick, purple cloak, the gold rings of a king gleamed on his arms.

Hereward hid his surprise, and bowed his head in a show of deference. Here was Sweyn Estrithson himself, king of the Danes, not one of the monarch's many sons that he had expected to meet. This opportunity was greater than he had ever dreamed; and riskier too.

The king nodded, accepting the show of respect. 'You know me?' he asked.

'I know of a king who is as fierce a warrior as he is wise a ruler,' Hereward replied. 'And one who now has bloodied the nose of William the Bastard and may yet cut his legs from beneath him.'

'And my huscarls have told me the tale of the Bearkiller, the bane of Normandy's duke.'

'Then we have ploughed the same field.'

Sweyn broke into a gap-toothed grin and swept his right arm to usher Hereward into his tent. The Mercian nodded to Kraki, Guthrinc and Hengist to wait outside. It was warm in the ruddy glow under the hemp cloth. In one corner, hot coals glowed in a copper bowl. More fragrant leaves smouldered on the embers, hiding the reek from the cess-pit beyond. Furs had been heaped in one corner as a sleeping place. The king sprawled on them and waved a hand for Hereward to sit on a plank supported by two logs. Sweyn clapped his hands and a pretty brown-haired girl slipped in – English by the looks of it, Hereward thought. She carried a pitcher, and from it she poured two wooden cups of beer. When she offered one to Hereward, she blushed, clearly knowing who he was. He smiled in return.

The king raised his cup and said in a commanding tone, '*Wæs þu hæl.*' Hereward echoed the toast. 'Your folk have visited this camp every day since we put to shore, monks from the abbeys and men from the fields alike,' Sweyn continued, 'and every day I hear pleas to drive out the conqueror and rule this land as my kin did in days gone by. They take my men into their homes and to their feasts and give them what little meat and drink they have.'

Hereward sipped his beer. 'William's rule has been a long, cruel winter for many. They would feel the sun on their faces.'

'The Bastard will not let his prize slip through his fingers easily.' The king lounged back, but Hereward could feel Sweyn scrutinizing him, weighing his worth. And he too knew the truth of his host, a man who had ordered his huscarls to slaughter a church-full of guests when he had heard one of them had ridiculed him. 'When we took Eoferwic, we thought his days were done,' he continued. 'But he fought back and left your north a desert. Never have I seen such blood, rivers of it, and I have fought battles where there have been bodies as far as the eye could see. Pestilence and starvation spread among the poor souls who yet live. Some say William would rather see this a land of the dead than lose his crown.'

Hereward's knuckles whitened as he gripped his cup tighter. 'The End of Days,' he muttered, shaking his head. 'No, it will not come to pass.'

The king smiled. 'You would set your face against God's judgement?'

'William the Bastard is a man, and he does not speak for God. I will do all within my power to bring him to his knees.'

Sweyn nodded, seeming to like this show of defiance. 'Your king has crushed all uprisings now, save one. The one you lead. He thinks his throne is safe, and that you are nothing more than a flea.'

'Let him think that. More joy to see his face when he finds the only fleas in the east are ones that ride the backs of wolves.' He drained his cup. 'This winter has been hard, but still we stand. And with more men, we could take the fight to the Normans, and drive them out.'

The king called for more beer, and once the girl had filled his cup, he said, 'We make common cause, then. Is that what you are here to say?'

For a moment, Hereward hesitated. He recalled Alric's words as he left Ely to follow Hengist to the camp of the Danes: 'Take care lest you make a deal with a devil worse than the one you know.' Yet here was the moment where the fate of the English could turn on his words. 'We can offer you safe haven, a home protected by the strongest defences, where William's men can never touch you.'

Sweyn kept his gaze fixed on his guest, urging him to continue.

'This land is filled with traps and death,' the Mercian added. 'We know the secret paths that will keep your battle-wolves with the living. With the English beside you, you will be able to thrust a spear deep into the heart of William's army.'

'Even so, your numbers are small,' the king mused. 'What more can you offer?'

Hereward grinned, recalling the moment long months ago that he had sown the seed of his plan, needing only men to see it bear fruit. And now here it was. 'Riches beyond your dreams,' he said. 'And the power of God himself.'

The king's eyes brightened.

CHAPTER THIRTY-FOUR

5 April 1070

Pink apple blossom fluttered in the orchard. The sweet fragrance drifted down to the column of weary warriors as they marched through the great gates of Wincestre. Their shields were dented, their cloaks stained with mud and blood, but they raised their heads to the chorus of cheering crowds greeting King William's return from his victorious campaign to bring peace to the unruly north.

As he rode, Balthar searched the bright faces of the folk lining the streets to the royal palace. He had hoped he would glimpse Godrun there, so desperate was he to see her. Yet he knew she would find him changed, in many ways, and for the better, he hoped. Those gruelling experiences in Northumbria had stripped the fat from his body and carved lines into his face. More, they had worn the edges off his arrogance.

As the spring sun warmed his cheeks, he thought back to that bitter chill in the mountains when he had rejoined the army. He had feigned ignorance of Faramond's fate, though it still haunted him in the dark of the night. But the hardships of that winter had brought more immediate concerns. William had been forced to contain a rebellion among his own men, starving and exhausted and losing brothers to the cold. And then they had fought hard for Cestre where their enemies had not been prepared for the arrival of an army in the frozen season. The folk there had been cowed in no time and William had put them to work building a new castle. The feast had been great indeed, though he barely remembered a morsel that passed his lips. The uprising had been quashed and William's possession of the crown had been sealed. Only the trouble in the fens remained, and that was like the grumblings of old men compared with what had already been crushed. Soon that too would be ended, at the hands of the Butcher. After so much hardship, the road south had seemed long indeed. But now he was home.

As he passed through the gates into the palace enclosure, he trembled with relief. He was not alone in that. Looking around, he saw the grins on the faces of the commanders as they slapped each other's back. For the first time in many a month he heard laughter.

The king leapt from his horse with surprising grace for a man so large. Balthar felt William's eyes upon him as he dismounted in turn. The monarch must have seen the eagerness in his face for he called, 'Run away, Fox, and not to your wife, I would wager.' Balthar's ears burned as the king's laughter followed him into the still hall, but he cared little. Through echoing chambers he ran, searching every place Godrun might be about her chores. He found her in the store, filling a pitcher with wine for the returning monarch. His appearance must have shocked her, for her eyes widened and her hand flew to her mouth. 'Are you well?' she ventured at whatever she saw in his face.

Unable to contain himself any longer, he pulled her into his arms and forced his mouth upon hers. The pitcher crashed to the floor, the good wine draining into the grooves among the flagstones. Her surprise held her rigid for a moment, but then she gave in to his kisses. When she wrapped her arms around his neck, he felt stunned by his response: not lust or love, but desperation. He knew he could not afford to let her go again.

'Come with me,' he requested, grabbing her hand, 'to your bed. I cannot wait another moment.'

'The king will call for me to serve him,' she protested.

'The king will understand.'

'He knows?' She wrenched free of his grasp.

'More than knows. He has given us his approval.' She stared at him in disbelief. 'I will ask him to make you mine alone, so you will no longer have to endure the vile advances of those other men.' He smiled. 'I told you I would protect you.'

When he had finally convinced her, he led her along a meandering route from the palace to her home so they would not be seen. Inside the hut, he pulled off her dress with feverish hands and pushed her down upon the bed. She gasped, seemingly surprised by the intensity of his desire, but she offered her thighs to him without protest. Beguiled, he was, and he would not have it any other way.

His seed spilled across her belly too quickly, and with that release, he felt as if every dread, every doubt, every piece of guilt, every harrowing experience rushed out of him as one. Tears rolled down his cheeks and then he began to cry, huge sobs that racked his entire body. Even his shame at such a display could not contain them.

Godrun wrapped her arms around him, shocked by the outpouring. Yet she said nothing and seemed not to judge him, and for that he felt thankful. When he had recovered, he bowed his head and murmured his apologies. He did not want her to see him that way, and he tried to make light talk, demanding to know the latest palace gossip. But she would have none of it.

'Tell me,' she insisted, fixing a stern eye upon him. 'If we are to be close, we must have no secrets between us. You have helped me too much since I came here, and now I would aid you, if I can.'

'There is nothing you can do,' he sighed, but she pressed and after a few moments he was telling her the grim tale of what he had seen in the north and of the king's cruelty and the misery the monarch had left in his wake. The grimmest facts he chose to omit, out of kindness. Nor could he bring himself to tell her of his own role in guiding the king's hand to such atrocities. Afterwards, he sagged against her, saying, 'Once I believed I knew everything, and now I see I know nothing. I feel lost, Godrun, and alone.'

'You are not alone. I am here.' She stroked his head and whispered, 'You are a powerful man. The king listens to all that you say.'

'And laughs at me.'

'No. He raised you on high because he needs you. You are his way to understand the English, and to bring them to him, in obedience. You cannot be lost, for you still are that same man who guides the hand of a king.'

Balthar felt his stomach churn at those words. 'I . . . I do not think I want that work any more.'

'Then what path do you think God would want you to tread?' Her lips brushed his ear and he shivered with delight.

'The path of righteousness. I believed we would see peace and wealth under William's rule. All the suffering of the invasion could be forgotten, if only we accepted the Normans. Now . . .' He creased his brow, the thoughts forming even as he spoke. 'Now I wonder if I was mistaken.'

'In my home, I heard many say the same,' she said, resting her head on his shoulder. 'William is cruel. William steals and slays and the misery will not end until the English are all driven into the mud. I know nothing of these things.' She shrugged, then turned to him and smiled. 'But you are a wise man. If you believe the king is a threat to us all, then surely he must be.'

Balthar jerked at her words. From her lips, in so bald a manner, they sounded shocking. Yet was this not the only honest conclusion of the doubts that had afflicted him? He rubbed his brow in confusion. It felt as if his old life had been washed away in a flood in recent times, that world of slow advance to power, and dull family life, of numb hearts and grey thoughts. The king had raised him up, and he had committed himself to

William and all that he offered. But there, beside Godrun, it felt of little import any more. He shook his head, smiling. 'These doubts seem new to me, but I wonder if they first rose unbidden when I laid eyes upon you.'

'Me?' she said with a shy smile.

'You reminded me of who I once was, and of a world I had forgotten, or tried to forget.'

'You are a good man,' she murmured, kissing his cheek, 'and I know that whatever path you choose will be for the good of us all.'

In her eyes he saw such adoration that all his fears melted away. He wanted only to please her, and if it bought him peace, all the better. 'Good, yes, I will do good.' His mind was racing. 'The suffering William has brought to the English is a crime that must be fought,' he blurted. Only when the words had left his lips did he realize he had no idea what he could do about such a thing. Nor did he want to lose his head with a futile gesture.

Godrun frowned.

'What is it?' he asked gently.

'You say the king has not crushed all those who stand against him?'

'In the east a few remain, but they are no threat.'

'Perhaps you could aid them?'

He laughed. 'What could I do? Carry a spear and a shield while the Norman army bears down upon me? There would be no more kisses after that.'

'But you see and hear everything here in the palace. You know the king's mind,' she said, growing excited. She held out her arms. 'Why, could you not guide his ship on to the rocks? Or find some way to send aid to those poor souls in the east? No one is cleverer than the Fox,' she added, eyeing him from beneath heavy lids.

He felt a stirring in his groin at that seductive look. 'You have bewitched me, Godrun, with your youth and your joy and your innocence. I am yours for ever more,' he said with a laugh.

214

'You are right. I *am* the Fox, and more cunning than the king realizes. I will show you what power I command.'

This seemed to excite her, which drove him to even greater passion. She pulled him back on to the bed, nipping at his ear with her teeth. 'And I will show you much love in turn,' she breathed, 'more, perhaps, than you have ever had in your life.'

CHAPTER THIRTY-FIVE

29 May 1070

Shards of moonlight glittered off the rippling black waters. An oar sliced through the silvery illumination, and then another, as the fleet of large, flat-bottomed boats headed westwards along the Wellstream, the miles-wide channel that carved its way across the northern fenlands. Warriors squatted on the timber seats, their helms and mail shirts gleaming under the eye of the full moon. No one spoke. Across the wild fens, the wind had dropped and the warm night was still.

Hereward stood in the prow of the lead boat, one foot braced against the rim. Fire burned in his breast. After all the worry and the wait, the battle against the Normans had begun. When this night was done, the king could no longer pretend his crown was secure. The Mercian glanced back across the trail of vessels. Near eighty warriors followed his lead, English, Danes and axes-for-hire, lured by his promise of riches beyond measure. *Now we honour the fallen*, he thought. *Now we take back what is ours.*

Redwald loomed at his shoulder. 'Outwell is behind us,' he

murmured, knowing that any voice would travel far in that quiet land.

'Soon, now,' Hereward whispered in reply. 'Soon.'

The Mercian grinned to himself. During the long, cold winter, he had allowed his fears to devour him, he knew that now. His army breaking apart by the day, good men hacked down by the Normans as they scouted the snowbound wetlands. It had seemed that all their hopes were turning to dust. The arrival of the Danes had changed all that. He had gambled everything on Sweyn Estrithson allying his army with the English rebels and now they would all reap the rewards. His thoughts flew back six weeks to that mild spring day when the Northmen had tramped through Ely's gates. The cheers of the English must have been heard all the way to Wincestre. All there knew that now they had a force to be reckoned with, and the days of struggle and thin hope had passed. The Danes had brought with them carts laden with meat and grain that had been given to them by grateful folk on their journey from the coast, and good venison and boar that had been hunted on the way. There was to be no want in Ely on their arrival, Hereward had insisted on that. And though these fierce men had strange customs and sullen ways, the English had welcomed them into their hearts, as was the English way.

King Sweyn had stayed with the remainder of his army, clustered with his commanders in his blood-red tent as they planned the coming battle against the Bastard. Hereward felt a cold satisfaction that vengeance was coming fast. There could be no turning back from this day.

He glanced across the heads of his men. Their faces were crusted grey with ashes, each one a promise of the grave for any Norman who stood in their way. Some looked determined, others keen. No fear. That was good. Guthrinc winked at him. He winked back.

Redwald squatted by his feet, watching the moonlit trees ahead. 'It is sad Alric cannot share in our great victory this night.'

'He is not a fighting man.'

'No, better he stays behind and ministers to the women and children. He is not one of us.' He paused for reflection, adding, 'A good man, but not one of us.'

A hunting owl screeched as it swept across the Wellstream. When the haunting cry died away, Hereward felt a tremor in the boat as it approached the point where two other streams flooded into the channel. Still swollen by the spring rains, the waters churned violently. But his men knew the moods of the Wellstream. They were ready for this.

He cupped his hands around his mouth and mimicked the screech of the owl. The call leapt from boat to boat. Hereward rested his hand on Redwald's shoulder and the younger man looked up at him with untroubled eyes and a trusting smile. For one moment, Hereward felt a pang of regret for the few good times during his childhood, and then the boat slammed into the swirling current. He dropped to his haunches, gripping the edge.

At the agreed warning, the warriors heaved on the oars. The boat rolled as if it had crashed over rocks hidden just beneath the surface. Hereward braced himself. One side flipped up at an acute angle, then smashed back down. The other side rolled up just as steeply. 'Hold steady,' he urged through gritted teeth. He could hear his men cursing as they fought with the oars. The timber frame groaned, flexing against the current. Aft it was wrenched to one side and the boat went into a spin. Oars stabbed the water. Hectic splashing drowned out the sound of laboured breathing. The warriors thrust the boat into the spin, and the vessel whirled one rotation. Then the oarsmen rowed in unison. The boat seemed to heave, and judder, and then, as if breaking free from invisible hands, it shot forward along the channel.

Hereward released the breath he was holding. The violent spring currents had torn boats apart in times past, however well-made they had been. His relief ebbed when he heard a cry and a splash. Turning, he saw that a Dane had been thrown

218

over the side of the next boat in its convulsions. His fingertips clutched at the edge of the vessel as the claws of the currents tore at him. The desperate faces of his brothers glowed white in the moonlight. They lunged to grab his wrist, but the boat shook so violently they could barely keep their own feet.

And then he was gone, his mail shirt and heavy furs dragging him down beneath the black waters. The other men cried out his name and jabbed the oars beneath the surface in the hope that he would grab hold. But he would have been swept away by the current, Hereward knew. If his body were ever found, it would not be until the summer and then far from this place. The waters of the fens were cruel. The Wellstream claimed three bodies a year, folk said, and many left offerings of bread and spears once the snows had melted, to placate that hungry river.

Even though he had never learned the Dane's name, he bowed his head in memory of the lost man. It would not be an omen.

The rest of the fleet made it through the turbulence without further loss of life. Silence fell upon the warriors once more. They bowed their heads with grim determination as they rowed harder up-river. The Wellstream drove like a spear into the heart of their enemy. Never would they have been able to approach so quickly and unseen by the Norman patrols if they had been forced to follow the old tracks. As the reed-beds thinned, the desolation of the fens gave way to thick woods and steeper banks. The horizon, always so far away in Ely, seemed to close in around them. Hereward sensed his men grow tense as they neared their destination.

When they rounded a bend in the river, the Mercian himself stiffened. On higher ground, a church tower was silhouetted against the starry sky. The thatched roofs of houses tumbled down the slope from the enclosure surrounding the minster.

'Burgh,' Hereward murmured to himself. His thoughts flew back to the last time he had visited the abbey, when his uncle, the abbot Brand, knighted him under duress. Brand was now dead, and a new abbot guided the monks, no doubt just as much in thrall to Norman power.

With hand signals and hushed tones, the orders were given. The oarsmen guided the boats to the river's edge and moored them with stakes driven into the mud. Once they had disembarked on to the muddy path – the place where local fishermen would drop their willow baskets to catch eels – Hereward raised his blade towards the sweep of glittering stars. His men grabbed their spears and axes from the bottom of the boats, and their shields from where they had been hanging along the sides. All faces turned towards him as the warriors gathered four abreast on the Wellstream's edge.

'Some say these are the End-Times,' Hereward began, his voice low but his words carrying powerfully across the rapt men, 'and that the king is the Devil who has brought us to these dark days. The north is a wasteland. On the wind, we hear the cries of the sick and the starving. The blood of an unjust war against the innocent has turned the rivers red. Aye, Death is abroad upon his white horse.'

He lowered his sword and swept it towards Burgh. 'This night we show William the Bastard whose days are truly ending . . . his own. Follow me now, wolf-brothers, and let our weapons drink deep of the mead of battle. Glory waits for us, and gold. And on the morrow, a new dawn breaks.'

He saw eyes burning with fire and lupine grins, and spears thrust towards the heavens in a silent cheer. As he turned towards Burgh, his blood pounding in his chest, he felt struck by a revelation that warmed him. The affairs of men turned in a gyre, like the falcon that flew from his wrist when he was a boy. Once he had been little more than a ravening wolf, driven by rage and hungry for blood, shunned by all civilized folk. Now he was a leader of men who had been taught the value of friendship and honour and justice. Once, not too many weeks gone, his army had stared disaster in the face, and now they had victory within their grasp. He thought of his father, and the miseries of his childhood, and how he had once believed that had charted the course of his life. But no path was set. God or fortune or will could lead any man out of the dark.

Hereward grinned to himself. All would now be made right with the world. He whirled towards the church tower, glowing silver in the moonlight. 'We are the English,' he cried, knowing there was no longer any need for secrecy, 'and the day of reckoning is here.'

Chapter Thirty-Six

The roar of the attacking English rang through the still night. Hereward thought how it must have chilled the very souls of any Normans who heard it, a dread that would be doubled the moment they looked down on the skull-faced horde thundering towards the palisade.

'Redwald, Guthrinc,' he called as they scrambled up the ramparts. 'On my order, let fly your battle-serpents.'

The two warriors plucked arrows from the leather pouches on their backs as they ran. Hereward knew he had chosen them well for no man there was better with the hunting bow. When they were in range, they dropped to one knee and nocked the shafts to their lines. The night, too, had been well chosen. He waited until he saw the heads of two Norman guards appear above the stockade, caught in moonlight so bright it might as well have been day.

'Now,' he snapped.

The arrows whipped out. The guards, focusing their attention on the melee against the fence, never saw them coming. One plunged into a helm's eye-hole and the man screamed, pitching backwards from the fence as he clutched impotently at the wavering shaft. The other arrow found a Norman throat.

Hereward heard the choking gurgle for only a moment before that man too fell.

Cries of alarm rang out from the other side of the palisade. The sound of running feet echoed from the hall where the English scouts had told Hereward the small Norman force slept. The Mercian grinned. All was unfolding as planned. Ivo Taillebois, William de Warenne and the bulk of their men were far away to the south. He laughed as he thought of the hated enemy waiting in the woods all night for a raid that would never happen. His men had sown the whispers of that attack for days in the surrounding villages, knowing it would reach the ears of Norman spies.

More guards appeared on the fence. They had clearly seen their fallen brothers for they kept their heads low.

'To the Bolhythe Gate,' Hereward yelled. His warriors surged along the eastern wall towards the southern entrance to Burgh. Beyond the gate, the street led straight as an arrow to the abbey.

From the southern ramparts, Hereward looked out over a moonlit wasteland of tree stumps, vast swathes of land blackened by burning, heaps of waste where shrieking flocks of birds would feed each day, and large stagnant pools. Deep ruts had been carved into the road leading to Burgh by the merchants' carts. He turned to face the gate, as high as three men and no doubt barred by a heavy oak beam on the other side.

'Break it down,' he commanded.

Four Danes heaved up the trimmed and bark-stripped trunk of an oak that had been left outside the fence by the wood-cutters at the end of the day's labour. As they charged towards the gate, the rest of the army thundered alongside them, throwing the weight of their bodies against the barrier. The wave broke with a crash. The gate groaned and splintered, but held. With a roar, the Danes pulled their ram back for another strike.

Hereward whipped his arm to the right and left to direct Guthrinc and Redwald to positions on either side of the throng. They knelt once more, nocking arrows to creaking bowstrings, and aimed at the top of the stockade. When a guard raced along the walkway, Redwald let fly. The shaft clanged on the Norman's helm and ricocheted away. Cursing in his guttural tongue, the man dropped down low. The two English archers fired again and again whenever any Norman dared raise his head. Hereward nodded his approval. The English within Burgh would be roused and the gates shattered before the enemy could hurl rocks or fire down upon his men.

The tree-trunk rammed against the gate time and again. The barrier bowed. Shards of wood flew out. From the high walkway the guards' yells grew more urgent as they realized their defences were about to fail.

'The moment you are through the gate, cut down any Normans you find,' Hereward bellowed to his men. Barely had the words left his mouth, when he heard a tumult growing deep within the settlement. His brow knitted. No more warriors rested within Burgh that day, his scouts had been certain of that. The rising wave of anxious voices swept closer until it crashed against the other side of the gate. English voices.

Hengist turned to him, puzzled. 'The lambs of Burgh aid the wolves who steal their food and their coin?'

Hereward watched his skull-faced warriors hammer the gate. He thought of the stories of the Wild Men of the Woods he had heard told by superstitious folk across the fens as rumours of his army had spread, and he guessed the truth. 'They fear us more than they fear William's men. We have done our work too well,' he replied, his face darkening.

'The gate will never fall with so many men pressed against it,' Hengist said, listening to the swell of voices from the other side. 'We are undone by our own.' He ran one hand through his stringy blond hair and looked to his leader, waiting for the order to withdraw.

Hereward shook his head. 'This night is a battle-cry that will ring out across the land. If we run like whipped curs at the first hardship, we tell everyone that we are too weak for the struggle ahead. We may as well lay down our spears and bare our throats to the Norman king. Would we be known for ever more as the men who betrayed the last hope of the English?'

'What say you, then?'

Hereward gritted his teeth. Only one road lay ahead, and he must take it, though it damned him for ever. 'If the folk of Burgh attack us because they are afraid, they will only run when they are more afraid.' He felt his heart sink, knowing that this weapon would cut both ways. He shook his head, pushing such troubling thoughts from his mind. 'Burn the gates and the walls,' he shouted to his warriors. 'And then set Burgh itself afire.'

CHAPTER THIRTY-SEVEN

And Burgh did burn. Grey clouds of choking smoke swirled up from the blazing gates. Whitewashed only days before, the seasoned timber of the walls was already blackening and cracking. Shadows flitted across ash-encrusted faces as the English army shook their spears at the sable sky. In the ruddy light, Hengist danced, untroubled by the fierce heat. Warriors shouted to be heard above the deafening roar as they handed out sizzling brands for the moment the barrier would fall. And beyond the palisade, a chorus of screams tore out.

Hereward lost himself in that conflagration. As the rest of the world fell away, his head filled with that flickering wall of orange and yellow. On his tongue, he tasted only the bitterness of the smoke and his nose wrinkled at the scorching air. Deep inside, he began to feel the first stirrings of the devil he always carried with him. The fire called to it and it answered. The screams of the Burgh folk facing their greatest fear was nothing. The rush of excitement rising from his belly was all. Monster, he was, at heart. He could not deny that.

'Hereward. Give the order.'

He stirred himself, realizing that Redwald had been talking to him. He shook his head to dismiss the lure of the flames and yelled, 'When the gates fall, burn the houses. But do not set fire to the abbey.'

'Folk will be afraid of you after this,' his brother said. 'If they dare utter your name.'

'War makes beasts of all of us.' Already the folk of Ely feared him. Now his name would make good English folk across the fenlands tremble. Never would he have guessed this road lay ahead when he vowed to challenge William the Bastard. He yearned for Alric's words of comfort, anything that would light his path through this dark. But then the gate cracked like a tree falling and a gale of flames swirled up. In a surge of sparks, the barrier collapsed inwards. Beyond the inferno, folk fled back up the street amid a cacophony of shrieks and yells.

Holding his shield high to protect his face from the heat, Hereward bounded over the flaming ruins of the gates. As he landed, he dropped into a crouch and drew his sword. Guards raced through the wall of smoke to defend the breach.

Hereward's jaw tightened. In battle, the Normans had sacrificed speed for protection. Long mail shirts dragged them down. Tall shields guarded the legs and chest as one, but hindered movement. They thought their more lethal weapons gave them an advantage, and sometimes that was so. But not here. Not in this chaos of fire and smoke and the confusion of battle in narrow streets. First blood would be his.

When the first Norman burst from the grey cloud, he was ready. Before the knight could swing his blade, the Mercian hurled himself forward like a hungry wolf. Their shields clashed, throwing the guard off-balance. He flailed wildly with his sword-arm, but Hereward ducked beneath it and thrust his own blade up under his foe's chin. His eyes shone at the gush of blood, and he felt the thirst that he thought he would never quench.

As the guard slid off his blade, Hereward whirled to meet the next attack. Ruby droplets showered from the edge of his sword. With a grunt, the second knight hacked down towards the Mercian's shoulder. As Hereward danced back the guard

227

thrust his blade towards the heart. The Mercian's shield splintered as he deflected the strike. Hereward peered over the remnants of the shield's rim and saw the knight's gaze flicker in pools of shadow within the eyelets of his helm – a sign that he knew his death was close. Fire and blood roared through Hereward's head. All sounds of battle ebbed away and in that quiet, small world, he felt calm descend on him. He stepped to his right and swung Brainbiter in an arc. The Norman's bared throat opened up.

Before his foe had fallen, Hereward crashed back into the din of battle. He turned, yelling, 'To the abbey.'

Five English surrounded each one of the few Norman guards. In a moment, they had overwhelmed them. Guthrinc plunged his spear into a knight's chest, lifting him high so he kicked and squealed like a skewered pig before the iron tip burst through his back. Another fell under a rain of Danish axes.

Near the palisade, fire consumed the rows of huts and halls. Men torched the thatched roofs and the dry grass that had grown up around the timber walls. The conflagration swept across Burgh, leaping from home to home. Hereward's thoughts flew back to his bloody struggles in Eoferwic four years before the invasion when he had first realized fire was one of the greatest weapons of fear. How long ago it seemed. And fear was everywhere in Burgh that night, running as wild as the inferno. Screams filled the night. Though most of the Burgh folk fled to the far reaches of the settlement, a few brave souls drew water from the wells to try to quell the flames.

Redwald smiled grimly. 'They should not have stood with the Normans.'

Hereward shook his head. 'They were afraid. They did not deserve to suffer so.'

'You had no choice. Victory here today is all that matters.'

The Mercian knew his brother was right, but still he felt cold at what he saw around him. He pushed aside his doubts and ran up the baked track towards the abbey. Once he had broken out of the choking smoke, he sucked in a soothing breath of clean night air. The war-cries of his men sounded behind him. Beyond the minster enclosure fence, the stone tower of the church loomed. Torchlight danced in the dark grounds as the monks fled their homes.

'Harm no churchmen or face my wrath,' he bellowed, half-turning to the mob of battle-crazed warriors at his back.

The gate to the abbey grounds hung shut. Though a half-hearted attempt had been made to bar the way, the English warriors had smashed through within moments. As they flooded into the enclosure, Hereward ordered the Danes to search the minster buildings in case the monks had tried to hide their treasures. Their eyes gleamed with lust for gold.

Hereward thrust open the heavy door of the church and stepped into the cool, dark interior. The sweet scent of incense hung in the air. Overhead, the timber roof was turned a dull red by the raging firelight that streamed through the small arched windows. 'Give me more light,' he demanded. Hengist and Redwald searched along the walls until they found several fat, stubby candles. When these had been lit, the shadows swooped away.

Hereward stood in the centre of the nave and looked towards the high altar. Hanging above the entrance to the altar, a great gold crucifix gleamed in the half-light. On the head of the Christ, precious gemstones sparkled in the crown.

'What do we take?' Kraki growled.

'Take it all.'

'Everything?' The Viking eyed his leader askance.

'Leave nothing of value behind.'

Kraki shrugged and cracked his knuckles. 'Hard work but good reward,' he grunted, stalking towards the altar.

Redwald raised his head to look at the Christ. 'You do not fear God's judgement?' For the first time, Hereward heard a note of uneasiness in his brother's voice. Surely good-hearted Redwald had no fear of damnation?

He smiled. 'I do not rob God. I save these treasures from the plundering fingers of William the Bastard.'

'How so?'

'He has sent one of his warrior-knights, one Turold, to be the new abbot. But it is just another way to seize the abbey's treasures.' Hereward sheathed his sword and stepped towards the altar. 'Better these jewels and gold lie in our hands than the king's.'

Redwald shook his head in bafflement. 'How do you know this . . . this Turold is on his way?'

Hereward grinned. 'I have my ways, brother. I learned long ago that battles are won not by spears alone.'

Redwald grew silent, no doubt awed by the vast wealth that would soon be on its way to Ely. Hereward clapped a reassuring arm across his brother's back. 'With the riches we take this night, we can buy whatever food or weapons or axes-for-hire we need. We can build a great army on the back of this. And as word spreads across the fens, and beyond, men will flock to our banner. William can no longer pretend we are flies buzzing at his table. He will have a fight on his hands. And,' he added, with a confident nod, 'all men will know we have God on our side, aye, even William himself.'

'You speak in riddles, brother,' Redwald grumbled. 'But I bow my head to you, like all here. No army could ask for a better leader. The king will be shaking upon his throne when he hears of this night.'

The two men strode towards the altar. A rope tied to a spear had been thrown over a roofbeam and Hengist shinned up it like a squirrel. Once he was crawling along the narrow timber overhead, another warrior scrambled up to join him. Together they tugged and tore at the iron chain fastening the Great Crucifix to the beam.

'Use your arms, not your teeth,' Guthrinc boomed. A loud curse echoed, drowned by the laughter of the English warriors.

But the Great Crucifix could not be freed. Hereward ordered the men to take the jewelled crown and Hengist clambered down the Christ figure to remove the gold foot-rest. The candle-light shimmered off more inlaid precious stones. The other men began to heap the spoils in the centre of the nave. Hereward counted twelve jewelled crosses next to a mound of gold plate and goblets, books with gem-encrusted covers taken from the scriptorium, and eleven gold and silver feretories which he knew the monks used to transport relics between abbeys.

One other treasure was still missing, perhaps the most valuable of all. Silently thanking Abbot Thurstan for his information, Hereward ordered Guthrinc to lead a search of the church. The men detailed to climb the tower returned with the great decorated altar frontal which the monks had tried to hide.

'A fine haul,' Guthrinc said with an approving nod.

'And yet there is one thing greater,' Hereward said, 'though it would not buy you even a night with a Frankish whore.' He ignored the men's curious gazes and pointed to a small chamber on the north wall. With a suspicious grunt, Kraki strode off to investigate. When he came back, he was carrying a large oaken chest carved with images of angels.

He set it at Hereward's feet and snorted, 'Too light to be filled with gold.'

The Mercian stooped to flip open the heavy lid. A browning bone nestled in white linen at the bottom of the box. The warriors stared at it, brows furrowed.

Only Redwald recognized the bone for what it was. 'A relic,' he murmured.

'The arm of St Oswald,' Hereward said. 'Here is the power of God. It heals the sick, makes the blind see and the lame walk, so they say. And it brings good fortune to the ones who protect it.'

Redwald looked to him, his eyes bright. 'Then this was why you came to Burgh. Not only for the gold.'

'Gold buys us time. This . . . this buys us victory.'

'Alric knows?'

Hereward looked around the faces of his men and felt satisfaction at the awe he saw there. His course was right. 'It was he who first set me on this path, when we spoke at Ely of the works of St Etheldreda,' he replied. 'You see how folk

231

tremble, afraid, when they make their vows to be true to us over her shrine.'

Kraki nodded, a sparkle in his eye. 'Then God is now one of our Devil's Army.' A murmur of support rustled around the gathered English warriors, growing to a cheer.

As the clamour died away, the door crashed open. All heads turned. It was one of the Danes Hereward had set as look-out at the abbey fence, a blond-haired man with a pockmarked face.

'The Normans are here,' the Dane shouted. 'They gather to the south and west of Burgh, ready to attack.'

Redwald shook his head in disbelief. 'This cannot be. We lured the king's army far away.'

'How many?' Hereward demanded, his voice cold.

'Enough to crush us all.'

The Mercian silently cursed himself for being too confident. 'It seems,' he said through gritted teeth, 'that the Normans are cleverer than I thought. We have been led into a trap.'

CHAPTER THIRTY-EIGHT

'What kind of man is this, who is prepared to burn the homes of his own folk?' Ivo Taillebois asked as he looked out across the wall of flame along Burgh's southern edge.

Harald Redteeth grunted at the Norman's failure to see what lay beyond his nose. 'A man prepared to win at any cost. You would do well to heed what you see here this night.'

'Then we are much alike, this Hereward and I.' The Butcher showed his yellowing teeth. The blood of the English rebel still stained his cloak, though it had been three days since the man had been tortured to find out the truth behind the stories he had been spreading around the fenland villages: a planned deception by the English to draw the king's army away from Burgh. Harald wrinkled his nose. To take a knife to a man who had been whipped and beaten within an inch of his life. Where was the strength in that? They were a strange breed, these Normans. Cruel and brutal, when there was no need to be. Cold, like their churches. Sometimes he wondered if any of them had ever lain with a woman.

The wind changed direction and a thick cloud of grey smoke rolled among the oaks like an autumn fog. The fires of Burgh became an orange glow, but the roaring filled the night. Harald looked round at the ranks of Norman warriors. Like sentinels, they stood, in their long mail shirts and helms and with their tall shields and swords, as if they were about to ride into glorious battle instead of attacking a mud-grubbing pack of English farmers. He grinned as the whispers of the *alfar* reached his ears. Yes, for all their shortcomings, the English had proved themselves more than a match for the invaders. Even his hated enemy, Hereward. He had misjudged him. When first they had met, the Mercian had seemed little more than a wild animal, without honour. There was more to him than that.

But he would still cut off his head and kick it into one of the deep bogs.

'We have enough men here to slaughter them. Why do you wait?' he asked.

Taillebois shrugged. 'We take no chances. Like snakes, those English. Every time you think them beaten, they slither out and bite you again. Let them look to us, and make their plans to fight or flee. And while they talk and doubt and plot, Abbot Turold will ride with his men from the east. There will be nowhere for Hereward to run. He will be ours, at last. And then we will earn the king's thanks. What do you think of that, Viking? More gold for you to spend on whores and feasting and drinking?'

The Butcher raised his right arm and barked an order in the Norman tongue. His men began a steady beat of sword hilt upon shield. As the thunder rolled out towards Burgh, the army moved forward through the trees. Harald sighed with relief. He was sick of all the talk and the sneaking around and the planning. At last it was the time for men.

234

CHAPTER THIRTY-NINE

Turfrida jerked awake beside the dying embers in the hearth. With a gasp, she struggled to bring her thoughts back from the world of dreams. Somebody was hammering on the door. Shivering from the night's chill, she pulled her thickest cloak around her as she struggled to her feet. Her belly felt as heavy as a sack of corn. As nausea washed through her, she pressed the back of her hand against her mouth to steady herself. Soon, now, this child would be born and then perhaps she could walk more than a spear-throw without needing to sit or piss.

When she wrenched open the door, she saw Edoma there. The girl's eyes darted and she tugged anxiously at her cloak.

'What is it?' Turfrida snapped, more irritably than she intended.

'A messenger came,' the girl babbled. 'From Hereward. Madulf heard the news from him and bid me fetch you. The Norman army is moving and your husband fears for your safety.'

'He thinks they will attack Ely?'

Edoma nodded, but her eyes were unsure. 'So Madulf says. Hereward has made plans to defend us. But the fighting will be bloody, he says, and he does not want you here when you are with child.'

'I cannot leave these folk behind,' the older woman protested. ''Twould not be right for them to suffer while I am treated like a queen.'

The girl bit her lip, worried. 'You must come with me,' she insisted. 'If Hereward finds I have failed him—'

Turfrida showed a quick smile. Though he had always been gentle with her, her husband's temper could burn hot if his orders were ignored. 'Where would he have me?' she asked, softening her voice.

Edoma breathed deeply with relief. 'There is an old wife in Somersham who will care for you until the battle is over, and help you with the birthing, if that is to happen soon. I will take you there.'

Turfrida grumbled under her breath, but she could see there would be no arguing with the determined girl. She returned to the hearth and found her leather bag. In it, she put her comb, a dress and a linen under-smock, the brooch her father had given her on her wedding day, and some of her charms and the dried herbs she used in her rituals. Though her child drained her spirits, if she could listen to the whispers and aid Hereward, she would.

At the door, Edoma made to take her arm, but Turfrida told her not to fuss. 'I am not lame,' she said, fixing an eye upon the girl.

Edoma nodded and smiled brightly. Oh, to be a girl again, with none of the world's troubles, the older woman thought sardonically. For a moment, she looked back on simpler times, in Flanders, when she and Hereward had just been married. A hard road had always lain ahead of him, but never had she foreseen so much suffering and strife and worry. She prayed that soon it would be done and they could return to the life they had promised each other.

Ely slept soundly. The sweet-scented night-breeze rustled through the branches, and in the distance a fox barked. In the bright of the moon, the shadows carved deep valleys across the silvered grassland. As the two women walked down the street, Edoma pressed a finger to her lips and smiled.

The guard at the gate was nowhere to be seen. Likely emptying his bladder, Turfrida thought. Edoma eased the gate open a crack and they slipped through on to the winding track down to the jetty. Once the ramparts had fallen behind them, the girl whispered, 'If the Normans have eyes and ears in Ely, they should not know where you are going.'

'Hereward worries too much about me.'

'Better that we are safe, aye? The Normans are cruel masters. They have hanged many a woman to make the folk pay for slights and sour words.'

Turfrida knew the girl was right. At the jetty, the whispering water lapped against the shore. A fisherman's flat-bottomed fen boat bobbed at the end of a rope. 'I will row you to where Madulf waits,' Edoma whispered. 'He has a horse to take you on, so you will not have to walk far.'

The older woman felt thankful for that mercy. She cupped her belly with her right hand as Edoma took her arm and helped her into the rocking boat. She struggled to find her balance with her new weight. Her body felt strange to her, and she did not like it.

Once they were settled, the younger girl paddled out across the water with steady strokes. Turfrida stared out over the peaceful mere shimmering in the moonlight. While Edoma searched the shoreline for her meeting place, her brow furrowed, Turfrida closed her eyes and put her head back. She hummed a song her mother had taught her when she was young. 'Days long gone fill us with yearning,' she murmured, to herself.

When she felt the boat change direction and the oar-strokes grow more insistent, she sat up and looked round. Ely was lost behind a band of lofty oaks. The waters curved around a finger of higher land into the wilder areas of reeking marsh where Hereward had warned her never to venture without a fenland guide. Edoma's brow was furrowed. 'Where is Madulf?' she grumbled. 'How does he think I will find him in the woods at night?'

'There,' Turfrida exclaimed, pointing at a glimmer of candle-light among the trees. The glow disappeared for a moment, then shone once more. 'He calls to us.'

Edoma shook her head, still muttering under her breath. Keeping one eye on the intermittent light, she paddled towards the shore. When they reached the shallows, she splashed into the black water and pulled the boat into the whispering reeds. Once they were close enough to dry land, she held out a hand and helped Turfrida into the long grass.

'Madulf will keep you safe,' she whispered. 'He has ordered me to return to Ely. He thinks I am a little girl who will bring the Normans to us with my chatter.' She showed a sour face, which made her look like nothing more than that little girl. Turfrida hid her smile.

'Thank you. Take care on the water alone. When I see Hereward, I will tell him how well you helped.'

Edoma bowed her head shyly. 'And may God go with you,' she murmured. She climbed into the boat, less gracefully than she might have hoped, and paddled away. Turfrida watched her go for a moment and then turned into the trees. The branches creaked in the breeze, but she could not hear her guide and the light was now hidden.

'Madulf,' she called in a low voice.

The candlelight glowed for a moment, luring her on. She thought of the dead-lights that sometimes glimmered in the marshes later at night, the souls of long-gone sinners, so the local women said, and she shivered. She stooped under low-hanging branches. Dry wood cracked under her feet. The light appeared again, hidden just as quickly. Twigs caught in her hair and brambles tore at her ankles. She wheezed from the exertion. Her belly felt heavier than ever.

After a few moments, the candlelight appeared from behind a broad oak. A figure stepped out, half-lost in the dark among the trees.

'Madulf,' she murmured. 'If I had to walk many more steps—'
The words died in her throat. It was not Madulf. His hair

was black, as was his cloak. Turfrida felt her insides turn to ice when she saw the feared face she had last glimpsed in Flanders so long ago now. 'Emeric,' she gasped, 'the witch-hunter.'

'You have heard of me. Good,' the churchman said in heavily accented English. Two other men stepped out from behind trees, Normans by the look of their shaved heads. Emeric gesticulated and his assistants grabbed Turfrida before she could flee. She tried to cry out in the hope that Edoma would hear and raise the alarm, but a hand clamped over her mouth.

'Now,' Emeric said, 'we shall see what God thinks of you, witch.'

CHAPTER FORTY

Silhouettes flitted across an orange glow as the folk of Burgh battled to contain the blaze. When the thick clouds of choking smoke shifted, the thunder of the approaching Norman army drowned out the terrified yells. The king's men beat their shields, summoning Death to pick over the bones of the slaughtered in the coming battle. Iron sentinels, they were, grim-faced, backs like rods, disciplined and battle-honed.

They would reckon the English rabble, Hereward thought as he raced to the gate of the abbey enclosure. They would learn. His men poured from the buildings clustered around the church, arms laden with the last of the treasures. A gleaming mound of gold and silver and jewels now stood almost to the height of a man's chest. The mercenaries and the Danes eyed it jealously.

'We fight?' Kraki barked, scowling as he glimpsed the advancing army.

'We fight,' Hereward shouted back. 'They outnumber us, but not by enough to be sure of victory. Burn the rest of Burgh. Once they have walked through the fires of hell in their heavy chainmail and helms, they will be easy meat.'

Kraki turned and bellowed the order. A group of Danes

snatched brands and ran down the slope, torching the houses they passed.

Guthrinc eyed Hereward, his face giving nothing away. 'William the Bastard burns homes too,' he said.

'We will build them new ones when we have won,' Hereward snapped, knowing in his heart that the other man was right. 'Would you have us bare our throats when the Normans come?'

The other man shrugged. 'I say only, take care that victory is worth the winning.' He turned and shouted to the warriors, 'We have the high ground. Make those bastards fight for every step they take.'

Hereward pushed back his hot anger. He had to keep a clear head – and hold his devil at bay. Turning to the heap of plunder, he ordered his most trusted men to load the riches into the sacks they had brought with them.

Barely had the words left his lips than Hengist thrust his way through the warriors. 'You must come,' he gasped, breathless from running. 'All is not as it seems.'

The two men raced across the abbey grounds to a long, low, timber-roofed hall. Inside, a small fire crackled in the hearth and a single candle guttered. It was the infirmary, Hereward saw; dried herbs and plants had been stored on shelves along-side bowls of foul-smelling pastes. Hengist crunched across the reeds scattered on the boards to a low bed in the shadows against the far wall. On it lay a monk taller than Hereward by a good two heads, his feet hanging over the end of the bed. One arm was thrown across his face and his brown hair was greasy with fever-sweat.

'Leofwine the Tall,' Hengist said, leaning over the sick monk, 'here is Hereward, war-leader of the English. 'Speak, as you spoke to me.'

The cleric slid his arm back and squinted to see with his rheumy eyes. 'Hereward. Yes, I know of you,' he said in a creaking voice. 'Your own uncle said you were a bastard who could not be tamed. Now you are grown you have found your true path in life, I hear – fighting an even bigger bastard.'

'There are bastards aplenty in this life. At least I have always been honest,' Hereward said wryly. 'Speak to me, monk.'

Leofwine pushed himself up on his elbows. He shook with ague. 'King William is sending one of his warrior-priests to be abbot of Burgh.' He screwed up his face in a sour expression. 'Turold is his name. He will aid Ivo Taillebois to bring order to the fens. The Butcher has already met with him.'

Hereward shrugged. 'This is not news.'

'Then, Man-Who-Knows-All, you have no doubt heard of his new orders,' Leofwine sneered. 'He comes not next week, as he once planned. He rides this even with an army of one hundred and sixty knights.' He spat a mouthful of phlegm on to the reeds and coughed long and hard. 'Rides hard, so I am told, from Lincylene. Earlier this night, we heard word from Stamford that he had watered his horses and taken on food for the last of the journey.'

'Turold means to close off our road back to the east,' Hengist insisted. 'There can be no other reason for his speed. This is part of the Butcher's plan to trap us here.'

Hereward nodded. This made sense. With Turold's army, the Normans would have more than enough men to crush them.

'He is sly, the Butcher,' the monk continued. 'He has learned he cannot fight you upon your own ground, and he has set more than one dog running to bring you down, I hear.'

Hereward smiled with contempt. 'Let him try. His time runs short.' He clapped a hand on Hengist's shoulder. 'Tell Guthrinc and Kraki. Draw the men back. It seems we cannot stand and fight. We must leave before Turold arrives.'

'How?' the other man enquired. 'The Normans will not let us walk away without a fight.'

'Go,' Hereward urged, his face hardening. Hengist ran from the infirmary. The Mercian turned back to the sick monk and said, 'If you think me such a bastard, monk, why do you warn me?'

'No one here wants this Turold. Prior Aethelwold knows full well the Norman will heed no English voices, and will send our riches back to William.' Leofwine lay back on his bed and closed his eyes.

'Even a man like me would be better than that, eh?' Hereward laughed quietly to himself. He peered down at the monk and added, 'Is God to take you?'

'The sickness has broken. Soon I will be well again.'

'Then I wish you good health, Leofwine the Tall, and I bow my head to you for the aid you have given. I ask you for one further mercy. When the Normans come, they will lie about me and what I have done this night.' Hereward glanced towards the door, listening to the sounds of battle ringing through the night. It drew closer by the moment. 'Tell all that my army fights for the English. For you, Leofwine, and for your fellow churchmen too. We will not let the Normans steal the last of our birthright. Do not let lies turn the English against us, for whatever hard things we do, we do for the good of all.'

'I will do as you say,' the monk said weakly. 'Now go. I am weary of this talk.'

Hereward raced back out into the smoky night. On the edge of Burgh, the wall of fire roared higher still. The clash of iron upon iron echoed. He peered down the slope from the abbey and saw his men hacking down any Normans that battled through the inferno. Yet the enemy's attack was half-hearted, he could see that now. The bulk of the army held back beyond the ramparts, the Butcher sending only a few men at a time to brave the blazing gates. Enough to keep English minds occupied and to prevent any thought of escape.

'How can we flee?' Guthrinc shouted as he ran up with Kraki and Hengist. 'Unless we grow wings and fly over the Normans waiting at the gate.'

'Find the prior who fled the abbey when we attacked and bring him here,' Hereward ordered.

He grinned at the doubt he saw in the men's faces and waved them away. After long moments, the three men returned. Hengist herded a short, stout, bald-headed man at spear-point. Five other monks trailed behind, wringing their hands.

The prior scowled at Hereward. 'You have burned Burgh and stolen God's treasure and now you mean to slaughter men of God?' he shouted above the sounds of battle and the roaring of the fire. 'Truly you are the Devil.'

'You are quick to take offence, monk. But there is more at stake here than your life.' The Mercian stared at the prior with cold eyes. The churchman squirmed and averted his gaze. Hereward beckoned Guthrinc over and whispered in the big man's ear. When he was done, he hooked a fist in the prior's tunic and dragged him through the abbey gates and down the track towards the fire. Kraki, the monks and a crowd of warriors followed. Hereward could sense their eyes on his back and he felt pleased that none of them could predict what he planned to do.

Once he felt the intense bloom of the flames scorch his face, he hurled Aethelwold to his knees and held out one hand to Kraki. The Viking read the gesture and passed his axe to the Mercian. The monks began to sob, clasping their hands together and begging God for help. Hereward ignored their pleas. He forced the prior's head down and raised the axe over his head.

Bodies littered the track in front of the gate, his own men and Normans together in one blood-soaked trail. He looked past them and through the swirling flames until he glimpsed the next rank of the king's men approaching, shields held high against the heat. They slowed, then halted when they saw him.

'You know me,' he bellowed over the crackling of the conflagration. 'You have your eyes and ears in Ely. You know why they call me the Devil and what I will do. Tell your master to lead his battle-wolves back into the trees or I will slaughter all the men of God in Burgh. And on his soul must it be.'

The Normans lowered their shields, unsure. Hereward shook the axe over his head. The king's warriors hesitated for only a moment, seeing the cold conviction in their enemy's face, and then they fled. The Mercian allowed himself a low laugh. The monks had fallen to their knees, wailing, and the trembling prior was muttering a prayer.

'Rise, Father. You are not to die this day,' the Mercian said. 'In truth, you have been saved.'

Aethelwold looked up with burning eyes. He stood on shaking legs and stuttered, 'You are mad.'

Hereward grinned. All eyes following him, he strode to the nearest corpse, one of the fallen Danes, pushing aside his unease at what he was about to do. 'This fallen battle-wolf deserves better, but in death he will help save us, his brothers,' he said, grasping the dead man's hair and pulling the head back. With one clean sweep of the axe, he sliced through the neck. The monks cried out.

'Here is the first of your men of God,' Hereward bellowed. He whirled the head around by the hair and flung it over the wall of fire. It bounced across the ramparts where he knew the Normans would see it. 'If they doubted me, they now know I am true to my word,' he said to the other men, holding out his arms.

'What use is this?' Kraki demanded. 'Even if they let us pass through the gates, they will still be upon our backs the moment we make for the boats. They will slaughter us on the banks of the river where we cannot defend ourselves.'

'Then let them wait,' Hereward replied. 'And wait.' He grabbed Aethelwold's dalmatic tunic once more and began to drag him back up the track. 'Come, Father, your prayers have been answered,' he said in a sardonic tone.

When they reached the abbey grounds, he called his warband to him, and the rest of the monks too. 'We have bought ourselves time,' he said, 'and while the Normans wait for us to step out into the open, we will be on our way to Ely with our prizes.' He saw his warriors glancing uneasily down the track to the fire and added, 'We are not leaving the way we came. Follow me, but hold your tongues once we reach the wall.'

As the questions flew fast, he ran out of the minster again, and towards the eastern wall, dragging the prior along with him. 'The Normans will be watching the river-gate,' Aethelwold gasped.

'True. Only a fool would leave that way.'

Hereward followed the wall north from the river-gate until he reached the north-eastern corner. Guthrinc waited there with a small group of Danes, his face flushed and his hands dirty. A small portion of the timber had been battered down. The Mercian nodded, pleased, and turned to the prior. 'Leofwine the Tall has told me of your new abbot. Your days here in Burgh are soon to be grim.'

'We have no say in the matter,' Aethelwold snapped.

'No, for any sour words from you would only bring the king's wrath down upon your head. You must suffer any pain this Turold sends your way.' He paused, grinning. 'Unless you come with us.'

The prior eyed the Mercian askance, his eyes suspicious.

'The Normans will think we have taken you prisoner and so you will be spared the king's punishment,' Hereward continued. 'And you can spend your days in Ely, watching over the bones of your saints, until this war is won and you can return to Burgh.'

The prior's eyes widened and for a moment he couldn't speak. 'It seems I have misjudged you.'

'I am still the Devil, Father,' Hereward replied with a wry smile, 'but in an age of hardship you must take what help you can.' He turned to Kraki and whispered, 'When the time is right, lead our battle-wolves to the boats. Keep the monks apart from the treasure.' The Viking grunted his understanding.

Drawing Brainbiter, the Mercian beckoned for Redwald, Guthrinc and four of the fiercest Danes to follow him through the gap in the wall. He prowled through the shadows along the palisade until he glimpsed the Normans caught in the moonlight by the smaller river-gate. There were five of them, and one more on horseback, ready to ride off and raise the alarm if the English tried to escape that way. Kneeling, Guthrinc nocked an arrow and drew his bow. He nodded to Hereward, understanding what was expected of him.

The shaft whipped through the air. As the mounted knight fell backwards, dead, the other warriors jumped to their feet. Their cries were lost beneath the roar of the fire. Hereward ghosted forward. His blade whispered once and the nearest warrior fell. Before his foes could gather their wits, he rammed his sword up into the armpit of the next soldier. Like wolves, the Danes fell on the remaining three. Hereward watched the slaughter with satisfaction. The Normans had tried to trick them into a trap. They had given their best, and still they had lost.

Sheathing his blade, he watched his men and the monks flood out from the gap in the wall. Kraki waved them towards the boats. At the rear, men lumbered under the weight of the sacks of treasure and the relic chest.

Hereward raised one fist to the heavens in celebration. How long he had desired that victory, and how sweet it tasted. Yet it was only the start. More fighting lay ahead, more bloodshed. But now there could be no doubts that with the Danes beside them, and God on their side, the English could win back their land.

CHAPTER FORTY-ONE

The sun was rising across the fenlands. Streaks of pink and purple flowed through sky and into glassy mere as the fleet of flat-bottomed boats drifted home. The exhausted army could have been alone in all the world. Only oars dipping with lazy strokes and hide hulls creaking against the currents disturbed the tranquil morning. Overhead, marsh harriers wheeled. In the prow of the lead vessel, Hereward shielded his eyes to watch the elegant birds of prey perform their intricate dance. For a while he flew with them.

Ely loomed up, twirls of grey smoke from the morning fires rising to the pale blue sky. He gazed back over his silent warriors and saw grins blossom whenever his eyes were met. He felt proud of his war-band. Not a single man had failed him.

'What now?' Redwald asked, looking up with an easy smile.

'Rest. Fill our bellies. And let word of our victory spread.'

Redwald thought for a moment as he watched a dragonfly skimming across the dark water. 'You believe we can win?'

'Do you have doubts?' Hereward asked, surprised.

The younger man flashed a grin. 'No. No doubts.'

Once the boats had moored, the chattering crowd of warriors and monks milled along the mere's edge. Weariness ebbed away in a flood of euphoria at their great victory. Hereward led the troupe up the winding track to the dewy ramparts and through the gates into the just-waking community. The Danes flooded back to their camp where the rest of their brothers waited, shaking their axes in the air as they bellowed for mead.

Prior Aethelwold trudged up the slope towards the abbey. His beaming monks trailed close behind, whispering to each other with excitement. How bright they looked for men who had lost their home, Hereward noted. The threat of their new master must have haunted them indeed. He walked alongside the small knot of English warriors hauling the heavy sacks of treasure and the relic chest. While Aethelwold and the new arrivals were welcomed by Abbot Thurstan, Hereward ordered the men to hide their plunder beneath the floor of a hall next to the church. He nodded with satisfaction as he watched the relic being carried into the church. Folk would come from all around to marvel over it and seek God's grace. And then the word would spread like a summer fire.

'Keep guards upon the door of the treasure house at all hours,' he murmured to Kraki. 'There are men here who would kill for such riches.'

'*I* would kill for such riches,' the Viking grunted in reply.

As Kraki strode off to find fresh men to watch the hall, Alric hurried over from the gate. He clapped a hand on his friend's arm. 'William still sits on the throne? You have failed us all.'

'I am leaving him for you, monk. You can talk him to death,' the Mercian replied, grinning.

'Hengist has already talked enough for both of us. The children dance around him as he weaves a tale of this last night that would not shame a scop. Your great victory has put fire back in his belly.'

'Hengist is a good man who has suffered much. He has earned some peace.' He nodded towards the church. 'Go. Greet your new friends from Burgh. I would tell my wife I am well.' As he made to go, he saw the monk frowning.

'I cannot find Turfrida,' Alric said. 'I took her fresh bread at dawn, as I do each day, but your home was empty, the hearth cold.'

Hereward shrugged. 'She is in the camp, then, helping out the sick with her plants and pastes and foul drinks. Even though she is heavy with her own child, she will still help any who ask. Or,' he laughed, 'she is out in the woods, whispering to the trees and the birds and learning their secrets.'

Reassured, Alric hurried towards the church and Hereward strode to his house, his belly growling and his limbs aching for rest. But he found his home as empty as Alric had said, and he felt sad that for the first time in many a day his wife was not there to greet him. He ate some of the bread the monk had brought, and some cold stew, and he swigged back a cup of beer before sleeping soundly until the sun was at its highest. And still Turfrida was not there.

Curious now, he strode down to the Camp of Refuge. It was warm, and the narrow tracks among the makeshift houses were crowded with folk gossiping about the night's raid. Men clapped him on the shoulder and young girls flirted as he moved among the throng. The children would not leave him alone. How he hated that. Everywhere he asked after Turfrida, but no one had seen her since the previous evening.

As the day drew on, he began to worry. Ely was brimming with life, but it was a small place and everyone knew his wife. Someone would have seen her if she were there. With the shadows lengthening, he forged out of the gates and searched the quiet glades and along the banks of streams where she hunted for her plants, or practised her mechanical arts. Alric strode down from the ramparts, then Guthrinc, and Redwald, and Kraki. They barely spoke. Every inch of the isle, they walked.

The sun set.

Through the long reaches of the night, Hereward waited by the hearth, staring into the flames, listening to every footstep that passed his door, every creak of the settling timber, every whisper of the breeze in the roof.

In the chill dawn, his panic began to mount but he tried to

push his fears aside. He ventured out to the walls. His friends were already waiting. They took the fen boats and rowed along the edge of the mere, pushing a long stick into the shallows.

On the next day, they rowed out into deeper water. News of their search had travelled across Ely, and the mood had darkened. People spoke once more of Dunnere's daughter, who had not been seen since the English army settled in Ely. When he returned to snatch a bite of bread or fish, Hereward sensed eyes on him, but every man and woman looked away rather than meet his gaze.

Once night had fallen, Acha found him desperate and brooding on the mound, watching the stars reflected in the mere. She sat with him in silence for a long moment, and then said, 'Doubt my words if you will, but I would never wish for this misery, nor would I see your heart ache so. I pray that she comes back to you.' Her hand touched his, so briefly he barely realized it before she had slipped away into the dark. He heard the heartfelt emotion in her words and he was surprised how much it touched him.

Near sick with worry, he could not sleep, catching only fitful dozes in the church, nor could he bear to return to the home he had shared with his wife. He refused to believe her dead, but mounting grief crept up on him and settled into his heart like a stone. He tried to distract himself with plans for the coming war, but even they could not console him.

Early in the morning, desperate for any sign, he forced himself to go back to his cold dwelling and picked through Turfrida's meagre possessions. Each item called forth a sharp memory. He felt an ache that he had not experienced since he looked down on the body of his mother, her blood draining into the boards of his father's hall. But as his hand hovered over the old chest she had brought with her from Flanders, his senses prickled. Something was missing. He sifted through his memories, turning over the necklaces and charms with increasing desperation until a revelation struck him. The brooch her father had given her on their wedding day, her most precious possession – gone. Her comb too. He reeled back, barely daring to believe. Rushing out into the pale light, he raced to Redwald's home and dragged him from his bed.

'Turfrida is not dead,' he shouted with a defiant shake of his fist. 'She took her brooch . . . her comb . . .'

Redwald wiped his bleary eyes with the back of his hand and looked up at his brother. 'Do not raise your hopes,' he began.

'No,' Hereward almost shouted. 'I know her. If she were travelling those are the two things she would take with her.'

'Where would she go? And why would she tell no one?'

'I have no answer. But I will find one. Wake the others. We will meet at the abbot's hall, and plan—' He stopped speaking and cocked his head. Someone was shouting his name.

Out in the street, one of the guards ran up to him. 'A stranger, at the gates,' he said breathlessly. 'He has words for your ears alone.'

Hereward followed the guard to the palisade, annoyed by the distraction. Folk would occasionally arrive at Ely to test the truth of the tales of the wild men of the woods or the blood-soaked battle-prince before they made their decision to join the army. Outside the gates, a ruddy-faced ceorl in a mud-spattered tunic waited, his hands clasped in front of him. His eyes darted around as if he thought he would be cut down at any moment.

'I am Hereward. What is your business?'

'Your ears only,' the peasant muttered, eyeing the guard. The Mercian hid his irritation and stepped closer.

'I have word from the Norman lord,' the man began, unable to meet Hereward's eye, 'about your wife—'

Cold flooded Hereward. He grabbed the stranger by the tunic, almost lifting his feet off the ground. 'Speak,' he snarled, 'before I carve out your heart.'

'She is in the hands of the witchfinder,' the man stammered, the blood draining from his taut features. 'She is to be tested.'

Hereward felt sickened. Visions flashed across his mind of atrocities inflicted by the Church upon women suspected of being witches. Missing noses and ears, scars and burning. And death more often than not.

'The Norman lord said you can save her from harm,' the ceorl continued. His eyes grew faraway and Hereward could see he was repeating word for word a message that had been branded into him. 'But you must give yourself up to him, at the new castle in Lincylene. And you must come alone, without your Devil's Army. If you fail to do this in good time, your wife will be put to death.'

CHAPTER FORTY-TWO

The warriors came in the grey twilight. As the master of the flame lit the torches over Ely's gates, five wild-bearded Danes swept in, their furs reeking of stale grease, their clanking hauberks scarred from numerous axe-blows. They had travelled far through the treacherous wetlands, losing one of their number to the waters along the way. They were in no mood for talk. Ignoring offers of bread and stew from the English hosts, they marched to the camp where their own men sat swilling back horns of ale around campfires.

In the abbot's hall, the fire blazed in the hearth to dispel the coming night's chill. Long and deep were the shadows, and the meaty scent of baked eel from the evening meal still hung in the air. At the head of the long table, Hereward hid his fears behind the mask of a ring-giver, aloof, cold, reflective. Redwald watched his brother, wondering what thoughts passed through his head. Since he had met the stranger at the gates, he had been a changed man. Yet he would tell no one what had transpired between the two of them.

Kraki shook his fist in the air and cursed in a tongue Redwald didn't recognize. Guthrinc nodded, smiling wryly, which seemed to send the Viking into even greater spasms of anger. They were arguing over the tactics for the coming war. Hereward seemed to hear none of it, as though their words were little more than the droning of flies.

What could be more important than the battle for which Hereward had planned for so long? he wondered. And where was the joy his brother had shown that morning when he believed his wife had left Ely of her own choice? Redwald looked around and saw he was not the only one to be puzzled by his brother's demeanour. That interfering monk, Alric, watched from the shadows near the door. Though it seemed he scarcely left Hereward's side, he never took part in the battle-talks. How great he must consider himself to be, so unconcerned by the petty struggles that dominated the lives of other men. Yet now the monk's face was drawn, his gaze never leaving Hereward.

'Are you blind or ale-soaked?' Kraki roared. Redwald jerked his attention back to the war-council. The Viking leaned across the table as though he were about to take Guthrinc's neck in his huge, scarred hands. 'The trickle of men coming to our gates is turning into a flood once more. All tongues speak of Burgh, and William's bloodied nose, and God's glory shining down upon the English.'

'And you would send those men, as untried and untested as children, into the storm of Norman axes and swords?' Guthrinc's voice was light.

'We strike now!' Kraki hammered a fist on the table. The cups flew over, flooding ale across the table-top.

'Enough,' Hereward commanded. 'We sacrifice no man who comes to us in good faith. We fight when they are ready. Make them ready.' As silence fell, the Mercian looked around the faces, glowering, and then stalked out into the night. Alric followed. Redwald could hear the harsh back and forth of their muffled conversation as they swept across the enclosure towards the church gate.

With an apologetic smile, Redwald held his arms out. 'He has not eaten all day. Some food in his belly will do him good.'

255

'Finding his woman is the only thing that will make him well,' Guthrinc said. 'The leech has no salve to cure that ill.' Kraki grunted his agreement.

'Then I hope he finds her soon,' Redwald replied, 'for there are times when I think she is the source of all his strength.'

'Her and the monk,' the Viking interjected, shaking his head at the strangeness of it all.

'Aye, we are all riddles.' Guthrinc poured himself more ale and swigged it back in one. 'That is the way God made us, so there must be some sense in it.'

'Hel take me if I can see it,' Kraki muttered.

The sound of running feet echoed outside the door. Hengist crashed in, breathless. 'Danes,' he gasped. 'Here.'

'We know there are Danes here,' Kraki snapped. 'Your madness has you in its grip again.'

Hengist shook his head. He seemed to have more of his wits about him since Burgh, Redwald thought. Truly that was another form of madness if the thought of war with the king made him sane. 'Messengers from Sweyn Estrithson. Their mood is grim. I smell trouble.'

Guthrinc and Kraki jumped to their feet, striding to the door. 'Fetch Hereward,' Guthrinc ordered. 'His mood may be foul, but he will come.' Hengist raced into the night.

'What would trouble the Danes' king?' Redwald enquired, doubtful.

'News that William is to attack their camp by the whale road?' Kraki mused. 'That is what I would do. Drive the Danes away and leave us with half an army again.' He looked to Guthrinc, adding, 'We thought that sly bastard would try something like that.'

Cries and the clash of iron jerked them from their conversation. As they ran out of the hall, following their ears, the tumult grew louder. Redwald thought it sounded like a mob brawling and a vision of his brother caught in the grip of his terrible rage flashed across his mind. Outside the treasure hall, torches danced. Warriors surged amid the bark of orders in the guttural

256

Danish mother-tongue. Redwald slowed, unable to comprehend what was happening. His gaze fell upon the guards Kraki had placed outside the hall, now lying face down on the ground. *Dead*, he thought at first until he saw one stir. The treasure-hall door hung open and warriors were carrying out armfuls of the gold, silver and jewels that they had plundered from Burgh.

'Stay your hands,' Kraki bellowed, 'or face my axe. I care little that there are more of you. I can reduce that number in a thrice.' To make his point, he shook his weapon in the face of the nearest Dane.

'Hold.' The order rang out and the warriors slowed and came to a halt. All eyes fell on Kraki, Guthrinc and Redwald as the one who had made the command pushed his way through his men. Redwald recognized Nasi, a tall man, beardless, with blond hair tied with leather thongs. He was one of the two seasoned warriors Sweyn Estrithson had put in charge of the war-band he had released to the rebel army. Most of the English liked him. He laughed easily and bragged less than his brothers, but he had been first into battle when the Normans had attacked at Burgh.

He turned his ice-blue eyes on Kraki. 'I would not have wanted this.'

'What is *this*?' Guthrinc asked, folding his arms.

'My king has ordered us to give you no further aid in battle, and to take the gold to our ships, where it will be safe.'

'It is safe here,' Kraki growled.

'Aye. For you.'

Kraki flinched, raising his axe. The Danes bristled at the threat, levelling their own weapons. Guthrinc waved his hands palm down to calm the situation. He saw the danger, as Redwald did. The Danes were always quick to anger. He had seen men laid flat with a single punch for one wrong word. And gold always made those passions burn hotter. 'You do not trust us?' Guthrinc asked.

Nasi did not reply.

'We have been good spear-brothers. We shared the mead-oath.

We face a common foe. And when we promise gold, we always are true to our word.' Guthrinc smiled to ease the tension.

'True. We have faced death shoulder-to-shoulder. That bond can never be broken.' Nasi held out his hands, the meaning clear: he had no say in the matter.

'Sweyn Estrithson doubts us because he does not know us.' Kraki forced himself to lower his axe, following Guthrinc's lead. Redwald watched him struggle; he was not a man known for calm during conflict. 'Let him speak with Hereward. He will ease your king's worries.'

Nasri nodded. 'Sweyn will listen to Hereward. But for now, we have our orders. The gold must rest on our ships. Are we to fight?'

And what a one-sided fight that would be, Redwald thought bitterly. Three men alone, with the rest of the English dozing by their hearths or drunk. 'Where is Hereward when we need him?' he muttered under his breath, just loud enough for the other two men to hear.

Kraki thrust out his chest, stepping towards the Dane. Guthrinc caught his arm. 'This is not the time.' He leaned in and Redwald heard him whisper, 'If we take a stand, they will cut us down and take the gold anyway.'

Kraki snarled like a cornered wolf. Cursing, he turned on his heel and walked away so he would not have to see the Danes carrying off the hard-won treasure. At the abbey gate, he bellowed, 'Hereward. We need you.'

Guthrinc, coming to join him, glanced back at the milling Danes. 'I do not like this one bit,' he muttered. 'Once that gold is on their ships, what chance have we to bring it back to dry land?'

'You think that is their plan?' Redwald asked. 'And it was their plan all along?'

Kraki shook his head. 'Sweyn could have taken that gold without our help. Something else is amiss here.'

'There,' Guthrinc exclaimed, pointing towards the church. Two Danes lurched out of the door, hauling the relic box between them. 'This is about more than gold,' he added, his face darkening.

Redwald looked over to the monks of Burgh who had gathered by the enclosure fence. When they had seen their precious church treasures being taken from their grasp once again, they had raised their arms to the heavens, calling for God's help. Now they grew silent, staring in dismay at the relic box, more valuable to them by far than all the gold from their abbey. As the two Danes carried the chest towards the gate, Prior Aethelwold could contain himself no longer. He ran out and threw himself to his knees in front of the warriors, grasping for the box. The other monks swarmed behind him, crying for mercy.

Redwald lost sight of the warriors at the centre of the heaving circle of desperate churchmen clawing for the chest. Guthrinc clutched his head, knowing what was to come. With a roar, the Danes rushed the monks, tearing them off one by one. But each churchman only threw himself back into the fray. Redwald saw anger rising in the warriors' faces. Their tempers snapped as the monks continued to battle, and axes were wrenched high. It would be a slaughter.

'Enough,' Kraki roared. With Guthrinc at his side, he hurled himself towards the fight. Redwald cursed at the pointless sacrifice. The fools would be dead before they saved even one monk's life. He edged back towards the gate, preparing to run.

'Halt.' Arms outstretched, Nasi stepped between Kraki and Guthrinc and the churning mass of monks and warriors. 'Take no lives,' he barked to his men before looking Kraki in the eye. 'We want no bloodshed,' he said, lowering his voice, 'but the king has given his orders.'

Kraki and Guthrinc slowed as the Danes lowered their axes. 'One drop spilled,' the Viking said, stabbing a finger at Nasi, 'and you will pay with your life.'

Though the Danes put their weapons aside, they gave no further mercy. They ripped the monks off the mass of bodies, cuffing them and hurling them aside. Redwald watched the

259

churchmen sprawl across the abbey enclosure, bloodied and dazed. But no lives were taken, as Nasi had promised, and Kraki and Guthrinc held back, glowering.

Once the monks had been dispersed, the warriors formed a circle around the two men carrying the chest and escorted them out of the abbey gate. His left eye caked with blood, Prior Aethelwold knelt, praying for aid in a loud voice. His monks wailed and tore at their hearts around him.

'Where is Hereward?' Kraki roared, shaking a fist in frustration.

'He is gone.' The three men turned to see Hengist trudging towards them. 'He took some bread, his spear and his shield and left Ely. And the monk with him.' His face fell, revealing the dismay he had been trying to contain. 'Hereward has abandoned us.'

CHAPTER FORTY-THREE

'If you take one more step, you will pay a price that you will regret,' Hereward growled. His voice carried through the dark beneath the willows and across the moonlit mere.

Alric inhaled the chill air reeking of rotting leaves and black mud, but he did not flinch. 'You would not strike me. You have learned many lessons since we first met and you are a better man for it. Now learn how to take a friend's hand when it is offered.'

'You think you can help me? How? By praying for a host of angels to bring me what I need?' The Mercian shook his head wearily, his anger draining away. 'Go back. Must I tell you again?' He turned and looked towards the north. His destination, Alric thought. Since they had left Ely behind, following the hidden tracks, Hereward had always been heading in that direction.

'I know the byways of your soul as well as you know this land.' Alric softened his voice. He could see his friend's anger was born of despair. 'We have grown like brothers, the two of us, over the years of battle and bloodshed and joy and feasting, have we not?'

Hereward said nothing, refusing to meet the other man's eyes.

'I have seen you take a spear to the arm and an axe that near cleaved your helm in two,' the monk continued, 'and each time you rose and fought on as if the blows were naught. But I have never seen you so wounded as when your wife was lost.' He rested his hands on his knees, taking another deep breath. The trek from Ely had been too fast, too hard, and the constant arguing had worn him down. 'This . . .' he waved his hand wearily at the moonlit path ahead. 'This can only be about Turfrida.'

'And if it is, what business is it of yours, monk?' The shadows of the branches hid the warrior's expression.

'Take the hand of friendship, Hereward. Do not return to the man you were, that wild beast who snarled and snapped at all who passed and thought he needed none but himself.'

'I cannot be that man,' the Mercian shouted, stabbing a finger at his friend. 'Would that I could. And then I would not be here, tearing myself apart over two paths.' He stalked to the edge of the black water and squatted down, bowing his head as if in prayer. 'Your world is easy. Right or wrong, God or Devil. And my world used to be too. But now, whichever path I choose, the other will end in blood, and the death of good folk. There is no right or wrong. Both are right. Both are wrong. And my choice will damn me whatever.'

Alric winced at the anguish he heard in his friend's voice. For a moment, Hereward stared along the white path of moonlight across the dark lake, and then he rose slowly and drew his shoulders back. When he turned, he was grinning, all signs of his turmoil gone.

'We have walked a hard road, you and I,' he murmured, 'and I am glad you have been there at my side.'

'The road is not done yet.' Alric furrowed his brow at this change in conversation.

Hereward pulled bread from his leather pouch, broke it in two and handed one piece to Alric. 'This war has given some purpose to my days,' he began. 'It is a just one. We fight for our fathers and our fathers' fathers and all the things they built

262

with their hands. We fight for the folk suffering under William's cruelty, and to stem those rivers of blood he has set flowing across this land. Never would I have thought men would follow me into such a battle—'

'But they do,' Alric interjected. 'They would give their lives for you.'

Hereward bit into the bread and spoke: 'We have achieved much. With the Danes at our side, with Burgh's gold and the power of St Oswald, we now have a force that could shake the crown from the king's head. I did not do that alone. You showed me the way.'

Alric chewed on his piece of bread, reflecting. He was reassured by Hereward's words, but there was something in the man's tone that troubled him.

'I am no longer needed in Ely,' the Mercian said, so bluntly that Alric thought he had misheard.

He gaped. 'You are needed more than ever.'

'Others can lead as well as me, and they will.'

The bread paused halfway to Alric's mouth. 'What do you mean?'

'I have chosen Turfrida. Now all is well in Ely, I could choose no other.' He swallowed his bread and added, 'Only I can save her life.'

'Where is she? How do you know what has happened to her? Tell me,' the monk began.

Hereward shook his head. 'That is not for you to know. All that matters is that I will be gone—'

'For how long?' he murmured.

'Some time.'

The monk searched the other man's face. Those words held too much weight. He held out an imploring arm. 'Your army needs you, Hereward.'

'You must return to Ely and let the English know they must choose a new leader,' the Mercian insisted. 'Redwald can command their respect. He is clever and good-hearted and brave.'

Alric winced inwardly at the thought. 'Redwald . . . he is not you, Hereward,' he said hesitantly, not wishing to offend. His thoughts flew back to the shocking confession he had heard, and the admission of murder, and his suspicion that more terrible things lay unspoken.

'My brother is better than me. With him at its head, the English army cannot lose.' Alric opened his mouth, but could not find the words. 'Swear you will tell the others,' Hereward pressed. 'The army cannot be left without a leader. The final battle is near. Now we have set our trap, the Bastard will attack any day. A time of blood is coming fast, and only the strongest will survive.'

'I will tell them what you said,' Alric replied, relenting. *But I will offer my own counsel*, he thought. Redwald could not become leader.

Hereward nodded, seeming relieved. He gripped his friend's arm and held it for a moment that seemed to go on for ever.

'What is it that you are not saying?' the monk whispered, fearing the answer.

Hereward seemed on the brink of replying and then shook his head and smiled. 'You have been a good friend,' he said softly. 'Do this one last thing for me and all will be well.'

With that, Hereward turned and slipped into the shadows among the willows. Surprised by the warrior's speed, Alric hesitated for a moment. When he tried to follow, calling out his friend's name, he heard only the whisper of the breeze in the branches and saw only the all-consuming dark.

His mind raced with all that had been left unsaid. He turned and began to make his way back along the edge of the rustling reed-beds, only then registering the words of Hereward's farewell: *Do this last thing for me*. He felt a growing chill. It sounded as if his friend were going off to die.

CHAPTER FORTY-FOUR

Blood gushed into the pail as the butcher slit the boar's throat. Frenzied squeals rang across the yard at the back of the palace in Wincestre. Once the beast had crashed on to the mud, two lads dragged the carcass through the open doors of the barn to the carving table. Taking care not to splash any blood on her apron, a girl lifted the bucket and carried it away to make the pudding. More meat lay on the leather hides in the gloom of the barn, waiting to be butchered. Balthar could see geese with their necks broken, two cows and another boar.

'A feast? I have heard nothing of this,' Edwin of Mercia said, peering into the barn. 'What do you know of it, Fox?'

Balthar smiled and folded his hands in front of him. He had heard nothing of any feast, but he was not about to reveal his ignorance. 'The king makes his plans and announces them when he is ready.'

'Be sure you tell us when the time is right,' Morcar said, forcing a smile.

The three men stood in the shadows between the stores on the other side of the yard where they could not be seen. Balthar knew the Mercians hated him. He could see it in their cold eyes and sullen expressions and the way their fingers clenched on the gold hilts of their swords whenever they stood near him. Yet these days they nodded when their paths crossed, and they asked after his wife and sons. No contemptuous words ever left their lips, no mockery, no dismissive jibes. The king's brutality in the north had scared even them. They had come to realize he was a man capable of any extreme to achieve his desires, and the monarch's Fox knew his mind better than any. Balthar liked that feeling of power.

'What news have you for us, then, Fox?' Edwin asked.

Balthar understood what the other man really wanted to know: if the king was preparing to move against the English earls. 'The king's eyes are elsewhere for now,' he replied, 'to the east where the Danes have now joined forces with the English fighters in Ely.'

Edwin and Morcar exchanged a look. 'Never would I have thought Hereward could have raised such an army,' Morcar whispered.

'This Hereward is proving a great enemy,' Balthar said. He leaned in and whispered behind his hand, 'Why, there is even talk that he could topple the crown from the king's head.'

Edwin raised his eyebrows. 'Is this true?'

'His army grows by the day,' Balthar replied, glancing around. 'A few more loyal men is all he needs.'

Edwin nodded thoughtfully. The Fox hid his smile. He had sown his seeds well. He knew Edwin and Morcar had their own men, but they were well hidden somewhere between Wincestre and Mercia. All it would take would be a few more shoves to drive the frightened earls out of the court and into the rebels' arms.

'We always liked you, Fox,' Morcar lied. 'When the feast is called, sit with us and let us drink mead together.'

'An honour,' Balthar said with a bow. He watched the two brothers stride away, heads locked in conspiratorial whispers. There was much truth in what he said, and more in their fears. Soon the king would tire of keeping these enemies close and he would have them killed or shut away from the light.

Once the two men had disappeared, he hurried into the palace and found Godrun as she carried logs to the hearth. Her face lit up when she saw him. Glancing over her shoulder, she pushed him behind one of the screens. He kissed her, savouring the curves of her body pressed against him.

'How went it?' she whispered hopefully.

'Edwin and Morcar are like two hungry dogs. I throw them a few scraps and they follow me wherever I lead.'

'You are so brave,' she said, taking his hand. 'You risk so much. The English will surely love you as much as I when William is gone.'

Balthar smiled and nodded. He was not sure that the crown could ever be taken from the Norman's fingers, but for now he was enjoying his new role, and more, enjoying the attention it was gaining him from Godrun. His subterfuge seemed to excite her and she took him to her bed whenever they found a free moment. He felt like a youth again, spilling his seed time and again. And that meant fewer hours in the company of his dour wife. He told her the king made too many demands upon him. She was more than satisfied with the coin he took home, and the prestige of being married to a man of such power and influence. All in Wincestre knew of him, a great and powerful man who commanded the king's attention and enjoyed the greatest rewards. If only they knew that he had earned the name the king had given him. He smiled to himself at how skilfully he passed on all the secrets and whispers he heard in the king's palace, first to Godrun, who whispered them in turn to friendly Englishmen in town. And so he enjoyed the very best of two worlds and he was happy. But more, he felt he was doing good works for the first time in his life, and through it clearing a conscience that had become weighed down with guilt. Somewhere in all this intrigue he would find his path back to God.

'We must take care,' he whispered, kissing Godrun on the forehead. 'The uprising still simmers in the east and the king's patience wears thin. He is at his most dangerous when his temper frays. Anyone could feel the weight of his ire.'

'But it is good that Ely is still free,' she said, wide-eyed. 'If Edwin and Morcar send their men—'

'Hush.' He pressed a finger against her lips to silence her. Cocking his head, he listened. A dim commotion of shouts and horses and running feet rumbled from outside the palace. Puzzled, he snatched one last kiss, murmured a goodbye, and hurried out.

The palace enclosure throbbed with swarming bodies. The king's guards milled around the yard, unsure how to react to the spectacle unfolding in front of them. But the gates hung open and the commanders barked orders to stand back. Through the midst of the Normans, a mob of wild huscarls strode, fierce in helms and furs and chainmail. They looked like bears hunting in the mountains, Balthar thought, their heads turning constantly as they glowered at the warriors surrounding them. A figure walked in the centre of the horde, but the Fox could not see his face behind the wall of shields and bristling spears and axes. The Norman commanders cleared the way and the huscarls swept into the palace.

Balthar thrust his way past the Normans and inside, concerned that he knew as little as the common fighting men. As the huscarls approached the door to the king's hall, it swung open. William himself stood there, grinning. The knot of warriors parted to allow the figure at the centre to stride forward; the Fox edged along the wall to get a better look. He glimpsed a man built like an oak, with wild black hair and beard. The stranger gave a gap-toothed grin.

'King Sweyn Estrithson of the Danes,' William boomed, flinging his arms wide and laughing.

Balthar gaped. For months now, the Danes and the Normans had been engaged in a bloody dance throughout the east, and now William was greeting his opponent like a brother. What could this mean?

The two kings disappeared into the hall and the doors slammed shut behind them.

CHAPTER FORTY-FIVE

The new castle loomed over the high-town. In the merciless summer sun, the whitewashed timber of the keep shone across the great river plain from the top of the steep-sided hill. Age-old wood-framed houses and the great hall of the Mint clustered in the fortress's shadow within the stone walls of old Lincylene. Shielding his eyes, Hereward let his gaze drift outside the walls where the jumble of newer houses tumbled down the hillside to the broad, black ribbon of the River Witham. Sails billowed and lines cracked on the ships moored along the quayside. Bare-chested men sweated in the sun as they unloaded iron from the south and lead from the west, and chests and bales of prized goods from foreign shores, perhaps amethyst pendants from the hot lands to the south, or delicate pottery from Byzantium. The din of hammers from the workshops and the shouts of merchants along the river and in the marketplace carried across the still countryside. He wrinkled his nose at the reek of the cess-pits and the bitter smoke from the furnaces, sharp even at that distance.

Hereward drew his shoulders back. What lay ahead did not daunt him. He would not enter Lincylene cowed and whimpering and beg for Turfrida's life. A warrior, he was, and if there was even the slightest chance that he could free his wife and escape, he would seize it. Cunning would win him that prize, not the edge of his sword, he knew that: slow and careful, like the fox at night, not savage like the wolves.

Leaving the dusty track, he pushed his way into the cool of a wood. He trampled through snaking brambles until he found an ancient oak as broad as four men abreast, its roots so twisted that dark caves and crevices had formed beneath them. Scraping out the leaf mould and rich, black soil, he slid his spear, shield and sword into the dim recesses where not even curious children at play would find them. Now he would not be a warrior, but a freeman seeking work and food. No man would think him a stranger, with his Danish blood and Mercian accent. He was amongst his own here. The chin hair he had let grow would hide his jaw-line, his eyes shadowed by the hood pulled low over his head. With a stoop of his shoulders to make him appear shorter, he feigned a limp and set off for the straight north road that the monks said had been built by the Roman invaders in times long gone.

As he joined the stream of creaking carts and merchants trudging in the sweltering heat, he glanced up at the town from under hooded eyes. Now he could see why the king had made Lincylene key to his strategy in this last rebellious part of his realm. On its high hill, surrounded by thick stone walls, the new castle commanded the area. From that eagle's perch, the Normans could see across the river plain and up to the thick forest of the wolds to the north-east, perhaps even to the marshes beyond. Only a siege that lasted weeks would break its back. He looked around and saw how vital this place was for the trade that had brought wealth to every part of the land. All life in the east passed through here at some point, so Mercians said. The north road made travel from Northumbria and Wessex easy. Another old Roman road that the locals called Fosse ran towards the west. The Witham carried the ships to the whale road in the east, and to the west was the wide valley of the Trent, which could be navigated, via the Ouse, to Eoferwic itself. Who controlled the trade routes controlled England. But more than that, from this stronghold William the Bastard could send out his iron army to crush any foe, whether English rebel or Danish invader. He lowered his head. He had seen enough.

When he passed through the gates into the low-town, he hid his distaste. After so long with only the soughing of the wind and the murmur of the water for company, his ears ached from the din of the teeming town. He forced his way through the stream of bodies reeking of sweat in the heat. The stink of rotting food and human waste choked the back of his throat. Yet a brief smile touched his lips. For all the discomfort, here he could lose himself, just one more soul struggling to pass through the day.

Through the low-town he picked his way, following the streets up the hill. The Normans were everywhere, some in hauberks and helms, fixing a cold eye on everyone who passed. These ones saw only enemies. Others were dressed in the finest linen tunics, the colours bright, only their shaven heads revealing their origins. How many could he have killed that day. He pushed aside his hatred and thought only of Turfrida. If all went well, there would be time enough for vengeance.

Away from the river, the crowds thinned. In a tavern not far from the walls of the high-town, he filled his growling belly with stew and moistened his dry mouth with beer. With his back to the wall and his eyes on the door, he could watch everyone who entered. He kept his ears open. Work continued at the castle, he heard. William had ordered the timber keep to be replaced by a stone one at the earliest opportunity, and new ramparts were being dug.

Once he had heard enough, he limped out into the baking day. Shouts and jeers were now ringing from the direction of the marketplace. Curious, he made his way to the edge of a growing crowd. On a mound on the eastern edge, a Norman commander with a face like granite looked out over the throng. Two of his men held the arms of a stout youth with hair like thatch. His eyes were wide with terror, his face bloodless. A third Norman stood near by, holding a long-bladed knife.

The commander held up his right hand and the crowd fell silent. Hereward glanced around and saw faces flushed with excitement or dark with cold judgement. No fear of the Normans here, nor anger it seemed. He felt troubled by this sight.

He looked back to the mound as the commander said in faltering English, 'Beornstan the White, accused and found guilty of the crime of rape. With force, he took the girl Winfred, daughter of Ulger the Smith, five nights gone. Here, now, his punishment.'

The crowd watched, rapt, as the youth began to whimper. One of his captors ripped down his breeches. The other grabbed the youth's prick and yanked it out. Fear rooted the lad to the spot; he offered no resistance. The third Norman stepped forward, rested the long knife against Beornstan's balls and began to saw upwards. Hereward glimpsed a spurt of crimson before he looked away. The youth's screams tore out, drowned in an instant by the jubilant yells of the crowd.

'He got what he deserved,' a doughy woman beside him affirmed.

'Aye, the little bastard's done it before and never been caught,' her friend replied.

As he pushed back through the throng, Hereward felt a growing uneasiness with the satisfaction he heard expressed. Too many folk seemed pleased with their new masters. The Normans brought justice where it was needed, and punishment was swift. Since the brutal crushing of the north, the king had restrained his crueller urges, at least here, in the east. The war would have to come soon, or these sheep would be too content to rise up.

Climbing the hill, he reached the solid stone wall encircling the high-town that the Romans had built when they had ruled this place. The gate was oak, new and robust, and five guards watched over it. No easy way in presented itself. Anxiety tightened his chest. He had no idea how long he had, or even whether he was already too late. But he knew he had to stifle his desperation. However much he wanted to hack through every bastard Norman to save his wife, he knew if he acted rashly it would only lead to his death, and no doubt Turfrida's too.

That night, with the coin in his pouch he bought a berth in the sleeping hall in the low-town. As a rule, it would have been full of drunken sailors snoring loudly, but in that hot night they slept under the stars aboard their vessels. At dawn, he slipped out into the silent streets and made his way once more up the steep hill. Even there, surrounded by his enemies, he felt no fear, only a grim determination to save Turfrida.

When the men working on the castle trudged up to the gate, bleary-eyed and reeking of night-sweat, he slipped in among them, just another strong pair of arms forced to do the Normans' bidding.

The labour was hard. He spent long hours digging the new ramparts in the blazing sun alongside the work-band, with only cups of ale and a few morsels of bread to keep him going. But he watched everything. Nobles came and went, purposeful, their conversations low and intense, and not only those who had been granted land around Lincylene. Warriors rode out of the gates in the early morning and disappeared into the wild country. Other fighting men strode into the bailey before the sun was at its highest, fresh from the south. Hereward sensed a throb of keen anticipation everywhere. His eyes flickered to every face that passed as he dug into the hard, stony soil. After Burgh, the Normans should be worried. They knew the English had new allies in the Danes, a formidable army that could strike at any moment. Word of the burning of the town and the looting of the abbey rushed across the land like the spring waters. Yet he saw no concern anywhere.

The workmen stripped off their tunics in the blistering heat, their skin reddening by the hour. At first he had felt uneasy and exposed when he had thrown aside his hood and cloak. But he had smeared his face and hair with his filthy hands like many of the other men and in no time they resembled the children who played along the muddy banks of the Wellstream. The Normans paid no heed to dirty English dogs, anyway.

During the most intense heat of the day, he sheltered in the thin shadow beside the stables. As he mopped the sweat from his brow, he glimpsed two familiar figures striding across the bailey towards the keep. Ivo Taillebois was as grim as ever, his eyes narrow slits, his mouth a slash in his stony face. But the nobleman William de Warenne beamed and waved his hand in the air as he spoke. How easy it would be to smash in their skulls with a stone. But Hereward gritted his teeth and pushed the urge aside. Not long after, he looked over to the gates where a knot of newly arrived warriors milled and saw Harald Redteeth. Once he had overcome his disappointment that the Northman had not died from his wounds the previous year, his loathing burned hotter still. He could not look at the Viking without remembering the head of his friend Vadir hanging from Harald's filthy hand. Vengeance would not come soon enough.

The Northman suddenly jerked his head round as though Hereward had called to him. Half-hidden by the spoil heap, the Mercian knew he could not be seen. Yet he felt the hairs on his neck prickle erect. The Viking stared for a long moment and then moved out of the gates with the other warriors.

The first day Hereward laboured in silence. On the second day, when his face was familiar, he struck up short conversations with the other men. He sifted through the talk of weather and food and women and found the gold: hints of a coming battle, overheard plans for the construction of more castles and sturdier ones, built in stone, to keep the king's peace. Yet none of this held value beside what he truly needed to know.

As the third day drew to a close, he leaned on his shovel, his muscles aching from long hours of digging. When the castle gates rattled open, he looked up and grimaced to see the cold features of Emeric the Witchfinder. It seemed only yesterday that he had been in hiding with Turfrida as the Norman churchman hunted her through the woods in Flanders. His jaw tightened as he watched the cleric make his way across the bailey to the third of six timber-framed stores.

'Aye, he's a cruel bastard,' the man beside him muttered when he saw where Hereward was looking. 'Sometimes you can hear the screams.'

Hereward jerked round. 'Who screams?'

'I heard tell the Normans keep a woman in there, a witch, who could shake the very foundations of the king's rule.' The man crossed himself with a hand missing two fingers. 'Her torments were great indeed, so one of the guards said, for only when the devil had been driven out of her could all our souls be safe.'

Never had Hereward felt such anguish. He turned away and closed his eyes, thinking he might be driven mad by the thought of his wife's suffering.

'Get some food in your belly,' the other man said, eyeing him with concern. 'This work is hard, and under this sun it can turn even the strongest man's head.'

Hereward nodded, pretending it was the heat that had drained the blood from his face. In his mind's eye, he saw the witchfinder at his feet, beaten to death, and at that moment he wanted nothing more. Yet one wrong step would end his life, and Turfrida's too, most likely. Throwing aside his shovel, he all but ran from the bailey, not stopping until he was in the lowtown. No sleep came that night. But he contained his fury and made his plans.

CHAPTER FORTY-SIX

The Norman commander raised his gauntleted fist. At the centre of the bailey, his warriors fell silent and awaited their orders. Their helms gleamed in the hot sun. They held their spears erect and their shields tight against their chests. Hereward watched the band of fighting men as he wiped the sweat from his brow. They looked too sure of themselves, he thought, too many grins, too many eager glances. Were they merely content in their ignorance of the threat the English posed? Or did they harbour some secret knowledge at which he could only guess?

The nobles and guests of the Norman lords milled around, raising their cups of wine in celebration of some coming victory. Hereward grimaced as he looked at their faces, seeing arrogance and pride and contempt. He wished he could burn them all there and then. With disdain, he returned to his digging, only to sense eyes upon him. No one seemed to be looking his way, but he could take no risks so close to bringing his plan into effect. Putting his head down, he eased behind the other workmen.

The gates groaned open. The Norman commander dropped his fist and with a cheer from the crowd, the warriors surged out into the high-town. Once the gates had creaked shut behind the disappearing men, the nobles and guests trailed back into the keep, wafting their hands by their flushed faces.

For a while, Hereward struggled to lose himself in the work, tormented by the knowledge that every moment he wasted Turfrida suffered more. She was strong, he told himself, and he prayed she would endure, but he knew the child she carried would sap some of her vigour.

When next he looked up, the sun was at last slipping towards the west. The shadows lengthened across the bailey. While the other men kept their heads to their labours, he edged behind the spoil-heap and began to dig a low trench. Soon the work-master whistled low and long. With sagging shoulders, the relieved men threw aside their shovels and trudged towards the gate. The Mercian ducked down behind the pile of earth, listening to the grumbles slowly fade away.

As the gate groaned open, Hereward crawled into the trench he had dug and clawed earth over himself. Soil tumbled across his face, into his mouth and his nose. Once his frantic scrambling was complete, he lay as still as he could and listened. No one came. In the stifling gloom, all he could think was that he had dug his own grave. Sweat soaked his tunic and his throat became like sand. Muffled sounds reached his ears: snatches of dim conversation, hoofbeats near the stables, a guard hailing a friend.

The thin light faded until he swam in darkness. The sounds of the bailey ebbed. Silence lay heavy on the castle. Still, though, he could not risk leaving his hiding place, not until all his enemies were in their deepest sleep.

As if to echo his worries, vibrations throbbed through the ground around him. He stiffened. Someone was prowling around the spoil-heap. He choked back his breath, praying the trench would be well hidden in the dark. The gentle steps stopped for a moment, as if the walker were looking around, and then moved on past him. Once they had faded away, he sucked in air through gritted teeth. The pounding of his heart slowed. His plan had been a good one.

For what seemed like an age, he choked in the stink of the soil, hearing only the rasp of his laboured breathing. Time held no meaning there. He found his thoughts drifting to his childhood, miles away in Barholme, and his mother singing to him gently at twilight. The peace of those evenings settled on him once more. But it was fleeting. Again he felt the blows from his father's fist on his cheek, the ringing in his head, the pain in his belly from where the shoe had thumped. Still no anger came from those distant memories, only a terrible regret as if his suffering had been all his own fault.

More footsteps thudded in the dim distance. He jerked from his lucid dream, his chest tightening. This time he heard another sound too, a faint scrabbling not far from where his head lay. Rats, scavenging for any crumbs of bread dropped during the day's work. The scurrying circled his hiding place. Those hungry vermin would not be frightened away by anything. Once he had seen a rat as long as his forearm attack a baby while the parents were sitting close by at the hearth.

The footsteps drew closer. He swallowed. Now he could not risk driving the rats away. The weight of one of the squirming creatures pressed down upon his face. He worked his mouth, hoping the movement would shift the thing, but his actions only seemed to make the rat more frenzied. Claws began to tear at the earth. Eager snuffling reached his ears. It smelled him there, fresh meat on which to gnaw.

His body was as rigid as an iron rod, his breath burning in his chest. The feet shook the ground next to where he lay. After a moment, he heard the sound of splashing, a bladder being emptied. Unperturbed, the rat raked the soil away from his face. Sharp nails tore at his skin. The vermin's rough nose darted in, pressing next to his eye. He could feel the vibrations of its jaw. Any moment it would start to rend with its fangs.

The splashing slowed and then gushed down once more.

The rat lunged. Before the fangs tore his flesh, Hereward wrenched up in a shower of black soil. The writhing vermin spun through the night. The pissing man, a guard, reeled in horror at the terrifying apparition rising from the cold earth beside him. So shocked was he, his cry caught in his throat. He stumbled back, soaking his shoes, his hands clawing at the air.

Hereward pounced, driving the man down on to the towering pile of earth. He clamped a hand across the guard's mouth and ripped the head to one side. The snapping of the neck sounded like a dry branch breaking. Leaving the limp body for the rats, he crawled around the heap and crouched, listening. All was still. The brief struggle could not have been heard.

A single torch burned beside the door of the keep. A sea of darkness washed up against the small island of light. On previous evenings, he had watched two bored men guarding the gate. With the walls of the high-town so secure, no more were needed, and they had seemed to pay little attention to the world around them. Even so, he knew he would only have a little time before the remaining guard began to search for his missing companion.

Keeping low, he loped around the edge of the bailey. The night was warm, still scented with the meaty aromas of that night's meal. The row of six stores loomed up out of the dark, and he found the one he had seen the witchfinder enter the previous day. For a moment, he listened at the door. No sound came from within. Easing the door open a crack, he slipped inside.

A fat candle guttered by a flight of earthen steps leading down into the pitch black of the undercroft. His throat constricted. It was too quiet. Apprehension shifted to fear for his wife's safety and he quickly turned it to cold anger. All the Normans would pay for the torment they had inflicted on his wife – the witchfinder, Ivo Taillebois, William de Warenne, yes, and the king himself. Blood would follow blood. He steadied himself, then picked up the candle and edged down to the lower level. At the foot of the steps, his nostrils wrinkled. He could smell loam, but behind it other scents lurked: charred wood, sweat, iron.

Shadows swooped away from the candle flame. Letting his eyes adjust to the gloom, Hereward looked around the undercroft. At another time it would have stored supplies for the castle. The floor was packed earth. Halfway along lay a circle of grey ashes and charred wood, and within it thin rods of iron. He wrenched his head away quickly, sickened by the visions that burned through his mind. Tilting the candle, he made out a bundle of rags heaped in one corner. In another stood a pitcher and a cup, some strips of hide, a pail, a broken spear, an adze, a whetstone.

His attention flickered back to the rags.

The thunder of blood in his head drowned out the sound of his running feet. He dropped to his knees beside the unmoving form. For a moment, he was gripped by the sight of brown hair, now matted with grease and sweat and blood. His thoughts rebelled, refusing to make sense of what he was seeing. A part of him wanted to call his wife's name, but the word choked in his throat. Then, with trembling hands, he turned Turfrida over on to her back. Her belly swelled beneath her filthy, torn dress. Her too-pale face was smeared with dirt. As his gaze drifted down, he saw her bare arms were a patchwork of wounds and burns. How she must have suffered. He fought back a wave of devastation.

But then her eyes flickered in the candlelight and he stifled the urge to cry out with relief. He snatched up her cold hand and stroked the back of it with his filthy thumb. She frowned as she looked into his face, not sure what she was seeing, or not believing. Her thin smile seemed to take a tremendous effort, for it faded quickly, and when she spoke her voice was barely more than a husk. 'You should not have come.'

'And leave you here, the thing that is most valuable in my life?' he whispered.

'It is a trap.'

'I know.' He shook his head, trying to dispel visions of the witchfinder with his glowing rods and his blades and his mallets, and of Turfrida screaming and pleading for mercy. He felt hollowed out by what he knew had transpired. 'They will pay,' he croaked. 'Pay with their lives.'

Turfrida raised a trembling hand to silence him. 'No . . . be still. You must hear me. They took me to lure you here. A choice, that is what they offer . . . My life for the end of your war. You must stand up and vow in the marketplace here in Lincylene that you believe William is king, that you were wrong to raise your spear against him, and that all English should lay down their weapons and bow their heads to him.'

'And then they will take my life,' he said with a grim smile.

'You cannot do this. Your fight is just, and my life is nothing next to that.'

'You think I would condemn you to death?' he whispered.

'I do not think you would condemn the English to misery and blood under that Bastard's cruel rule. This is a choice no man should ever have to make.' She tried to grip his hand, but she was too weak. 'You must forget me, Hereward. Fight on. The English need you.'

He leaned forward and kissed her forehead. 'I do not play by the king's rules. I make my own. One guard waits at the gate, and he will be dead before he can speak. Then I will carry you from here, and we will be away from Lincylene long before William's dogs can hunt for us.'

She smiled again. 'My love,' she whispered.

'I will return in moments.' He squeezed her hand and turned, darting back across the undercroft to the steps. Relief filled him. Bounding up the stair, he slipped out of the door into the night.

A figure waited, swathed in the dark. Hereward froze, wondering if he could kill the stranger before a warning was called. 'Stand your ground,' a familiar voice growled. The shape stepped forward, and the Mercian saw it was his father.

Hereward gaped. Why would Asketil be there, in a Norman stronghold, so far from his home in Barholme? 'You are a prisoner too,' the warrior whispered. As his thoughts raced, he realized his father did not look as aged and feeble as the last time they had met. He seemed taller, his shoulders pushed back, as Hereward remembered him from his youth. A fire burned in the old man's eyes.

'I knew it was you I saw skulking with the filthy ceorls earlier this day,' Asketil snarled. 'Though I searched the bailey, I had no doubt you would soon appear. You could not ignore the lure of your whore.'

Hereward winced. 'Come, let me take you from here—'

Asketil shook his fist at his son. 'I will not rest until I see you cut down, like the wild dog you are.'

'But . . . we are blood,' Hereward replied, incredulous.

'And you have dishonoured that blood. *I* am loyal to my king.' He turned and yelled into the dark bailey, 'He is here. Hereward is here.'

Stunned by his father's betrayal, Hereward was rooted. In an instant, the waiting guards encircled him. Spears flashed up to his chest on every side.

Asketil turned his back on his son. 'I have brought honour back to my kin,' he sighed. With disbelief, Hereward watched his father walk away towards the keep. The old man's words floated back: 'You have always had no worth, but now you have failed the poor souls who put their trust in you. Your doomed fight is over. Your army will be broken. And then you will be put to death, so all the English know that you are as nothing.'

CHAPTER FORTY-SEVEN

3 September 1070

The raven banner of the Danish king fluttered in the sea breeze. Beneath it, wind boomed in the striped sail of the Long Serpent as the royal flagship prepared to leave England behind. Sweyn Estrithson looked up from the prow and saw the weather was good. On their sea-chests his men sat, wrapped in furs against the chill of the long crossing as they gripped the oars. With a nod, the king signalled all was well.

Alric shielded his eyes against the dazzling sun and watched the *langskip* pull away. It was the first, but it would not be the last. With mounting anxiety, he looked across the rest of the vast fleet. The decks bustled with activity. Along the water's edge, by the salt marsh, warriors pulled down tents and kicked out the embers of the night's fires. Others hauled chests and sacks into the surf to stow on their vessels. The scout had been right. The Danes were going home.

'This cannot be,' Aethelwold proclaimed, throwing his arms into the air. 'They take the saint's bone and our church's treasures.' Alric lunged to restrain the distressed prior, but the churchman threw himself down the slope towards the stony beach. The monks of Burgh surged after him.

'Did we expect any less when we allowed them to load the gold on their ships?' Redwald muttered as he strode up, Kraki and ten other warriors massed behind him.

'You think we stood a chance to stop them?' the Viking snapped.

Alric grimaced. He had sensed the tension between the two men from the moment he had returned to Ely with Hereward's message. Kraki clearly did not believe Redwald was up to the task of leading the army and had made that point vociferously. Only Redwald's refusal to accept the command prevented a confrontation. The younger man was no fool. He preferred to whisper in a small voice and let others reap the consequences of his actions. Yet since that day the English had been leaderless and Alric had found all sides looking to him to keep the peace.

'We lose our leader, we lose our army and now we have lost our gold and God's power,' Madulf bemoaned with a shake of his head. 'We have nothing to protect us from the king's wrath.'

'We have what we always had,' Kraki growled, shaking his axe.

'If only Hereward were here. He would know what to do.' Dismayed, Sighard leaned upon his spear.

'But he is not. We must make our own way until he returns.' Alric watched the Burgh monks rushing through the remnants of the camp, trying to find someone who would listen to their pleas. 'Let us see if there is aught we can do.'

He strode down the slope and crunched across the pebbles, hoping he appeared more confident than he felt. When he approached a red-headed Dane folding a sapphire-coloured tent, the warrior thrust him aside with such force he fell upon his arse, flushing as the man laughed. Undeterred, however, Alric moved on until he caught sight of Nasi. The commander of the Danes at Ely was ordering two men to drag a stuffed sack towards the ships.

Alric hailed him with a wave. Nasi shook his head wearily,

but turned to face the monk. 'Save your breath,' he sighed. 'We return home.'

'With all the gold and the arm of St Oswald? Where is the honour in that?'

Nasi's eyes darted furtively and then he beckoned the monk to one side where they would not be overheard. 'Our king has given his order. It is not for us to question it,' he whispered. He glanced around, adding, 'William the Bastard has paid him off. All the gold and silver we have taken is ours to keep, and more with it, some say. And the bone of Oswald too.'

Alric frowned. The king was clever. A little gold was a small price to pay to kick the legs out from under the rebellion. 'You leave us with nothing.'

The Dane held out his hands and gave an apologetic shrug. 'Another day will dawn and another feast will come.'

For you perhaps, the monk thought bitterly. 'We have set our trap to lure the king's army in and now we have no one left to fight them. We will be slaughtered.'

Nasi could not reply.

Alric looked towards the fleet and gaped as the monks of Burgh splashed through the surf towards the nearest vessels. Nasi followed his gaze and grinned slyly. 'Better they sail with us than fight for their treasures here on the beach. They think the king will hear their pleas once he is drunk on mead in his own hall.' He shrugged. 'The faith of a churchman, a wonder to behold.'

When the Dane returned to his work, Alric bowed his head and made his way back up the beach. The journey had been futile, but he had expected no other. For Hereward's sake, he had at least tried. As he strode through the long grass on the dunes, he heard the English warriors bickering away in the trees. Tempers frayed on all sides. How long could they hold the army together without Hereward to lead them?

Through the low-hanging branches he pushed, towards the sound of the arguing voices. Barely had he taken four steps into the shadows under the canopy, when he sensed movement behind him. Thinking Nasi had come after him, he half-turned. A bolt of pain seared through his head and he felt himself falling.

Darkness came.

How long passed, he did not know. Once again, he felt sure he was back in the monastery in Jarrow, his place of safety, being scolded by Brother Oswyn for being a poor scholar. As he came round, he felt the world moving beneath him. Rough wood prickled his cheek. His head throbbed as if he had spent all night drinking mead. Hands folded into his tunic and pulled him into a sitting position. When his vision cleared, he found himself looking into the face of Nasi. Salty wind stung his face and a booming filled the air. He knew then where he was.

'You chose to join me on the wave-skimmer after all, monk,' the Dane said with a grin.

With mounting horror, Alric looked round. No land could he see, no safe home, only the heaving blue waves and an uncertain future.

CHAPTER FORTY-EIGHT

The sky blackened in the north. Bolts of lightning danced along the horizon. As the wind tore across the water, the swell began to heave. Alric looked to the growing storm, fear and nausea battling inside him. Upright in the prow, Nasi barked orders to his men, keeping one eye on the vast array of ships dipping and cresting on the waves. The Danes were seasoned sailors and treated the whale road with respect. Yet they gazed with unease towards the tempest as they hunched over their oars. That troubled him even more. Aft, the steersman wrestled with the steering oar against the turbulent waves. The weather-vane tipped with the iron heads of ravens spun wildly.

'God will watch over us,' Aethelwold murmured, more to ease his own terror than to comfort Alric.

'I have endured one shipwreck. I should not wish to face another, even with the Lord at my shoulder,' Alric muttered. Memories of black water closing over his head flooded his mind and a shudder ran through him.

The prior dropped to his knees and mouthed a prayer in front of the relic chest. The four other monks on the vessel clustered around him as the deck rolled under their feet. As they picked up the prayer, Alric looked around and saw a curious thing.

The Danes near by eyed the box with the same uneasy stare they kept for the storm. At first, he could not understand why that would be so. When he saw one of the warriors cross himself and raise his eyes to the heavens, he had it. Men who braved the sea were more superstitious than those who lived out their days on dry land. These hardened fighting men feared they would be punished for stealing the relic from the churchmen who guarded it.

Lightning briefly turned the world white. Then thunder cracked overhead and the day became as night.

Alric crouched down beside the praying monks, finding some shelter from the blasting wind below the rims of the shields on the rack running around the boat. Screwing up his eyes, he wished he were back in Ely, anywhere but where he was.

Adding to his misery, his head still throbbed from the blow that had struck him. The attack as yet made little sense, though he had turned it over in his mind a hundred times. A hooded man had paid good coin for a Dane to take his dazed form aboard a ship, so Nasi had told him. Only one answer seemed possible: that he had played too large a part in the leadership of the army since Hereward's departure, and the Normans had sent their eyes and ears in the camp to get rid of him. He felt proud at that; and scared too.

Another flash and thunder-crack, then within moments rain as hard as stones lashed on a buffeting gale. Alric buried his head on the sodden deck. Under his trembling hands, he felt the ship rise high as if it had been plucked up by God. When it crashed down, the monks cried out as one, all of them rolling along the planks. Alric clamped his eyes shut tight. This was how it had started last time. A vision of towering cliffs of black water flashed across his mind, and then he felt once again his lungs filling, his vision darkening, and his panic as Death clutched for him. He feared drowning more than any other death. Along the Northumbrian coast he had seen men pulled from the sea, bodies black and bloated, eyes eaten by the fish.

Seawater sluiced across his face. Choking, he jerked his head up and saw a growing pool in the bottom of the vessel. Cold terror flooded through him. The tar-covered moss and animal hair that jammed the grooves between the planks was failing in the rough waves.

'Here. Make yourself useful,' Nasi bellowed. He tossed a wooden hand bailer. Alric snatched it up and threw himself into the pool, scooping the brine over the side. When he glanced up, he saw Nasi still standing upright next to the dragon-headed prow, his hair plastered to his head. His face remained as calm as if they sailed across the mere at Ely. Alric felt comforted by that sight. The pounding of his heart eased a little and he even found it in him to peer over the side. At times the waves seemed higher than the mast. The rest of the ships were lost in the deep gloom of the storm, if they had not already been dragged down to the bottom.

But then the strakes flexed, groaning against the rivets like a wounded bear, and dread gripped him once more. A wave as high as a church tower plucked the vessel up and flung it down into a trough. Alric cried out, afraid the ship would shatter into pieces. How could this be happening to him again? Was this how God punished him for his sins?

The wave-skimmer whirled, rose up, crashed down again. Alric spun through the pool of water, jerking up and gasping for air. He could see only iron waves and iron sky. And somewhere the prior was screaming, 'God save all our souls!'

CHAPTER FORTY-NINE

Dark water engulfed Hereward. From the depths, he struck out, upwards towards a halo of thin, grey light hovering overhead. He blinked once, twice, and as his vision cleared a cold face fell into view. The face of Death, it seemed, and it was. Harald Redteeth peered down at him, his pupils as wide and black as that deep ocean from which the Mercian had just escaped.

'Alive. Good,' the Viking muttered, his breath reeking of meat. He drew back, settling on his haunches.

The Mercian's left eye was caked with blood, his face mottled with bruises from the beating he had taken when the guards fell upon him. His wrists and ankles had been bound together with hempen rope. He shook his head to clear the haze and looked around. He was in an undercroft, but not the same one where Turfrida was being held. The dank air smelled of loam. At the far end, near the earthen steps leading up to the door of the store, a candle flickered, but he could not tell if it was night or day outside. A heavy beat echoed high overhead, rain drumming on the roof boards. The hot period had broken.

'Come near,' he urged with a grim smile. 'I have torn out the throat of a wolf with my bare teeth. I can do the same for you.'

Harald Redteeth shrugged. In the palm of his right hand, he balanced the axe that hung at his side by a leather thong. The blade was notched and scarred, the haft worn by years of use. 'This is my axe, Grim. It was given to me by my father, and to him by his father,' he said, examining the weapon approvingly. 'That is what we do. Pass down the things of value so there is a chain linking us with the past that shaped us. You English, you do the same with your knives, so I am told.' He looked to Hereward who showed no response. The Viking nodded reflectively. 'With these blades, we carve our lives, and our place in the land, and in the years. And when I hold this axe, I feel my father's hand upon mine, and his father's upon his. That is how it should be.'

He laid down his weapon and picked another axe off the mud floor. Hereward had not noticed it until now. Harald Redteeth turned the axe over, examining it from every angle. It was clean, shiny, the edge sharp. He wrinkled his nose. 'This is a Norman axe. They have a way with weapons, those bastards. Sharper.' He ran one filthy-nailed finger along the cutting edge. 'Stronger. They are built to kill.' He tossed the weapon aside and it clattered on the hard ground. 'They mean nothing. They are not passed on. They do not tie a man to his blood or days long gone.' He narrowed his eyes and pointed one finger at Hereward. '*You* know what I mean.'

Hereward watched the Viking stand and prowl around the shadows of the undercroft, his hauberk rattling with each step. He came to a halt in the half-light, his red-dyed beard glowing like fire. Hereward sneered. 'The Butcher has sent you—'

'The Butcher has not sent me,' Harald interrupted, cracking his knuckles. 'I am not here to do you harm. Where would be the honour in that, a man tied up like a dog?'

The Mercian strained at his bonds until his wrists burned. 'You would do well to kill me now,' he said. 'For when I am free I will end your life for what you did to my friend Vadir, in Flanders.'

'No more than what you did when you killed my battle-brother Ivar, in a burning house, denying him entry to the Halls of the Slain.' The Viking glowered. 'We have a blood-feud, you and I, and it can only be ended one way, between men, on the field of battle, whether it be by your death or my own.'

'Yours, then.'

Nodding, Harald Redteeth drew closer and folded his arms. 'We shall see.'

'My wife, Turfrida. She yet lives?' Hereward held his head up, trying to show no sign of weakness, but a tic gave away his fears. How close he had been to spiriting her away from danger until his father had betrayed him. His stomach heaved at the memory. His mind shied from all thought of Asketil, a man filled with such loathing he would set aside all blood-ties to try to destroy his own flesh.

The Viking nodded, scowling with disgust. 'Stealing a woman, and a woman with child at that . . . making her suffer to break your spirit . . . there is no honour in this course.'

'And yet you raise your axe for these very snakes.'

Redteeth bristled. 'I take their coin. And it serves me that they are your enemy.' Calming himself, he prowled away once more and when he turned, he said in a low voice, 'And so you must dishonour yourself by denying the English and the battle you fight. Force your own folk to bare their throats to the conqueror's fangs. And if you do not, your woman will die in agony.' He spat. 'No man should endure that choice.'

Hereward kept his shoulders back, but he felt a deep cold run into his bones. Never could he sacrifice his wife and his unborn child. Nor could he renounce the English, and every man and woman who had believed in him. He saw no way out of this misery, and only suffering and death on all sides.

If Redteeth recognized those fears in his face, he said nothing, and Hereward felt grateful for that small mercy. The Viking shook his head wearily and strode back towards the door. At the foot of the steps, he half-turned and said, 'The Butcher will be here soon, with that noble cur who follows him around.

They will demand of you your decision, and one way or another your life will be over.' He shrugged, humming a strange tune to himself. After a moment, he added, 'A horse is tethered by the house where your woman is kept. The castle gates are open, and will stay that way until the carts have brought food for this night's feast.' He bowed his head in thought for a moment, and then added, 'A man who was not bound could put both to good use.'

Hereward snarled at the final taunt as Harald Redteeth climbed the steps and went out. But in the flickering candle-light, something glinted in the corner of his vision. He looked round and saw the Norman axe, still lying on the mud next to him.

CHAPTER FIFTY

R ain lashed the castle grounds. Lowering black clouds turned the day into night as the figure crept out of the store near the keep. Torrents of water gushed across the sun-baked mud and grass of the bailey. Shin-deep grey pools formed in the hollows. Thunder cracked overhead, and in the stables the frightened horses whinnied and stamped their hooves. Hereward gripped the Norman axe, creeping low against the wall. So heavy was the downpour he could barely see the gates. It was the perfect cover for what he had to do.

His sodden tunic was already clinging to his skin as he reached the store where Turfrida was imprisoned. Blinking the rain from his eyes, he eased open the door and slipped inside. When the thunder rolled away, he heard the piercing scream hidden beneath it. His wife was not alone. Devastated, his head spun at the agonies he heard in that throat-rending cry. No more would she suffer. Hereward gritted his teeth and crept down the steps.

A steady beat of rain dripped through the roof. More water sluiced down the earth walls of the undercroft and pooled across the floor. An orange glow suffused the far end of the space, from a fire dancing in a circle of stones. Iron rods lay in the coals, the tips glowing yellow. His nose wrinkled at the cloud of sulphurous smoke drifting through the store. Another scream tore from his wife's throat, and he almost cried out in response. *No more*, he thought to himself. *No more*.

As the smoke shifted, he glimpsed Turfrida huddled on the floor in the glimmering light by the far wall. She had rolled into a ball, her hands pressed against her face. Her round belly strained against the filthy linen of her dress. Two figures loomed over her, their backs to him. One was a guard leaning on a spear. Tall and strong, he was, like an oak, a worthy opponent in any battle. In the heat of the undercroft, his helm had been set aside and he wore only a sweat-stained tunic and breeches. Hereward saw the other man was Emeric the witchfinder. He clutched an iron poker, the tip glowing red, and he slowly waved it over Turfrida's shaking form.

'Witch,' he murmured. 'How many times we have met here. I would have long since shown you God's mercy were you not the bait for an English rat. And so we must still pull the devils from you one by one, this day, and the next, and the ones beyond that, until the vermin has met his fate.'

'Soon you will be dead,' Turfrida croaked, 'and no one will mourn for you. The *vættir* have said this is so.'

Her words seemed to drive the churchman into a rage for he swung the poker up as if to strike her. The Mercian flinched, too far from the cleric to strike. The poker hung in the air for a moment, before Emeric lowered it and said with a smile, 'I pity you, but this is in God's hands now.'

Hereward felt sickened by what he saw. Other men might be destroyed by seeing their wife in such torment, but not him. He turned his pain deep inside him, as he had all his life. In reply, his rage called to him from the dark chambers of his soul. He could not, would not, contain it any longer.

With a snarl, he bounded across the undercroft like a wolf. His thoughts fled. His vision closed in. He swung the axe. The guard barely had time to raise a defensive arm as the blade came down, cutting through flesh and bone and almost severing the head. Blood splashed into the fire, sizzling. The man fell without a sound escaping his throat and Hereward was already turning on the witchfinder.

Emeric swung up the hot poker instinctively, but it was a half-hearted defence. With the back of his hand, Hereward swatted it out of the cleric's grip. It bounced across the floor into a puddle, hissing and steaming.

The churchman stooped and snatched a knife from the ground, no doubt one he had planned to use on his captive. He was fast, like a snake. Hereward saw Emeric might even have drawn blood, but Turfrida slammed her feet into the back of the witchfinder's legs. The knife tumbled from his grip, and as he sprawled on the ground, she snarled, 'Let God save you now.'

Hereward grinned at his wife's defiance. Here was the woman he had married, filled with fire despite the agonies that had near sapped the life from her. Yet when his gaze fell upon the witchfinder once more, he forgot Turfrida. Only one thought burned in his mind. 'Kneel,' he growled.

The churchman must have glimpsed some terrible thing in his captor's face, for he began to shake uncontrollably as all resistance drained from him. Falling to his knees, he bowed his head and clasped his hands together, pleading, 'Mercy.'

'I will show mercy,' Hereward replied. Emeric pushed his head back and closed his eyes with relief. 'Mercy for all those who might have suffered under your cruel hand.'

And he brought the axe down.

How long passed, he did not know. Blood hammered in his head, and his heart burned like a smith's forge. When he was done, he looked down, but he could not tell what lay before him. His tunic was stained black, his hands and arms dripping. Setting the axe aside, he fell to his knees and pulled Turfrida into an embrace. Relief flooded him.

'My husband,' she murmured. 'I knew you would save me.'

Yet in truth it was she who had saved him. Lifting her up in his arms, he whispered, 'I will never let harm come to you again. This I vow.'

He carried her to the steps, and out into the deluge. As the rain rinsed the blood off him, he thought how pale she looked. The horse was tethered where Harald Redteeth had said it would be. Within moments, they were riding through the castle gates, down the winding streets of Lincylene and out into the rain-drenched country. All was well, he told himself. All was well. His wife and unborn child were safe. He had survived to take the battle to the king, finally. And yet, as he looked towards the grey horizon, one thought seared through his mind: the beast inside him had thrown off its shackles and he was afraid it would never again be chained.

CHAPTER FIFTY-ONE

Gulls wheeled across the blue sky. Aft, in the distance, the last of the roiling storm-clouds swept away. Alric clawed his way upright with the aid of the mast and attempted to wring out the hem of his sodden tunic as he peered out over calm seas. He smiled to himself. Peace had returned to the world, and with it a sense of purpose.

Diamonds of light glinted off the waves. Ahead he could see a brown smudge of land lit by the full glory of the afternoon sun. He crossed himself and muttered a prayer of thanks. Nasi strode by. 'That was no storm,' he said with a shrug. 'It was only a sneeze.'

Yet as Alric looked around, he saw that of the vast fleet that had set sail from England, only three ships now accompanied them. The Dane followed his gaze and added, 'Perhaps more than a sneeze.'

'All lost?'

'Some will be at the bottom,' he agreed, his mouth tightening. 'The others could have been blown anywhere from Normandy to Ireland. On this journey, God has not smiled on us.' His eyes flickered towards the relic box. Aethelwold and the monks knelt around it, still at prayer. Nasi moved on, passing among his men at their oars. He muttered something in the flinty Danish tongue and they all laughed loudly in response.

As the rocky cliffs drew near, Aethelwold stumbled along the brine-slick deck, shaking from the chill breeze. His soaking tunic dripped a trail behind him. 'Sometimes I think these Danes are mad,' he whispered, watching the crew throw their heads back and sing of the sea and women and blood. 'Death almost takes them by the hand and yet they treat it as nothing. And you . . . you seem untroubled by how close we came to leaving this world behind,' the prior added suspiciously.

'God saved us. He did not smile upon the Danes. They have lost much of their treasure and have little to show for all their fighting in our land. There is a reason for all things, so we are told, and I think I now see with clearer eyes.' When he had thought he was going to die, sucked down to the cold, black depths where the serpents swam, a calm had descended on him. What if God had divined a path for him, but he had been too busy peering into the dark to see the light ahead? He believed he knew why he had been stolen from his home, why he was there heading to a strange land, why he had been carried past death when so many others had been taken. He had great work to do, and it would test him to the limit, but he would not fail.

Aethelwold looked to the three ships sailing close behind. 'What if the king is dead? Who will hear our pleas?'

'You waste your breath,' Alric replied, a little more harshly than he intended. 'Even if Sweyn Estrithson lives, he will never let you take St Oswald's arm back to Burgh. It is worth more than gold itself to a king. It is power, God's power. Wars have been fought over less. You know these things.'

Aethelwold raised his head in defiance. 'We have been charged with protecting the holy relic. God will see this thing done.'

'You sail to your deaths.' The prior flinched, but refused to meet Alric's eyes. 'Sweyn Estrithson slaughtered a church full of men at prayer because they said one word against him. These Danes knew what would happen the moment they agreed for you and your brothers to sail with them. Do you think these warriors who spend their days spilling blood for gold have hearts filled with kindness?' He watched the cliffs loom ever closer, grey slabs of rock that seemed to suck the light from the air. 'Once the king is in his hall, he will listen to your pleas, and nod, and then take your heads. When you have been burned, he will count his gold and pray over his new bone and tell the world that God now aids the Danes.'

'Then you will die too,' Aethelwold snapped.

'Whoever set me on this ship knew what my fate would be.'

'Yet you look towards the land of your fate as if it were a home-fire. You are as mad as these Danes,' the prior raged, stalking back towards his monks. Alric nodded; he had long believed that to be true.

The light was fading as the four ships reached land. Warriors splashed into the surf and hauled on oak-fibre ropes to beach their vessels on the stones. Once the drain-plugs had been knocked out of the hull to empty the water from each vessel, the men collected their shields and spears and sea-chests and gathered on the beach. Pitch-covered torches hissed into life in the gloom.

Alric watched the Danes eyeing their ship furtively as they gathered in the circles of light. Only when Nasi said to the prior, 'Fetch your box of bones,' did he understand why. They had carried the reliquary aboard with barely a second thought, just another piece of plunder. Now they were afraid to touch it.

Once three monks had clambered back into the vessel to retrieve the relic chest, Nasi led the way up a winding path to the top of the cliffs. A track wide enough for a cart plunged through dark woods. Night had fallen by the time they were wading through the thigh-high grass of rolling heathland. Soon woodsmoke drifted on the breeze and Alric could see more torches burning ahead. Behind ramparts and a palisade stood the king's royal manor: a vast hall and a stone church with many smaller halls and houses surrounding it. Inside the wall, on three sides, narrow streets lined with smaller houses and huts ran off into the dark.

As they passed through the gates, folk swarmed around to hear the news. Faces paled in the dancing light, and the mutterings of the crowd turned into anguished cries: a reaction, Alric assumed, to an account of the storm, and the possible loss of the royal ship. Within the hour scouts were galloping out to spread the word that the search for Sweyn Estrithson must begin immediately.

'Stay in the church until our king returns,' Nasi said to the English clerics as they waited, weary and cold, by the gates. 'And take your bone-chest with you. Do not wander freely. My men are quick with their spears and ask questions later.'

Inside the cold church, they lit candles and said prayers at the altar before making beds of clean straw in the tower. The brothers quickly slumped into a deep sleep after their ordeal, but Aethelwold sat in the shadows of one corner, brooding. Alric thought he had fallen asleep too, until a voice rustled out of the gloom. 'I see now that you were right. They will never let us leave with St Oswald's arm. I have sacrificed all these lives because of my foolishness.'

'We are not dead yet,' Alric replied.

'There is nothing we can do,' the prior said with a note of hopelessness. 'We cannot fight our way out. You heard the truth buried in Nasi's words. They are holding us here against our will until the king passes his judgement. We are already doomed.'

Alric knew he could not argue. Once he heard Aethelwold's snores, he muttered a quiet prayer for guidance. This was the reason why he was here, he was sure of it. The first hints of a way out had come to him aboard the ship in the aftermath of the storm, yet it was a road he was afraid to travel. Sleep would not come easily, he knew.

The next morning, he prayed until his knees ached. The Danes brought stew and bread and ale and the monks picked at the meal with little enthusiasm. Alric chewed a few mouthfuls, but the apprehension that nagged at him stole his appetite. As he watched the prior slip into a black mood that seemed to infect all the brothers, he felt the burden upon his shoulders grow heavier still.

Two more days were passed in prayer, then on the following morning Nasi slipped into the church and announced, 'We have received word. The king has survived and will be in his hall within three days.'

And then our time is done, Alric thought.

As darkness fell, he crept up to the altar while the other monks ate and raised his head to the heavens. He had no choice, he knew that now. Across the royal manor, the Danes would be swilling mead and slipping into the drunkenness that seemed to claim them every night. The time was right.

Soon after the night was torn by cries of alarm. Smoke billowed through the church and the roar of the fire echoed off the stone walls. Through the haze, Alric could see the glimmer of the flames consuming the altar and soaring up the king's luxurious tapestries towards the wooden roof.

'Help me,' he yelled through the billowing cloud as he heard the monks stumble down from their roost in the tower, coughing and choking. He lumbered around blindly, the relic chest clutched in his arms. His lungs were raw from the smoke and the heat and his eyes watered so much he could no longer see the way out. A burning roofbeam crashed only a spear's-length away, and for a moment he felt sure that he had doomed himself.

But then Aethelwold and another man staggered up through the dense smog. They grabbed his arms and dragged him towards the door. Relief swept through Alric and he murmured his thanks to the Lord. Outside in the night, the monks gathered around him, throwing their arms in the air in joy. 'We feared the holy relic lost,' the prior said, tears streaming down his cheeks. 'Praise be to God on high for guiding your hand.'

Danes flooded out of the halls, pointing in horror at the flames licking through the church roof. Nasi strode up with a face like thunder. 'What foul deed is this?' he accused, looking across the monks.

'This is God's work,' Alric proclaimed, sweeping one hand towards the blazing church.

'Blasphemy,' Aethelwold gasped.

Alric set the reliquary down and showed a face filled with wonder. 'As I prayed at the altar, God spoke to me. His light shone forth from this box, blinding me, and His voice shook the very walls.' The monk bowed his head and pressed his palms together in supplication. 'Those who stole this holy relic from its home will feel the full force of His wrath, unless this matter is ended now and the arm of the saint is returned to its resting place.'

'This is God's word?' the prior demanded, his eyes wide.

'This is His true word, I so vow.' Alric flinched as the words left his mouth. Would God strike him dead there and then?

But the moment passed. Nasi looked from Alric's face to the reliquary and, after a moment, he took one step away. In that simple movement, the monk saw his victory.

Slowly the Danes edged backwards, casting uneasy glances towards the circle of monks. Alric turned and watched the church roof collapse with a rumbling thunder that sent a whirl of sparks soaring high into the air. As the flames licked through the crumbling place of worship, he felt sickened by his lies and his blasphemy: what a crime he had committed against God. He prayed that he would be forgiven. He let his thoughts fly across the dark ocean to England and Hereward. Once, life had been simpler, torn between the dark and the light. Now, for the first time, he truly understood his friend.

CHAPTER FIFTY-TWO

The woman's screams rang out into the warm Ely night. No other sounds drifted from the open doors, no drunken singing, no arguments, no whining children. The fenland community seemed to be holding its breath, waiting, praying. On the Speaking Mound, Hereward sat looking out over the dark wetlands. As much as he tried, he could not prevent those cries reminding him of his wife's agonies in Lincylene. He wondered if he would ever forget what he had heard and seen in that place. His anger began to burn once again at the memories. Since his return that had seemed to be the only emotion he knew.

A figure strode out of the dark. Redwald nodded, smiling. That summer had browned his skin and taken some of the apple-cheeked innocence out of his features. 'How goes it?' he asked.

'The child has not come yet,' Hereward muttered.

Redwald laughed, cupping an ironic hand to his ear. 'Ah, I thought your wife was calling her husband to his chores.'

The Mercian forced a grin, but he could not ignore his fears that Turfrida's suffering had left her too weak to survive the childbirth.

Redwald seemed to see through his attempt, for he stressed, 'She is strong. Stronger than you and me, I think, sometimes.' He squatted beside his brother, adding, 'You are not the same man who left Ely for Lincylene.'

'I am the man I always was.'

'You speak in riddles.'

Hereward scowled, his worries rushing out of him. 'How could so much change in so short a time? No Danes to swell our army. No gold. No old bones. When last I was here, we seemed on the brink of bringing the king to his knees. Now . . .' He shook his head in disbelief.

'The monks say God has deserted us,' Redwald grumbled, 'that He is punishing us for the attack upon Burgh Abbey. He allowed the Danes to take St Oswald's bone and He departed with it. They pray even now for His return to Ely.'

'I have had my fill of churchmen,' Hereward simmered. He clenched his fist until his knuckles whitened. 'And you tell me Alric has abandoned us too.' Without the monk to guide him, he felt adrift. In a matter of days, the world seemed to have been turned on its head. His friend had sailed away without a single word of parting to those who had sheltered him, and his most hated enemy, Harald Redteeth, had aided his own escape. Surely this could only be another sign of the End of Days.

'You do not need Alric. You have me,' the younger man said gently as if he could read his brother's thoughts.

'And for that I give thanks, always.'

Redwald bowed his head. 'I have a confession.'

Hereward frowned. 'Speak.'

'From the moment we first met, you always treated me with kindness.'

'Why would I not? Your father had been murdered by out-laws, your mother dead of the sickness . . .'

Redwald jerked his head away, hiding his expression.

'What is wrong, brother?'

'Brother! There it is. You did not have to regard me as your

305

brother. You should have been angry when Asketil took me into his hall, and made you share all that you had.' Hereward had never seen him so anxious.

'I only did what all would have done for someone who had suffered so,' the warrior replied, resting a comforting hand on the other man's shoulder.

After a moment, Redwald reached out and unfurled his fingers to reveal a short-bladed knife with a whalebone handle carved in the shape of an angel. 'The knife your father gave you on your coming of age. You thought it lost. I . . . I stole it. You showed me only kindness and I stole your greatest prize from you.'

'I know.'

Redwald wrenched around, his eyes wide with shock.

'I have always known,' Hereward continued, his smile forgiving. 'You had nothing in your life, and no father to give you your own knife. I understand why you took the blade. And you needed it more than me.'

The younger man swallowed. 'You are too good—'

Hereward laughed and shook his head. 'This is why you are so filled with sorrow? An old knife. Memories of days long gone.'

Redwald held the knife hilt out to Hereward.

The Mercian shook his head. 'Keep it. I have no use for it.'

'It ties you to your father, and your father's father, and all those who came before.'

Hereward looked out into the night, his mood darkening. His thoughts flew back to Lincylene and the look of loathing upon Asketil's face. 'Keep it,' he repeated quietly.

Redwald released a juddering sigh. 'I have done terrible things, Hereward.'

'In these times of war, we all stray into the shadows sooner or later. You are a better man than me, Redwald. If I could not forgive you anything, I could never forgive myself.' Here was the only thing of good to come out of his blighted childhood. He would protect his brother always. 'Do you hear my words?

Think no more of these things. Look only to times ahead, not things gone.'

After a moment, Redwald allowed himself a tight smile of agreement. 'Very well.'

'Good. Then we have matters to attend to, you and I. I need a man beside me I can trust.' Hereward looked out across the rooftops of Ely. 'Turfrida was lured away from the safety of these walls. The girl Edoma took her, at the orders of Madulf, so she said.'

'Tricked by him? You think Madulf works for the king?'

Hereward said nothing.

'Why did you not seize him upon your return?'

'This matter should not be dealt with in anger. Let him think he has not been found out. When I am ready . . . when the child is born . . . I will act.' Hereward gritted his teeth. 'Every time we turn over a blade of grass, we find another of the Bastard's snakes lurking here. There must be an end to it, if I have to test every man and woman in Ely.'

'Folk are still frit. Their memory of Saba's ending is as sharp as the blade you used to take his head.'

'Not scared enough. Someone must pay for what happened to my wife, and pay with their life.'

After a moment, the younger man said in an uneasy voice, 'Let me speak freely. I fear for you, my brother, and I fear for all here in Ely. We are back where we were. The Normans are massing and soon they will attack. We cannot challenge the king with the men we have.' Steeling himself, he took a deep breath and added, 'Give up this war. Leave here. Return to Flanders, or travel further afield. Or throw yourself upon the king's mercy.'

Hereward recoiled as if burned. 'Never.'

'I would not see you dead.'

'My life means nothing. What we fight for has far greater value.'

'Then do it for your wife's sake,' Redwald said, holding out his hands. 'The Normans have shown they will stoop to any depths to strike at you. Will you see her life put at risk again?'

Hereward lowered his head. That thought had haunted him since he had left Lincylene.

'We cannot win,' the other man pressed.

'I know your thoughts are for me, and Turfrida, and all folk here in Ely. But it is too soon to think of running away with our tails between our legs.' Hereward gripped his brother's forearm. 'All is not yet lost. I have planted other seeds. We must wait a while longer to see if one bears fruit.'

Redwald's eyes narrowed. 'What seeds?'

Hereward grinned, but before he could reply, Edoma raced up the slope from the direction of his house. 'Hereward! You must come,' she called breathlessly.

The Mercian hastened down the track behind the girl. Outside the entrance to his home, women milled about, whispering to each other in the light of a torch. They clutched bone crosses to their breasts, and some held amulets, or plucked at rabbits' feet. He could smell the spices in their leather pouches, and the fresh-baked bread they held under their arms as was the tradition, ready to offer to the new mother if the birth were successful. Shadows danced across their faces, but he could read nothing in the expressions and his heart fell.

At the door, Edoma beckoned to him. She did not smile and her eyes seemed too dark. He was afraid of what he would find. After Lincylene, he realized how near death dwelled.

'Come,' Edoma urged as if she were scolding a small child.

Hereward hid his fears and stepped across the threshold. Inside, candles cast a soft golden glow across the walls. His nose wrinkled at the sweet scent of the birth-leaves smouldering in the hearth embers. Around the low bed, three grey-haired women stood with their backs to him. When he stepped forward, the old mothers turned as one, their faces as brown and wrinkled as old leather. Hereward stiffened, but then he saw their smiles as they moved away from the bed. A sigh of relief racked him.

Under a linen cloth, Turfrida lay on the bed, her face shining, her hair plastered to her head with sweat. She too was smiling.

A baby suckled at her breast. 'Welcome your son to the world, my husband. Hereward, son of Hereward.'

Barely had he time to marvel at the child before the women flooded in with their gifts of bread and salt and spices, and as the word spread through Ely, men gathered outside his house, calling his name and cheering. Kraki thrust a horn of mead into his hand, and clapped him on the back so hard he almost pitched forward. Full-throated singing rang out over the wetlands, and for a few hours he forgot his troubles.

As dawn rose, he returned to his house. Turfrida was looking down at their sleeping child, her eyes gleaming with affection. 'Here,' she murmured, holding out the child. 'Hold your son.'

He peered into the baby's face, and then shook his head. Turfrida's brow furrowed as he stepped away. How could he tell her that in the child he could only see his own past. He wanted nothing to do with it. 'I must have words with you,' he began, pacing the room.

'Such a grim tone so soon after such joy. What ails you?' she asked.

'The time is even riper now,' he replied, glancing at his son. He sat on the edge of the bed and took her hand. 'You must leave Ely.'

Turfrida's eyes widened. 'Never.'

'It is no longer safe for you here, and it is not safe for our son. We have enemies among us. And the Normans will now go to even greater lengths to harm me through you.' He bowed his head, his voice falling to a whisper. 'I do not want to be apart from you. But I have sworn to protect you and this is the only way.'

'No,' she insisted.

'It must be. I will hear no other.'

Her eyes blazed. 'Will you carry me off, kicking and screaming?'

'If I must.' He felt stung by the hurt he saw in her face, but he knew it was the right course. Sending her away now was the only way he could be sure she would be safe. She glared at him in defiance, but he held her gaze until she realized he would never change his mind.

Slowly she lowered her head and pulled her child closer to her. 'Where will I go?'

'I have spoken to Abbot Thurstan. You will be taken to Crowland Abbey. The monks there will care for you and . . .' He glanced down at the boy, '. . . our son. They will treat your wounds and your burns and help you recover from the birth. No one here will be told of your whereabouts. The Normans will never find you.'

She blinked away tears. 'For how long?'

'We will meet again when this war is done.'

'And when will that be?' she snapped. 'Months? Years? When I am old and grey, and your son is grown and does not know his own father?'

'Better that, than you dead, and our child dead,' he replied, more harshly than he intended. He softened, adding, 'You will never be out of my thoughts.'

She lowered her head and whispered, 'Nor you out of mine.'

When he embraced her, he thought she would never let him go, but he had to remain strong. For the rest of that day, he finalized the arrangements and when he was sure she was strong enough, he gave Abbot Thurstan the word. In a misty dawn, he led her out of the house and down to the gates. Turfrida wore a plain cloak and hood to hide her face, and the baby was swaddled in a thick woollen blanket in a sling across her back. Few would give her a second glance on the road north to Crowland.

At the gates, she held him tight for a long moment, and when she pulled back, she was smiling. Hereward felt proud that she had hidden her tears. Nothing could be gained by making it harder for both of them.

'Take this,' she said, pressing a polished grey-blue stone into his hand. A hole had been drilled through the amulet and a leather thong attached. 'Without Alric or me to look after you, this will keep you safe.'

He thanked her and slipped the amulet over his head. 'But Redwald will still be here,' he added with a smile. He saw a shadow cross her face and asked what was wrong.

'He is your brother and I know you hold a place for him in your heart,' she began, 'but watch him, Hereward.'

He frowned. 'What do you say? Redwald has always been loyal.'

Turfrida pressed two fingertips against the centre of his forehead. 'I will say no more. But watch him well, and keep these words locked here.' She kissed him deeply before he could ask her again, and then she walked away.

Outside the gates, a Crowland monk waited with a donkey in the still morning. Pearly mist wreathed around his feet and drifted down to the water. Turfrida turned to her husband, her face lit by the rising sun. She smiled and placed a hand upon her heart. 'Though miles lie between us, we will always be together here.'

Hereward watched her wind her way down the slope towards the causeway. His thoughts flew back to the first time he had seen her, at the battle-fair outside Bruges. He remembered the golden autumn sun and the crisp air scented with woodsmoke, and he recalled the way she held his eyes while the knights surged around them both. That moment had changed the course of his life.

The drifting mist swallowed her, and the sound of hooves ebbed away, but still he watched for long moments after, remembering.

CHAPTER FIFTY-THREE

The mob of grim-faced warriors waited in the pool of torch-light outside the hut. There, in the deep of the night, the Camp of Refuge was silent and still. That would change. Fingers flexed and fists bunched as vengeful eyes darted towards Hereward. He nodded. 'Drag him out.'

Kraki wrenched open the door and stormed inside. Three of the burliest men followed him. Startled shouts rang out. A moment later, the Viking stepped back out and grunted to his leader. The three warriors dragged Madulf into the dancing light. His eyes were bleary from sleep, his mouth wide in shock.

Sighard scrambled out behind his brother. 'Are you mad?' he protested. 'Leave him be. He has done no wrong.'

'You are coming too,' Kraki growled, stabbing a finger at the younger man.

Before the two brothers could complain further, the warriors hauled them from the camp, across the dark slopes and through Ely's gates. At the Speaking Mound, more men had gathered in a circle of amber torchlight. Near the summit, Hengist waited, a long-bladed knife at his side, like the one the butcher used for paring meat from bone. Beside him, Edoma shifted, her face near bloodless. She kneaded her hands together, her unblinking stare locked on the approaching Madulf.

Shouting and cursing, the prisoner struggled with his grim-faced captors. A fist cuffed him round the ear and he slipped into a daze. At the top of the mound, the warriors flung him down on to the grass.

Hereward climbed the slope in front of the younger man and folded his arms. 'On your knees,' he growled.

'I have done no wrong,' Madulf complained. With the back of his hand, he wiped the snot from his nose. He looked first to Sighard, and then to Edoma, holding her eyes for a long moment. In that gaze, Hereward saw a silent urging; to keep her lips sealed, perhaps. The Mercian nodded and Hengist slipped his blade against the captive's chin. Madulf stiffened, his eyes widening in terror.

'We will start with the ears,' Hereward began, his voice carrying across the assembled warriors. 'Then the nose, and then the eyes.'

'No,' Sighard cried out. He yanked free of the men who held his arms and clawed his way up the mound. 'Please,' he gasped, reaching out a pleading hand. 'My brother has been true. Why do you threaten him?'

Hereward showed him a cold face. 'My wife was pricked and stabbed and burned and taken to the edge of her life because of your brother.'

'Never.'

The Mercian turned to Edoma. 'Speak.'

'Madulf came to me, at night, with a message . . . from you . . . from Hereward . . . he said,' she stammered. The girl swallowed, looking to the man she had accused. Her brow creased in disbelief that he had betrayed her, and all of them. 'He said you had ordered me to take Turfrida out of Ely, to a place where she could be made safe before the Normans attacked.'

Madulf's mouth worked for a moment before the words croaked out. 'No . . . I . . . I never did such a thing.'

'He has a lying tongue,' Kraki sneered. 'You can see it in him. Cut him now and be done with it. I need my sleep.'

Hereward glowered at the kneeling man. 'I would have vengeance for the agonies wreaked upon my wife. And I would let the world know that such a thing will never happen again.' He stretched out his arm towards a newly erected wooden spike on the top of the mound. 'Once we are done with you, your head will have a new home. All who pass will see the fate of those who risk my wrath.'

Madulf blanched. Sighard searched his brother's face in disbelief and then fell to his knees, pressing his hands together. 'He is weak and filled with anger and jealousy. Whatever he has done, he did it without thought. Show mercy.'

Hereward ignored the pleading man and looked around the rows of faces turned towards him. 'The Normans are drawing their forces together, ready to attack us,' he stated in a loud voice. 'They think we are doomed and believe the time is right to end the days of the English. Yes, we are beaten down, but we are not broken. And we will fight to the last drop of our blood as we have fought these past seasons. Some say I should turn away from this course. Run. Hide. Save all our necks. I say to them now, my mind is made up. I would rather die on a Norman spear than live a life with a head bowed to the bastards who have stolen all we have.'

He saw the faces of the warriors were rapt. That was good. 'Any man who will not follow me should leave Ely this night,' he continued. 'There will be no shame. An honourable death is not for all. I want only brothers at my back, battle-wolves I can trust, fighters who will laugh in the face of doom.'

A ripple of assent ran through the crowd. He glanced at Madulf, remembering the pain he had seen etched into Turfrida's face. That memory felt even sharper now that she was no longer at his side.

'Once before I took a head to show what would happen to those who were unfaithful to us. That warning went unheeded,' he said, raising his voice. 'One blow, clean and swift. I showed him a kindness. I was wrong.' He grasped Madulf's hair and drew the young man's head up so he could look at his accusers. 'All has changed. No more mercy ever again, no more kindness. We can only win if we are as hard as William the Bastard, I see that now. The snakes that crawl through Ely will be found out. And any man or woman who gives comfort to our enemy will suffer such agonies they will plead to die.'

The prisoner's chest heaved with silent sobs. Hereward shook Madulf's head by the hair. 'Speak now,' the Mercian said. 'Confess. And go to God with your sins cleansed.'

Hengist drew the blade across the captive's face, past his right eye, to his ear.

Madulf sucked in a deep breath to steady himself. 'Do it, then,' he said in a clear voice. A calm seemed to descend on him. 'My soul is clean. I will not confess to a crime I did not do.'

Hereward squatted and peered into the young man's eyes. After a moment, the Mercian smiled. He looked to Guthrinc at the front of the crowd, who grinned and nodded, his eyes sparkling. 'You are a bastard, but you know how to draw the truth out of a man,' Guthrinc said.

Madulf gaped, looking from one to the other.

'Set him free,' Hereward said, rising. 'He speaks truly.' As Sighard wrapped his arms around his brother, the Mercian saw the confusion in the faces of his men. One day they would understand. Fear was the greatest weapon they had: William the Bastard understood that more than most. Sometimes it cut shallow, and sometimes the wounds ran deep, but men always responded with the truth in their nature.

'If young Madulf tells the truth,' Kraki yelled, 'then the girl must have lied.' He spun around, but Edoma was nowhere to be seen.

'Find her,' Hereward ordered.

'Edoma?' Sighard gasped in disbelief.

'The Normans are clever,' the Mercian replied, peering into the dark for the missing woman. 'They chose someone who could move through the camp without drawing eyes. And one

315

who could play lovesick fools like you two to get the information she needed.'

'Not just us,' Madulf muttered. He cast a sheepish look at his brother. 'She visited another's house in the night, perhaps more than one.'

Not long after, Guthrinc strode up. 'Edoma has fled Ely. The guards let her through the gate moments ago.'

'Take some men. Find her if you can,' the Mercian commanded. 'I would see her pay for what she did.'

Hereward watched Guthrinc lead a knot of warriors into the night, knowing the chance was slim that they would find the woman in the dark. Soon she would be back among the Normans, but her days of revealing the English plans would be over. One small mercy. 'Double the men upon the walls,' he shouted to Kraki. 'Now the king has lost his eyes and ears here in Ely, he may be driven to strike sooner. We must be ready to fight for our lives.'

CHAPTER FIFTY-FOUR

The wooden cup shattered against the stone wall. A bear-like shadow loomed over the shards as the king stalked around his torchlit hall at the palace in Wincestre. His eyes burned and his face was contorted with rage. 'Still the rising in the east has not been put down?' he bellowed, clenching his fists. 'Do I employ children, or simple-minded fools?'

Balthar the Fox stiffened as he peered around the edge of the screen near the door. William was as unpredictable as a cornered beast when in the grip of his temper. He could see the blood drain from the faces of the king's regents, William fitz Osbern and Bishop Odo. Both of them knew well the outcome of his black moods from the long years of his brutal rule in Normandy.

'Must I now leave Ely a wasteland like the north?' the monarch roared. 'Soon there will be no England left to rule.' A pitcher of wine flew across the hall.

Tall and thin, Odo of Bayeux looked like a hawk with his sharp nose and low brow. He folded his hands behind him, trying to appear unmoved. 'Our scouts say they do not have the men to mount any attack—'

'Yet,' the king snapped. 'How soon before some wounded

earl takes shelter beneath their banner?' William came to a halt by the hearth and peered into the flames. 'This must end now,' he continued in a low voice. 'This night. The bastards in the east are the last of the English standing against me. We shall not give them the chance to build their army, and then Ivo the Butcher may yet find the strength to crush them.'

'What would you have us do?' fitz Osbern enquired. He was a head shorter than Odo and broader, with a near-permanent scowl.

'Move slowly. We want all here to believe that we and the English are one,' William replied, one foot resting on the stones around the hearth. 'But we have kept too many serpents here in Wincestre where we can watch over them. No more. Our plans creep out before our own men know them. Sometimes I wonder if any English here can be trusted.'

Balthar felt a chill. Could the king suspect him?

William turned to his two trusted counsellors, his fury simmering. 'By dawn, those sly dogs Edwin and Morcar must be where they can do no harm. And seek out any others you believe are not loyal to this crown. I would be done with all this plotting.'

Without waiting to hear any more, Balthar slipped out. His heart was hammering and sweat slicked his brow. He raced through the deserted palace, his thoughts shifting as fast as his feet. He could not be sure the king's men would come for him, or for Godrun, but he had to presume the worst. When his head perched on a spike at the town gates, it would be too late to act.

Down the dark back-ways he stumbled until he reached Godrun's dwelling. She cried out in shock when he burst in. 'What is wrong?' she gasped.

'The king is ready to move against his enemies this night, real or imagined. We must be away.' He rushed around the hut, grabbing what few possessions she had.

She caught his arm. 'He comes for us?'

'We can take no chances. Edwin and Morcar are doomed, of that I am certain.'

318

'Then this is your chance,' she said, her voice hardening with defiance. 'Go to them. Tell them to flee, with their men. Join the uprising—'

'Are you mad?' he snapped. 'If we delay, we too could be doomed.' He felt stung by the disappointment he saw in her eyes and he calmed himself. 'You are right,' he sighed. 'My wits were addled for a moment. I will find the brothers now and tell them what must be done.' She smiled and that pleased him. 'Wait here until my return. We must be away from the palace before dawn.'

'Your wife . . .'

He shook his head. 'There is no time. She will be well.' He pushed aside the pang he felt at abandoning his sons, but God willing he would see them again soon. 'Here,' he said, holding out the short-bladed knife his father had given him. 'Keep this about you. If anyone comes for you, protect yourself.'

'I do not know how,' she said, unable to take her eyes off the blade.

'One stab. Like this. In the belly.' He thrust the air with the knife. 'Then run. No one will answer their cries here. But if the Lord watches over us, you shall not need to use it. I will be back with you in no time, and then . . .' He let the words hang for a moment and then ended the sentence with a hopeful smile. He felt surprised at how excited he felt. Despite the danger, here was the chance of a new life. He wondered where they would go. To Ely, or into the west? He kissed her once and then hurried out into the night.

His anger at the king burned harder with every step he ran, through the streets back to the palace. William's words haunted him. *Soon there will be no England left to rule.* How could he ever have been so deluded?

At the hall the Mercian brothers shared, he pushed his way inside without announcing his presence. Edwin and Morcar jumped up from a bench, overturning mead-cups. On edge, they both went for their swords. Balthar held up his hands to

319

calm them. 'You must flee,' he hissed. 'The king is coming for you this night.'

They did not question him, as he knew would be the case. Too long had they lived with the certainty that one day the wind would change. 'We owe you for this, Fox,' Edwin said as he levered up three boards with his knife. From the dark space beneath, he pulled a chest, no doubt containing his valuables. Morcar disappeared into the shadows to collect his own possessions. 'You may not be the king's whore that we all thought you were.'

Balthar flushed. He deserved no less, he supposed. But was that really how he was seen? 'Odo and fitz Osbern will be here before dawn with their men. If they find you gone, they will scour the town for you. I can show you a way out of Wincestre.'

Edwin grinned and called to his brother, 'We have our own Fox now.' He turned back to Balthar. 'What do you want? Gold?'

'I want only that you take your men to Ely and join the uprising. With your aid, the crown can be claimed for a king who does not see the English like rats in the grain.'

Edwin threw on his cloak, grunting, 'We have had our fill of risking our necks. With gold aplenty and an army to keep us safe, we can seek a place to hide where William will never find us.'

Morcar staggered back into the light, a small chest gripped under his left arm and a heavily laden sack dragging behind him. 'Let us not be hasty, brother. Ely may be the safest haven of all.'

'I do not have the stomach for battle,' Edwin said.

'Not even if this new king were a Mercian?' Morcar grinned. 'A man who could bring all the English together as one.'

'This is not the time for such talk, brother,' Edwin said, clutching the chest to him.

The Fox hurried to the door and peered out. Once he was sure they would not be seen, he beckoned for the brothers to follow and they hastened out. Across the palace, the sound of running feet echoed. The guards were already being called to take the regents' orders. Torches sizzled into life on the other side of the yard. His heart thundering, Balthar led the Mercians through the dark along the perimeter fence. While the earls collected two horses from the stables, he ran to the entrance to the palace grounds. When he had sent the guard to fitz Osbern, he pulled open the gate. There would be no going back now, he knew.

Once the Mercians had led their steeds through, he eased the gate shut and with silent tread picked a winding path through the dark back-ways. At the western wall, the Ridgate stood unguarded. Balthar nodded, pleased with himself. This gate was ancient and rarely used, only large enough to admit a single rider. The three men lifted the oak bar and swung it open. The gibbous moon lit the still countryside. 'Find it in you to join the fighters in Ely,' he urged as the two earls mounted their horses. 'You have it within your hands to change the course of things.'

'We will ride towards the fens once we have met with our men,' Edwin said with a nod. 'But then we will do what we do.' And with that, the two brothers rode out of the gate and into the night.

He had done what he could. Balthar ran back through the quiet streets, his fear that he had taken too long mounting by the moment. At Godrun's house, he wrenched open the door and dashed inside. His heart leapt when he saw she was still there and well.

'Is it done?' she asked hopefully.

He nodded, leaning back against the closed door as he sucked in deep breaths to calm his thundering heart. 'Edwin and Morcar have gone in search of their men. They ride towards the fens, but as yet they have not decided their true course.'

Godrun closed her eyes and clasped her hands together as if in prayer. 'Then this torment is finally over.'

'Not until we are beyond Wincestre's walls,' he cautioned. 'Let us hurry.' In the corners of her eyes, tears glistened in the firelight and he saw her hands trembling. He felt guilt at how he had neglected her. Even he was afraid. How scared must this young girl be. 'Come,' he said gently. 'All will be well. A new life awaits us, together.' He held his arms wide and she rushed into his embrace.

Pain seared through his stomach. With an agonized cry, he staggered back. Shaking, Godrun gripped his knife in her little hand. Blood dripped from the blade. As he looked down, she lunged again and again, her face contorted with hate.

'Why?' he stammered, falling back against the wall. He slid down to the floor in a heap, convulsing in shock. His life-blood pumped through his fingers and puddled around him.

Godrun loomed over him, blinking away tears, not of fear but fury. 'Every time you pawed my skin it was all I could do not to empty my stomach,' she snarled.

Balthar gaped stupidly. Her words made no sense to him. He reached out one sticky hand and breathed, 'Our love—'

She spat at him. 'While good English men and women suffered, you grew fat eating at the king's table. You traded their lives for comfort.' She shook with revulsion and that wounded him more deeply than the knife she wielded. 'All you have you built upon the bones of your own. You deserve to die.'

Hot tears streamed down his cheeks. 'I learned my lesson. I tried to help—'

'Too late.'

As she turned her back on him to collect the small bag filled with her meagre possessions, he reeled as the truth finally broke through his resistance. 'You never loved me,' he croaked, still barely able to believe it. 'All these long months, you led me along to learn what you could . . . to help the English fighters . . . All the kisses, all the words of love . . .'

'The Fox,' she sneered as reached the door. 'So cunning he could never see what was under his own nose.'

He blinked away his tears, and when his eyes cleared she was gone. Even then, his heart still ached for her. Pain racked him as he sensed his life's blood draining through his fingers, but his

322

thoughts were of all he had lost through his own failings, and all that had been stolen from him. How foolish he had been, how weak. Bowing his head, he began to pray, his last hope for redemption.

The hut began to darken.

CHAPTER FIFTY-FIVE

1 October 1070

The sound of many voices raised in song shattered the still of the fenland dawn. At the gates of Ely, the guards stood on the high walkway and peered into the pearly mist swathing the meres and marshes. The rising sun cast a rosy hue over the drifting clouds.

Still bleary-eyed, Hereward shook his head to dispel the last of his dream and clawed his way out of his bed. Pushing past the watchman who had woken him, he strode down the leaf-strewn track towards the gates. All around him, warriors raced to fetch their spears and shields from beneath their beds. He saw their brows lined with apprehension, the hollow look in their eyes. Doomsday was coming, or so they thought.

But not this day. He had heard the Normans singing as they marched into battle and it was a sound like iron upon stone. These voices chimed like solstice bells. Hauling himself up the ladder to the walkway, he leaned on the palisade and stared into the drifting white clouds. Beside him, the guards peered over the rims of their shields, ready for a flight of arrows to whip out of the mist.

Closer the singing came, and as it neared he realized the words were not English, or Norman, but the old Roman tongue. Shapes materialized in the white haze. The guards' knuckles whitened on their spears. And then the mist unfolded, like a cloth of linen being drawn back, and a column of men walked out into the dawn light.

Monks, Hereward thought, puzzled, *singing to the glory of God*. As they emerged fully into the light, he saw that four churchmen carried a frame made from ash branches lashed together. On it rested a familiar chest, the relic box containing the arm of St Oswald. When he recognized Aethelwold striding among the clerics, hands pressed together in prayer, he realized these were the monks of Burgh Abbey.

The guards on either side of him gaped at the spectacle. Then one of them pointed to a figure walking apart from the other clerics. It was Alric, grinning as if he had played the greatest trick of all. Hereward flung himself down the ladder and ran out through the gates.

Alric beamed, throwing his arms wide, and they embraced for a long moment. 'I thought you dead,' Hereward said, adding with a feigned scowl, 'or worse: that you had abandoned us.'

'There was a time when I too thought myself dead,' the monk replied. 'But not high seas nor Danish spears nor fire could keep me down.'

'Heaven was not ready for your complaining, more like.'

Alric stepped back and swept an arm towards the relic box. 'And see, I have brought you a prize. God smiles upon the English once more.'

'That is good,' Hereward said. Still he felt afraid to hope that they were climbing out of the pit of misfortune that had claimed them. 'Now if only you had brought me an army too.'

Alric nodded, his face darkening. 'We must speak. On our long trek from the coast, we passed many Norman scouts and fresh camps. I think the Butcher is moving his army into place ready to attack Ely.'

'He has been preparing for this battle since you left,' the

Mercian replied. 'He takes his time. It seems he wants to leave nothing to chance. I would stake good coin that he is afraid any failure will bring the king's wrath upon his head.'

'The delay may be his undoing,' Alric said hopefully. He watched the singing monks trail through the gates. 'It may give you space to build your army.'

Hereward grimaced. New men were arriving at Ely by the day, but still not enough to swell the numbers to a level sufficient to defeat the size of army that the Butcher was massing. 'As the days pass, I worry that more English are beginning to accept the Norman rule,' he said. 'They hunger for peace after so many years of war and suffering. One day we may be seen as the enemy loose in this land.'

'Then we must make plans to turn this war around,' the monk said.

Hereward frowned. 'You seem changed. What happened out there across the whale road?'

'I will tell you all. But only when my belly is full,' Alric laughed, clapping an arm around his friend's shoulders. His humour faded and he narrowed his eyes, looking around to be sure he would not be overheard. 'I did not choose to leave,' he whispered. When he saw his friend's surprise, he added, 'Aye, I thought you would not know the truth. How could you? My skull was all but dashed in and the Danes were paid good coin to spirit me away. Paid,' he continued, looking round once more, 'by someone here in Ely.'

Hereward grinned. 'Trouble yourself about this no longer. We have already driven out the king's eyes and ears and now they flee for their life from the hard judgement of the English.'

Alric sighed with relief. 'I feared that all your throats would have been slit in the night. But you are in good spirits. Tell me . . . Turfrida?' he ventured with a note of hesitancy.

Before the Mercian could reply, a guard hailed him from the gate, where stood one of the scouts who had been out in the wetlands searching for Edoma, his face flushed from his haste.

'Your eel stew will have to wait, Alric,' Hereward muttered, already turning in response.

'You found her?' he asked as he strode up to the two men.

The scout shook his head. 'Not her. Another. Four Norman knights hunt a girl by Lugh's Bog, too many for me to help her on my own.' He hesitated, his brow knitting. 'She looked like Dunnere's daughter.'

Hereward stiffened. 'Fetch Redwald, Guthrinc and Hengist,' he commanded, 'with spears and shields in hand.'

As the scout raced off, Alric held out his hands in disbelief. 'Dunnere's daughter? It cannot be. No word for more than a year and she turns up now?' Blood drained from his face. 'Unless she is a ghost . . . and this is yet another portent of the End-Times.'

The Mercian gave nothing away, but if it was Dunnere's daughter, there was hope. As the other warriors raced down the track with the scout, he dashed from the gate. Alric followed. They hurried down the slope, plunging into the sea of white mist. Their rasping breath grew muffled, the world around them deadened.

Hereward led his men across the causeway and then turned north. The secret paths appeared out of the reeds and willows and he chose the fastest route, no matter how dangerous. Four knights would show little mercy to any woman travelling on her own, let alone one as comely as Dunnere's daughter.

'Why such haste for this woman?' Redwald hissed as they ran.

'Because she could save all our lives,' Hereward replied.

When they reached the edge of Lugh's Bog, they slowed, straining their ears to hear any sound. Few ventured here. The marsh reeked of rot and occasionally foul-smelling bubbles burst as if something moved just beneath the surface. Thick walls of tangled willow, sedge and reed clustered hard on every side.

Hereward raised his arm to bring the others to a halt. Dim voices rumbled through the mist, call and response tinged with the excitement of boys at play. He swept his arm left and right. Hengist crept one way, Guthrinc and Redwald the other. Drawing his sword, he prowled forward with Alric at his heel. Drifting white clouds folded around them.

Laughter echoed. Another cry. The Mercian grimaced as he cocked his head, trying to discern the direction of those smothered sounds.

Crashing erupted in the willows just ahead. Looking over his shoulder and laughing, a Norman knight burst out of the mist. Hereward leapt back in surprise, betrayed by the distorted echoes. Just as shocked, the knight cried out as he turned his head. A querying call in his own tongue answered from further along the edge. Realizing they had been discovered, Hereward roared like a bear and swung his blade. The knight tried to duck, but he was wrong-footed in the marshy ground. He half-stumbled and the sword sliced into the side of his neck. Clutching at the spurting wound, he fell, but his screams tore through the haze. They died in his throat as Hereward hacked down, near-severing the head. He loped on before the man's gurgles had faded away.

Footsteps raced all around, whether friend or foe Hereward did not know. Distorted cracks and rustles faded in and out. Another gurgling cry reached his ears, choked short: a Norman he was sure. A few moments later he pushed past a curtain of willow branches to find Guthrinc with one foot on a fallen warrior's chest, trying to wrench his spear from the body.

Hereward prowled on, searching through the mist. From the depths of a reed-bed, a knight leapt with a cry. His blade swung down. The Mercian threw himself to one side and the sword narrowly whipped past him. His battle-honed arm moved faster than his thoughts and he thrust Brainbiter into his foe's chest before the Norman could recover. The knight tumbled backwards into the bog, trailing a crimson arc. In a flurry of sticky bubbles, he slipped below the surface and was gone.

One left, he thought with grim satisfaction. But the Normans were a distraction. The girl was the only thing that mattered.

He ignored his concerns that there had been no sight nor sound of her and pushed on through the trees. The mist unfolded to reveal Alric, beckoning. He loped after the monk to a clearing where Hengist was sitting on the final body, wiping clean the tip of his spear in the sedge. The Mercian whistled and Redwald and Guthrinc appeared soundlessly. 'Find Dunnere's daughter, if she is still here,' Hereward ordered.

They searched along the edge of the marsh, calling in clear English voices. After a while, the mist began to clear and shafts of warm autumn sun punched through the branches. As they followed the trail of crushed reeds and broken branches made by the Norman knights, Hereward heard a woman's hesitant voice hail from the western end of the bog.

On the edge of the reeking mire, he found her crawling out from a hiding place among the tangled trunks and thick sedge. Her dress was filthy with the mud of the road, her fair hair lank and greasy and tied back with a piece of torn cloth. She looked up at him with a face like thunder, and he thought how changed she was in appearance; her eyes seemed older than her years by far. Her time in Wincestre had taken a toll. Behind him, the other men ground to a halt, marvelling at the woman who had disappeared from Ely in such mysterious circumstances.

'Godrun. You are well?' he said, ignoring her black expression. He made to embrace her, but she took a step back.

'Well?' she repeated, her eyes cold. 'Yes, I am well. Those four dogs did not harm me, if that is what you mean.'

Hereward nodded, relieved. How long he had waited and hoped for this moment. Unable to contain himself, he asked, 'Tell me your news.'

'I have done my work well,' Godrun began in a flat voice. She snagged her fingers through her hair, pulling out a dry leaf. 'No one could have done it better.'

'I had no doubts. That is why I chose you to go to Wincestre. All men are children, and fools too. They will let women lead them by the nose, as their mothers did when they were young.'

'What did you see in me, Hereward? Why did you choose *me*?' she demanded, her eyes blazing.

'Tell me,' he repeated. He pushed aside his guilt. The task he had set her was always going to be hard, he had known that from the moment he asked. But too much had been at stake and he knew that she, if any, could get him the result he needed.

She choked off her reply and glared for a moment. When she spoke her voice was strained. 'The earls Edwin and Morcar have left Wincestre. They ride back to Mercia to meet with their armies. They will oppose the king.'

'And they will join our fight?' he pressed, almost grabbing her shoulders.

'They are ripe for the plucking,' she replied flatly.

'How long has this plan been birthing?' Redwald asked incredulously.

'I told you, brother, I sow my seeds and wait to see what sprouts,' Hereward replied without turning round. He held Godrun's eyes, seeing the hurt in them.

'I hate you,' she spat, finally losing her control. Tears of anger flecked her eyes and her cheeks burned. 'The things you made me do—' The words died in her throat and she looked away, her hand flying to her mouth.

'We are all in your debt,' he began gently.

She held up a hand to silence him. 'Do not give me easy words of comfort,' she said with contempt. 'I am broken now. I cannot go back to my father and the life I once had. I have no good summers ahead of me.' She swallowed, choking back tears. 'I would end my days if I could.'

Nothing he could say would ease her pain, he knew that. Her scars ran too deep. 'Then I will speak plainly,' he said, holding out one hand. 'This war demands terrible things of all of us. We look into the dark and see no light. We look into our hearts and do not recognize the things we find there. It makes us hard. But we carry this burden so others do not have to. Your father. Your brothers. All in Ely.' He paused, watching her eyes brim. He remembered all the women he had seen suffer, and wished he could have spared her this. But he could not. 'Your sacrifice may well have saved them all.'

With gleaming eyes, she held his gaze for a long moment. Though he knew she understood his meaning, he could see she had not forgiven him. He felt stung by that look. But that was his burden. When she walked off ahead, he turned to Alric and whispered, 'Go with her. Offer her what comfort you can. But ask her not what she endured in Wincestre.'

Once the monk and Godrun had disappeared among the willows, Hereward turned to his warriors. 'Godrun has bought us hope,' he said, his voice hardening with defiance, 'and perhaps more than that . . . an army that can cut right through the bastard Normans. Our days to come are in our hands once more.'

CHAPTER FIFTY-SIX

Angry voices jolted the still of the greenwood. Black wings thundered up from the dense canopy as roosting crows shrieked their warnings at the two arguing men. In slanting shafts of late-afternoon sunlight, a throng of warriors watched their leaders confront each other. These were huscarls, mail-clad and fierce, and seasoned spearmen who had fought the brutal campaigns in the north. On their arms, gouged and splintered shields told the story of bloody battles won and lost. Behind them, their snorting horses rested after the long ride from the plain to the west of Wincestre.

Hengist crawled on his belly along the broad branch to get a better view. He flexed his legs to ease the aches from his own hard ride from the north-east, here to the edge of the fenlands. His throat was dry and his sweat had soaked through his tunic, but not for a moment could he have slowed his pace. Resting on the creaking branch, he looked down on the earls Edwin and Morcar, once rulers of great power, now mere men. How that loss must sting them, he thought. They paced around each other like bad-tempered dogs, snapping. Their drawn faces spoke of worry and doubt.

Hengist nodded as he scrutinized the two earls. Godrun had

332

said they were ripe to become allies of the Devil's Army and he could see that was true. They had a hunted, friendless look about them. Yet he could not forget Hereward's warning. They were hard men, these Mercians, and quick to use their swords at the slightest suspicion. Approach them with care, his leader had cautioned. As the discordant voices reached his ears, he knew this was not the time. Once they had calmed, he would step out, arms outstretched to show he carried no weapons. And then he would deliver Hereward's message. He looked across their force waiting among the trees and saw the forest of spears. He grinned. With these men swelling their army, the Norman bastards would truly have a fight on their hands.

He took a deep breath, still feeling the strain of the last two days. He had begun to fear he would never find this wandering army in the wild countryside, even with the information Godrun had given him. But he was here now, and he would not let his battle-brothers down. No one would call him mad again.

'Our best hope lies in the fens,' he heard Morcar insist. 'Only among the bogs and waters and trees will we be able to hide from the king's wrath.'

Edwin waved a dismissive hand towards his brother. In that one gesture, Hengist saw where the power lay between them. 'You are a fool if you think William the Bastard will ever let us alone,' Edwin said. 'He will not rest until all those who might stand against him have been crushed. He knows how to keep the peace in an unruly land and he knows how to keep the crown. With this.' He hammered one leather-gauntleted fist into his palm.

'What say you then? Run, like dogs?'

'And keep our heads upon our shoulders. We have gold enough to live like kings.'

Morcar ran one hand through his thinning hair, his face creasing with the strain. 'And go where? We have few friends across the whale road.'

Edwin softened his voice to try to win over his brother. 'We have friends in the north. Malcolm, King of the Scots.'

The smaller man turned away with a furious shake of his head. 'And travel across a land now under the grip of the Normans? The risk is too great.' From his hiding place, Hengist saw him snatch a suspicious look at the waiting men before he leaned in to whisper to his brother. Trust was thin on the ground even there, and rightly so. If William the Bastard suspected Edwin and Morcar could become a threat, he would have ensured at least some of their men were in his pay.

Edwin seemed to ignore his brother's words. He grimaced and fluttered his hand again. Walking back towards the warriors, he said, 'Enough. I have the gold and I will ride north. Join me or take your men and follow your own path. And on your own head be it.'

Hengist saw Morcar's cheeks flush. The man who had once ruled Northumbria had lost face in front of his fighting men and he was not taking it well. 'Go, then,' he snarled. 'This parting of the ways has been a long time coming. You will regret your choice, brother.' He raised his arm and flicked it towards the east. As he turned towards his horse, near-half of the army found their own mounts. Within moments, Morcar's horde was riding away without a backward glance.

Hengist looked from one war-band to the other with dismay. Hereward had not prepared him for this possibility. He could not carry his master's message to both camps; which one should he choose?

Afraid that success was slipping through his fingers, he scrambled backwards along the branch. Swinging himself down, he dropped on to the forest floor like a cat. The rumble of hoofbeats filled the air and the ground shook as Edwin's men departed. Hengist raced along the hidden track to the south, regretting how far away he had tethered his horse.

By the time he reached the beast, his mind was made up. He climbed on to his ride's bare back and urged his mount towards the north. Morcar might lose himself in the wilderness, but at least the former earl would remain close to home. If there were a chance to bring Edwin and his army to Ely, it had to be seized now.

Branches tore at his hair and lashed his face. Lying low across his horse's neck, he rode as fast as he could along the narrow track. The sun was slipping towards the horizon, the shadows lengthening among the trees and the air growing sharper. Night was coming too fast. He pushed his steed on.

As he weighed the best way to approach Edwin without risking the edge of the earl's blade, he heard shouts and cries and the clash of iron upon iron from ahead. He pulled up his horse and cocked his head, listening. Could Morcar have turned his men around and now be fighting his brother for his honour?

He jumped off his horse and tied it to a tree. It would not be good to be caught up in the battle. As he crept forward to get a better look, he heard the thunder of hooves rushing towards him from the battle ahead. With his back pressed against a broad oak, he hid as the riders raced by. 'To Morcar,' one of them called.

Hengist frowned, puzzled. Who then fought Edwin? He loped through the trees until the storm of fighting seemed to rage all around him. Peering from behind a lightning-blasted ash tree, he saw bodies littering the forest floor. Everywhere was confusion. Riderless horses bolted. Warriors ran, for their lives, or to defend Edwin. Swords flashed in shafts of sunlight. Shields cracked and spears stabbed. And then he glimpsed the familiar hauberks and helms of the Normans. The king's men were carving their way through the wandering army.

Edwin had been betrayed by his own men, that could be the only answer. Morcar had been right. The Normans would not have been able to find the army by chance. Hengist cursed under his breath. There was nothing he could do here now. He had to hope that he could find Morcar's trail to the north-east.

But as he turned to creep back towards his horse, he heard the pounding of feet draw near. He crouched behind a dense tangle of bramble heavy with berry. Three men came running

335

by, casting desperate glances over their shoulders. One of them, he saw, was Edwin.

As the men scrambled over snaking roots, Hengist heard the whistle of an arrow. The shaft slammed into the fleeing Edwin's chest and he fell to one side, dead.

In shock, Hengist threw himself back against the ash tree. The arrow had not come from the direction of the battle.

For a while, nothing moved. Then, after several taut breaths, a shape separated from the pooling shadows. He squinted, troubled by the silhouette he saw. As the figure slipped away through a patch of late sunlight, Hengist glimpsed a sight that left him sick to his stomach. The man who had killed Edwin and perhaps had ended the last hope of the English was Hereward's own brother, Redwald.

CHAPTER FIFTY-SEVEN

The candle guttered on the shelf. Shadows swirled across the hut as the woman raised her head from her straw mattress and looked around. 'Who is there?' Turfrida asked, her eyelids heavy. She squinted, trying to pierce the dark around the door. Only a few hot coals glowed in the hearth, enough to take the autumnal chill out of the air. She had been dozing fitfully. Sleep came rarely since she had left Hereward behind for Crowland. Too many dreams plagued her, and her child seemed just as troubled, waking and crying far too often during the dark hours. Did it sense something amiss, she wondered, glancing towards the heap of swaddling clothes in the sleeping-basket? For children were wise. They still heard the whispers of the *vættir* and saw things no grown man or woman saw.

Turfrida pressed herself up on her elbows, her eyes clearing. She shuddered. A shape darker than the shadows around her was watching her from the door. 'Night-walker or man, step forward and reveal yourself,' she hissed, her hand flying to the talisman on the leather thong around her neck.

After a moment's hesitation, Redwald stepped forward into the wavering light. Turfrida felt a chill. His face was impassive, but she saw a gulf between the apple-cheeked, innocent features

337

and the cold, dead stare that had always disturbed her. How Hereward never recognized what lay in those eyes had always amazed her. Or perhaps Redwald only revealed it to women.

He began, 'Hereward sent me—'

'Save your lies. I can see into your heart.' He flinched at that.

'More witchery?' He crossed the room and warmed his hands at the hearth. 'It is cold out tonight.'

Turfrida climbed from her bed and pulled on a cloak. Gooseflesh prickled the skin of her forearms, and not from the cold. 'What do you want?' she demanded.

'You never liked me,' he said, rubbing his hands together.

'And you never liked it that I had Hereward's ear,' she snapped, tugging the cloak tighter around her.

'How high he could have risen if only I had guided him. How low he now will fall.'

'There must be some gain here for you,' she said coldly, ignoring the unsettling tone she heard in his words.

'Gain?' he repeated, pursing his lips. 'It is too late now for gain.'

'How did you find me?'

'Hereward told me, in the end. He trusts me.'

She screwed up her nose. 'I have never known a man so sly, spinning half-lies and setting friend against friend with only a few words, all to your own end. You weave your web and wait to see what flies fall into it.'

He shrugged. 'Yet you said nothing.'

'You are Hereward's brother. He loves you. It was not for me to hurt him with sharp words.' She paused. 'He will find out soon enough, I always knew that.'

He eyed the baby's basket and sighed. 'Once I thought there was hope that Hereward could lead the English to victory, and that we could return to the world we all knew. I was taken in by a king's thegn. I lived among riches. I never went hungry. And I rose to stand beside the highest in the land.' His voice cracked with passion. She watched him clench his fist, his hand shaking. But then the fire seemed to drain out of him and he hung his head, reflecting, she thought, on what might have been. 'But you, and that monk, have led my brother in circles and now that chance of victory has passed,' he continued, his voice low. 'The strength of the Normans grows by the day, and we grow weaker. When they attack, it will be as if a storm of spears falls upon us. We could still throw ourselves upon the king's mercy, keep our heads upon our shoulders and live to claw some kind of joy out of this miserable life. But, no, Hereward will never have that. He would rather we fight until the last. And die. For what? The English are already turning to the new king. We will be forgotten before the flesh has even rotted from our bones, and all will have been for naught.'

Turfrida snorted with contemptuous laughter. 'Only one thing will stop my husband winning this war. Weak men, like you. Men who whine like frightened children and run crying at the first sign of hardship,' she spat. 'This war will be lost by men who betray the strong and good-hearted for their own gain. If the English stand together as battle-brothers, William the Bastard's days are done.'

When he looked at her, she thought she saw sadness in his eyes. At that moment he seemed little more than a lost boy. 'It is too late for that,' he said in a quiet voice. 'We must do what we can to save ourselves.'

'I know why you have come here,' she said gently, stepping closer to the hearth. 'You have failed to turn my husband away from his plans for war, and so you would have me persuade him. I cannot, Redwald.'

He laughed quietly to himself. 'I know you would never do that. You and Hereward are too much alike. No, my only hope is to throw in my lot with the Normans. King William needs clever Englishmen, I hear, and I will rise to the top once more. That is my destiny. That has always been my destiny.'

Turfrida eyed him, scarcely able to believe what she had heard. Had their struggles driven him mad, like poor Hengist? But then she realized what lay behind those words and she felt a chill. She glanced towards the door and regretted it immediately.

In a casual manner, Redwald stepped back a few paces so he was between her and her path to escape. 'You think to make of me an offering to the Normans,' she said, her face hardening.

He shook his head. 'How little you know me.' Before she could reply, he lunged. Shock gripped her at his speed. But then she felt a sharp pain in her belly and when she looked down a dark stain was spreading across her white linen sleeping-dress. Redwald slowly drew his arm back and she glimpsed the short-bladed knife, sticky with blood. Staggering, she clutched at her stomach and felt the hot essence bubble up between her fingers.

'What have you done?' she gasped.

'What I should have done long ago.'

He pushed past her and she fell upon the bed, her head spinning. When she glanced back, she saw him looming over the child's sleeping-basket. His expression remained emotionless as he stabbed the blade down into the tight bundle of swaddling clothes, then again, and again.

Turfrida smiled despite her pain.

His face flushed as he realized the truth. Snatching back the heap of cloth, he saw the sleeping place was empty. In sudden rage he hurled the basket across the hut. Turfrida closed her eyes, relief washing through her. The child would be safe with the wise woman who had taken him for the night to ease her burden. The son would still be reunited with the father.

'You will not escape justice for what you have done,' she wheezed. 'My husband will hunt you down and slaughter you, brother or not.'

Redwald wiped the blade on the hem of her sleeping-dress. 'There will be no hiding any more. A monk saw me when I slipped through the gate. I would not make an enemy of Hereward, but he must cut his way through an army of Normans if he wishes to reach me.'

The candlelight seemed to glow brighter and for a moment she was sure Hereward was standing there, watching her. Regret flooded her. Never again would she see her husband or her son. She felt a deep sadness, for them, not her, for they would have to live out their days in the shadow of this loss. 'Why have you killed me?' Her words seemed to come from another.

'So the Normans will know I am true.' He turned her on to her back and leaned over her so that his face filled her whole vision. She saw no more emotion there than in a butcher who had killed a pig. Those eyes. Black and dead.

'How will they know you have truly done this thing?' she gasped.

He smiled.

CHAPTER FIFTY-EIGHT

Fog shrouded the field of the dead beside the abbey. Under its grey cover, four grieving men hunched in silence around a yawning grave. Heads bowed, the cloaked and huddled mourners listened to the solemn intonation of Crowland's abbot drifting out across the grassy mounds of ancient burials. No bird called. No breeze moaned through the sombre yews. So still was it, they could have been alone in all the world. Deep in the dark hole, bound tightly in a white linen shroud, Turfrida was being laid to rest.

Alric screwed up his eyes. How that pathetic bundle tormented him so. The account of what the monks had found in her hut the night of her death tramped through his mind until he felt he would never be rid of it. Yet when he looked up, he encountered another sight worse by far. Hereward's face appeared to be graven in stone. His mouth was a black slash, his eyes hollow and haunted. All night and day, Alric had prayed for his friend, afraid of what this terrible crime would do to him. But Hereward's grief had been sealed deep inside him, and though Alric had tried to find words of comfort, none of them would reach the foot of that black chasm.

As the abbot's final Latin words rolled out into the deadening fog, Hereward unclasped the hands that had been held tightly in front of him. On his palm, he showed a polished blue stone on a leather thong. He dropped it into the grave, saying in a low, strained voice, 'Take this with you when you run with the *vættir*, so you will be safe. My wife . . .' Alric thought his friend seemed on the brink of saying more, but he simply nodded and walked away without a backward glance.

Leaving Kraki and Guthrinc at the graveside, Alric hurried after him. Now more than at any time Hereward should not be left alone. He knew well how grief ate away a man's heart.

Before he could reach his friend, a monk stepped from the direction of the abbey. A small bundle nestled in his arms. 'Your son,' the monk said, proffering the child.

Hereward peered into the depths of the cloth for a long moment and then said, 'I do not want him.' When the monk began to stutter questions as if the Mercian had not understood his intentions, Hereward's face darkened and he growled, 'Keep him here. Raise him, teach him, make him a good Christian man, one of your own. But do not tell him who his father is.'

He spun on his heel and strode away into the fog, leaving the dismayed monk behind. Alric ran to catch up. 'Why,' he asked breathlessly when he arrived at his friend's side, 'would you not take your son back to Ely?'

'Children are weak,' Hereward growled. 'They bleat and they moan and they are a burden to all. I have no time to raise him. I have men to kill and a war to fight.' He seemed done, but then added, 'He needs a better father. The monks here will serve well.'

Alric began to protest until the Mercian silenced him with a murderous glare. The matter was closed. Past graves glistening with dew the monk walked in silence at his friend's side. As they neared the stone bulk of the church, he snatched a glance and saw Hereward staring deep into the fog. 'What are you thinking?' he ventured.

'Autumn mist,' the Mercian muttered, his thoughts far away from that place. 'And the rising sun.'

Alric smiled, pretending to understand, but his thoughts worried at him. One thing they had not yet discussed, one thing that cast such a terrible shadow he had been afraid to raise it. No longer could it be ignored. He took a deep breath and began, 'Redwald—'

'Redwald could not have done this thing,' Hereward interrupted in a flat tone.

'The monk who saw him enter—'

'The monk was mistaken,' Hereward insisted, his anger crackling. 'I know my brother. He is a better man than me, a bearer of a good heart. This crime . . .' The words choked in his throat. 'Only a devil could do such a thing.'

'You do not know him,' Alric snapped. For too long he had kept Redwald's confession sealed inside, and all the fears and doubts that sprang from it like briars had threatened to throttle him. No more. 'I have heard his confession, when he believed he was dying, in Ely. This murder is not beyond him.'

Hereward whirled, his eyes blazing. 'You lie,' he snarled, raising his fist.

Alric stood his ground. 'You would accuse me of that, after all we have been through together?'

The hand hung in the air for a moment before it slowly fell. The monk saw it was shaking. 'Tell me,' Hereward whispered.

'His confession lies with God. I cannot betray the trust your brother placed in me.' He swallowed, choosing a careful path between helping his friend and damnation. 'But know that your brother is not the man he showed to the world. Devil, yes, I would call him that.'

Hereward waved a dismissive hand. 'You accuse him, yet you can tell me nothing of these crimes? No, I will not have it.'

Alric pushed his face forwards, forcing the warrior to look into his eyes. 'Then you must choose who you trust more, your brother or me.'

'How can you ask such a thing?' Hereward hissed.

'Because you are my friend,' the monk all but shouted, 'and you deserve to know the truth, though you hate me for ever more.' When Hereward flinched, he forced himself to calm. 'Seeing me every day, knowing that I held his darkest secrets, that must have made him afraid. Of all in Ely, only I knew who he truly was. He would have killed me if he could, I am sure of it, but at that time he was afraid of being found out. When the Northmen made to sail away, he seized his moment. He thought the waves or the Danes would do his bloody work for him and I would never be seen again.'

Hereward searched the depths of his friend's eyes and then let out a howl of such pain that the crows took flight from the trees around the abbey. The beating wings sounded like distant thunder through the fog. The warrior swept away into that grey cloud and for long moments after Alric could hear his roars, like a wounded beast roaming around the abbey.

In the abbey church, the monk prayed long and hard for his friend. But when he ventured out into the chill once more, he came up sharp. A vengeful apparition stood by the graveside, wreathed in mist. Alric shuddered at Hereward's fierce expression as he stared into the void at his feet. As the monk neared, the Mercian looked up. His pain had gone, or had been pushed back inside. But his eyes were plagued by a look that Alric had not seen since their first days together, when Hereward had threatened to tear the world apart with his rage.

He sensed someone standing near by. Hengist waited in the mist, his head half-bowed as if he carried a great weight upon his shoulders. 'Edwin is dead,' Hereward said. 'Morcar and his army are missing. We must find them before the Normans reach them or all is lost.'

Alric nodded, relieved that his friend had been distracted by this new purpose. 'And then?'

Hereward looked down at the grave. 'And then I will find my brother and carve out his beating heart.'

CHAPTER FIFTY-NINE

The sun was setting in a crimson blaze. On the steep slopes of the hill below, the darkening rooftops of Lincylene were limned with fire. Redwald slid down from his horse in the lengthening shadows and strode across the mud of the bailey. The sack banged against his thigh with each step. The grounds were still and his jaunty humming carried out through the chill air to the door of the castle.

As he neared, he heard his name called brightly. A woman ran out from the deep shade around the keep. Edoma grinned, her fair hair flying. She never slowed and crashed straight into his embrace, her arms thrown around his neck. Her soft mouth clamped on his and his thoughts flew back to hot nights of passion, sweat-slick bodies, and slaps and punches and bites that she had taken eagerly and demanded more, and harder. Whatever he wanted, she had let him do to her, and in that exchange they had sealed their relationship. He would never call it love, but it filled one part of the vast, empty space inside him.

She broke the embrace and snatched his hand, urging, 'Come. All is ready.' He had to all but run to keep up with her as she dragged him playfully towards the castle. Once through the door, her mood grew more serious.

'They are waiting?' he whispered.

She nodded. 'I have told them all about you,' she murmured.

As they moved to the steps, he passed a Viking with hair and beard dyed blood-red, somewhat familiar, his eyes like black holes in his skull. Redwald shivered as he climbed to the first floor, convinced he could feel the man's cold gaze upon his back.

Edoma stepped into the chamber first, her hands clasped behind her back and her head bowed in deference. But he saw her eyes flash coquettishly; she could not help herself. 'He is here,' she announced to the room. 'Redwald, brother of Hereward.'

'But not by blood,' he said as he stepped in. The Butcher and William de Warenne stood by the hearth with cups of wine in hand. Another man waited in the corner of the room, on the edge of his vision. Redwald was shocked to see it was Asketil, and for a moment he wondered if he had been lured into a trap.

But then the old man softened his stern expression and walked over to embrace his adopted son. 'No, you are not of my blood,' he said quietly, 'but would that you were.'

Redwald could see that Asketil was no captive. He carried himself with the confidence of a man who walked his own land, just as Hereward had said. Yet why the grey-haired thegn stood alongside the men who had stolen all he had would have to remain a mystery for now, he knew. He had his own game to play and it was a dangerous one. As Asketil broke the embrace, Redwald looked back to the Butcher. He saw no kindness in the Norman commander's face. Here was a man who would not respond to pleas, only strength. He had judged the situation well.

'There is no hope for the English,' he said, looking from the Butcher to William. 'Hereward will lead them to their doom.

His battle-lust has hollowed him out. Blood is all he wants, and death. All reason has fled.'

Asketil nodded. 'No more would I have expected.'

'I would ask forgiveness of the king . . . of all of you . . . for the crimes I have committed against you in my ignorance,' he continued. 'And I would ask a chance to make amends.' He bowed his head, feigning respect. He had wagered his own life in coming here, he knew it. Yet being bold was the only way to gain high reward.

The Butcher swilled his wine, his cold stare seeming to suggest he would happily snap Redwald's neck with his bare hands. After a moment, he shifted his gaze to Edoma. 'You believe there is some value in this dog?'

'I do,' she replied. 'I know him well.'

'And you, Asketil. You speak for him?' Taillebois enquired.

'He is the son I should have had. Let him earn your mercy and you will find no man more worthy of your trust in all Mercia.'

William de Warenne poured himself another cup of wine. 'And how will you earn this mercy?'

'I am here to swear an oath to the king,' Redwald said in a confident voice that commanded attention. 'I will tell all I know of the English in Ely and I will join the fight against them, if you need me. I would spill my blood for the king.'

'And you will spill the blood of ones you once called "brother"?' the Butcher asked. Redwald heard a note of contempt in the commander's voice. He cared little. Soon he would have passed Taillebois by and the Norman would be bowing and scraping to him.

'I will do whatever the king wishes,' he replied, holding the man's gaze.

'And why should we trust you?' William enquired, sipping on his wine. 'Hereward has shown he is cunning. Setting his own eyes and ears among us would not be beyond him.'

'I have already slain Edwin of Mercia, an enemy of the crown. But I prove that I am worthy with this.' Redwald bent down and slowly and deliberately opened the sack. Such a foul stench flooded out that all there recoiled. With a gentle shake of his wrist, he emptied the sticky, blackened contents on to the floor. Edoma cried out, her hand flying to her mouth.

Redwald nodded. 'I bring you the head of Hereward's beloved wife.'

CHAPTER SIXTY

Milky strands of mist rolled through the hollows of the forest. Moisture dropped in a steady beat from the high branches where the leaves glowed gold and brown and red in shafts of late autumn sunlight. Still, it was, that early morn with only the hungry cries of roosting rooks to disturb the peace. Hidden beneath the blanket of fern, the Norman force waited, unseen by any who might pass.

Harald Redteeth lay on his belly on the spongy leaf-mould and cocked his head. In that vast, near-impassable forest, he could hear the whispers of the *alfar* more clearly than anywhere else this side of the great black sea. They were uneasy, those restless spirits of tree and leaf. They smelled blood. Aye, and blood there would be, an ocean of it if the Normans had their way.

Under the fronds beside him, the Butcher lay. His face was as cold as ever. No smirk, no sign at all that the victory he had long desired lay within his grasp. 'Hark,' the commander growled. 'They come.'

Redteeth pushed the warnings of the *alfar* to one side and listened. The dim sound of hoofbeats rumbled through the ground. The chink of mail carried on the breeze and the tread of many feet. He folded his fingers around the haft of his axe, Grim, and readied himself for glorious battle. At his back, he could feel the weight of Ivar the Grey's gaze and he murmured, 'Not now, brother. Soon.'

The Butcher jerked his head around and glanced at him as if he were mad. 'Quiet,' he snapped in a low voice. 'Would you give us away, you fool?'

Harald gave a gap-toothed grin, resolving to plant his axe in the commander's head when the time was right. He felt the urge to whistle a jaunty tune and with a great struggle restrained himself.

The sound of the approaching army grew steadily louder. Did he suspect his days were short, this Morcar, who once had all Northumbria at his feet and now ran from the king's wrath? The Viking pushed aside a handful of fronds and peered down the slope into the deep hollow where the mist swirled around the lower trunks of the ash trees. Taillebois had planned the attack well, he would give him that. Once in that natural bowl, they would find their easy escape routes cut off. Surrounded by an army with the advantage of high ground, they would feel the fire of battle lit beneath them and they would stew in their own juices.

'Hold until I give the order,' the Butcher commanded.

Harald heard the words passed on from man to man hidden in the undergrowth until they faded away beneath the sound of dripping dew and rustling leaves. Harald grinned again, to himself this time. First Morcar would be slain, and then, once the last hope of building an English army had been snatched away, he would ride with the Normans to Ely, and Hereward, and the vengeance he had long desired. He thought back to the previous night when Taillebois had addressed his men in the bailey at Lincylene. One small group had been sent to lure Hereward and his army out to the northern fens. By the time the rebels returned home, every Norman soldier in the east would be waiting for them, a wall of iron cutting them off from their safe haven in Ely.

The column of men trudged into the hollow. Redteeth squinted, taking in the hunched shoulders and bowed heads, the shambling gait, the spears used as staffs to help them along. They were weary, from too many days of running and hiding as they picked a winding path to Ely to avoid the Norman scouts that crisscrossed the region. Little did these men know they had long since been found and their road identified.

The Butcher pushed himself up on his arms, watching his prey move further into his trap. Harald lifted his axe, ready to move. Taillebois nodded to himself, satisfied there was no going back for the enemy. He thrust himself up and yelled, *'Dex aie!'*, *God aid us!*, the battle-cry of his homeland.

As one the Norman army rose up from the fern. *'Dex aie!'* thundered from every lip.

Redteeth watched shock light on the faces of the exhausted English as he hurled himself down the slope. Around the vast circle of the hollow, the entirety of the king's men assigned to the fens began to move, a wave of iron about to break on the enemy army. Horses reared up. Cries of fear rang out. Men at the front of the column tried to press back. The warriors behind them moved too slowly and blocked their path. They milled around, clattering shields and tangling spears. Confusion reigned. Someone yelled out to form a shield wall – Morcar, the Viking guessed. Too late. The Normans would be upon them before any order could be found.

Harald Redteeth gritted his teeth. His feet pounded down the steep slope. He was afire, his blood thundering through his head, his axe in hand. This would be a fine slaughter. The English stood no chance.

All around the hollow, a storm of battle swept as the two sides clashed. The thunder of axes upon shields boomed out, and a cacophony of battle-cries and screams. The Viking threw back his head and laughed as he ran.

Mist swept around the legs of a young English warrior as he fought his way out of the morass of his brothers. His eyes widened in terror when he saw Harald, and he levelled his spear, his shield juddering as he bumped it up his body. He could not have been more than fifteen summers, Harald thought, but if he was old enough to fight, he was old enough to die.

The Viking thrashed his axe down with such force the round shield almost split in two. The lad staggered back in shock. Gamely, he thrust his spear. Redteeth smashed it aside with his weapon and, without slowing, slammed his shoulder into his opponent. The English warrior went down on his back, his shattered shield spinning away. Harald loomed over him. The boy knew his days were gone, but he did not beg or cry. The Viking liked that. 'I give you a glorious death,' he said, swinging his axe high.

At his back, a roar resounded, so loud it sounded like the awakening of a giant. Redteeth wrenched his head round, his axe wavering.

Around the entire rim of the hollow, pale figures emerged like ghosts from the glow of sunlight filtering through the autumnal canopy. Ash-streaked, bodies black with the mud of the fens, their shields painted grey and brown, the better to hide them among leaf and wood. The Devil's Army.

The Viking heard his victim scramble away. He cared little. All around the sounds of battle had died away as if the Normans and Morcar's men held their breath. Harald turned slowly, surveying this new army. Hereward must have brought every man of fighting age that he had, leaving Ely undefended. He risked everything on this coming battle. Redteeth gave a grim smile. How clever Hereward was, cleverer by far than the Norman bastards. They had set a trap, and a better trap had been set for them in turn. Now they were caught between two hammers.

He shook his axe furiously and roared, 'Come, then. Let us bathe in blood and die like men.'

A moment of silence filled the forest as the echoes of his words died away. Then the English crashed their weapons against their shields, and the spectral forms swept down the slopes.

CHAPTER SIXTY-ONE

'Kill them all,' Hereward bellowed. 'Leave no man standing.' The ashes crusting his face hid the depths of his cold fury. Through the waves of fern he bounded, and down the steep slope towards the king's men. His men thundered in his wake, but Hereward only had eyes for the Norman bastards. He grinned when he saw the flicker of fear on those graven faces.

Confusion swelled in the Norman king's army. As he ran, Hereward glimpsed Morcar's men fighting back with renewed vigour now they saw they were not alone. The Normans were torn, with enemies on both sides. Whichever way they turned they would show their backs to a foe.

A wall of the long Norman shields rose up before him. Emerald, scarlet, ochre, dragons, griffins, the Holy Cross, a barrier of vibrant colour that belied the grim men of iron that stood behind it. Hereward swung his axe high, focusing on one set of eyes peering over a shield's rim. Brainbiter would be no good in this fight. One wrong angle and the blade might shatter against the strong Norman mail. But the axe, that could hack through anything with the right arm behind it.

For a moment, he felt suspended in glory. A halo of sunlight ringed his vision and all the sounds of battle, all the cries of fury and agony, the pounding of feet and the clash of weapon upon shield, all of it seemed to rush away. The world slowed. Each beat of his heart boomed in his head. The fire in his gut licked up. Blood, that was all he wanted, enough blood to wash away the misery that had stained his life. Those cold eyes held his, growing larger and larger still.

And then the moment broke.

The wave of English crashed upon the Norman rocks. Never slowing a step, Hereward leapt the last few paces and swung his axe down. His opponent raised his shield and the blade smashed through the rim. As Hereward wrenched his weapon free, the king's man thrust with his double-edged sword. Too clumsy, Hereward thought, and too easy to predict. He slid around the blade and brought his axe down in a short, furious blow. Hand and sword both fell away in a gout of blood. His enemy's scream was lost behind the rolling thunder of battle.

Off-balance in his agony, the Norman staggered back a step. Hereward rammed his shoulder against the shield, pitching the warrior further back. In an instant, he was through the shield wall. He hacked his axe into the neck of the warrior to his left. Before the cry had left his victim's lips, the Mercian lashed the weapon into the shoulder blade of the fighting man on his right.

And then he felt the battle-madness sweep through him. As he whirled, all he could see were flashes of faces and barbs of sunlight reflected off helms. His axe cut high, then low, never ceasing in its flight. Mail burst, flesh parted, bone shattered, gore flowed. Bodies crashed to the ground like trees before the woodcutter. The boom of the blood in his head sounded like waves against a ship's hull. Faces came and went. He thought he saw his father there, and Redwald, but each time their features blurred into those of one of the king's men screaming in his death-throes.

Underfoot, the ground churned into a soup of blood and mud and piss and shit. His nostrils wrinkled at the death-reek. As he realized he had carved a space about him covered with the

355

fallen, the battle-madness began to recede. He looked around with clear eyes. It was a slaughter.

A hand caught his arm and he whirled. It was Guthrinc. 'Too many of our men die,' he yelled. Hereward knew who he meant, the fresh ones, who had never lifted a weapon before they appeared in the camp.

'They came to Ely to give their lives for our fight. This day they make that gift.'

He cast his eyes over the seething battle, spears tearing high and low against the shields of the king's men. English warriors were falling everywhere as Norman spears, axes and swords thrust back. He glimpsed the faces of men whose names he had not yet had time to learn, some who had only arrived in Ely the previous day. Long had he resisted sending them into the horrors of battle too soon, but now he had no choice. The outcome of this day would decide the course of this war. The lives of every man in Ely were only part of the huge stake he had gambled.

'We will win,' he shouted defiantly. 'See – our enemy has been cut back to a half of their number. Soon they will be over-whelmed.'

'But at what cost?' Guthrinc yelled, racing back towards the fighting. The towering English warrior thrust his spear over the top of a Norman shield and into the man's face. Beside him, Kraki roared a battle-cry as he swung his axe down. For a moment, Hereward glanced back up the slope to where the lone figure of Alric observed the battle. Would he win this day and lose every friend he had? If that were the price he paid, so be it. He had stood alone before.

He turned again to the battle and cried, 'Fall back.' At his command, his men rushed back up the slope as they had been ordered before they left Ely the previous night. The Normans stared in incomprehension. Hereward grinned as the crack of bowstrings echoed across the hollow. Arrows rained down on the Normans. Over the top of the shields the shafts flew, plunging into eyes, ramming through mail into chests and arms. The cries became a chorus. He had his rats in a barrel and he would slaughter them one by one. After a second volley had been loosed, he shouted, 'Attack.' His archers fell back and the spearmen rushed forward.

His archers could only be used sparingly for fear of hitting too many of Morcar's men, but as he looked across the bottom of the hollow he saw they had done their work. The tight ranks of the enemy had been fractured. Into the gaps, the English flooded. It was the beginning of the end.

Hereward felt a rush of euphoria. He raced back to the fighting and hurled himself into the line beside Kraki. 'Come now when I have done all the hard work,' the Viking grumbled.

Hereward swung his axe down with such force it cleaved a helm and skull near in two. As his enemy fell away, he looked across the sea of men and locked eyes with Harald Redteeth. The red-bearded Viking was laughing like a madman as he hacked right and left with his axe. Hereward grimaced and began to carve his way through the king's men towards the mad Northman who had killed his friend Vadir.

Barely had he advanced a foot, when his senses prickled. Through the swirl of battle, he glimpsed Ivo Taillebois waving his arm in the air and bellowing some new tactic, lost beneath the roar of battle. The hated enemy army began to fall back.

CHAPTER SIXTY-TWO

The axe fell one more time and blood spurted up. Harald Redteeth thrust the dying man aside and drove into the midst of Morcar's army, cutting and slashing as he went. Behind him, Ivo Taillebois waved his men on, snarling encouragement.

The Norman commander had made a brutal decision. At their backs, he had left a line of his warriors to die in battle with the men of Ely. The bulk of his force now drove towards the weary English at the centre of the hollow. The Viking glimpsed the furrowed lines of incomprehension on his allies' faces and laughed. He could see the Butcher's plan as clear as day and it was the only one they had left.

This battle had been good, but death had come too close. Now he understood the whispered warnings of the *alfar*. Even his battle-seasoned arm was shaking with each axe-strike. Another helm flew, taking the top of a man's head with it. And as the body dropped, Harald had a clear view of their prey. Morcar huddled at the centre of his forces. His long, horse-like face was slick with sweat, his eyes wide and staring as he searched for death on every side.

'Follow me,' the Viking roared. He swung his axe with

renewed vigour. Behind him, he sensed the Butcher and his warriors falling into place. Their spear formation drove straight into the heart of the English army.

Harald glimpsed Morcar begin to look around in panic. But he was surrounded by men trying to protect him unto death and he had nowhere to turn. The Viking chopped through the last of the line and loomed over the shaking earl. Snagging one fist in the Englishman's tunic, Harald hauled him up high. His axe blade bit into Morcar's neck and held.

'Stop or he dies,' Redteeth bellowed.

The Butcher took up the cry, and so did his men until it rang out over the din of fighting. Morcar's huscarls were the first to lower their arms. They glanced at each other with uncertain eyes. Moments later, the men of Ely slowed their attack and then paused. Harald watched heads turn towards Hereward, waiting for an order.

The Mercian needed Morcar alive or he would not have command of the earl's force, the Viking knew. And then all this bloodshed would have been for naught.

'Do not give them time to think,' the Butcher growled.

Harald dragged the earl through his bewildered men. The Normans formed a knot around them, less than a tenth of the original number who had set the trap that morning. Up the slope, they surged, as fast as they could go.

'Hereward will take his time,' Redteeth said. 'He has the numbers. He need do nothing rash.'

'Time is all we need,' the Butcher replied, looking down at the watching English. 'Time to breathe and think. A few moments ago we had none of it.'

'Do not harm me,' Morcar cried. 'I have gold. I will pay well for my freedom.'

Harald shook him as if he were a fresh-caught rabbit. 'Hold your tongue, you filthy coward. One more word from you and I will take your head, even if it sends us all into the Hall of the Slain.'

Once they had passed over the lip of the hollow, they heard

the roar of the English echo behind them. 'Run,' Taillebois commanded. 'Towards the water.'

The Viking grinned. The Norman commander was clever, he would give him that. In all that part of the dense forest, the stream would give them the fastest and most easily defended route out of danger. He wrapped one arm around the slight earl's chest and hauled him on a weaving path among the oaks and ash trees. The Normans crashed through the ferns all around. Gnarled roots and clustered trunks slowed their progress, but the Butcher held a clear line for the stream they had passed the previous day.

Behind them, Harald could hear the English army cresting the rim of the hollow. On either side, dead branches and fallen twigs cracked repeatedly. The Mercian had sent fleet-footed scouts to keep pace with them. He nodded. As expected. That was what he would have done.

The forest floor began to slope down. The Normans stumbled over outcropping rocks and plunged through bushes, brambles and fern as they made their way towards the sound of gushing water. Within moments they came to the edge of a broad white-topped stream cascading over stones, heavy from the autumn rains. Harald shook Morcar roughly for good measure and then plunged along the muddy bank. Soon the water began to cut deep into the ground and the weary warriors splashed into the icy flow to follow its course.

Harald grunted as he heard the rasping breath of the men around him, clearly already tiring. The English were not called the wild men of the woods for naught. This world of trees and water was their home and they would not give up pursuit easily.

As they forged along the stream with all the speed they could, the banks soared up on either side until they reached high overhead, topped with a dense wall of tree and thorn. If the English wanted to attack with numbers, they could only come from behind, and then with only four abreast. In the chilly shade at the foot of the narrow gorge, the Normans breathed a little easier.

'Keep moving,' the Butcher ordered. 'When the water opens out, we may be able to lose them in the wilderness. Then we will find a village, and some horses, take what we need and ride for Lincylene.'

Yet Harald watched a shadow cross the Norman commander's face. Of all the men the king had sent to keep the peace in the east, these few were the only ones that remained. Even if they survived, William's wrath would be great indeed.

At a whistling, Harald jerked round. A flaming arrow shot through the air. A cry rang out, but the man was dead long before he plunged into the water and extinguished the flames licking across his tunic and hair.

More pitch-soaked shafts whipped down from the top of the bank and struck home. Hampered by their mail and shields, the Norman soldiers scrambled along the rocky stream as fast as they could. But every time they paused, fiery death rained down on them.

'They will have picked us all off long before we get out of here,' Harald snapped.

The Butcher cursed, looking around as he fled. But Harald laughed as he splashed on. 'Now we have a fight,' he roared. 'Let us see who wants to live the most.'

CHAPTER SIXTY-THREE

The ruddy glow of the setting sun rimmed the horizon. Across the darkening landscape, the wetlands caught fire. A chill breeze blew from the north, drawing whispers from the reed-beds and the willows.

The knot of Normans looked out over the lonely country. 'The fens,' Harald Redteeth muttered. 'We should not be here.' An uneasy silence fell as the remainder of the king's men weighed what lay behind those words.

After a moment, Ivo Taillebois said, 'We travel north, along the edge of these wetlands. Soon we will find the tracks that lead to Lincylene.'

The Viking grunted in contempt at the commander's confidence. At their backs, the dark forest brooded. Ten more lives had been claimed as they made their way along the watercourse to the edge of the trees. Arrows whistling from the dense vegetation. Rocks falling from the high banks, crushing skulls and spines. One by one they were being picked off, a flock of sheep at the mercy of a pack of circling wolves.

'We should kill the English dog. He will only slow us down,' one of the warriors muttered, nodding at Morcar. The earl's eyes darted in apprehension.

The Butcher considered this for a moment, then said, 'We may still need him to bargain our way out of here.'

'They are men who hunt us, not ghosts,' Redteeth said, looking around the warriors. 'Never forget they are flesh and blood.' He tapped his forehead. 'Here is your true enemy. Fight it.'

The Butcher glowered at this usurpation of his authority. Harald cared little. He took the coin of the Normans while it suited him. But once Hereward was dead, he would be away, with a few grudges paid in the passing. He showed his gap-toothed grin, then strode off north along the edge of a broad mere soaked in inky shadow. He eyed the thin red haze limning the horizon and wished they had more of the day. The harsh cawing of the rooks in the forest slowly died away. Only the rustling of the reeds remained. He looked up and saw that the chill wind had brought grey cloud from the north. There would be no moon to light their way, no stars. No torch could be lit for fear it would draw the English to them. He was used to the brilliance of snow-covered plains, but those bastards could see in the dark, he was sure of it.

He glanced back at the straggling line of men, shoulders hunched, eyes darting furtively. The heart had been kicked out of them, so many of their brothers had been lost that day. And now they were moving through a land that was strange and threatening to them. They needed their castles, their stone walls and ramparts. These wetlands were like a living thing, luring in the unwary and then swallowing them whole. The *alfar* were strong here, and other, darker things, he had heard. One of the English spears-for-hire said the *wuduwasa* lived in this miserable place, feeding on the bloody bones of men. If he met it, he would cut it like any other beast. But he knew the Norman warriors had heard that tale too, and it scared them. He cursed under his breath as he pushed his way through the curtain of willow branches. Were it left to him they would have found somewhere to hide out, and defended it until first light. The Butcher's decision to move through this treacherous place by night would be the death of them.

On the horizon, the last of the light died.

As if the rising dark were a signal, a cry of alarm rang out from the rear of the pack. Harald grimaced. *And so it begins.* He barged his way through the men, only a step behind Taillebois. Three warriors twisted and turned, their spears jabbing towards the wilderness behind them.

'You will bring the English down upon us,' the Butcher snarled, cuffing one of them.

'They are already here,' the man replied in a tremulous voice. He could not tear his gaze away from the empty landscape. 'Lambelin walked behind us not a moment ago. And now he is gone.'

The Butcher drew his sword and joined his men in searching the dark. 'The coward. He ran away rather than fight to save his brothers.'

Redteeth squatted, studying the muddy ground. After a moment, he reached out and touched the broken vegetation. His fingers came up sticky and dark, and he held them to his nose and sniffed. 'Blood. They took him while he walked only paces behind you.' He looked up and saw the men shaking.

'We heard nothing,' one of the men stuttered.

Harald lurched up and grabbed him by the tunic, thrusting the edge of the axe against his face. 'Keep your ears and your eyes open,' he snarled, 'or you will be the death of all of us.'

The Butcher thrust the tip of his sword against the Viking's neck. 'One more word out of you and I will take your head,' he said through gritted teeth. 'I command here, never forget.'

Redteeth grinned and nodded. This was a march to the very doors of the Hall of the Slain, it was clear now. The only question that remained was at what point he should abandon these fools to the fate that clearly awaited them. But he had to choose his time well. He and Hereward had been joined by blood and he knew the Mercian's mind. The English warrior would hunt him down and kill him first, and let the Normans be damned.

Taillebois snatched his sword away, his anger simmering. He

whirled to the three Normans and hissed, 'Watch your backs. Or you will be rotting in the bog with Lambelin.'

He marched back to the front of the column, urging his men to step up the pace. Their legs were shaking with exhaustion and their hauberks weighed them down, but fear gave them strength. Harald pushed only to the centre of the group. Bodies were better than shields.

Near running, they edged the mere and then moved out into the heart of the wetlands as the forest fell behind. Taillebois ordered a man to go ahead with his spear to test the ground lest they plunge into one of the hidden bogs. So dark was it, they could barely see further than the man in front. Every now and then, a man would stumble and fall, his brothers dragging him back to his feet. The pace could not be slowed, they all knew that.

When the lead warrior hissed a warning, they ground to a halt. An owl shrieked in the distance as it hunted. 'Go slow,' the Butcher warned. 'A bog lies ahead, but our scout has found a causeway.' Harald heard the Norman commander hesitate and knew what he was thinking. On a causeway, they could be trapped, with only two directions to choose.

As Taillebois deliberated, the Viking heard a whistling. Before he could call out a warning, a strangled cry rang out. A man fell near to him, a shaft protruding from his chest. Harald dropped low. But the unnerved Norman warriors milled about, shouting in the dark as they tried to shove each other towards the causeway. Another man cried and fell. And another. Redteeth scrambled on his hands and knees towards the front of the column.

'How can they see us?' one soldier cried, his voice breaking. He pitched back an instant later, trailing blood from the arrow rammed in his chest.

'Are you mad?' Harald shouted. 'Get down. Make yourself as small as mice—' The rest of his warning was lost beneath the sound of thundering feet as the men raced for the causeway. Cursing at their foolishness, Harald loped behind them.

Suddenly, orange flared out of the dark. The burning shaft thumped into the back of a Norman soldier. Screaming, he ran four more paces as the flames leapt up his body, and then he pitched on to the wet ground. The fire roared up, a beacon to light the night for the English dogs.

The glow lit fear-filled faces as the Normans panicked and scrambled on to the causeway, haring as fast as they could along the narrow, treacherous path. Harald had no choice but to follow them.

Once they had escaped the revealing glare, Redteeth heard the man in front of him praying for dawn. A moment later he cried out as he slipped off the causeway and plunged into the marsh. Another warrior tried to grab for his arms and followed him into the sucking mud. In an instant, both men were gone, dragged down by the weight of their mail shirts. As the sounds of their thrashing faded away, the Viking shook his head wearily. These fools would do the enemy's job for them.

The fleeing warriors slowed. The causeway was made of flint and almost impossible to make out in the engulfing dark. Mile upon mile lay ahead of them before they would reach the safety of the castle at Lincylene and the Viking could almost feel the despair rising around him.

On and on they trudged. The path carved a straight line through the stinking marsh. Occasionally Harald glimpsed indistinct shapes in the dark, small islands covered in willows and sedge. Each one could hide an English archer. Not for a moment could their guard be lowered. The reeds swayed in the breeze and murmured and mocked. The trees moaned, the bog gurgled. Bubbles burst, reeking of rot. They could not even trust their own senses in that place. After a while, the strain began to tell. The Viking heard more whispered prayers, edged with desperation, and voices raised in anger as men blamed their brothers for near-slips and stumbles. It seemed as if they had been walking for an eternity.

As they approached rising ground, a bark of shock brought the column of anxious men to a halt. Harald struggled past the rest to the front, taking care not to lose his footing. 'What now?' he growled. A warrior pointed a trembling finger at a pale shape hovering in the dark ahead. He squinted and saw it was a head, resting at the point where the causeway met dry land. The mouth gaped and the eyes had rolled up so only the whites were showing.

'Lambelin,' de Taillebois muttered.

'Go back,' one of the warriors urged. 'They must be waiting for us.'

As the men began to turn, Harald called for them to hold fast. He squatted, resting the palm of his right hand upon the flint. His skin tingled with the vibrations running through the causeway. 'They want us to go back,' he growled. 'The English are coming up behind us. Fast.'

Panic gripped the remaining soldiers once more. They spilled out on to the rising ground, forcing Harald and the Butcher ahead of them. Taillebois called for caution, but it was no good. The Normans stumbled into the trees and the undergrowth along the marsh edge. The Butcher yelled out once more that their indiscipline would be the death of them and this time a few calmed. But not for long.

As Harald turned, he glimpsed movement all around. Spectral shapes formed out of the gloom. From swaying reed-beds and pools of black water they rose, from the sucking mud where surely no man could ever live, from the trees and the bushes and seemingly out of the very earth itself. At first they appeared as insubstantial as mist. But then with a cry that could chill the blood, they rushed from the night, taking on form and fury as they came.

Terror took hold of the Normans. Harald watched them run. Axe-blades flashed, splitting skulls, severing limbs. Spears burst through chests. A man went down and hands grabbed his ankles and dragged him off into the murk, though he dug his nails into the mud to hold himself fast. The Viking watched the white, contorted face disappear, a scream tearing from his throat.

The Butcher caught his arm. Five warriors were gathered around him, their spears and swords pointed towards the gloom. 'We have lost Morcar,' he hissed. 'Our only hope now is to run.'

Redteeth saw through Taillebois's words. The Butcher intended to sacrifice his own men. Their slaughter would be the distraction that hid his own escape. Disgusted that the Norman made no attempt to save those he commanded, the Viking said nothing. The Butcher would pay the price for his dishonour, sooner or later. Within moments, they were running through the willows. The screams of the dying echoed on every side. One by one those cries faded away until Harald could hear nothing but ragged breath and the hammering of their feet. Only seven of them remained, he marvelled, just seven out of the entire Norman force that had ridden south from Lincylene. Hereward had proved himself a great warrior indeed. It would be an honour to take his life when the opportunity presented itself.

But as they squelched through soft ground beside a wall of waving reeds, a spear shot from the gloom and took one of the warriors. Away in the trees, he glimpsed the ghosts keeping pace with them. The Butcher had seen them too, for he glanced once at Harald before suddenly turning on his heels and darting in the opposite direction. Harald heard him crash into the reed-bed and then he was gone.

When another warrior went down on the tip of a spear, the Viking skidded to a halt and shook his axe in the air. He was only running to his death, he now knew. Better to stand his ground and die in battle like a man. 'Hereward,' he roared. 'Come. Fight me. Let one of us die with honour.'

Three cries came in quick succession, the last of the Norman soldiers dying. For a moment, only silence hung among the trees. He raised his axe and looked around. Movement flickered on the edge of his vision and a blow crashed against the back of his head. His helm flew from his head and he fell, dazed.

When his senses returned, he fumbled for his axe but it was

gone. Those skull-faced night-creatures stood all around in silence, looking down on him with fierce eyes. Before he could speak, they parted and a figure walked through their midst. Hereward loomed over him, his face an emotionless mask. He felt a sword point at his throat, under his chin, forcing him to raise his head as the iron bit into his flesh. He looked deep into the Mercian's pale eyes, and for the first time in his life felt unsettled by what he saw there.

CHAPTER SIXTY-FOUR

Torchlight danced across the ash-encrusted faces of the English as they watched their leader prepare to take the head of his enemy. Hereward pressed the tip of his sword into the Viking's scarred flesh. A bubble of blood rose up, but still Harald Redteeth did not flinch. For this man, death was not a grim stranger to be feared, he could see that. Both of them had known too much of endings.

Silence lay heavily over all. Not a man moved. Hereward felt an unfamiliar calm descend. For most of that day, the blood-lust had raged through him. He had hacked and sliced with no thought but of stealing the last breath. Now he weighed a life in his hands. The Viking's eyes were all-black, as if he had been consumed by the night from within, and in the torchlight his dyed beard and hair glowed like the embers of a home-fire.

'You killed my friend Vadir. You lopped off his head and tossed it away as if it were nothing.' He paused, scrutinizing the Viking's unflinching gaze. 'And you saved the life of my wife. You are a bastard, and the world would be better off rid of you. And you are a man of honour.'

Harald Redteeth grinned. 'Aye, here is a riddle to hold any feast in its thrall.'

The trees rustled in the chill breeze, and if Turfrida had been there she would have said it was the voices of the *vættir* as they observed this momentous event. For one moment, he felt his wife's presence in those willows too, and he shivered.

'This blood-feud of ours will be ended,' he murmured. 'But not this day.' He drew his blade back and sheathed it.

Harald Redteeth heaved himself to his feet and levelled his gaze at his enemy. 'One day we shall find our ending.' With a nod, he turned and plucked his axe from where it had fallen. Without a backward glance, he pushed his way through the English and was gone.

Guthrinc stepped up to Hereward's shoulder and sighed. 'This night will come back and bite you in the arse.'

Hereward shrugged. 'Amid all this bloodshed, honour is like a beacon in the dark. These things matter.'

He looked around the faces of his loyal men. At his command, they had offered up their lives, and they had fought with a courage that far exceeded their raw skill. He felt proud of each and every one of them; he could have asked no more.

'We have won a great victory this day, one that will ring out across this land,' he called. 'You, here, are the last hope of the English. And you have earned the glory that they will shower upon you. A greater battle lies ahead, one that will finally bring William the Bastard crashing into the mud. But you have shown here that it is a battle we can win.' He grinned. 'Now, to Ely. And let us feast as if there be no tomorrow.'

A cheer rang out across the chill wetlands, and that night Hereward thought he had heard no greater sound.

CHAPTER SIXTY-FIVE

War was coming, and his horse would be red.

In the light of the feast-fire, the faces of the Ely folk might glow with hope, but Alric could see in their shifting eyes that they knew it would be so. War, and his three brothers too, as each seal was opened. And then, as sure as night followed day, would follow the Final Judgement. For Ely, for England, for all men.

As Kraki roared a mead-oath from the top of the Speaking Mound, he put on a grin and raised his own cup. It had been a great victory, no one could deny that. The king's army in the east had been turned to dust, his sheriff, the Butcher, humiliated. And yet in that moment of glory lay the threat of all their tomorrows. The king would come as he had come to the north. And all the dead they had buried these last days, all the young men who had never before raised a spear in battle, would be as nothing to what lay ahead.

They all knew it would be so. He could see.

And yet he marvelled as he wandered among the crowds enjoying the battle-feast. The men sang and cursed and laughed and swilled ale down their throats as fast as their cups could be filled. Women whirled around the bonfire to the lilting tune of bone whistle and harp, their faces flushed with abandon. Children jumped dogs over the high poles, and wrestled so close to the blazing logs their scolding mothers had to drag them back from the heat. This was not a night for tomorrow; it was a night for days gone by. It was a night to say this is what our fathers built with their hands, and their fathers before them; this is what we have, and if we have it not in days to come, still we will know the fire it brought to our hearts and the warmth to our lives.

He sipped his ale and felt deep currents move him.

The throng was the largest yet, reaching down through the dwellings almost to the walls themselves. Ely folk, and earth-walkers from the Camp of Refuge, and now Morcar's men, their eyes bright as they basked in the warm reception they had received. Alric eyed the girls' favours trailing from their wrists and the ale-cups thrust into their hands by carousing men.

Through the crowd, Hereward walked, the way parting before him. He smiled and nodded to all who called his name, but Alric could see his thoughts were elsewhere, at a lonely grave beside the abbey at Crowland. The monk wondered if the day would ever come when those eyes lost their haunted look.

He watched Hereward lean in close and whisper in Acha's ear. The conversation seemed intense and after a moment the woman's face darkened. With the history that lay between the two of them, Alric felt himself grow suspicious, but only for a moment. With a nod, Acha hurried over to Godrun. The blonde-haired girl sat on her own, staring into the flames. Her face was blank, but the monk sensed her troubles heavy upon her. Since her return, she had barely spoken to anyone, even her own father.

Alric grunted his thanks to a serving woman as she handed him a chunk of sticky boar-meat, and then he wandered up to his friend. 'Is something amiss?' he asked, looking to where Acha now sat close to the younger girl. The two women chatted and smiled.

373

'Acha has agreed to watch over Godrun,' Hereward replied. 'She has a good heart, though she tries to hide it.'

'And succeeds most of the time,' the monk muttered.

'You have felt the edge of her tongue,' the Mercian said with a laugh.

'Who here has not?' He eyed his friend as he finished the sweet boar-meat and licked the grease from his fingers. 'God's road can be hard at times, but you walk it better than any man I know.'

'Do not try to make me a saint. No one will fight over my bones when I am gone.' He looked around at the revels and nodded with satisfaction. 'After the hardships we have endured, these folk deserve one night of joy.'

'And you think they are prepared for what lies ahead now that the iron circle closes upon Ely?'

Alric felt pleased when he saw the fire in the other man's eyes. 'Let the Bastard come. He thinks we are trapped here, on Ely. He thinks we quake and quail at the thought of the great king striding to our door with his mighty army. Instead, we lure him in as the hunter lures the rabbit. Why sweat and moan as we march to Wincestre when we can bring the king here to die in this land that is our fortress?'

The monk searched his friend's gaze for some sign that might assuage his fears. So much had been stolen from Hereward – wife, mother, friend, yes, and father and brother too. How easy it would be for him to give in to that devil who promised succour with blood and fire. But what if victory could only come if that devil were freed? What then? He choked down his worries and put on a grin. 'Then let us eat well and drink mead until we fall over,' he said, sweeping one arm out towards the feast. 'For the war will begin soon.'

'Aye,' Hereward agreed. 'And it will be a war that will shake the very halls of heaven.'

Alric watched his friend walk towards the drunken cheers of Guthrinc and Kraki. His worries refused to die. Into the roaring flames of the feast-fire he peered, as if answers might lie within, but there were none. And then he looked to the red, gold and white sparks that swirled up into the night. They were carried far out over the quiet wetlands, accompanied by the sound of song and laughter. Somewhere near by, an owl shrieked and took wing. A cold breeze had picked up and, in its stirring, the willows out in the darkness seemed to whisper, *Beware . . . Beware.*

Beware.

Historical Note

As I embarked on this second volume detailing Hereward's resistance to the Norman invaders, I again spent many days travelling across the fenlands of eastern England. It's a part of the country that can, at times, seem bleak and windswept. But on other occasions, particularly when the sun's out and the sky is blue, it's pleasingly unspoilt and relaxing. History lies all around, and that's the true attraction for anyone who loves the past. Prehistoric tracks and medieval cathedrals, Roman defences and Elizabethan carriage routes.

But the research I had to complete was, for me, of a completely different stripe: historical geography. Or geographical history. The Fen country has changed phenomenally in the thousand years since Hereward walked there. At the time of the Norman Conquest, this was a land that altered by the day, by the hour. Water flooded across it, at times turning lakes and meres into what was almost an inland sea with ferocious currents, the settlements rising up on small islands. In other sections, treacherous bogs were all but impassable beyond the narrow flint causeways that crisscrossed the area. Bounded to the west by a dense, near-impenetrable forest and to the east by the sea, the Fen country was almost a natural fortress.

Land reclamation, drainage, the changing environment and modern agricultural techniques have created a gentler, pastoral world far removed from Hereward's wild land. I spent long days looking at ancient land records and old maps, and talking to academics to try to comprehend the true nature of the Fens at that time. By the end I had realized it was impossible to understand that bloody rebellion without truly understanding the Fens.

One other thing: eagle-eyed readers may notice a change in the style of place-naming from the first book in this sequence. I've now decided to use the eleventh-century names of towns and rivers wherever possible, and I apologize for the inconsistency. In my defence, I can only say that it *felt* right. I'm not a huge fan of long lists of character and place names at the beginning of a book so you are left to your own devices, but I feel most readers can easily decipher the modern spelling of, say, Snotingeham or Wincestre. The only one worth noting here, I think, is the Wellstream, which Hereward and his men travelled along to reach Burgh. Before the reclamation of the fens, it was a three-mile-wide channel surrounded by quicksand, that drained the River Nene.

ACKNOWLEDGEMENTS

Laura Hall at Lincoln Visitor Information Centre; the staff of Ely Museum; the staff at Ely Cathedral and Peterborough Cathedral.

ABOUT THE AUTHOR

James Wilde is a man of Mercia. Raised surrounded by books, he went on to study economic history at university before travelling the world in search of adventure. Unable to forget a childhood encounter – in the pages of a comic – with the great English warrior Hereward, Wilde returned to the haunted fenlands of Eastern England, Hereward's ancestral home, where he became convinced that this near-forgotten hero should be the subject of his first novel. *Hereward* was a bestseller. Wilde indulges his love of history and the high life in the home his family have owned for several generations in the heart of a Mercian forest.